THE RADIO REVOLUTION

Historical Fiction based on Radio Free Hawaii (The Radio Revolution in Honolulu 1991-1997).

First Hawaiian Edition

Sheriff Norm Winter

Website: Stirringneuorns.com
A CATWALK ORIGNAL
670 Auahi Street A6
Honolulu, Hawaii 96813
Phone: 808 545-5002
C 2017

© 2017 Sheriff Norm Winter
All rights reserved.
ISBN: 0999228390
ISBN 13: 9780999228395
Library of Congress Control Number: 2017949825
Catwalk Originals, Honolulu, HI

DEDICATED TO JEFFERY LAU AND JENIFER WINTER

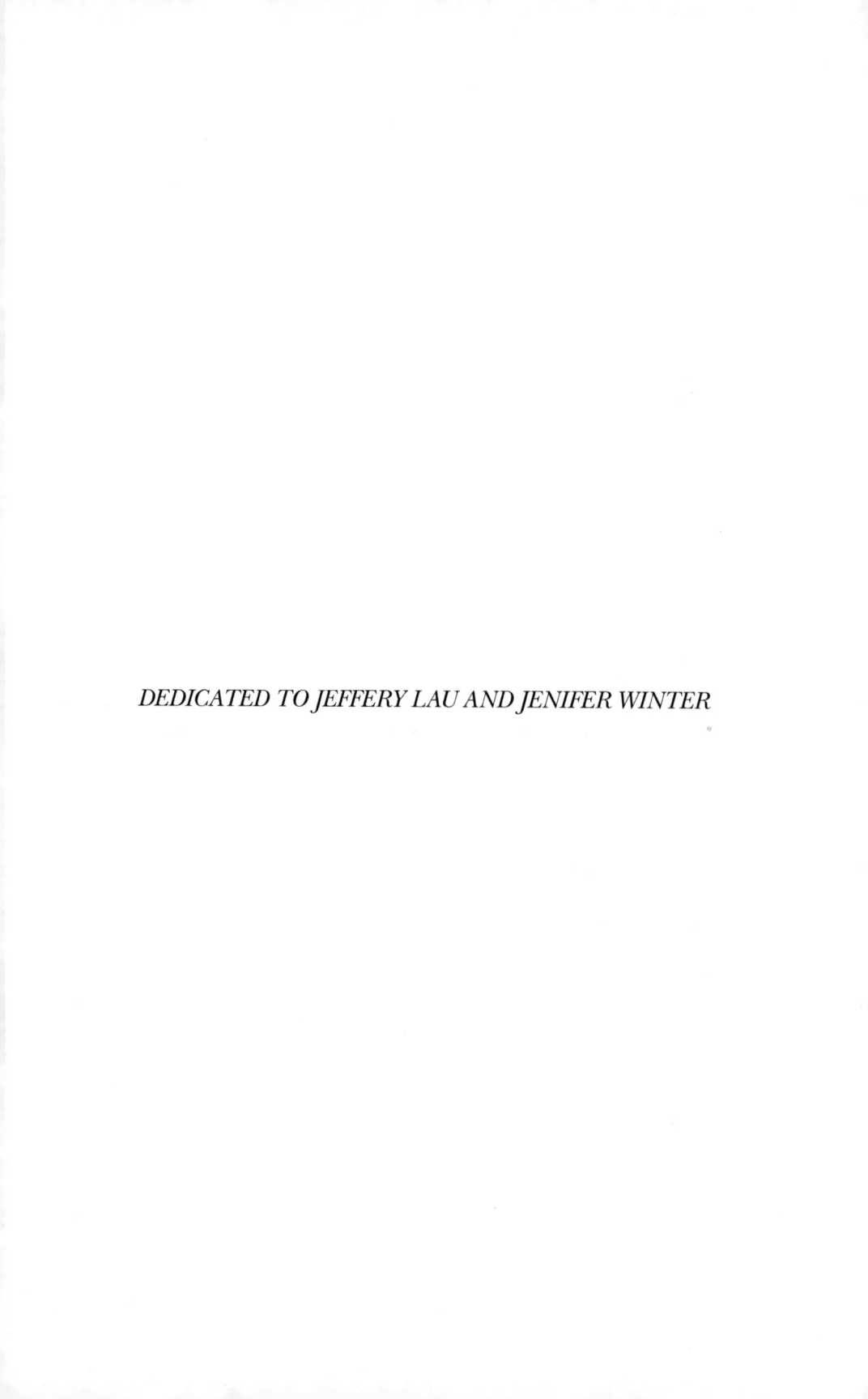

1

MAYBE I DO HAVE A HEART

Kaua'i, October 25, 1989

I have an insecure wife. She says she loves me. Nevertheless, she just locked me out of the house and suggested I go to Hell.

Why? I've been fired from seven jobs in eighteen months. It's not that I'm a lousy worker. I'm a great worker who sizes up the problem and goes about trying to fix it. Problem is, my *bosses* are lousy workers who talk about the different meows of their cats or whose super hero can wallop the other guy's super hero, with absolutely no understanding to the fact the American political arena is about to push the non-wealthy over the cliff.

Love is forever. But it has a bad habit of leaving the realm of forever when your consciousness realizes, "I'm not here anymore." It might be just as well. If I stayed, my consciousness would be spewing out senseless muck. So the "forever" is *there* and I'm over *here* with a bunch of homeless people in a cement, camp ground in Polihale.

Polihale Beach Park is a massive sand dune on a little island in the Pacific called Kaua'i. The island itself has a weird connection to other worlds that the rest of the planet is deprived of, and Polihale is at the ass end of that island. It's a heavy place of pathos swallowed in a deep rich beauty with blaring ocean waves that pound against godly mountains.

Why do I say godly? The mountains look like two-thousand-foot totem poles with the faces of Gods carved on their tops. It is here that the lives of the Earth exit into other worlds. I know that sounds crazy, but it is a perfectly natural concept to the people of Kaua'i. And you can feel the exit of life as the waves beat against the two-thousand-foot totem poles of the gods.

People call me a radical, which they misinterpret to mean I'm incorrigible, a rebel who is out to destroy their security. A radical, however, is a person that sees the problem and tries to find a way to fix it before the same people face a disaster that obliterates their security. I thought I could fix it in the business world, but here I am in Polihale realizing the problem goes deeper. The root of the problem lies in the Constitution of the United States of America.

What does a radical do when he's faced with changing the Constitution of the United States of America? This radical, drinks a beer, shouts out a few blasphemies to his friends or anyone who will listen, and then conveniently stuffs the disaster into the back of his mind. Some radical.

I realized at age sixteen: radio is the way to change the world. Why? It's a *sound alone medium.* You hear a sound and your mind imagines the visuals that go with the sound. It excites your imagination. You hear music and your emotions are activated by the sound alone medium. If a DJ's voice sounds sincere, a warm intimacy between you and the DJ is felt. It's like you and DJ are in a room together. If you hear listeners talking on radio, you feel more a part of the radio world. If radio opens the door to all kinds of music and ideas, you feel a part of the world, listening to radio.

My theory at age sixteen was that with radio you are stirred into actively listening and feeling part of the world. Your consciousness is suddenly wired to the world and you are a part of the whole, sharing your feelings and ideas with others. When enough people share ideas with each other, it becomes a snowball and ignites the whole world with motivating thoughts. Yes, utilizing your imagination in the midst of being a part of the world - that is a way out of the pit the world has put itself within. Radio could be the world's savior.

Now, I'm reconsidering. What does a sixteen-year-old know?

But then again, love won't save the world. Sorry, John Lennon. Love is forever and a great fix-it, but it wilts when consciousness yells, "I'm not here anymore."

Money won't do it. Sorry, Rockefeller. Money attracts the uncooperative people who work harder to get it so they can do whatever they want, and what they want is to shit on the cooperative people.

Religion won't do it. Sorry, Pope. Pledging allegiance to the invisible might make you feel better because it can't talk back, but when people get into a group and decide everybody has to think the same, imagination is crushed, and the larger the group, the worse part of the human nature ascends to the top.

Politics won't do it. Same problem. The larger the group, the stupider it gets and political systems are huge.

So I came to the conclusion at age sixteen: radio is the best way to change the world.

When radio was vibrant in the thirties, forties, fifties and sixties, didn't Orson Wells' "War of the Worlds," and Hitler's fanatical, emotional speeches combined with Churchill's emotional speeches, and the Beatles crushing the rigid views of the time leading to the Woodstock concert - didn't they all change the world?

If you were there, you know radio certainly did change the world. Of course now radio is a limp rag you can't even wring out. And the culprit? I already mentioned that. It's the Constitution of the United States of America.

It's cold out here on the beach and the wind just blew my belongings and my tent into the waves. Sand is stinging my face and blowing into my eyes and I am beginning to believe Kaua'i people are right: this is where the torture of the earth's life departs. Trouble is, a whole bunch of that life must have been blasted dead in some war or terror act and its departure isn't too soothing. Yeah, and it is a six-mile hike back to the main road and then I've got to hope for the mercy of a speeding car zooming along in nowhere with this questionable visibility.

Here I am, Mr. Nature, trying to rough it without a car so I can think the deep thoughts, like what is my place here on this planet amongst the planet's natural surroundings? Stupid. What was I thinking? Coming out to the wild surf without even a car? And three nights from now, here in Kaua'i, I've got to meet my stupid ass words head on. What have I gotten myself into?

But there are cars here in Polihale. I'll take shelter under one until it decides to leave, then beg for a ride if it can tread out of the sand and find the main road in near-zero visibility.

I slither under a four-wheel drive, but it is still cold and the wind and sand seem to find me there anyway. I cover my head with my shirt as the sand burns my belly. I hear noises, humans squealing, and some yelling verbiage, people shouting to others in a group. I assume they are saying to each other, "Get in the car, quick!"

I hear pots and pans clanking against the cement alcove, preparing to head for the ocean, and the tarp roof of the alcove is flapping loudly over the howling wind. The car rocks a bit and the engine starts.

Oops. Dumb idea, getting under it. But it doesn't move. They just turned on the heater.

I should get in the car.

I belly crawl out and knock on the door. The door opens. "You poor man, you don't even have a jacket, jump in."

I hesitate. The front is a two seater.

A girl pulls me in anyway. She's a pretty one, and the driver looks like a Don Juan. In the back are two glassy-eyed young men, one with dreads, the other with dirty sandy-blonde hair and a snarled beard.

The girl puts her arm around me, "Don't take it wrong, I just want to get you warm. My name is Mandy."

I'm out of her league anyway. I'm pushing fifty. "Hey, this is the best welcome I've had in a long time, thank you!"

Mandy is beautiful at second look: a full figure, bronze flesh, probably a mixture of a thousand cultures and races and her brown eyes seem to flash into amusement, then solace, then a dreamy distant look. When her eyes are dreamy it is like she isn't even there. I know that look, it is the sign of intelligence as if, why am I here? I belong somewhere else.

Now she smiles like she is the sun itself.

Damn, I wish I was younger!

Mandy says, "Are you one of those lost ones looking? Show me your hand. I read palms. Left one first; that's your past."

I show her my left.

Don Juan says, "She's really good, you know."

I'm trying to figure out why she thinks I'm a "lost one."

She says, "Straight as an arrow, your heart."

She's wrong about that. I feel pretty close to heartless now.

"You have the triangle. You will never leave Hawaii." She's right about that. I came here twenty-five years ago and even being forced to live in the streets a spell, I was determined to stay.

"You've got the elliptical cross. You're an earth shaker."

I smile. "I guess people might say that about me."

She is still hugging me. I am getting a rise. I am really feeling her presence and really, really liking it.

She reaches for my right hand. "Gosh," her eyes light up.

"You are starting a new life, a famous one; you are going to be bigger than the movie stars."

Thought that myself, but at the moment I had pretty much given up on it. But here, now, I'm a homeless middle-aged man barging into a car in a raging sand storm, and this girl has sized me up pretty well. Yeah, she is right about me starting a new life. And I sure am thinking of some big ideas. Maybe she is good with this fortune stuff.

She looks at me very curious and intently. "What *do* you do?"

I didn't want to tell these kids my vocation. Kids know radio sucks. "Trying to make radio not suck, but failing miserably." I lift my hands in an act of hopelessness, "That's what brought me here."

The dread in back, in a half laugh, says, "How can you possibly make radio *not* suck?"

I was on the defensive. I forgot about the girl's arm around me and turned around facing the Dread in the back seat next to the Sandy one.

"By allowing people to have a real radio station. A radio station for the people, not for a bunch of idiot conglomerates who want everything to sound the same and then try to shove that sound down your throat. It is even in the 1934 preamble to the Congress's Radio Act. But in 1969 after Woodstock, the preamble for the people was eliminated by Congress, and radio has sucked ever since, in fact it gets suckier every year, if that's possible."

The Sandy in the back smiles, "Wow."

The girl presses against me and kisses my cheek. "I love you."

She didn't mean it the way I wanted it to mean but I got a boner anyway. Don Juan seems a little uncomfortable.

I divert the situation with a question, "What's your name, driver?"

"Why you ask?"

"My name is Danny, Danny Fall." That is my stage name. My real name is Danny Boy Heinzwaffle. But I would never mention that name to anybody. "I told you who I am. Why not you?"

"I'm from Brazil."

I gave a little room, "Then a traveler, right? Looking for something?"

"Yeah, I've found it." He puts on his possessive pose. His arm and hand loops around Mandy, grabbing her shoulder.

Mandy is the one who looks disturbed now.

The Sandy one in the back tries to cool the tension. "We are all just friends here, trying, struggling, to find ourselves in this fucked-up world."

Mandy smiles to the back voice. Don Juan smiles saying, "Yeah, that's the way it is, but a woman needs to be one with her man."

A man doesn't need to say that unless he is not one with his woman. But I don't dare extend that logic.

Mandy turns to Don Juan saying, "I'm glad I'm helping you and you helping me, it is just the world is bigger than two people."

Suddenly it is me who wants to say to Mandy: *Jesus, I love you.* While Don Juan is clinging to her, she is gripping my ribs harder than before.

I'm thinking, I know of women who want to take on the world, to be fair to everybody, to give of themselves freely and who in the end go through torment that jades them for life. I suddenly don't want that to happen to Mandy. I want to keep her light going. God knows mine died so many years before. I'm desperate. I want hers to shine forever. Shit, There's that love word again. Forever.

I throw it out there. "About ten miles down the big road is a nice bar and restaurant. If you can find a way to get there, I'll treat you all. Till this storm winds down."

The sandy-haired guy in the back says, "You want some weed?"

I figured it was a test to see if I was cool.

"Hey, I am a square, no interest in altering my mind except maybe calming it and making my emotions come to the surface with booze. You smoke, fine. Not me."

Mandy takes a hard look at Don Juan. "He's really trying to do something."

The Dread in the back says, "Cool it Juan, he just offered us a free meal. Can't be that bad."

Shit, his name is really Juan.

Juan takes the car out of park, the four-wheel-drive spins. We jump ahead a bit, but then slip back. He revs the car again, we jump again. I hear the motor screaming then popping as it sucks out the sand. We suddenly scoot forward. I hear the rumble as the car finds the dirt road. I use the word "road" loosely, even at five miles an hour I feel like we are in an earthquake.

Mandy's arm is still clinging to my ribs. She whispers, "I can feel your heartbeat."

Her right breast is next to it. Juan doesn't notice, his eyes are focused on the so-called road a bit obscured by the sand storm.

I keep up the banter to get everybody's mind off the tension. The outside sand flurry, the howling wind and the lack of visibility might help divert the tension, as well.

"Do you know what youth say when I ask what *kind* of music do you like?" There's no answer.

I go on. "They seem to fight the question. Frequently, more than half the time, they stammer and finally say stuff like, 'I like all kinds of music.'"

Tension is still churning. Mandy tries to put her head on my shoulder. It hits and bounces back with each pot hole in the road. Her right breast is still adjacent to my pounding heart.

I reiterate, "They fight the question and instead say a*ll kinds* of music."

She says. "Are you a radio programmer?"

"I'm a consultant now, and consultants do research. And yeah, three out of four males 18-24, when I ask what kind of music they like, respond, 'I like all kinds of music,' or something to that effect. Why do they do that? Anybody here got an answer?"

There was silence. Yet I kept silent.

Oddly it was Juan who first responded. "Because they don't have any fucking idea of how much different music is out there. If they heard some of it, they would call a lot of it shit."

I smile. *Ah, got him talking.*

As always I'm a bad ass trying to get to the bottom of things. I say, "True, but why fight the question? Can't they say stuff like, I like reggae and pop or rock, but no, they insist in saying stuff like any kind, or all kinds of music, despite the question being what *kind* of music do you like?"

Sandy in the back jumps in, "Well, two out four 18-24s' probably don't have any real taste when it comes to music, it is just blah, all the same."

I keep pushing. "It's very odd for 18-24s not to be opinionated about the music they like. They are in the final process to find out who they are and music, for most, is one of the identifiers. Nevertheless, when asked directly what *kind* of music do they like, it is like they don't even listen to the question, they respond, '*All kinds.*'"

Mandy says, "Maybe they don't want to be categorized. You are already categorizing them by putting them in blocks of ages. Maybe they are fighting the survey."

"That's a slither of the truth," I say. "But it goes deeper. We are living in an age where free enterprise is being suffocated by massive conglomerates trying to completely control the market. They make their employees follow strict guidelines, they give them little chance to find personal identity through their work, and youth has a real hard time jumping into that world. Even free enterprise feels the pressure to act the same now. You are right, Mandy, they don't want to be categorized, especially males 18-24 in my research. They are screaming to bust loose."

Mandy says, "I'm nineteen, and a girl, I sure don't want to be categorized in a survey."

Sandy, in the back, says, "Hey Danny, you might be on to something. I feel out of place in this world, like where can I get involved? I'm twenty-six, and sure I like reggae but I might answer 'all kinds,' too. I like variety."

Juan jumps in, "The world sucks, the spiritual way is all that there is left. We need to lift ourselves up in spirit to get away from this hell."

Mandy squeezes his hand in approval.

The Dread is silent but when I turn to him, I detect his approval.

I'm crying inside. I remember what it was like when I was a kid. Jobs everywhere. You were treated like an individual having a chance to find yourself in your work. Then twenty years later in the eighties, conglomerates overran free enterprise and started controlling the market. The workers have to follow strict guidelines or be fired for any slight deviation. And when conglomerates get a certain size they go on runaway, they can make a slew of mistakes to lose profit and still they rumble on. If you want to improve the situation, they just dump you because being a big shit is more important than creating value in the market place anymore and improving profit. Twenty-five years later, the kids aren't even trying. It is so hopeless. They'd rather search for the invisible than deal with Earth.

This stuff is hitting me like daggers. I'm crying. Maybe I do have a heart.

2

WELCOME TO RADIO 101

Earlier, nine days previous, October 16, 1989, in Honolulu, Hawaii.

KYTI Radio Station general manager's name was only known as Jackson. He sat behind his wide desk in a soft, fluffy, leather chair, listening to his hysterical radio programmer scream. "He ruined my station!"

Jackson remained unfazed. Radio programmers, who are in charge of the music and presentation of a radio station, come and go but General Managers have contracts too expensive to break without utter incompetence. Jackson had survived twenty years as a General Manager of various stations only moving when he got a better offer. Besides his basic concern was sales and Tony, his program director, was but a slight blip in the day's itinerary.

He looked at his watch. "First off, Tony, forget the word 'My Station.' This is a corporation and you and me are pawns. May I inquire what ruined the corporation's radio station?"

Tony was pacing up and down in the spacious red carpeted office, "Danny's shit got on---unbelievable shit. The advertisers, our listeners-" Tony's hand flew in the air, "Everybody is outraged!"

"Who complained?"

Tony stopped pacing, "Nobody complained. You know radio. Advertisers will just cancel. Listeners are just gonna turn the dial. You know that! We've got to appeal to the silent majority, not the lonely heart fools and weirdos that request songs on a radio station." Tony went on. "How in the hell did Danny get that record on the playlist?"

"The corporation is paying Danny Fall's consultant firm 40,000 dollars per year to consult. They run surveys, ask our listeners, test the music with potential listeners. But you, Tony, won't even listen to him. You won't even talk to him. Do you know why they are paying him 40,000 dollars per year? Because everybody who listens to Danny - their ratings leap."

Tony says, "My ratings went up without him."

"The corporation's ratings went up, not yours. And I might add, just a nudge, not a leap."

Tony resumed pacing, "How did that song get on? It's pure blaring noise, even the name of the band is bad, It's called 'Clash,' and the song is called London's Frying or something; it sounded like it too. Fortunately, I rushed in and lifted the needle before a full minute of the song escaped to the airways during prime time. But it was on the playlist all last night and in high rotation. I didn't put in rotation because I listen to everything before it goes on the air.."

"No, you don't listen or even talk to Danny, so I had him talk to the music director."

"You went over my head?"

Jackson took his hefty frame out of his plush chair. "Damn it, Tony, you just don't get it. It's not my radio station, it's the corporation's. They paid Danny's firm 40,000 dollars and you won't even talk to him. The corporation would have lost 40,000 dollars if I didn't have the music director do your duties that you refuse to do."

"You had Bobby put that song on behind my back?"

"I work for the corporation, not for your back, Tony." Jackson sat back down and looked at his gold watch. Three minutes until his tirade to the new sales staff. "Plus I'm not going behind your back. You are not working here anymore. You're fired!"

Tony stopped his pacing. "What?"

Jackson called accounting on the intercom. "Give Tony his full check, up through today. He just quit." Then Jackson put down the intercom. He pointed his finger to the door, "Now get out. I've got things to do for the corporation."

Tony just stared at him.

Jackson rose again, "Get the hell out; you're gone."

Tony staggered backwards, turned to the door, and shook his head. He turned around as he was opening the door, "You are gonna pay for this, Jackson."

"I already have. You've cost me big."

Jackson made a phone call. "I need a rap on Danny Fall. Can't afford him working for anybody in this town, got it. And fire that damn consulting firm. My program director is losing it. He quit on me. Danny is deliberately trying to destroy our station. Be sure the world knows that. Spread the word. Let the world know somebody is paying Danny to sabotage leading radio stations. And find out who is paying him to do it. Ask if anybody knows who the saboteur is. Got it?"

"To the max, Jackson. Didn't I warn you about Danny? Every station is afraid of him."

Jackson was the most respected general manager in Honolulu. Every station he worked for got better. But he was clueless as to why he was able to do that. He just had an uncanny ability to sniff out shit, and radio was full of it. Danny wasn't shit, he was a radio genius and the most popular DJ in Honolulu for five years before he tried to start his own radio station. The backers had dumped him after six months, mostly because of his political views. But radio geniuses needed to be corralled, brought to their knees to fit the corporate picture.

When he's starving, I'll get him. He spends money like water, anyway. For now, I'll make it impossible for him to get a job anywhere else.

Jackson knew Danny wouldn't leave Honolulu. He had put all his chips here. Two years later people were still asking radio stations to put him back on the air. Danny was gold here if he could just settle down. Jackson was gonna let him sweat it out, bring him down to reality.

He rose and went to the sales meeting. Five new sales reps were sitting in chairs around a large conference table waiting for his appearance. He walked in shouting,

"Keep your sorry asses down! This is the last chance for you to sit on them for the next five days. I want an hourly report from every one of you. Pep will give you the times each hour to call. If my phone isn't blazing, you won't last the week. If I'm on the line with someone else, I'll just punch on the conference button. You don't call anybody else, just me. And tell me the fuckin' truth.

"Now about Clients. Just visit em, no phoning, and visit em again, and again, until you get the sale. Only talk on the phone if they call you or you are calling me or Pep.

"Pep will give you a list. Every damn name on the list desperately needs to advertise with us whether they know it or not. We've done the research. You'll get the details as to why each one individually needs us. You got the easy part. If they want special treatment or better rates, talk to Pep, and Pep will talk to me. I want to know their dialogue: what you say to them, what they say to you, and if you don't get the sale, we'll detect what went wrong in your dialogue and send you back until you get the sale.

"Now get out of here. I hate meetings."

3

SUNSET GRILL

Returning to the Evening, October 25, night of the sandstorm, Western Kauai, Hawaii

Through the darkness, the four-wheeler moves into the parking lot at the Sunset Grill. The sand is gone and in the soft lights of the parking lot, so is most of the paint on the car.

The Sunset Grill is a casual place with an outdoor patio. As we approach, the waitress raises an eyebrow. We look homeless and the sand storm makes us look worse. I could tell she might refuse to serve us.

I smile. "This is the rock band Sublime. We need a quiet place so we are not disturbed."

The waitress looks at us up and down. "I've never heard of you."

"That's fortunate, that's why we are on a little island in the middle of the Pacific. But just to be safe, give us a quiet place out of way, if you can?"

She gives us a satirical shrug and motions us to a remote table reserved for smokers. As the kids sit down, I take the waitress aside. "We'll take two bottles of any kind of Merlot and five hamburger steaks with pilaf."

"I'll need to card the others," she says.

I slip her a twenty, "Hey, we're out of the way, aren't we? Nobody will notice."

She smiles. "I know. But sometimes the liquor commission sets us up."

I was prepared. I pull out two one hundred dollar bills wrapped in a napkin and handed it to her, saying, "They don't set you up this way, do they?"

She unravels the napkin, looks around, hesitates, nods, then leaves.

I turn and sit down.

"Hey, we don't even have a menu. Some waitress," says Juan.

"You're getting free food and drink, take what you are gonna get. You'll love it."

"Who's Sublime?" Asks the Dread.

"A fantastic rock and reggae band in Long Beach. Gonna be huge if I get a radio station to play them."

"You throw your weight around a lot."

My eyes turn to Juan. "You're right. It sucks. I'm just around people like that, so it rubs off on me. Sorry. But I don't think we would have a chance to be seated without some kind of bullshit. We look a bit tacky."

The waitress brings two open bottles of wine saying, "Nobody has heard of this Sublime band."

I smile, "They will."

"Where do you guys play?"

"We're from Long Beach, the ghetto of LA."

She smiles, "That, I'll buy."

Juan says, "I'm vegetarian."

Idiot kid.

"Damn kid, loosen up. The world is here for you to adapt. Shit, you're only how old? You got time to adapt. This is the best damn hamburger steak ever made. Don't like it, eat the plate, no meat there."

The waitress folds her hands across her chest, looks at Juan's belligerent face and smiles, "Bet you guys love your manager."

I nuked the conversation. "And I love these kids, too."

I pour five glasses of wine, four out of one bottle and one out of the second. Dread says, "I don't drink."

I just reach over and set his glass next to my own glass. "Look guys. We are all stranded, left out of the circle. Let's stick together and make the circle bigger so we can fit in it."

"What can we offer you? You got money. You push your weight around. We're not like that." Juan waited for an answer.

"You got it upside down, kid. I'm nothing without you. You are real, real in a shitty, fake, bullshit world. I need you."

"You don't even know us," says Juan.

I look at Mandy. "Mandy reads palms, I read eyes. I know you."

"Like hell you know me, don't buy that."

"You lived in the streets in Brazil, probably never had much of a home, stole from tourists a lot, smuggled into the US, got in with a rich older woman who you left behind in Texas. That about sums it up. Right? And the three of you have been together for a year or two before Juan showed up. He's the newcomer. And the three of you just moved to Kaua'i probably from San Francisco."

There was shock on the faces. "Yeah, I'm good, too, Juan; I used to tell fortunes myself."

"Never been to Texas, but you know that, don't you, you've been tracking me. You're a cop!"

"I just looked in your eyes and listened to your English, dumb ass. And you just said that vegetarian stuff to be cool with Mandy. Twenty-one-year-old vagrant males who have starved half their life are never vegetarian, even American Rastas."

The dread says, "Yeah, but I try to be Ital. I'm just too hungry to complain."

"Yeah, and you are close to thirty, yeah?"

"I'm twenty-seven, I'm not an old man yet."

"So what's the problem?" Mandy asks.

"The Constitution to the United States of America." I didn't want to elaborate on our first get together so I didn't say another word. But I was surprised. She noticed there was a problem.

Juan looks at Mandy. "He's crazy."

Mandy looks serious. "Didn't you say I'm a good fortune teller? He is going to be more famous than movie stars, remember?"

"I thought the Constitution of the United States was a great document. It is just what people do with it that sucks," says the dirty-blonde hair one.

"Ah kid, It's got a 'puka' that is making the rich richer and the poor poorer. That's what we are gonna fix."

"A puka?" Says Juan.

Dread adds with a laugh, "That we are *gonna* fix?"

"Puka. A hole. It's a Hawaiian slang word---for stuff that doesn't fit in the hole, or falls through."

The waitress proves to be a bit of a juggler. She comes with five plates in a precarious stack, three in one long arm, two in the other. She flops the hamburger steak plates on to the table a bit too loudly. "Anything else?"

"Just some water for the Dread." I say.

She laughs, or is it a smirk? "You don't even call them by their names. I'm surprised they put up with you. What do you have on them?"

"A job to change the world."

She shakes her head. "Musicians are crazy."

I turn to the kids. "Just eat and drink. Talk comes later." I guzzle a gulp of wine and gradually clean out the second bottle. I am thinking no one seems to fight it; it's like they accept me and go along with the "We."

What's going on that I don't know?

4

ON THE MOVE

In Lihue, Kaua'i there are three relatively cheap motels; an anomaly on an island flooded with swank hotels. I put Mandy and Juan in the Kaua'i Palms Motel, and was forced because of no vacancies, to put the Dread, the Sandy one, and me down the street a block, in the Motel Lani.

I figured Mandy would go with whatever I said and Juan would follow, but the Dread and the Sandy one were far more jaded about this world and would need some logical thinking to get into the program. But I had the advantage. They were homeless and had nothing else to choose from. It would be far harder when I had to explain the same thing to complacent America. I am happy with kids in general. They are just deposited into a shit hole by conglomeration, and they are greater than that. 'Why?' They finally got me off my ass to do something about this conglomeration thing. Maybe I can become a real radical.

"Can't figure you out," says the Dread. "Why are we here?"

"I thought I already mentioned that, to change the world. Take a shower and get some sleep and we'll talk in the morning."

Dread says, "My name is Gregory. Okay, gonna take a shower."

"Like Gregory Isaacs, good name. Don't clog up the drain with sand. We are all gonna shower."

As the Dread leaves, Sandy says, "My name is Brad, Danny. You want us to start a revolution?"

"Yep, but a non-violent one---I hope. And I like your name with a 'ley' on the end. The Sublime's singer and song writer's name is Bradley."

"You really like that band, don't you," Bradley says.

"All the great bands come from England. 'Sublime' is an anomaly, they come from Long Beach. The leader of the band is so upset with the world. He is a super 18-24, and defiant as hell."

"Why haven't I heard of them?" Bradley says.

"Because radio doesn't listen to the people. If radio doesn't play them, the world doesn't hear them. It's that simple. A lot of great bands out there. Crass, the Clash, Sex Pistols, Siouxsie & the Banshees, Joy Division, Smiths, The Cure, Nine Inch Nails, Depeche Mode, Bob Marley. You don't hear them unless you go to clubs or you talk to hip record stores. Great music is being suffocated by radio. Radio only plays the sounds left behind a decade ago."

Bradley just shakes his head. "Everybody has heard of Bob Marley."

"Bob is so big he seeps out of everywhere. But you don't hear him on radio, do you? Oh yeah, maybe one song, 'Jammin,' because it was redone by a local artist."

Next morning, I corral the kids and shuttle them to the oldest running restaurant on Kaua'i, Hamura's Saimin. It's around the corner. We take over the work table, then comes a waitress.

"You need to be out of here in twenty minutes. You want the regular or the special?"

I got this habit of pissing off the locals when they get territorial. I mean, Kaua'i is the ultimate place to live in the world, but if you weren't born here or spent suffering years getting entrenched, the locals, they get real protective of their golden place. Now this waitress, who looks like the center on a B-football team, she has just reduced our time down to twenty minutes.

I suck into the question to get to the horizon. "Why only twenty-minutes?"

"Lunch time is for the locals on this table."

The other lunch counter is real long and winds itself into the shape of a snake with itty bitty stools meant for midgets. You plop your ass down with one thought: When can I get a real chair? Great for encouraging turnover of customers, just eat and flee and then rope in the next crowd.

"We need the table. It's critical. And it might take more than twenty minutes."

She notices I stood my ground. She put her eyes into a penetrating, perhaps shock expression. And I am talking loudly, deliberately, looking for a savior.

I am lucky.

A carpenter with his apron comes over and says, "Wow, I heard the voice." He turns to the rectangular looking woman, yes, our sweet loving waitress, and says, "He's cool, this is Danny Fall, Gota. The guys will understand."

I say thanks, and tell Gota, "I will pay the meals for the regulars who haunt this table in twenty minutes and our carpenter friend here."

I hand her a hundred, and say, "We might be here awhile." My words don't seem to register with her.

She looms over me, "Regular or the special?"

A short menu makes it quicker to decide. Faster turnover. I get the message. Be quick. "We'll take the special."

Juan says, "What's the special?"

I reply, "What you get."

A minute and half later five bowls of saimin with a whole garden in it are placed heavily on the table.

Juan says, "Soup for breakfast?"

Mandy says, "Shh, it is almost lunch."

Gota adds forks to the table. It is a subtle insult. But Juan doesn't even notice the chop sticks and goes for the forks immediately.

I start with the problem in a loud voice. I want to prove to these kids I am for real and I am bent on setting them up with a plan.

"If you work for the government, your purpose is to serve the people. But if the government gets paid more, or has more stability, or better benefits, then the people that work for the government aren't going to be interested in serving."

The patrons notice me. Some stop eating.

I go on in an even louder than normal voice. "They are working there for better benefits to themselves—at least the majority are. And this gets compounded when you work for the Federal Government. Why? Because the Federal Government can make more money anytime it wants to. So federal employees get better benefits and are paid higher than the average salaries of the nation. They are there to serve the whole nation so their salary shouldn't be higher than the average income in all of America, including averaging in the poverty stricken.

"A good example is the US Congress. They get paid better, have better health care like the rest of the federal employees, and when they get fired by the people, they smile knowing they aren't really fired for they will get a pension for the rest of their life equal to 40% of the money they made in the five years they were overpaid in Congress.

"So who runs for the US Congress? The majority that run are doing it to make better income and a huge pension. The majority are not running to serve the people. And the ones who are running to serve the people usually are less funded and it's harder for them to make it. And Congress is controlled by the majority, so even if the service-minded make it to Congress, and try to serve, there is not much they can do when they get there, being the minority. And that isn't even the big problem. That's only the beginning of the problem."

From the audience someone shouted, "Danny Fall is on the mic!"

There were whoops and cheers. I was glad. The kids would begin to realize my presence. I nodded and went on.

"The United States of America was proud to be a free enterprise economy. But that was the past, not the now. Capitalism gets to a certain point when it goes on runaway, where businesses get so huge they can make a billion mistakes and still roll on seemingly unstoppable. And, when they get that big..."

I paused. "They try to control the market. Big business, the conglomerates try to control the market for their advantage. The more competition they isolate or destroy, the more they control the market. No longer are they trying to create 'value' like improving services, or even being sensitive to demand. When their workers see a way to improve value and be more sensitive to demand, they fire the workers, they don't care about that stuff anymore. They only want to control the market and destroy all things that made free enterprise flourish.

"They don't mind subverting the economy so they personally can get more. And where do they go to help themselves with better control of the market? They go to the US Congress. They lobby. And who are they lobbying to? The ones who ran for Congress for their own benefit. And what do these congress people do? They pass laws in their favor for kickbacks and campaign funds. They don't care about creating value in the market place anymore and of course their very last thought is helping the poor, the poor that conglomeration has created! The farthest thing from their mind is to serve the people, they are in Congress to serve big business---the conglomerates and enjoy the gravy.

"So, what are we going to do? We are going to change that!"

I slam my fist on the table. Soup ejects from the bowls.

One of the workers on a midget stool says, "Right on Danny. You best get back on radio!"

The restaurant customers are clapping.

Mandy smiles at Juan. "See. He is really going to try and do it."

"But how?" Questions Juan.

"Wait, we'll see." Smiles Mandy.

Someone on a midget stool says, "Danny Fall *isssss* back!" The crowd joins in on the long "is" and in unison cries, "Back." More cheers.

There is a crowd outside waiting to get in. The B-Football center, that rectangular Japanese waitress, is going about trying to pick up half eaten bowls to hurry everybody out for the next crowd. The crowd outside starts opting for take-out. Seeing the situation, I go about shaking hands and corralling the kids for departure. The questions are universal. "Which station are you going on?" "Will we be able to hear it on Kaua'i?"

Back at the motel we jump in the car and I tell Juan to head for the south side. I am so high about the response in the restaurant I forget to address the car thing. I got a four-day comp at the Hyatt. Might as well use it before we leave for Honolulu.

Kaua'ians are in love with trees. They plant them everywhere. And when a tree falls in a wind storm it is treated more like a tragedy, and it is immediately reseeded, even before one cares about the loss of his or her roof top. The car drives through a tunnel of trees, a highway where you may need to use your headlights even in the day due to the thick nest of leaning trees. Behind us is a police car. Not good. I had been wondering where our car came from, and am thinking I should have lambasted that question at the kids long before we left the Sunset Grill, last night. Big mistake. The police car puts on its siren.

Juan jumps on the pedal.

I reach over and yank his leg off the gas pedal to slow down the car. "Don't be stupid. We'll be fine. I know it's stolen. Pull over and don't say a word. So help me God, don't say a word even if the officer asks you a direct question. Let me answer it for you. Everybody, got it? No one talks, but me. No matter what the officer says to you, don't say a single word. Got it?"

Juan moves the car on to the shoulder. The officer pulls over. I know what he was doing. He is calling for reinforcements. I have to intercept him.

I get out and run to the officer, my hands in the air. "I can't believe I did this, officer."

The officer puts down the phone. He cautiously get out of the car.

I keep ranting. "I know it was reported stolen. It's crazy, officer. We were in a horrendous sand storm in Polihale, and this car had been parked over eight hours the motor still running, and we were desperate, the five of us needed shelter, and the car looked abandoned, we jumped in it for shelter, kept the engine running for the heater, so when the sand started sucking into the engine, we took off to clear it. Look, the wind stripped the car of most of its paint."

"I know about the Polihale wind storm. But that ended eighteen hours ago. You are complicit, at minimum," the officer says.

"Hey, I am just taking it to the Grand Hyatt, we are going to turn it in then. Couldn't see it be that much of a problem. Can't we take a taxi from here? It was my idea, and these kids were stranded there, too. It was an emergency."

I nervously watch the kids approaching, Mandy seemingly holding on to Juan to keep him from running away.

"Hey Danny, I know you. You cause enough trouble on radio. But commandeering a stolen car? I gotta take you in."

I say, "But leave these kids out of it, okay? It was my idea."

The officer points to Juan, "But he was the driver."

Mandy trembles, and stops. I know Juan is an illegal.

I just shake my head, looking humble, and say, "Yeah, officer I know. You gotta do what you gotta do."

The officer goes to his car phone.

"Kids, 'Just cool it. Don't move. Don't talk."

He comes back. "Do you guys have any personal stuff in the car?"

I say, "Not a thing. We lost everything to the sea in Polihale, we were lucky to get out alive."

"Damn Danny, I couldn't do it. I called you a taxi. But get your ass back on the radio. That's trouble enough. If I took you in, you'd probably never get another chance to get back on radio.

"It would be all over the papers, 'Danny Fall Steals a Car.' And, the five of you had better start running toward Poipu. I told the taxi you were joggers, but one of your friends was having a hard time breathing. And I got help coming in a few minutes. So run fast."

25

Relief on five faces. I say, "Thank you, Officer."

We all start running. I was the third fastest guy on the football team in high school but to my shock I can't keep up with even Mandy, and Juan is almost out of sight when the taxi appears.

Sitting in the backseat of the Taxi, *Shit, Twenty-five-years, plus smoking and drinking, it changes your body. Double shit, I sure could guzzle a bunch of beers right now. That was way, way too close.*

I check us in at the Grand Hyatt, and buy a set of summer clothes and bathing suits for everybody including me at the hotel apparel stores. We shower and the kids head toward the beach and pools.

I call my radio buddy in Honolulu to feel out the situation. Rabbit, a radio engineer and my best friend tells me the rumor. "You are getting paid to sabotage radio stations. You best stay on Kaua'i. Your wife took the kids and the dog to the mainland. When they take the dog, you know they ain't comin' back. And I bet she didn't pay the rent."

Fortunately, I had paid off my credit cards and had seven thousand dollars still left in my pocket. My credit line is at two hundred and fifty thousand on one card and unlimited on the other two. I figured all my other funds had gone with the dog. And I can't do much with the stocks; they are in both our names. I am in sad shape, considering six months ago I was a multi-millionaire. And now I knew why I was suddenly fired from the consulting firm: The rumor. I had five months left on the house rental lease at $3,000 a month. I tell Rabbit to tell the landlord my wife ran away with all the money and he'd best go after her, not me, 'cause I got none.

Shit, if my computer, stereo, and record collection are still there, the landlord is gonna take them.

I started in the streets in Hawaii twenty-five years ago, and I guess here I go again. I'm wondering if I should go back on radio. I really don't like being on radio but I'm just good at it. I prefer to be behind the scenes, to get a better perspective of how to manage the sound on radio. Radio is such a powerful instrument if it is done right, and being in the midst of it, like on radio, it is easy to lose your perspective. I'd rather guide the sound than be the sound.

THE RADIO REVOLUTION

My mind is ticking. I can tell. Juan is a natural. Call him, 'Don Juan with the Magic Wand.' Wave the imaginary wand on the radio, and the girls will swoon. It'll be like a kiss. Ratings will soar, especially with his accent.

Mandy is a natural, too. Hopefully I might get a break here on Kaua'i on a small time radio station to quietly start my crusade.

Hell, what a perfect place to start. Kaua'i is where great creations are formed on Earth. Then these creations are taken out to the world to make the world a better place to dwell within. I learned that on my first two days on the island when I was on my honeymoon seven years ago. Even the Dali Lama said, "All spirits enter Earth through Anahola, Kaua'i, and leave through Polihale, Kaua'i."

This is the beginning and the end of Earth. Perfect place to start. Hell, that's why I came back here. Start life at the center of Earth. Yeah, what was I thinking? There's no reason to go back to Honolulu now.

I go down towards the beach looking for a bar. Exotic recreational pools, cascading down, terrace after terrace, surrounded by tidepools of large golden fish, with the high rising waves thundering in the distance. It is an extensive walk and I am already feeling the stiffness from the run earlier through the tunnel of trees.

I order a Merlot. **B**ig mistake. It comes in a tiny plastic cup, the liquid about the size of a thumb nail. I gulp it down in two swallows and order a bottle of Coors beer, then another, then another. Things are getting better. I start thinking. How can I show America just how bad conglomeration has become and how it is destroying America? I smile. What a perfect example: radio. I'll test it out on the kids tonight.

5

HOW RADIO CAME TO SUCK

The evening comes. We five (Mandy, Bradley, Gregory, Juan, and me) go down the tiers of pools to a giant fish pond with large koi fish. They are swirling around in an early evening feeding frenzy. Stepping stones lead to an island in the middle of the pond where there is a thatched roof hut and tiki decorations. A sign hangs over a straw curtain, entitled, "Tidepool Restaurant." It looks Japanese but serves those little pretty display dishes, famous in fancy restaurants. The restaurants with the pretty decorated food you are supposed to nibble on---daintily. I'm not there for the food but for the quiet. It is 5:30 pm. The restaurant is just opening and I have reserved a small room where you could dip your bare feet in the fish pond if you had the urge. It is a bit romantic and you can hear the ocean waves thundering to the shore and smell the salt air as we settle under a string of Japanese lanterns. I didn't want to risk a thumbnail of wine so I order a bottle and two glasses for me and Bradley. I tell the waiter we have a meeting and wouldn't eat until later and the waiter smiles. Bow and tie waiters in fancy restaurants aren't as impatient as saimin waitresses. At least I hope not.

Always ready to lose it, Juan asks, "What is this meeting about? I thought this was dinner."

Mandy looks embarrassed in her thin see-through yellow blouse, not about the blouse, but about Juan's comment.

THE RADIO REVOLUTION

I know where Juan is coming from. He's been struggling for enough to eat all his life.

I say, "Juan, relax. You will never have to worry about food again. But you might have to wait occasionally, like now."

I go on. "We got a problem. The people of the United States think everything is fine. But it isn't. How can we let them know?"

"Go on radio?" says Juan.

"But what can we say to inform them of what is happening?" I say.

Mandy says, "Danny, what is happening?"

I say just one word. "Conglomeration."

Bradley says, "This has to do with what you said at the saimin restaurant, right?"

"Yes," I didn't say anything more, 'cause I want them to get involved in the conversation.

There was silence anyway. I finally say, "How do you make people see the light? You tell stories that show how different America was before conglomeration took over."

"Stories?" questions Gregory.

"Thanks to you, Gregory, for asking me at Polihale, 'How can radio *not* suck?' Well, there was a time when radio didn't suck. So the real question is, 'How did Radio Come to Suck?'"

The kids look shocked. So I repeat it, "Yes there was a time when radio didn't suck. What if we brought back that time? What if we made radio alive again, free of conglomerate pressure. Then let them listen to the other stations who are controlled by the conglomerates, let them experience the contrast, so their imaginations expand. They might become open to changing America and its Constitution. We do it by demonstration, not by a raving political discourse."

"I don't understand," says Bradley,

Mandy says, "Danny is opening the door to new thought. No one knows. Even Danny. But he knows we are being left out of society and he wants to get us and all others like us into society. He's looking for a fairer world. And he thinks radio can do it. Right?"

"We can do it, We five." I say. "Radio is just the tool."

"Why us?" says Juan.

"Juan you are a natural for radio, so is Mandy. Bradley is a deep thinker and Gregory is the heart and soul of our little group."

Mandy's eyes widen. "You do see a lot looking into eyes."

I suddenly realize Mandy is the leader of this group. She doesn't only control Juan, but Bradley and Gregory as well. And maybe me. Mandy stuns me. Her words are like razors.

I settle in with the story. "Tonight, I'm gonna tell you all a little story. You will tell this story when we get a radio station, with different props and characters maybe, yet still the same story. Then we will let people think, then look around at the world they are seeing, and hopefully they will begin to realize conglomeration is leading this world to hell. They'll see how a station run free of conglomeration is run, and how the stations absorbed in conglomeration are run, and when they see the difference, hopefully, they will get off their complacent asses and do something about America.

"Back in the fifties, radio didn't suck. Rock and Roll would never have made the impact it did on white radio, if radio was sucking like it is today. The year was 1957. Independent record companies dominated the charts. Radio stations had segues of Frank Sinatra to a surf instrumental, to an Italian song, one of which was the biggest selling single of the fifties---Nel Blu Dipinto Di Blu by Dominico Mudugo and there wasn't a word of English in it---- to Chuck Berry's wild rockers, to the screaming Little Richard, to the pop ballads like 'Old Cape Cod' by Patti Page, to a jazz number by Dave Brubeck or Cozy Cole who had the number one song, a jazz hit, to country songs like Gone by Ferlin Husky, to a drum solo like Sandy Nelson's 'Let there be Drums.' Stations played whatever was popular. They were not concerned with the "sound" of the station as they are today. Popularity was determined by the magazines Billboard and Cashbox charts which tracked sales in record stores. There were screams of payola, and there were independent record producers who lobbied radio stations for songs, but all and all the charts were honest. What was number one really was number one. And each region of the

THE RADIO REVOLUTION

country had songs that were especially popular in their area, and not popular anywhere else. A chart in New Orleans was radically different from a chart in Los Angeles, and in Hawaii a good third of the songs charted weren't on the Billboard top hundred chart. Today, no matter where you are in the country, you hear the same songs. And back then youth was addicted to radio, playing it twenty hours a day when school was out. When the Beatles hit, they changed the mentality of the whole world. And radio was what brought the Beatles to the hysterical masses."

Bradley says, "That's 'cause they had no TV or videos or video games and other distractions,"

"You couldn't be more wrong. TV and video games are attention sappers, but they are passive; they are not like radio which is the opposite: stimulating, and where you can do multiple things while listening to it. In fact, Bradley, you wanna know the power of radio, then?"

Bradley says, "It was a different world, then."

"Hell no! People don't change very much, even in thousands of years. Let me show you the impact of radio when it was free of the conglomerates.

"It was January 6, 1964. I had a record store in the upper Mojave Desert in between the grease cans and the bathroom at Jesse's Texaco gas station. I sold mostly 45 RPM records, the small ones, the ones with individual songs, one on each side. On Monday Morning I would go to LA and pick up records. I saw this Beatles record and knew a little about the band and bought 25 singles. Most record people didn't know anything about them. KFWB had a song discovery of the week they played every two hours. On this Monday Morning it was the Beatles song "I Want to Hold Your Hand." The first play was at six am. While driving back to the store, I heard the Beatles song in the car at ten am for the first time. I was forty minutes out of town. That was its third play. It hit me like a rock. I turned around, went back to the distributor and picked up 500 copies with a bogus check that had no chance of clearing.

Mandy reaches for my hand. "Calm down, Danny."

I feel a spark or something with her touch.

I calm down. I guess I am tense, thinking there could be another Beatles band somewhere but we will never hear it on radio, today. Conglomerates will muffle it.

Mandy smiles. Soothing. I speak more calmly. "So because I went back for more Beatle records, I arrived at the store an hour and thirty minutes late, at 1:30 PM. The kids were still in school; mostly only school kids bought 45s in those days. That was my clientele. Nevertheless, there was a line of people waiting for me to open the door. Their only question was, 'Do you have it?' Most didn't even remember the name of the band. I pulled down the wire gate went inside, and the phone was ringing off the hook. I answered it. Same question: 'Do you have it?' Remember, at 1:30 PM it had only played four times on the radio. Some people said they traveled seventy miles to my place to get it, 'cause I had the reputation in those days of having the new hot records. I sold the five hundred and twenty-five records by early next day and stayed open two extra hours that first Monday night.

"The check cleared! Radio was that powerful in 1964. They were still sensitive to the demand. Conglomeration hadn't set in then. Let me remind you right here: if this happened now in 1989, the new Beatles wouldn't make it to radio. It would have to travel the road Bob Marley had to travel in the late seventies. He's equally as popular, yet radio shunned him, so he just gradually increased sales and people don't care about radio anymore because people know in their subconscious, 'If you don't play Bob, you are not important.' Radio can't trick listeners as much as programmers believe. Those assholes think they can stuff whatever they like in your ear, and you will like it! Hell no."

Mandy shook her head. "You got a lot of steam, Danny."

Gregory said, "Subconscious?"

"Yes, Gregory, radio taps the subconscious. If it lets the world into it, it puts a spark in there. Subconsciously people know when radio is being honest. And when it is a lie, they say what you said Gregory in the car last night: 'How can radio not suck.'"

"Kids, that's how bad conglomeration is. It doesn't give a shit about the demand. It only cares about controlling the market. Let me repeat that. Conglomerates don't care about meeting the demand, they only are concerned with controlling the market to their favor."

Bradley says, "Wait, you are saying the America of the free is now controlled by a bunch of conglomerates?"

"Why ask, Bradley? You must know, at least subconsciously." I didn't want to elaborate.

Gregory says, "White people are so idealistic. It's okay, Bradley, but you don't see what we see. Danny is absolutely right, here."

I go on. "The Beatles and Bob Marley are proof. Beatles were instant. Conglomeration hadn't strangled the radio then. Marley was suppressed because by his time, a short ten years later, conglomerates had taken control of radio. Rock and Roll was suddenly gold, and the major record companies wanted to control it like misers. They wanted to possess it, just like you, Juan. You want to possess Mandy, 'cause she is gold. Same thing."

I went on, looking at Juan. "We don't need to own anything. We don't need it. Possessing things sickens us. When we own something, we try to protect it. That is sending our energies to nowhere."

Juan stares. He looks defiant.

"We don't need security. Security slows us down. It makes us think strange. You were in such an unstable world you looked for security, Juan---desperately. But getting it will destroy you. You need to get fearless, and let everything around you evolve, as it is supposed to without you conducting its direction."

Gregory, uncomfortable, tries to distract me. He says, "So how did this all happen, how could music allow such a thing?"

I wasn't listening. "Juan, you gotta get it. Now. You don't have time to drift backwards. Too much is before us to slow it down. I need you. Mandy needs you. I love all of you, but grappling for security is death now. You don't change the world by worrying about security."

Juan's voice wobbles. "I can't. I can't. My whole life is Mandy."

"No. Mandy was your life saver. Mandy is all our lives' saver."

I stopped. What am I saying? 'Mandy is our lives' saver?'

I just realized it. Mandy is all our lives' saver.

I continue, "Forget controlling. Enjoy her presence and her freedom to be her."

"I can't." Rebels Juan.

I got up from the table and went to Juan. "That's good. You are being honest."

"I'll be honest forever with her." Juan says.

I was quiet. I don't want to say anything. I go and sit down.

Juan is shaking. Mandy holds her ground and keeps silent.

This is a wise, wise woman, I think.

Gregory and Bradley seem to be staring out in space.

It was up to me to fill the void.

I say, "Mandy brought you into the group. Why? Because you are a beautiful soul. Nobody in this group has gone through what you have. Well, maybe Mandy. That is part of your bond to her. But to continue with Mandy in a meaningful role, you need to let things happen. Don't try to control them anymore. You are safe now. Let things happen. And the suffering and the death around your memories will fade. And you will have a chance to bite back. We all are left out of this world. But we all will have a chance to bite back."

I take a sip of my wine. Bradley does too. Juan seems distant. Mandy takes his hand.

Tears were coming out of Gregory. "Yeah," he says. "We been isolated from the world, and I know my band was popular but it never made it to radio, except a little on college radio. Danny is right. They don't play reggae on the radio. Conglomeration, controlling music, has shut our generation down."

"Kids, I gotta explain to you how this happens. How conglomeration turns into a huge cancer in economics."

Mandy says, "Tell us, Danny."

"Small business was the norm when I was young. Runaway chains and huge conglomerates weren't controlling the market place. Radio stations were not allowed to own another radio station in any market. That changed gradually and now you are allowed to own three stations in a market, and be in many markets with up to 140 radio stations.

"As I said, in the fifties the charts were dominated by small independent record companies. The major record companies thought Rock n Roll was going away, so they didn't venture into the market aggressively. But by the late sixties it was clear. Rock n Roll wasn't going away, and utilizing their superior distribution systems the major record companies started buying up the independent record companies and songs. In a free market that wouldn't be terrible; they were providing a superior distribution service and all, and the artists weren't getting shafted as much as they were with the independent record companies. It should have been just fine, *except*! And it was one big hell of an except.

"When companies get a certain size they start thinking of ways to control the market. Of course, in the beginning it seemed not to be too big of a deal.

"For example, Billboard was the only trade paper then. Cashbox had closed. To get a record on radio you needed to release a single, and that single needed to be reported as selling by the reporting record retailing stores. So what did the major record companies do? They cheated. They called the reporting retailers and ask for 'favors.' 'Can you give me a number one this week for this record?' The reporting retailer might say, 'Oh sorry, I've already pledged the #1 to Columbia, can you take a number six? And I sure could use some advertising moneys for my weekly ads in the newspaper. And oh yeah, do you have free goods?'

"That's how it began. The sucking of radio. And, of course, the independent record company's songs, no matter how popular, never made the charts very high and with radio following the charts, the new exciting music of the day that the independent record companies had generated in the fifties and sixties started disappearing from radio. This was the beginning of the major record companies' quest to control the charts. This take over began in the early seventies, and by the late seventies a great portion of the popular music of the day didn't make it to the airways, including Bob Marley. Artists like Siouxsie and the Banshees, The Sex Pistols, The Cult, Crass, The Clash, Gregory Isaacs, and Jimmy Cliff, though enormously popular, were either imports or on independent labels, and never made it to radio. FM radio, which wasn't dominate in the seventies, took up some of the slack, nevertheless a great many artists who were terribly popular still didn't make it to radio.

Bradley says, "I know most of these groups."

"How?"

"I hear them everywhere, like in the clubs and on the streets. There everywhere."

"But not on radio."

"Danny, radio doesn't count anymore. We don't listen, except maybe accidentally."

"See, radio taps the subconscious. You don't listen to radio because subconsciously you know it is not representing the world.

"And now things are far worse. Youths now, cluster in dingy coffee shops, wear black, and think radio is a horrible monster devouring their lives. Their poems are about necrophilia and depression. The rowdy, boisterous youth of the fifties and sixties is now meek, and wondering if the world is out to get them. If they have a concert anywhere, the police close it down because of noise complaints. Their music and identity are totally muffled. The Popular bands of the eighties are The Cure, the Smiths, Metallica, Slayer, N.W.A. and the Beatles of the eighties is Bob Marley. They never get heard on radio? Right?

There was silence.

Gregory says, "Shit, you are right on."

I went on. I was trying to control my anger. "What caused this disaster? You are the first generation to meet conglomeration head on.

THE RADIO REVOLUTION

The great squeeze in artistic freedom has begun. In the late seventies music started splitting into entirely new genres. In the fifties it wasn't even called genres, just popular music. So what the fifties would call music, there was, suddenly Punk, the Sex Pistols, Crass, the Clash, Social Distortion, etc. There was Reggae, Jimmy Cliff, Bob Marley, Gregory Isaacs, and Studio One artists. There was Disco. There was New Wave like the Cocteau Twins, The Smiths, The Cure, Sisters of Mercy. There was Ska like The Specials and early UB40. There was Rap like The Sugarhill Gang and Run DMC. But the major record companies were too afraid to try new sounds like the independent record companies had done in the fifties, so they tried to suppress all these new genres from happening, and radio didn't play them. Finally, in 1979, Disco became a radio format for a short five months before it died a brutal death of being overplayed with no variety between disco songs. Remember, stations were playing only a specific sound by the seventies: pop, soul, album oriented, country, and for a few short months, disco. And the real market of music was six or seven new styles of music like new wave, Gothic, glam rock, ska, punk, reggae, rap and heavy metal.

"Why had radio not played a variety format like the fifties? It was because major record companies encourage radio stations to play a "sound," so they could get artists to create that sound. It gave them the security that they could get airplay. Radiotron, the monster conglomerate of radio advertising, felt the need to disperse stations into sound formats (so they could get more revenues), so they went along with the major record companies encouraging radio stations to play a "sound," in order to get ratings and therefore ad dollars! Radio stations became adult contemporary, top 40, easy listening, album oriented, disco, country, and even in the late seventies, jazz. There was no mixing the sound and independent record companies who were introducing reggae, new wave, metal, gothic, punk, and rap, got zero airplay! England had a lot of these new sounds, but the American record companies passed a law making it illegal for record stores in America to order these sounds from England. The Major record companies of America had no interest in responding to the demand. They only wanted to control the market!

"And the control got worse! The major record companies didn't like the idea that Billboard only counted sales even though they had found a way to control the charts. So they lobbied and finally got Billboard to count only half of their chart in sales, and the other half in whatever radio was playing.

"Can you imagine that? Billboard was told: don't worry about popularity, don't worry about what people are buying, only worry about what we radio stations are playing. They wanted Billboard to report only what the major record companies wanted to be on the charts! And, of course, radio stations got so many favors indirectly from the major record companies that radio started playing whatever the major record companies wanted them to play. So the charts reflected only what the major record companies wanted. They had absolutely zero interest in what people wanted! Instead radio stations started using the word POWER, meaning whatever we play you WILL like! Of course, the lifeblood of the music industry, the independent record companies, sank into the background. And radio in the eighties sucks! You kids of the eighties - your musical tastes have been utterly suppressed. And you all think there is no place for you in this messed up, controlled world. Music is everything to youth. It's your identity. And if your identity gets squashed, how can you jump in this madness? Even if you couldn't label it before, am I right?

The kids look scared. For the first time they saw my rage. No one answered.

We just sat there staring at each other. I took a gulp of wine.

Gregory talks, "For me it is a double whammy being black and being in the eighties and my reggae band never got on commercial radio, though it sold real well anyway. But I think Bob, unlike The Beatles, didn't make it to radio because he was black."

I couldn't calm down. I started talking louder. "Bob was on an independent label 'Tuff Gong.' He owned it. It got distributed by "Island Records, in America. Island was an independent record company.

THE RADIO REVOLUTION

That's why, despite Bob Marley's Legend album probably being the biggest selling album of the eighties, it never made the Billboard top 100 Chart! But just recently Island was bought by Atlantic/Warner Brothers complex, a major record conglomerate, and oh, oh, oh, suddenly Bob Marley's Legend Album is on the Billboard 100 Album Chart! So now it's getting charted on Billboard and pretty soon you'll hear a lot of Bob on the radio. It is not an issue of black and white, Gregory. It is an issue of the conglomerates controlling the charts and keeping the independent record companies' songs off the chart, despite the fact that it is the independent record companies who have consistently brought the new exciting music of the day.

The waiter enters our little room, listens in shock to my anger, hesitates, and leaves.

"And guys, it's gonna get worse. Trust me, it is gonna get worse. We'd better find a way to stop it."

"How?" Asks Juan.

I calm myself, and actually laugh. "I'm thinking," I say.

Silence returned and the waiter cautiously entered the room for orders. Dinner came. Juan didn't complain about the size of the meal. The wine glasses were passed around. Even Gregory took a few sips. We all felt it. There had been so much intensity in my words, but I could tell. We were a team.

Mandy gave a toast. "Here's to the end of conglomeration." She laughed. Then said in a blaring voice so unlike her, trying to imitate me, "THE END OF CONGLOMERATION!"

We all laughed.

6

THE FAMILY

I'm staring out at the waves thundering against black rocks from the penthouse's second balcony.

The breaking of the waves is so powerful. They pound relentlessly upon the black rocks, foam discharging into the howling wind, as they gradually pulverize the rocks through the ages into black, then white, sand. Everything eventually turns white, I think.

Even in Hawaii where white boys are a minority, radio stations are owned *only* by the white boys. White boys like to throw around their power, dictate to their secretaries while sitting on top of their desks words so important the white-boy-owner thinks each word will reorganize the entire earth. They scream at the production managers (the guys who make the commercials), scream at the sales staff, scream at the program director, puff up with juicy-lucy-mountain burgers and have headlights blaring out of their mouths that make it impossible for any word to be returned to the bonfire in their brain.

Hey, like the white foam waves, crushing the black rock shoreline.

So it is a bit of a challenge telling them: your station sucks and you need me to change it completely.

It's even worse than that. I'm a white boy. I've got a bonfire in my brain. I'm mouthing off so nobody can rebound to my statements. And damn, I'm trying to rearrange the world. And if Mandy had a desk, I would sit on it if I couldn't get into her lap. In fact, there are only two things different. I don't own a radio station. And I don't have a production manager, a sales staff and a program director to scream at.

But I'm beginning to realize I can't leave these kids. I'm stuck in this mode until death. My whole existence is now dependent on these kids. In one day, I'm blind to anything else. They represent the screwed, young adults of the eighties. There is something in me that has to do this at all cost. *The world isn't the way they sell it to be.* When I was young I bought into it hook, line and sinker. We are free. Anyone can become President if they want to. But I was a quantum physicist, more than that, a mathematician even though I never went to a formal college. Everything is probabilities. Whites have a hundred plus chance to be President over blacks.

I'm pacing the balcony of the Penthouse at the Grand Hyatt. It is not that high up. There is a law on Kaua'i which states that buildings can't be higher than a coconut palm tree. The penthouse is three stories up overlooking the pounding waves splashing upon the coral reef, then withering into kisses upon the black rock beach.

Gregory comes up to me. "How are we gonna do this?" He asks.

"I never think like that," I say. "I don't know. I just intend to do it."

"Then you don't have a plan?" Gregory just shakes his head, and grins.

"Yeah, a beginning to a plan. You know math, Gregory?"

"It's not my forte."

"Well, there's a place where mathematics lives. Lives, and in that place, there is a knowing of what is right and what is wrong. More properly stated, in the world of mathematics balance is everything. Unbalance finds a way to erect itself towards balance, no matter how small the probability is. Conglomeration unbalances everything. Deep in the psyche of people, they know that balance must return. Hell, we might be the most complex mathematical creatures on the planet; we must know, deep inside, that conglomeration is a dead end. We just need to pick away at the ice of our skulls, 'til this inner balance reappears. Math is grouping grotesque, massive, clumsy conglomerations, balancing them like a juggler, until they give us a picture that is, maybe less in focus, but a picture nevertheless, that can lead us to a bigger picture of the real problem."

I continue after a pause, Gregory silent. "Still, we are in a tidal wave going one direction, so it's hard to stop and think, what is right and what is wrong? The pleasures seem to be luring us to ride the tidal wave, rather than sticking our heads into it and trying to swim against it."

I was moved by the thrashing of the waves. "Nature does it naturally," I say. I felt the magic of the ocean waves disassembling upon the black rocks providing a new picture, a new picture of balance.

It just came out of me. It just seemed natural at that moment. "How do you cope with this white world? Maybe you need to think about it before you answer, it is a complex"…. …Gregory interrupts.

"I'm not in the white world. When it makes its presence known, which I'm pretty good at not seeing, but when it does show its face and I recognize it, I sometimes pretend I don't see it, other times, when it is way too obvious, I just walk away, granted angry, but still I just walk away. It's nothing I can enter anyway. Sometimes I see it in the black world, then I just wanna puke. That's when it's the most obvious to me."

"You don't want to change it?" I ask.

"It's too big to change. It's light years away. It would take a million lifetimes to change it" Gregory is staring off toward the horizon.

"White people think things are getting better for blacks. You don't think that?"

"Cosmetically, yeah, maybe, but in reality, hell no. Juan is right. Bob (Marley) is our light. Go inward; don't mess with the world outside."

"So you really don't want to get involved with what I'm trying to do?"

"Danny, I don't know about you. I feel I'm just here to witness the effort. You are like nobody I've ever met, and I just want to see what happens. I can't believe I'm even here, 'cause this is the white world

THE RADIO REVOLUTION

to the max. It's obvious, but it hasn't made me angry, yet. It's crazy. I can't figure out why I'm here. Maybe, deep down, there is a bit of hope. Maybe you're digging in me to find it. Is that why we're talkin' like this now?"

"No. I'm looking for guidance from you."

"What?" Gregory started laughing. "You talk like you got all the answers. And I sure don't. I still don't get you, Danny."

"Well, if something comes to your mind, let me know, okay?"

Gregory just shook his head. "You are definitely hard to figure out."

"I don't like it when you say that, Gregory. I'm just being honest. I'm not hard to figure out. I just want to make this world better. Why be here, if I don't try. That's me."

"It's the way you try that I can't figure out."

"Then help me with a better way to try."

"Damn, Danny, I can't believe you're serious."

Mandy came out to the balcony. She might have heard some of the conversation but she didn't let on.

"Juan and Brad went to the hot tub. Can I join you guys?" She wrapped her arms around Gregory from behind, pressing her juicy breasts to his back. Her immaculately beautiful face. When she is relaxed it looks like a pixie, her slender arms and her tall stick figure facing sidewise towards me. She says, "I'm so glad you are still with us."

Gregory just smiles, still facing the dark thundering ocean as seen from the balcony.

I didn't know what to say to that. I remain quiet.

Gregory says to Mandy, "How are you and Juan coming along?"

"We had a long talk. I told him how I feel. At least he listened. What Danny said - thank you Danny - I think he is taking it to heart."

Gregory continues, "You think he'll join the club?"

"Probably. He belongs here, but expect moodiness for a while. He can't believe you are real," she taps my shoulder. "But he will. I'm sure of it."

Mandy laughs as she feels Gregory tense up, "I'm talking about Danny not you, silly, Juan has always known you are real."

I say, "I'm gettin' the idea this is one tight family."

Gregory says, "Yeah, we three are. Hopefully Juan will join the party. And for the first moment, I'm realizing you are a part of the family too---Danny."

Mandy laughs, still hugging Gregory her face turned toward me, "I knew instantly. I knew the moment I saw you fumbling with your tent like a six-year-old. I knew then you so didn't belong out here camping alone. I knew then Danny. You are my family."

Tears are actually coming out of my eyes. And I say, "It's wonderful to be a part of this. I haven't been a part of anything in a long, long, while." I realize I'm lying to myself. I've never been a part of something so beautiful.

Mandy moves from Gregory and hugs me in the same way from my back. It's too much. I turn around and hug her desperately from the front, then pull Gregory into our net. We all seem moved. Tears came forth from my eyes, perhaps the others, I don't know. My eyes were closed.

Gregory says, "I guess it's your initiation night."

"I don't understand," I say.

Mandy smiles. "It's the night I make love to you."

I am in shock. What have I gotten myself into? The woman before me is beyond beautiful. Looking into her eyes, it's like we're sailing through the sky for evermore, and together. How could I even look at her as a sex act? As a sexual creature? God, this is crazy. But I don't want her in the normal way. I want to be with her and become part of the family. I want to touch her magic. I want to let myself go and see where it will lead.

It is like my old world dropped away from me, seeing her for the first time.

She says, "I know you are scared. I know you have another life you are not ready to leave, at least, not completely. I know you want to touch me and make me sing. I know all this. Don't worry; we'll be

THE RADIO REVOLUTION

together for life, whether you want to go all the way or not tonight. I'm in love with everybody here. We know you haven't broken your barriers. We know you are one of us, but you don't know as of yet, how close we all are. We know this. And we are so, so, patient with beautiful souls, and you are one, Danny, you are an amazingly beautiful soul that is here to make the world sing.

"We need you. You need us. We, together, are a super team. And your dream to change the world. We are scared. We are worried. With your ways, you might lead us to oblivion, but we don't know for sure, and we know of no one else who is really trying."

I reply, "I don't know why I love you so much; all of you, even Juan."

Mandy says, "I see the way you treat Juan, like a father trying to wake his son up to the real world. That's why we are all here together. The other four of us never thought of changing this world. But now you are us and we are you, so we'll try, with you."

I am stunned. Nobody has ever seen me in this way before. No one has ever seen the real me and appreciated my presence on this Earth. Mandy did it instantly. And I was wrong. Not only Juan, but everybody in this group takes their signals from Mandy.

She sees the beauty that we are. I am in her web, completely. She is like a mirror to me. The others must feel the same. What is love? A mirror that allows you to see yourself, to see the beauty within yourself, whether you are in a gang in Brazil destroying others with guns and stealing from tourists, or me, a white asshole pushing the world around, not paying attention to how others are taking it.

Gregory is moved by her words too. "He says, "Forget what I said Danny, I'm here to help you anyway I can."

7

KEOKI'S

I have a friend in radio who was now the morning DJ on Kong Radio on Kaua'i. I'd hung around Ed back in the seventies when I was living on the streets, helped answering requests on Ed's Sunday Radio Show and I talked to Ed about my wild ideas for programming radio stations.

Ed was a staunch believer in the way radio is. Gotta be careful what you play, don't play anything unusual, don't play oldies requested during prime time, never play two female singers in a row. The people who don't call are your real listeners, they make your ratings soar, and the fewer songs you play the better your ratings will be. If your ratings fall, just shorten the playlist. Familiarity is everything.

Still, Ed was a good fellow. He listened to my radio theories, even got me appointments with program directors. Of course, my wild, creative ideas of programming could only get a smile from program directors bent on making everything sound the same. But when I became the highest paid DJ in Hawaii making a million a year, and playing music that would make any program director vomit (mostly old standards from the 30s and 40s), Ed was beginning to be more open to my ideas. And on Kaua'i, the center of the universe, Ed had more leeway to experiment with my theories. For Kaua'i might be the most progressive spot in America - spiritually, environmentally, sexually and socially and the source for the majority of Hawaii's traditional music, even though it had less than five percent of the islands' population.

I call Ed in the afternoon.

"I heard the rumor. What's going on?" Ed says.

I laugh, "Somebody doesn't want me in Honolulu anymore, I guess I'm too big of a threat. It's total bullshit."

"Yeah, there's no way I'd believe it. How long are you staying?"

"I might be here for good. Ed, how do I get a radio station on Kaua'i, pump it up to 100,000 watts, get repeaters on all the islands, and blast Hawaii off stagnant radio?"

Ed starts laughing. "You never change, do you, Danny?"

"Let's get lunch. What do you say?"

"Where are you?"

"Grand Hyatt." I say.

"No lunch. I'm stranded with family things 'til seven."

"Okay, eight at Keoki's."

"Keoki's? Somebody might see me. My job might be on the line!"

"You know why I'm here. You got a cover story, Ed. You're safe. Plus, we can talk about other stuff too, like me hiring you to teach my two new DJs and be my operations manager."

"With what, the scuttlebutt on the street is your wife took all your money, yeah?"

"Shit, Ed. This is bigger than radio. I need you."

Ed was silent, thinking. He didn't like the job he was in anyway, too much corporate bullshit, too many consultants and accountants changing the *naturalness* of radio. Danny was famous now. A legend, even had a half an hour interview on PBS in England. Sure, somebody might back him with a radio station again. "All right, I'll see you at eight. Hope you're prepared for Saturday night, Danny." Ed started laughing.

I didn't pay attention to Ed's comment. I confirmed it. "Eight then." I was smiling, too.

Keoki's is a typical open-air bar and restaurant on Kaua'i with its torches, palm trees, and gardens. Soft trade winds kiss your forehead and tease your hair. You sip a glass of wine, stare at a cloudy night sky watching a few strong lighted stars seep through on a new moon night and Juan, suddenly erupts, "Why are we here?"

Mandy and Bradley laughed. Gregory just smiled and shook his head.

I didn't answer, watching the waitress bringing the plates of pupus.

"Well?" says Juan. But then his attention got diverted to the food.

"Hey," I say. "Romantic night, guys. Why don't we take turns dancing with Mandy?"

We had gotten to the restaurant early because Kaua'ians don't believe in reservations, but it wasn't busy, and we had a half an hour before Ed was due.

The music was traditional Hawaiian but the singer was weak, especially on the falsetto notes. Gregory took Mandy's hand and ushered her to the dance floor. Bradley and I smiled at each other, watching Juan devour a Pork nachos.

Bradley says "You sure don't mind spending money."

"Yeah, I don't want to be caged into anything. Money can cage you."

"You never run out?"

"Once." I laugh. "I went crazy. I ended up in a mental hospital. My first wife and I went on vacation in the islands. Some vacation. She cashed in my ticket and left me stranded with no money or credit cards or a way to get back to Virginia. I guess she wanted to be sure I didn't come home. Now it's my second wife who just took all the money and kicked me out of the house and then ran off to the mainland with the dog and my two kids. But I ain't gonna go to no hospital this time. I got a new family."

Bradley smiles, "That you do. Mandy loves you, man, even more than the rest of us, I think. She told us, you gonna act crazy for a while, but just wait, you are gonna change the world for better."

"You guys take her word as gospel?"

Bradley smiles. "She's real intuitive. We were freezing in San Francisco even in the last days of summer and Gregory suggested we go to Hawaii because it was like Jamaica, which he loves. Mandy pops it up out of nowhere, 'Yeah, it is important we go there. There's something we can do there.'

"We wanted to do something. But there was nothing we could stand to do in San Francisco so we all were eager when she said that.

"So we landed in Honolulu with one of Juan's fake Id's and credit cards. But too many homeless there on Oahu. So we jumped a plane to Kaua'i and at the airport Juan copped a four wheeler and we hid out in Polihale. Five hours later you jumped in the car, and Mandy did her trip on you, and now we got something to do. We were just waitin' to do something. And more important, whatever we were gonna do, we wanted to do it together. You turned out to be the perfect solution."

"Thanks, kid. I appreciate that."

Gregory and Mandy are putting on quite a display dancing, whirly here and there and then in the middle of the song they start swaying in a hula style that had most of the patrons noticing.

They just got here from San Francisco? And they were dancing the hula? I was amazed.

The band started the classic "Beautiful Kaua'i'" and they continued in a hula fashion. I don't think any of the patrons had ever seen a black man dancing the hula, and the way they did it was magical. Gregory slid towards the stage and just before the chorus, asked for the mic and the singer, dubious, relinquished it.

To the everyone's shock, out came a haunting falsetto voice, and though Gregory hummed some of the words he didn't know, Mandy harmonized with him as they danced the hula.

The applause was enthusiastic and lasted over a minute.

Back at the table I asked, "My God, where did you learn to do that?"

Mandy smiles. "We came here because of Gregory. He was in a reggae band in Jamaica for three years. And he likes this latitude, 22 degrees north. It's like Jamaica. And we bought a bunch of Hawaiian Music in a store in San Jose. Lot of Hawaiians there, and also took Hula lessons there."

Gregory says, "There are a lot of similarities between Hawaii and Jamaica. Both love the reggae beat; Hawaii has its slack key guitars, and Jamaica has its slack key horns."

I added, "Every region has a different taste for music, that's something I miss in radio now that conglomeration has destroyed that. And your latitude on Earth is a big factor in the style of music."

Ed, despite having a dead leg caused by polio in his youth, found a way to a strut with a slide step and a swagger rambling to the table, displaying his giant wide smile. He greeted everyone with intensity, even diverting Juan from the food.

He smiles, "Danny made Honolulu crazy, and now I hear tale he is about to do the same with Kaua'i. Your spiel at Hamura's Saimin is already the talk everywhere I go. Danny, you need to be careful. In Honolulu everybody is rushing around busy, not listening too hard to your spiels, but out here, their ears are burning. We don't have too much to do out here. This is country."

"Beautiful country," smiles Mandy.

Ed looks at Mandy. Everybody at the table knew what he was thinking. "Not as beautiful as you, dear."

I broke the spell.

"Ed runs the tightest ship in radio. You learn from him and everyone in radio will be impressed."

Ed says, "Danny is a maverick on Radio, so don't listen to him. He does everything upside down.

"What did I tell you was the secret to radio, Ed?"

"'Always do the unexpected.' And I try. I just don't have the imagination you have, Danny."

Ed goes on. "Kids, let me tell you an embarrassing story. And it's gonna be *more* embarrassing this Saturday. In fact, that *is* why Danny is on Kaua'i this week.

THE RADIO REVOLUTION

"Danny came to visit me on the radio here as a consultant last year. I invited him to the morning show. I asked if he wanted to do the sportscast. If you live in Hawaii, you know who the Hawaii Rainbow Football Team hates the most, and it is the BYU Cougars. So two nights before, BYU had come to own us once again, and they did it, by beating us on the last play. There was all this talk in Monday's paper about refs calls. Everybody thought we should have won. So I let Danny talk about the column in the morning paper, the one about all the bad ref calls.

"Nope. Danny does the unexpected. He starts talking on radio, saying, 'You gotta give the Washington State Cougars a lot of credit; they gotta have a real good team. The Sunday paper said, 'Cougars snip the Rainbows.' Imagine that, a bunch of cougars from Washington State taking a bite out of our rainbows? Those cougars from Washington State must have rabies or something. I hope we don't have to play *them* again. Ever. Those Cougars crazy loco. And did you hear? They are in bed with bunch of horny cougar refs.'

"He was talkin' in a fake local tone. You hate to correct a DJ on the air; I mean, I couldn't believe Danny didn't know anything about football and BYU and the exciting game we had at Aloha Stadium. How could he make that mistake and say we played the Washington State Cougars not the BYU Cougars? So I popped in a commercial and said 'Danny, BYU cougars we played, not the Washington State Cougars.'

"Danny just smiled and said, 'I guess you got a few listeners after all. All the lines are blinking. Let's answer them live.'

"I'm not even allowed to answer live, somebody might swear, but Danny just picked up the line. And the worse possible words made it to the airways.

"'You dumb ass. What are you doin' on the radio, fucking ha'ole? Go back to the mainland, you dumb ass, that was the BYU Cougars that beat us again! Damn, do I have to take this now, from one more stupid ha'ole!'

51

"Danny just hung up the phone and said, to me live on the radio. 'You imagine that, some dumb local thinks we could have lost to the cougars of BYU. Those idiots. Where do your listeners come from, Ed? We would never never never, never lose to BYU. If it was the BYU Cougars, we would have thrashed them by forty or more points. They be looking for a rainbow to carry their wimpy asses home.'

"I finally got what he was doing. And I said, trying to hold back my laughter, 'Yeah maybe they were imposters, maybe a pro team or somethin.'

"Danny says, 'Yeah, there are a lot of cougars out there. There's the Houston Cougar Football Team, the Washington State Cougar Football Team, but I'll run naked down Rice street next time we play the BYU Cougar Football Team and don't beat them by forty points or more. I will. I will. I promise.'

"Now kids. We never have beaten BYU, at least not since we became a 1A football program. And every year it is the same question, 'Is this the year?' 'Is this year we beat BYU?' So sayin' we would beat them by 40 points or more was just bizarre. The phones kept ringing. I put the line on eternal busy. I was scared beyond belief.

"Danny says to me, 'You're not gonna have any listeners if you don't answer the phones live. Now.'

"'This is too hot,' I say, 'I probably already lost my job.'

"'Answer,' Danny says.

"I know Danny. He has an agenda on radio. He knows what he is doing even if the listeners and the station have no idea what he's doing. So I surrender. I opened the phone lines and he answers.

"The first listener, who probably likes Danny, says, 'Danny, you think the team we played was an imposter? I was there. Lavalle Edwards (the Coach) was there; all those Mormon fans were there. You've gone crazy.'

"Danny says, 'I looked at the score, 24-23. No way that was the BYU cougars. If the refs wanted to cheat, sure, why not bring in the BYU Coach, hey they probably paid him a big bribe to amp the charade.'

"Everybody called in. We didn't play music for an hour and a half. The telephone company called and said, cut down, you are clogging all the circuits, even the emergency lines. So then Danny does this reversal. 'Yeah, I know. We lost to BYU. It doesn't matter how we lost. But my word is gold. If we don't beat them by 40 points or more next year, I, at midnight, after the game, I will run down Rice street, with my beer belly, and legs that think running to catch a bus is a winded chore, and I will run down Rice street, back and forth, all night---naked.'

"That was last year. And the truth of the matter, we've lost ten times in a row, and Danny, I know, he will really rundown Rice Street naked this year. Cause that is Danny. That's why he is on Kaua'i' now."

I reply, "Unexpected, that is the secret of radio."

"Trust me, Danny. There are sixty thousand people here on the island, and half of them will be on Rice Street after the game waiting for you, including that local that called you a dumb ha'ole on radio. I know why you came back. To run down Rice Street all night, naked. More important, to live up to your word on radio."

Mandy smiles. "Danny will run down naked, and it will be a great radio event even if they put you in the slammer. Especially if they put your naked ass in the slammer."

Everybody started laughing.

Bradley says, "I'm beginning to see why you say you were crazy."

But I added, "But I won't need to. We will win by forty points or more this year. It is like what I told you, Gregory, math is balance and unbalance always rights itself even when the odds are unimaginable."

Ed says, "Well if we beat them by forty points I'll run down Rice Street naked crying 'Eureka, We've won.'"

"Don't say that on the air, Ed. You'll regret it, plus with your dead leg you ain't much of a runner. You are so slow the crowd will get a real good look at your you know what, which is slightly bigger than your dead leg. You *will* regret it."

Ed starred at Danny, "You really think we are gonna win by forty?"

"Yep. Most definitely," I say.

Ed says, "We just got routed by Colorado State last week and BYU crushed Colorado State 45-16."

Gregory says, "You really got faith in your math theory." He shook his head.

I admit. "Well, I'm really putting it to the test. That is what scientists do: experiment."

I went on. "Ed is the best DJ teacher there is. He is intense and proud to be a professional. You Juan, and you Mandy, you listen very carefully, and practice what he says until it is second nature. Ed's gonna control the day to day operations."

Ed asks, "Just a small question, Danny - where are we working?"

"Yeah, I don't know yet. Use them as interns for now, but no gophering them around, just teach them everything, and have them run your radio station board, and when they've mastered that, start letting them talk on the mic with you. Teach them how to set up your show. And all of you, talk un-expectantly. And when an opening comes, let them have a show. And I'll let you save your job. How? I won't come around. And two months from now, after the annihilation of BYU, we'll start the radio station."

"You mean, after you run naked down Rice street"

I didn't even respond to that. "While you guys are doing that, Bradley, Gregory, and I are gonna work on a plan to allow the listeners to completely control the music that gets played on our new, coming station. We are gonna bust this conglomerate radio idea wide open, and turn radio back to the people."

Ed says, "That's impossible Danny. How are you gonna do that--- All request radio?"

"Don't know. We'll figure it out."

8

INITIATION

Gregory is talking. "We open a radio station and ask people to call in their requests; what are we gonna do, play the songs in the order requested?"

I'm on my fourth glass of wine, sitting next to a kidney shaped glass table out on the second balcony of the Penthouse at the Hyatt. This balcony is facing a line of coconut trees on a moonless night. Me, Bradley and Gregory are talking about the plan to have the people run the music of a radio station.

Bradley says, "The basic problem is the requests will come in faster than the songs that get played. Won't work. After an hour or two, listeners will have to wait a day or two to hear their request."

Gregory suggests, "We could post a clock and tell the listener your song will play at this day at this time. And if somebody else asked it first, we could say it is coming on sooner. Kill two birds with one stone."

I lied. Counting Keoki's dinner with Ed, this is my seventh glass of wine.

Am I drunk? Yeah, Probably. I was asked to do something totally unexpected by Mandy at the diner and what did I do? I grabbed Ed with his one dead leg and dragged him to the dance floor, and we danced. Ed was a good sport. He even did the hula with one hip. Everybody at our table was rolling around in laughter. Maybe I'm not as sober as I think.

Bradley responds to Gregory's comment,
Jeez, I can't get these guys to drink much, can I?.

Bradley says, "They're not going to ask for the same songs. They're gonna ask for different stuff, especially when they start hearing different stuff."

Gregory says, "What do you think Danny?"

"I'm just listening and thinking." I was really just blitzed.

I say, "Both of you got good points." I concentrate on not slurring.

Bradley goes on. "This request thing isn't really going to be balanced. I mean, if we are gonna play what the people want as a group, we need a balanced representation. It might be best to make sort of a Congress of voters, and make sure those participating have a balance of different tastes, equal amount of females to males, and equal amount of ages reflecting the real population of the state. Even cultures and race need to be balanced to reflect the real population."

Gregory laughs. "Sounds like you got a problem. Making everything equal and reflective of the real population. And guess what, you got to reflect all the people who don't give a damn about radio and will never listen anyway, or even the people that don't pay much attention to the music. This Congress thing doesn't work, anyway. Look at the US government. That's what they tried. A balanced representation and look what happened. It is about as unbalanced as it can get."

I finally enter the conversation. "Radio isn't here to reflect the world around us. That is what makes it different. It is here to change the world."

These are the kind of things I say when I'm feeling it.

I correct my statement.

"Yeah - at first, the listener needs to feel this is the world about him. But radio goes one step further. It excites the imagination through the sound alone medium. We need participation, not balance. We need to stir creative thought through the imagination. That's what radio isn't doing anymore. That's what we've got to do."

"So playing requests is the answer, then?"

"No." I say. "You have already described the problem of requests. People are requesting for immediate satisfaction, and it is impossible to give it to them. We gotta go a different way for participation."

The adrenaline was over taking the alcohol. I go on. "An open door to suggest songs to be played. Imagine that. The door needs to be open to everybody, so people can feel a part of the world about them. They don't even have to participate. If they don't participate they still will identify with those who do participate and a new wave of creative music will appear, and imaginations will stir, and it will build upon that until a new imaginative world appears. We gotta open a puka, and just let it happen. Create a hole in the dike of conglomeration. And the human spirit will run free and blossom."

"You really believe that," says Gregory.

"Yeah," I say: I didn't mention it took seven glasses of wine for me to believe it.

"Then you are gonna need a ballot system," says Bradley. And ballots available everywhere. Like in the toilets of all the public bathrooms."

Gregory laughs saying, "With a big sign: Take a crap and vote."

I don't know if it was the, maybe the joke or the wine, but I almost fell off the chair laughing.

"And there is the internet too; that could be a vehicle," adds Bradley?

Gregory says, "How are you gonna control ballot loading? And how are you gonna collect the ballots? And how are you gonna tabulate them? And how are you gonna play something day one with no ballots yet? The ballot system isn't going to work. We need to do something else."

Bradley says, "There is either the request line, the ballots, or a special congress of voters. Or a combination of all three. What else could there be?"

He hesitates, then answers his own question. "We could bother people on the street, balance the amount we survey by age and sex and do it weekly in various parts of the islands. Then we could weight the votes by population, and combine all the surveyors votes and make a weekly play list. Might work."

Actually this thought had occurred to me. I had done surveys like that. But I got up and went looking for coffee. It was time to clear my head. I order coffee on the hotel phone. I don't like the coffee maker in the Penthouse, and asked if anybody wanted anything from the kitchen. No one responds and Juan is asleep with the TV on in another room.

Bradley and Gregory keep playing devil's advocate with all these ways to bring music to the people, and I just listen.

"How do we make people feel they are a part of the world while listening to stuff they don't like," says Bradley.

"There's a way?" Gregory asks.

I say, "Hey, it was that way in the fifties, why can't it be the same way again?"

Bradley shakes his head. "The world changes Danny, that isn't gonna work anymore."

I got a little upset, with the wine and all. I almost screamed it. "And that's why we will change it! Things change."

Mandy hears my outburst and comes to the balcony. She hugs me from the back again, and I crawl inside myself, embarrassed with my outburst. I feel her through my whole being and I'm afraid if I look into her eyes I'd be engulfed by her.

She says, "Let the think tank sleep on it for the night. Better ideas will come tomorrow."

I guess Mandy has been listening to our conversation.

Gregory smiles and Bradley comes over and gives Mandy a kiss on the back of her neck saying, "Good idea, Gregory and I will sleep in the second bedroom, you guys be sure to lock the master bedroom door."

Mandy leads me into the plush bedroom. I make a major effort not to stagger. She drags me to the wall and whispers, "Undress me."

I try to swallow. But my mouth is dry.

She has only four buttons on her blouse. I unhook the top one. She looks into my eyes.

My breathing quickens. She continues looking into my eyes.

She says, "The next one."

I suddenly notice she has no bra. I unbutton the next one.

She looks down.

She says, "The next one."

My hands are shaking. It takes me a full half minute to get the next one unbuttoned.

She looks at my eyes again. "Danny, I love you."

I am shaking but I go for the fourth, the last button.

She looks down at her breasts again. Her nipples are poking outward. They could be seen through the soft silk, yellow blouse. Her shoulders are quivering. She looks at her right shoulder. She looks at her left shoulder. I get the message. I slip her blouse gradually over her shoulders, slipping my hands down the back of her arms and discharging it to the floor.

She looks down. She looks at me. She looks down again at herself.

"Touch me," she says.

I just look into her dancing eyes, and swallow the emotion in my mouth.

There is something about seeing the neck, then the shoulders and then the collar bone of a woman and then trail your eyes down to her bare breasts. Women look so vulnerable, so enticing.

She repeats. "Touch me." and smiles, "Did you forget to lock the door?"

"Yeah, I might have been distracted."

She smiles again and goes to the bed. I lock the door, turn off the light, take my shoes off and return to the bed. *My God, she's naked now.* The shadows seem to be flickering over her naked body and she spreads her legs, inviting me. I feel the earth shaking in my feet. I undress. Suddenly she lifts her body and grabs me, pulling my naked body on top of her, drawing my lips into a long kiss that spreads fire up my spine as my body encompasses hers. Flesh upon flesh, naked.

She says, "Gentle now."

We barely touch each other's lips. Softy touching, retouching and tenderly putting her lips to mine, creating light, wet kisses.

I say it. "I love you."

She says, "I know. I loved you the moment I saw you."

"Me too," I reply.

I just slide into her, and remain motionless. We grip each other harder and harder. I don't know why I don't move. It's so natural, feeling my body attached to hers. I'm thinking I've never made love like this. I'm just at her beck and call. She seems to know what I want. I want beauty. I don't want to lose control. Just appreciate her presence. Then she starts making soft sounds. I start moving my body a little and her soft sounds start including heavier breathing. It makes me move a little faster as her voice rises a little in pitch. Her body shakes with each penetration and each withdrawal; I am forced to withdraw or worry I might come too soon. She hugs me, desperately. I am in and out of her minutes, minutes that seem like half an hour. And I just want to be in there forever. Forever.

Damn, there's that word again. Forever.

Morning came. I could tell it was late. The sun was high enough to penetrate the balcony and warm our faces. She got up and closed the curtain as I enjoyed looking at her naked form. She comes back to bed, puts her head on my chest, and says, "So you've figured it out, how to allow the listeners to program the music?"

That was the last thing on my mind. I was just plum joyful, ecstatic, I don't think there is really a word for the way I was feeling. I was so light I felt I was sailing, and her now mischievous eyes were dancing inside of me. I could see them when I wasn't even looking at them. I knew what they were doing without even looking, They were in me and her naked body lying near like it, too, was in me. We had touched so deeply. What in the hell else could I be thinking? It just popped out of my mouth. "I love you." Stupid but true.

She says, "It's wonderful."

It is. We are one.

9

THE PLAN

All day we stayed in our hotel rooms, the three of us discussing the plan to turn over the music to the people. Every possibility has major drawbacks. Then during the evening, the flower of our lives appeared. She had been scuba diving with Juan all day.

Mandy asked, "So what's the plan?"

Silence.

Then she smiled. "Take care of the listeners who care, and everything else will take care of itself."

I thought about last night with Mandy - the way she took me, the intensity of the act, and it came to me in a flash.

I say, "Screw worrying about ballot loading; we can detect it pretty easy. Screw worrying about people getting together to vote for one song. Hell, if they do, we'll play it. It takes a lot of energy to do that. Screw worrying about people who don't care about what we play. Screw 'em. Screw bands who get a group to vote for them. If they can do it, we'll play it.

"And whatever bad things happen in the ballot process, it will be a hell of lot better than having conglomerates decide what the radio station plays.

"And though I'm a minority on this I am gonna insist. If the same person votes every week for the same song, that person's song will eventually make the playlist. Intensity is everything. We will accumulate all votes week by week until it makes the playlist, and after it makes it, we wipe out all the accumulated votes and the song starts at zero again. Take care of the music intense listeners, let the ones with more desire and intensity tell the less intense what is good. Intensity is everything. The people who vote will rule however they want to do it. The rest of the world will accept it because it will be the best fuckin' radio that has ever existed."

"So we are gonna use the last ballot plan?" Bradley asks.

"Yes, Bradley."

I paced the floor in the living room. saying, "One: 'what are the songs I want to hear on the radio the most?' That question alone will make people think of songs that are not on the radio. And they can vote for up to ten songs. I thrust my arm out. "Yeah!"

"Two: 'what are the songs I want radio to *stop* playing the most (list up to three)?' That will get rid of all the over played songs on radio, and prevent ballot loaders from getting too much music to stay on the radio.

"And the least wanted to be heard song each week I will personally sledge hammer live on the radio during the weekly countdown. And we will never play it again." I thrust my arm out again. "Yes."

"Three: 'is there a song I think would be a hit if radio played it?' We will do Gregory's idea: the tin ear/golden ear. During the countdown show every Saturday we will play five song discoveries and the listeners can call in and say 'golden ear' or "tin ear.' At the end of the countdown show we will put all the golden ear winners in a run off and the winner will be played every two hours the next week. A lot of the biggest hits will come about this way." I kept marching around.

"And we will get a group of computers and Bradley, you can program them together and get volunteers to count the ballots weekly. And sure, we'll use the weighing program so that one age group or sex doesn't dominate the music choices. We'll break down 17 and under, 18-24, 25-34, and plus 35, for each sex. Eight categories will be weighed in the computer program. For example, if one category gets

THE RADIO REVOLUTION

twice as many ballots as another, the other category votes will count for two votes.

"Then we will get kids to volunteer to pick up the ballots in businesses, and businesses will agree because we will list their locations free on the radio. We'll use Gregory's idea, of going on TV first, soliciting ballots, and announce the day the station will begin. *Radio will never be the same.*"

I was starting to shout.

Juan smiled. "You know, I think this will work."

Mandy said, "I have a concern. You just said to let those who participate determine the votes, and now you are saying some participators will count more than others when you weigh the votes".

I stopped dead in my tracks. I thought about the fifties and sixties when radio played all genres, blues, soul, jazz, dinner music, easy listening, gospel, foreign language songs, country, rock n roll, and classical. And played them back to back. If a song was popular enough, it could break the genre barrier and be played on top 40 radio, which played the most popular songs, no matter what the genre. The songs played were based on actual sales in record stores across the country. All ages and sexes bought music. So the charts were balanced demographically with a bias toward the suppressed.

I said to Mandy, "Radio touches the subconscious, and stirs our universal mind. If we super serve one group over another, radio loses its power to reach the universal mind. We have to find a way so it can reach the universal mind, and make us all feel a part of the real world. Sharing musical tastes and learning what musical tastes reach the biggest spectrum of popularity through the voting process will bring us closer together. If radio allows all views, all genres, we will feel a part of the world while listening to radio. It will also excite creativity, because listening to radio excites your imagination in the sound alone medium. Radio comes out of nowhere. That opens your mind wider, and that stirs the mind towards a more imaginative world.

"That happened in the fifties and sixties. Rock n Roll first broke racial barriers because of the beat and more important, because of radio. Then in the sixties it went further. Sharing musical tastes through radio brought us more together, and the love and peace generation of the late sixties emerged, culminating with Woodstock in 1969. And listening to music in the sound alone medium created a platform for experimentation and creativity. Our minds were open to new things. Groups like The Beatles, Pink Floyd, Led Zeppelin, Jimi Hendrix, Bob Marley and many more had a way to reach us for acceptance. Then conglomeration set in, and radio began to super serve one group or another, and it lost its power.

"Overall female tastes in music is very different than males'. And your age makes a big difference too. If we are going to find a common denominator we need to ensure that no one age group runs rough shod over another, that's why the votes need to be weighed. We need to be encourage to share our tastes with others, and their taste with our taste. It'll bring the world together."

Mandy had tears in her eyes. "You're right Danny. The power of radio cannot ever again be thwarted."

Gregory asked, "Well, how did radio do that in the fifties and sixties?"

"They made an effort to count sales in record stores both LPs and 45s The charts were based on sales only and radio stations did their own surveys of music shops. Everybody bought music then, all sexes and ages, though there was slight bias toward males, and the suppressed people of Earth bought more music than the affluent. Then when the better selling songs reached radio, radio started listening to requests and the universal songs that broke genre went to the top."

Mandy hugged each one of us. She had tears in her eyes. She was overwhelmed with happiness. "Beautiful, beautiful, I'm so happy, it is the Radio Revolution and Gregory's band will at last get played." Tears slipped down her cheeks.

But we all knew why she was crying. This was what Mandy wanted the most. All of her loves working together.

I could feel it. We were going to be together forever. I felt so close to everybody I couldn't imagine our consciousness slipping away from each other. Screw consciousness.

Mandy went to shower. Juan asked me, "How did it go last night? Mandy was mum?"

Gregory raised his voice, "Never talk like that. We never talk about that! She never talks about others, either. That's the rule. You will get no information about our relationships with Mandy. And you better be quiet about yours as well."

Bradley, a foot shorter than Juan, went up to him and glared up into Juan's eyes and said, loudly, "Or we will push you out of the family. You got it?" He shoved a hand into Juan's chest.

Juan looked shocked.

I tried to cushion the blow. "Hey Juan, it is all new to me too. Just flow with it and we remember the rule."

We needed a group hug. I motioned to Gregory. He said to Juan, "It's just better this way." They hesitated, then hugged. I motioned to Bradley, he, too, went to Juan and said, "I'm sorry. I didn't mean to push you."

We have the family hug thing.

൭

I was happy with the plan. Of course I still had a slight problem. We didn't have a radio station. And the BYU/Hawaii football game was tomorrow night.

I had told Ed to pump up my boast on the radio: we win by 40, or I run naked all night long down Rice Street, Lihue's main street. He had been right; there might be a thousand people out there, even at midnight, to see me run naked.

I called Rabbit. "Know a bookie in Las Vegas that might give me huge odds, if Hawaii wins by 40 points or more? They were nine-point underdog on the Vegas Line, even at home," I told him. "I'll bet 10,000, get me 100-1 odds."

An hour later he got back to me saying Las Vegas didn't take those kind of bets. They think somebody risking that much money to take such shaky odds must know something. They have no idea you are just plum crazy. And on special odds bets, the house takes pushes. He added, "We can't do it."

"Rabbit, this is critical. Find out what they'll take! Call me back; I'm sitting on the line waiting." It was already past midnight.

Forty minutes later, wouldn't you know it, I was in the shower, but I heard the phone ring and rushed out stone naked. Bradley answered. I grabbed the phone from him. Rabbit said, "They'll split the bets with three houses if you can take fifty to one odds, not a hundred to one. But they'll only take the bet if you beat the spread by *fifty* points." He says, "The good news is that the Costa Rica spread is ten points, Tan is eight and half. Vegas is still nine. You gotta win by 41 points to win all three because the house takes the pushes. But just remember: as soon as I put the bet in, you've lost ten thousand dollars. Do you have it?"

"Yep, I'm using the max 5000-dollar cash I can get from my two unlimited credit cards and you know as well as me, when they find out I'm broke, those cards will be canceled. So this is free money now. Can't lose, even if I do lose."

"Alright, I'll put it in; the least I can do for a guy who gave me the down payment for my house. You know, they got a reporter at KGMJ going to Kaua'i tonight to film you running naked in front of thousands of people tomorrow night after the game. And KYG and KHI are playing the song 'the Streak' by Ray Stevens all day, and laughing on the air. I never knew so many radio people hate you. But I gotta ask you something, Danny. Why are you doing this?"

"I saw the game last year, Rabbit. We were down two scores in the last five minutes and suddenly they went to a way out spread offense, and we almost won. The BYU linebackers are slow. And Gabriel, the quarterback, is a solid short passer. They're gonna short pass them to death spreading out the whole line of scrimmage from one end line to the other, and all game long, cause now they know BYU's Achilles heel. We have way faster receivers than their linebackers. Plus, we are hungry. Plus, the fans are hungry. We've lost ten in a row to BYU, and our last win was fourteen years ago, and there are chaos patterns, and in football one of them is the fourteen-year cycle. A high fourteen years ago when we beat BYU then a dip to the bottom seven years ago, and then a rise again, almost winning the last two years, and tomorrow night the fourteenth year. Bam, the explosion."

"But why forty points?"

"Because it spontaneously came out of my mouth last year."

"Well we know, you always see stuff nobody else sees. But the problem is you don't see what everybody else sees. Good luck. I'll fax you the houses' tickets and commitments. It will take another hour. Then you'll have confirmation your bet is in, and 10,000 dollars is flying in the air somewhere."

"No Rabbit. 500,000 dollars is making a crash landing in my pocket. ETA midnight tomorrow."

"I love you, Danny. You make life and radio interesting. But I ain't going to Rice Street. Well... maybe to bail you out."

"Love you, too, kid, and thanks."

I had one more call to make in the plan. I called my mother-in-law's house in Sigurd, Utah - a town the size of a four story apartment building, except it is spaced out and surrounded with beautiful mountain ranges and good hearted Mormons. Why anybody would want to live in a town like that without even a gas pump or an open convenience store, and not a bar within thirty miles, was beyond me. The three days I was there, I was supposed to stay seven days but I conjured up a business emergency to get out early. What can you do for seven days staring at beautiful farm lands and majestic mountains? And my wife's parents looking at me like I was an alien?

I ring the number. I don't expect a happy voice on the other end. It is five o'clock in the morning in Sigurd, Utah, but there is nothing else to do there but sleep, so I ring the phone anyway.

Someone picks up the phone, "I say, this is Danny, I need to talk to Dorothy."

No voice answers, but I hear my dog barking.

"She's sleeping."

"I don't have much time, wake her."

"Just a minute."

It was a long minute. The dog keeps barking. The whole house must be up by now. But I don't hear the kids. Ages four and six are real noisy, normally.

Dorothy answers. "I tried to call you but no one knew where you were. I'm taking a break, I don't know when I will be back."

"Maybe never?" I was sounding stoic.

"Danny. I just can't stand it anymore. You're so irresponsible. Greg called me, told me you are finished. Your golden radio career is over and you're waltzing over to Kaua'i' to run naked in the street. It's just too much. You haven't brought me four consecutive pay checks in the last three years. We had an agreement: I control the money. Then out the blue you give Rabbit two hundred grand for a down payment on a house, and me, you still have me living in a rental, and when I ask for a house, you say, 'I can't own anything.' You can't even own a damn car. You make millions and you are constantly penniless. If I hadn't put money into stocks, your kids and the dog wouldn't have anything to eat right now."

"That's why I'm calling. We need to sell the stocks and split the money."

"It's not your money. It's mine. If I hadn't put that money into stocks it would have been gone. And I need you to sign over the stocks to me exclusively. If you don't, I'll start divorce proceedings and you might never see your kids again."

"Don't bother me with divorce. Write whatever you want. I'll sign it." I am shocked at my anger.

She is silent for a long while. Finally she says, "Do you want to talk to the kids?"

"Not now. I'll bring 'em to Kaua'i on Christmas and spring break, and next summer."

Dorothy was silent for a long time. Finally, she says, "You'll be living there and doing small time radio. I can't believe it." She starts crying. After a long sniffle, "And you'll have to pay for the airfare for the kids."

"Write it up, and be sure you give me free visiting access to the kids. That's all I ask."

"You really want out? I'm not sure yet."

"Dorothy, you know me; I can't be tied down to this money stuff. It's best this way."

"Danny, I love you; I just can't handle this. I'm sorry."

"Hey, it's good. We've got two wonderful kids and have had some great times. We just gotta put it in the memory bank for now." More silence. "I gotta go kid, I'm racing the clock. I'll call you when I have a stable housing situation, and then you can send me papers, and I'll turn all the stocks over to you."

Dorothy was crying. I felt horrible. "Bye, love."

The crying continued on the phone. I said, "Don't worry; it'll be okay. Maybe I'll love you more being away from you."

"Me, too," she burst out crying. again. Sobbing she said, "Bye." The phone clicked.

I noticed Mandy standing behind me. "Sorry Danny, I have a bad habit of eavesdropping. Are you okay?"

"What is there to say; a door of my life just closed."

"If you want to go back, I'll understand."

"No, Mandy. You make a call, you stick with it."

Mandy says, "Funny, isn't it. Time is that way. You walk through a new door, and you can't go back."

She was uncanny. She understood me. I looked at her deep brown eyes. They had that mischievous look again, and I said, "Mandy, we so, so alike. We are dancers, dancing around one pitfall after another."

She smiled. "This would be the perfect night to make love to you again, but I'm afraid Juan needs me."

I smile. "Go dance, girl."

She walks up to me, very deliberately, like she is in a march. She touches my cheek. "It is uncanny, we two."

I put my hand to her forehead, and mimic a kiss.

She does a face about and, raising her steps in a pronounced fashion, she marches to the bedroom.

My flamboyant ways were beginning to eat at me. I didn't have any of the stock monies. What if I lost the bet? I couldn't keep these kids going anymore. *Oh what the hell, don't look at a problem before it arises.* I went to the lobby to get the faxes.

They were already there. Rabbit was wrong. I had to beat the spread by 51 points. House took the pushes. It would take Hawaii to win by 42 points to win at all three houses. It would take 41 points to win at the Costa Rica and Las Vegas houses. But it would take the Tan house in Malta 42 points for me to win. I'm pretty brazen. But I was getting nervous. I should have tried to negotiate a better deal. Everything was on the line tomorrow night. *Hell, I live by my mouth, might as well put it to the test.*

The least of my worries was running naked down Rice Street.

10

THE GAME

We checked out of the Hyatt and Ed took us to Rob's bar on Rice Street. It was five-thirty in the evening, an hour and a half before the game started. I was envisioning the annihilation of the BYU football team. Their coach has the sternest looking face I have ever seen. He never cracks a smile, or a grimace, like the facial muscles can't move. Always an unemotional stature, win or lose. I was wondering what would happen to his face watching his national power football program be utterly annihilated on the field by the lowly Hawaii Rainbows. But I was a little concerned. He saw what we did in the last five minutes last year. Would he be prepared for it this year?

Even though it was an hour and a half before kick-off, there was a radio remote outside. Three stations on Kaua'i and two on Oahu had set up camp, undoubtedly all waiting to have a good solid look at my naked ass and unimpressive ding-a-ling..

The TV woman from Honolulu and her camera lady were there, too, with a massive camera that I was sure had a giant zoom lens on it. Of course, the radio and the TV guys wanted to interview me.

Ed hurried me through the crowd like he was my lawyer entering a highly publicized court room. He screamed at the radio and TV reporters, "We came to see the game, not a circus." Of course Ed's station had wisely placed his own remote inside Rob's bar and restaurant. We enter. Only the winners of Ed's radio station, a ton of servers, and Ed's radio staff were there. The bar was to open at 6:20. I wondered. Usually on college football day this bar was opened all day.

Half an hour later Mandy and Juan did a reconnaissance, going outside and coming back with the enemy placement and weapon assessment. To my shock I was informed that a giant flatbed, hauling a movie size TV screen had parked horizontal in the middle of Rice Street. And a block party was being set up. The booze was being sold by Rob's Bar in green and white tents (University of Hawaii colors). Rob's Bar had gotten approval for a street party right smack in the middle of Rice Street during the game. There aren't a lot of streets in the town of Lihue and there were going to be a lot of pissed off drivers taking bizarre detours through sugar fields and other dirt roads.

Of course, the real event was six hours away: The great interest in my ding-a-ling.

I did notice there was a door man at the door with a sign: Tickets $20.

I asked Ed, "What's the twenty-dollar door charge for?"

Ed responded, "My station gets the bar reserved for the winners on radio and my staff at the radio station plus free, food and drinks included. Robs gets the door money."

I shook my head. "Twenty dollars? Who's gonna pay that?"

Ed says, "You didn't notice, Danny? Robs took out all the chairs and even the center booths to make room; the tickets say standing room only. They shut down at two o'clock on a Saturday to set this up. If you want an end booth, it's two hundred and seventy dollars. And you still gotta pay for the food and drinks. They sold them out yesterday. That was the first day we announced the availability of the tickets."

Mandy smiles, "And Danny, there's a massive crowd outside waiting, most with pre-bought standing room tickets. You are going to have a crowd here for the game and after."

THE RADIO REVOLUTION

Ed says, "Danny, wasn't it you who told me about the amazing power of radio? We've been pumping it all day and yesterday and Robs bought thirty spots, two an hour, on my station as well. I might be right. You might have thirty-thousand to watch you run. But it's time to pump it more. We are going live on the radio," Ed looks at his watch, "In three minutes."

Maybe running naked down Rice Street, all night long, is more concerning than losing ten grand.

I swallow a lump in my throat.

Ed goes on Radio. "I'm here with the legendary Danny Fall. Last year he made an amazing statement after the BYU game on my radio show. 'We will beat BYU by forty or more points the next time we play them or I will run naked all night long down Rice Street.' I'm at Robs bar with a sold-out crowd and Danny Fall is here with me, awaiting the outcome of the game. Preparing to run naked down Rice Street all night long if we don't win by forty points or more. For those of you who want to, there is a big block party on Rice Street and a giant movie screen playing the game. So come on down - we'll be here all night. So, is this the year, Danny?"

I smile. "Are you kidding? Those cougar pansies. Of course we'll beat them by forty or more points."

"But will you really rundown Rice Street naked if we don't?"

"That's not an option, Ed."

"But will you, if we don't win by forty points or more?"

"If we don't win by forty points or more we will be in an alternate universe and yeah, I will run down Rice Street naked. Ed, everybody knows me. I live by my words on the radio. They know if an alternate universe appears and BYU loses by thirty-nine points or less, yes, I will run down Rice Street naked."

"What if they win?"

I laugh so hard the mic drops. Mandy picks it up. Ed, worried, checks the mic. I take it in my hand and say, "Dream on, Cougars. There is no universe where that could happen."

Ed, playing it up, says, "Yes, but it has happened the last ten times."

73

"When, Ed?"

"In the past fourteen years."

"Hey I'm looking, looking, looking, I don't see the past Ed. Don't screw up your mind with things that aren't here. Can you see a past, anywhere? The Rainbows are in Honolulu now. The pansies are there too, and worried shitless their fat fanny asses are going to be mutilated tonight." I raise my voice a few levels and in a squeaky voice say, "'Don't touch me. Don't touch me, Oh, you can touch me a little bit, you nice bruisers, no-no, don't be rough on me you big bruising rainbow warrior.'" I enjoy doing my pansy voice.

The standing room crowd had entered fifteen minutes ago. There are loud bellows from the crowd, cheering at my mimicry.

Ed says, "Danny, you know they've got the number one quarterback in the country. Your expectations might not be realistic tonight."

"If he can throw a complete pass with his pansy ass on the ground the rules say it won't count, Ed. Even horny Cougar refs won't allow that. And there're gonna be a few plays where his little wimpy ass will take minutes to be dug out of the ground. Don't have to be worried about him, Ed."

More cheers from the crowd.

Ed fans the flames some more. "Yes, but forty points?"

Hey, it would be a hundred, but you know how coaches are. They don't pile it on. They'll pull the reigns back in the fourth quarter, give everybody a chance to pound on those pansies. So, you can't count the fourth quarter for a lot of points. Just more joyful pounding. Forty is safe, sixty probable."

"But BYU is bound to score, too. You can't shut out the number one offense in the country, can you?"

"Yeah, those horny Cougar refs might give them a score, hoping to get one of those pansies in bed with them. Yeah, but forget it. If they score it will be meaningless." I raise my pitch and go into my squeaky voice again, "'Oh that was so sweet, thank you ref. We need to score. We need something tonight.'"

More bellows from the crowd.

THE RADIO REVOLUTION

"There you have it, everybody. Danny Fall will run naked all night down Rice Street if we don't beat the Cougars by forty points or more. The run starts at midnight just outside this bar."

Ed has told the Rob's security guys not to let any media in. "You get Danny Fall, and the media gets the outside." But the lady reporter from the Honolulu TV station was making a spectacle of herself, demanding entrance. I went to the door trying to calm the uprising. "You are welcome to sit at the bar, but bar seats cost a hundred dollars."

The security guy smiled. "And two hundred for your lady with that massive camera."

I didn't want to listen to her temper tantrum so I went back to the bar. It was nineteen minutes to kick-off.

Everybody was tense. A DJ on a speaker kept counting it down, "Ten minutes to detonation. Nine minutes to detonation." The lady and her camera lady finally blasted through the crowd and made it to the bar. Ed motioned some of his radio staffers to move. The lady with the camera pushed people out of the way to get a good angle. They synchronized for a live broadcast with the station. No time for a taped interview.

"This is Sarah Andrews in Lihue, Hawaii tonight, live. I'm here with Danny Fall, the guy who will do anything for attention. Even run down Rice Street tonight at midnight stark naked, if Hawaii doesn't win by 40 points."

I get mad. "And what are you doing? You just paid three hundred dollars at the door to talk to me. Who is the one who wants the attention?"

She says, "Your DJ career is over. Your wife left you and took all your money. Isn't that true, Danny? I don't see her here tonight. But still you want to be in the limelight, at all cost, even running naked down the main street of Lihue with a few thousand people watching."

I laugh. "Yeah, my wife doesn't need to be here. She has already seen my naked body. It's your chance tonight lady, but you won't see a leg hair, because Hawaii will decapitate the dreams of the BYU Cougar Football Team tonight." I raise my fist to the sky.

More cheers from the crowd.

The lady's feed to the station is suddenly cut off. She doesn't even get a chance at a closing statement. I say, "Um, if you want to see my naked body that bad, we could spend the night together, just you and me."

She and her camera lady burst away. The camera was wildly swinging, like the photo lady had lost control. Customers were ducking. The two ladies stormed out the door. The security guy approached. "Yeah, she paid the 300 dollars on a news station credit card."

He smiles. I smile. We high five. Mandy smiles, then says, "You sure don't have a way with women, do you?"

"Yeah I know. Maybe I need tutoring."

No one knew what was going through my mind. I couldn't believe I got myself in this position. I have a big mouth, and I'd really done it. Good thing everybody in the bar was on my side. And talking brazenly on the radio, a lot more people would begin to believe it was possible. If lots of people believed it could happen, it had a better chance of happening. We all work out of the same common mind, and that is why radio is so powerful. Our common minds come together in an imaginative way through real radio. Enough people believe, it will happen. And if Hawaii gets off to a good start, it will increase the belief, and it will happen. So the first quarter was critical to my bet, as well as avoiding being naked in front of thousands of people.

The bar came alive. This was the loudest I had ever heard a bar. Even with the TV at max volume you couldn't hear the announcer. The outside block party was roaring also. We were ten minutes into the game and Hawaii couldn't be stopped. They were using a weird split formation, a tandem of three receivers in a vertical line, each one behind the other one, and split way out to near the sideline, and another receiver split out on the other sideline. BYU was reeling, they couldn't even set up right on defense. They didn't have much time either. We were in a no huddle-offense, the first time Hawaii had tried that. The score was 21-0 and then it happened, a sonic boom exploded across Rice Street and the bar. BYU fumbled! And another

THE RADIO REVOLUTION

score. And another score. And the horny Cougar refs took away a safety and a block punt which ended up giving BYU seven points. But it didn't matter. Halftime score should have been 44-0, but with the refs participation it was 35-7. Of course I mentioned refs participation at half-time. "What? The refs think they are BYU players in this game?"

Things were going well. And I got the feeling the horny refs had sorta given up helping their bed friends. Seven sacks of the greatest college quarterback, and my half time comments included. "Look hard, you might find Ty Detmer (the BYU quarterback) hiding under the bench in the second half."

Two more scores in the second half and I was in the clear, 49-7. And the first play of the fourth quarter was a touchdown 56-7. It looked like I had made it. But with the second, third and fourth string in the fourth quarter, BYU did manage a score with three minutes left. And I got a bit concerned. One more score by BYU and I would lose. But their quarterback just kept getting sacked or running all over the backfield looking for help.

The gun went off.

I had won 500,000 dollars and had become the hero of Rice Street.

Usually in a football route fans leave early. But in the stadium on TV everybody stayed. I went outside with Ed. Half the island of Kaua'i was still there even though the police had stopped liquor at ten. We waved to everybody. Ed reached the microphone, and said, "Danny Fall is gonna walk, not run. With all his clothes on. Are we happy?"

The screams were blaring. There was a rush of bodies toward us. We needed to cool the moment. I went on the mic, "History has been written. BYU has been crushed October 28, 1989. Their tears sour the grass of the stadium. They had no idea of the power of radio. Their ranking as a top football program has met its waterloo. It was so bad the normally stoic BYU coach actually, at one moment, cracked a grim look on to his stone face looking at the score board with the score 56-7, and but a quarter to make a comeback. And the power of real radio will continue. I am going to start a state wide radio station in the center of the universe, right here in Kaua'i, and we are gonna bring back radio for the people, at long last. The people will control the music played. We will listen to whatever you say, and even the minority music preferences will surface to the air ways. Everybody will have a say in the music that is to be played, if they want to. All Hawaii will have a clear signal, even Hilo. It will be called the Hawaiian Island Music Report. The radio revolution will begin that day. On that day you can actually have a say in the music that gets played over radio. And the power of real radio will blossom."

There were bravo shouts. There were cries, "When?"

I shouted, "Soon. Very soon."

There was madness in the streets. It was crazy. Ed was in shock. How was I gonna do it? Gregory was in tears. He could suddenly visualize how powerful radio could be. Mandy was hugging Bradley, and Juan just looked dazed. How could this have happened?

"And remember Hawaii: I live by my word. Don't listen to naysayers. Listen to me. It will happen, and not only Hawaii. America will never be the same."

The cheers continued. I walked into the crowd and hugged everybody.

The five of us and Ed walked to his sister's house a mile and half away, hugging people as we went. Ed's sister, Edie, opened the door with open arms for all of us. It was two-thirty in the morning. The kids grabbed sheets to sleep on the floor. Ed motioned me out to the porch.

"Are you crazy? No one will back a radio station where the music is run by the people. Radiotron will black ball you big time; no chance of getting agency advertising. Danny. That's ninety percent of radio stations' revenue." Ed shakes his head. "Do you know what you are up against?"

"It'll be easy, Ed."

Ed says, "I love you, man, but I can't risk walking unarmed into a wall of gunfire. This is professional suicide."

"Ed, I got the money."

"From your wife?"

"No, I got new backers that won't be involved at all in the station; from Costa Rica, Malta, and Las Vegas."

"No, they just don't know what they are getting into. When they find out, they'll pull out."

"Nope, I stole the money. They don't even know how it happened. The money is all mine."

"Then we are going to jail."

"Ed, you said the golden word, 'We.'"

Ed says, "Let's crash. We'll talk in the morning.'

11

RADIO SHOCK WAVE

At his little office desk in his exercise room, the General Manager of Radio Station KYTI, and affiliates, Jackson, read the front page of the Sunday morning paper in Honolulu in utter shock: "'Bows' Bring the Hammer Down on BYU."

That was a known thing, so the shock of the victory had already passed. But the bad boy, the boy Jackson had 8-balled from Honolulu Radio, his picture, with a big giant smile, was plastered on the front page of the Sunday paper, and below the headline, on the left-hand column: "Danny Fall Eludes Nude Run."

Danny Fall on the front page of the Sunday Morning paper? What in the shit happened?

Jackson, in his rumpus room, choked on his coffee. Black drops splashed on the page. He read on. Screw the prediction. Anybody could predict something that stupid; a 40 point win. But only Danny would be lucky enough to pull it off. He read farther into the article. Danny was quoted as making an even more outlandish prediction. He was starting a new radio station that would air across the entire state.

Jackson gulped, and dropped the coffee cup on his protruding naked belly. It dribbled down to his yellow shorts, embroidered with little purple balloons. He hissed. "Ouch!" The hot coffee burned his balls. He hissed again. "That's damn hot," and frantically yanked his hot shorts off.

"'No one has had a station that could broadcast across the entire state, and from Kaua'i? And where in the hell does he think he is going to get the money to do it? It would cost a fortune. Nobody would lend him money with the rap I'm putting on him, sabotaging radio stations. Maybe some rich idiot fan, somebody with a political agenda? But Jackson knew Danny; as careless as he appeared flinging out crazy words... most of the time they came to fruition.

But not this! This was intolerable. He started calling. He called his cronies at the FCC asking about radio sales and signal buys. No one knew anything. He called his buddy at Radiotron, thinking such scuttlebutt would have reached his ears. Nothing. He called his buddies at the banks inquiring about loans. Nothing. He called his boss at home in Georgia, the head of the corporation, to appraise him of the situation. Nothing. All would check on it Monday. They couldn't do much on Sunday. No one knew anything up front.

Jackson eyes squinted. He tapped his fingers. Who would know? Rabbit, Danny's friend. He spun his rolodex, called the radio engineer. "What do you know about Danny's new radio station?"

Rabbit laughed. "Hardly! His wife took all his money, and he's hiding out on Kaua'i to avoid the landlord."

"Damn it, Rabbit, he isn't hiding; he is all over the fuckin' news. What's going on? You're his friend."

Rabbit was enjoying this conversation. "Jackson, I have absolutely no idea. I was as shocked as you reading the morning paper."

"I'll put it to you straight, Rabbit. You tell me, or I will see you'll never work again in this town."

"Don't get hard on me, Jackson. If I knew I wouldn't mind telling you. He's on Kaua'i. Why don't you talk to him yourself? Last I heard he was at the Hyatt in Poipu."

Jackson called the Hyatt. Danny had checked out.

It was Sunday. Feeling confident he would put a stop to this on Monday, he went to his exercise machine that recreated a walk through the black forest in Germany. He went more than usual this morning, diverting the machine up the Swiss Alps. *What in the fuck does that son of a bitch think he is doing?* Jackson couldn't let it go.

He shut down the machine in a mean sweat, put on new yellow shorts with little purple rhinoceroses knitted on the ass cheeks. He read the article again.

Rob's Bar was mentioned in the article. He called and was told Danny Fall was in a promotion with radio station KGT, organized by the morning DJ, Ed Kanoi. *That's my fuckin' affiliate station.*

Jackson looked on his rolodex and found Ed Kanoi's number. He called. No answer. He called Kaua'i's information line. Kaua'i' is a small world, and he found an operator saying that he might be at his sister Edie Rosa's. He got the number and called.

Ed's sister answered the phone at ten to ten in the morning.

"I need to talk to Ed Kanoi."

"He's asleep. It was a long night last night. I can have him call you back."

"If he wants to work in Hawaiian radio anymore, wake him up."

"Who are you? Are you his boss?"

"This is Jackson, Lady. Get him up."

Edie didn't know anything about a Jackson. But she was scared. Ed was helping to support her and her two kids. She went to the porch. Danny was up. "You know a Jackson? He's on the phone for Ed. He's threatening Ed's job."

"Let me take it."

"Jackson, what in the hell are up you to, now?"

"Danny?? Danny! What's going on, Danny?"

"Nothing. I'm just sleeping over at Ed's sister's place."

"Don't give me that shit. You opened your mouth big time last night. No radio station can reach all the islands. The expense would be unbelievable."

"You know I live by my word."

"Then talk to me."

"Did you threaten Ed's sister?"

"No, I just really wanted to talk to you. I don't even know who answered the phone."

"Come on, Jackson. You knew who answered. Why threaten a small time DJ just trying to make a living? He's just my friend. I've got no money, and he invited me to stay here tonight after the great victory of the Hawaii Football Team."

"Danny, what are you really planning?"

"To change radio, Jackson. That's what I'm planning."

"Are you crazy? You could make a fortune working for me."

"Sorry, Jackson. Only if it changes radio. I'm gonna change radio."

"Yeah, how?"

"I'm working on it. I don't have it put together yet. But that is my goal."

"How are you gonna change radio?"

I was mad at him. *You don't care about that, Jackson. But do me a favor. Stay clear of threatening families looking for their next pay check.*

"By allowing the people back in radio."

"People love radio the way it is. They'd love it more if you got back on the air. Come work here now and you'll get big bucks and everybody will be happy."

"Happiness isn't everything, Jackson."

"Well unhappiness is a lot worse. You just want to be unhappy? You think you can get away with this bullshit? Well, you are gonna be fuckin' unhappy, Danny."

I go a different direction. "Hey Jackson, I'm in love. I could give a shit over 'what is happiness' and 'what is unhappiness.' I let you determine that. Okay?"

"You're doomed to hell, Danny. I might be the only one that can pull you out of there. This is your last chance. I'll give you an hour to decide."

I say, "Come out here, and we'll talk."

The phone clicks.

I want to protect Ed and his sister's family. I realize Ed is in danger with this madman.

Edie hears the dead sound on the phone and looks at me. "Is everything okay?"

"Yes, Edie. Everything is alright. I'll take care of your family, I have money now."

"I see why everybody loves you. You really care about people. And you'll do anything for your friends."

I laugh. "I don't care about Jackson. And he's on Oahu. He won't bother you here."

"But he hung up on you."

"It means he'll call back."

Jackson took a quick shower, his mind a blazing. He dressed, stuffed a bag, and went to the airport.

Presently he called Edie again. "Tell Danny I'm in room 1302 at the Hyatt in Poipu and to meet me in an hour." The phone clicked. It was twelve-forty in the afternoon.

We were all in the living room, now-wide awake eating Danishes and coffee. Edie's face fell. "Damn it Danny, he flew in. He's at the Hyatt in Poipu. He said meet him in an hour, then he hung up. He's crazy."

I smile. "A good sign."

Ed looks scared. "Shit, he is the head of four stations, and ours is one of those affiliates."

"We are all going, guys. You, too, Ed. This will be fun."

Ed says, "Are you crazy? If he finds out what you are trying to do, he'll kill us, or do everything in his power to stop us. And I've lost my job."

I smile. "Don't worry."

Mandy goes up to Ed and gives him a hug. "Ed, trust Danny. He knows what he is doing, and the last thing he wants to do is hurt you."

Ed stares into those lively, mischievous eyes. "Maybe another hug, and I'll think about it."

Mandy shocks him by kissing him on the lips. Ed smiles. "I guess that settles it! I'm going."

Edie laughs. "Ed will do anything for a pretty girl."

THE RADIO REVOLUTION

"What's our plan?" Bradley asks.

"Just relax. Answer all his questions truthfully. Let him know how we plan to do it. Don't hold back anything. Jackson can't handle bullshit."

Ed starts pacing. "Are you mad?" Edie says he is going to see I never work again in Hawaii Radio."

I smile. "He told me pretty much the same thing. But don't worry."

I ask Edie if I could use the phone.

I dial. Everybody in the room listens to my side of the phone conversation. "Rabbit. I bet you had a nice phone call today."

"You sure know how to stir up a hornet's nest, Danny."

I respond, "So how do you get a radio station island wide?"

"You rob Fort Knox, buy a bunch of signals, listen to the FCC tell you it is illegal, and end up in court with a bunch of people suing you."

I laugh. "I was hoping for a better way than that."

"Danny, why did you say that last night?"

"I'm hot, Rabbit. I want to throw a curve ball into the mix."

"Well, it worked, big time. Jackson threatened to keep me from working in Hawaii if I didn't tell him how you are going to do it."

I laugh. "That's why I'm calling. How do I do it? He's meeting me in forty minutes and I need an answer."

"Danny, that was fucking amazing last night. The bookies think you are a time traveler. They want your predictions for this week, they'll pay a thousand dollars a selection. They want to make up their losses. If you want to play that game, you can make big bucks."

"I don't give a shit about that. Give me a way to have a signal on all the islands. Rabbit. Think. I got thirty-nine minutes to come up with a reasonable possibility."

Rabbit thought. "Cable? Yeah. Maybe cable. You could generate cable from Kaua'i to various signals in the other islands and then translate the signal back into radio waves. That's out of the range of the FCC. You could use radio signals on struggling stations, give 'em a few bucks, and they'll change their format. It might work, but you're talking thirty-thousand a month cable fees. Or, wait a minute - might be cheaper if you go with the underwater telephone lines. That would be in mono, though it would sound better than an AM station."

"Okay, sounds good. I'll get Jackson's blood pressure off the Richter scale with that."

"You could even go satellite, that would scare the shit out of Jackson." Rabbit was still going. "No, you would need two satellites, as one goes around the Earth, the other picks up the signal. That might be a big time expense, though. I really don't know how much. But the word 'satellite' might make Jackson crap right on the spot. You would need to charge listeners maybe thirty dollars a month if you go that way. The expense is huge. There might be a way to reduce the cost since there are a lot of empty satellites out there now. Corporations are buying them for the future. But they don't want to let them go cheap. Might be negotiable in the short run, like three or six months at a time. I got a friend at Exxon working on them; I'll give him a call."

"Hey Rabbit, I knew you'd come up with something. Get back to me on that. I got a twenty-minute ride to Poipu now. Call you later."

In the car, I gave the kids key sentences to say to Jackson to set off his high blood pressure. We arrived on time.

I knocked on room 1302. Jackson opened the door on me and five strangers.

"I didn't mean to meet all of Kaua'i. What's going on, Danny?"

"We're a team."

Ed winces.

"Well, let me talk to the quarterback alone."

"You wanted to know what's going on. This is what is going on."

"These kids are your backers?"

I nodded.

"I don't know if there's room in here."

"We'll sit on the floor."

I motion everybody in. Jackson hesitates, then shakes his head. "We'll, hello Kaua'i."

THE RADIO REVOLUTION

Jackson sits on the couch, the team and I take to the floor. "So how are you gonna do it, Danny? How are you gonna have island wide radio?"

"There is more to radio than radio and micro waves, Jackson."

I pause. Bradley continues. "There's cable."

Gregory adds, "And there are satellites."

"This is the radio revolution," Mandy explains with a smile. "And there are, under the sea, telephone lines."

"How are you gonna get a signal?"

"You mean lots of signals," I say.

"You gotta get FCC approval for mobile signals. You haven't done shit."

"How many struggling signals are out there that might want Danny Fall as a DJ, Jackson?"

"Don't try it Danny, I'll stop you everywhere you go."

"Not if I'm making you a bundle of money, Jackson."

"I'm listening." Jackson was all ears.

"Here's how we can do it. You give me a Saturday morning show. We'll call it the Hawaiian Island Music Report. It will air ten to two on Saturday. We'll place ballots in various retail locations all across the islands and we'll set up the same system on Oahu, Maui, Lanai, Molokai, and the Big Island and air it through the telephone lines or in some cases over cable lines and then translate cable into radio waves, and you give us your affiliates' signals to air the show 10 to 2 every Saturday and we will make you the landslide number one stations all across the state. But you'll have to allow us complete control over the music played. Your revenue will double because we will be playing what Hawaii really wants to hear. And they will love your radio station because it will be The People's radio station and anyone can participate in the music programming. You give us a commission of gross sales, and we all win. Just one show simultaneously aired over all the Hawaiian Islands on Saturday, 10-2, and control over all the music played on your radio stations, and your ratings will soar."

It was seven hours of bitter talking, wild word exchanges, every emotion running like a river except kissing and hugging. All were drained. But an elaborate fifteen-page agreement was at last drawn, written in Gregory's handwriting and wording.

Jackson knew with Danny's name the Saturday show would be huge. His biggest problem was giving up the music programming, even though his instinct told him it would work. How would he get the payola from the major record companies if he had no control over the music played? To offset this problem, Danny agreed he would delay the playlist a week, show him what was going to be on the next week's playlist, and let him go to the record companies for monies telling the record companies he could to be playing this or that next week.

I suspected what was going to be voted wouldn't get money, but it made Jackson more amenable.

Jackson figured he could fire the program directors at all the stations, give Danny the job of DJ presentation and control of the music, and save the DJs' bonus for being program directors. Being that a DJ's bonus for being program director was over 6% of the gross sales of the stations, Jackson could feel giving Danny 10% of gross sales, and 3% more if sales exceeded a set amount would be totally justified with the corporation. When Danny had been on his station before, Danny got 12% of gross sales, fewer bad debts, and revenue was almost doubled. Besides he didn't like his dipshit program directors and their arrogant ways. If they didn't want to be a DJ only, and lose three quarters of their pay, he had no problem. DJs were a dime a dozen.

There was another problem that went on in discussion for a full hour. Jackson wanted a share in Danny's company. A big share. Half the company. And half the rights, if this thing went national.

Finally, Bradley broke the stalemate, by saying out of the blue, "There is an enormous expense setting up ballots, tabulating them, maintaining a computer staff, utilizing cable and telephone lines for a simultaneous Saturday Morning Show and renting places on the towers with my father's funding. He would never allow an outside party into mine & Gregory's company."

Jackson says, "Well, Danny is an outside party."

I remind Jackson, "I don't own anything, I'm just an employee."

He knows my obsession with not owning anything.

Gregory adds, "My father is the first black State Senator from Kentucky and an Anti-Trust Lawyer, and I don't think he would go for you having a kick back, or a share, in two media companies. If it got out it might hurt his reelection. We can't allow that."

Mandy adds, "And I'm pretty sure your corporation wouldn't appreciate it either."

It was Mandy's words that struck a nerve in Jackson. He knew she was right.

"How much money are your parents putting up?" Jackson asks.

"I answer that one. "Four hundred ninety thousand." After paying off my credit cards that was the net bounty from the game.

Jackson asks, "Gregory, what is your last name?"

"Stefan, but if you call my dad, he may pull out."

"Your father is really a state senator from Kentucky?"

"He's on his third term now."

I was worried. I knew Jackson would check.

Jackson says, "I want to see the bank statement."

Now the kids are worried.

I respond, "I'll fax it to you when the money arrives. It will be here a week from Monday."

"No, I want it notarized by the bank and delivered by the President of the Bank. Which bank?"

"First Hawaiian."

"I'll call Henry, Monday. Take him to lunch, see exactly where this money came from."

"It's being transferred from overseas, some of it. It might take a week for all of it to get in the bank. So take him to lunch not this Monday, but the next Monday.

"And meet us here on Kaua'i' a week from Wednesday. Bring your lawyer, Jackson. I'll bring mine. The funds are in my account under my given name, Danny Boy Heinzwaffle. I'll transfer the funds to Gregory and Bradley's company, the following few days."

The kids start laughing.

I look at them hard. I say, "Yeah, Danny Fall sounds better, but a given name you can't help." They pick up I'm sensitive about it. They mute their laughs.

"Danny, why is the money going to you first. Is it a loan? "

"No. It's a capital investment."

"Okay, this is tentative, contingent on you really having the money. We'll confirm the meet up a week from Tuesday. But I want you to sign the final contract in Honolulu."

"No Jackson, you'll come here. We'll meet here at the Hyatt. We'll bring our lawyer, you bring yours. I'll even pay for the penthouse.

And Jackson, you got to do something now. Before we go one step further, I want you to call Edie and do me a nice favor, Jackson. Apologize to her. Ed's helping to support her, and you threatening Ed's job really scared her."

Jackson asks, "What am I apologizing for?"

"Just call her. Now."

"Are you telling me a deal this big is dependent upon an apology to somebody I don't even remember doing anything to and who, doesn't have anything to do with the deal?"

"Jackson, you need the practice." I laugh. "Call her now. Apologize. I won't tape it. I promise. Everybody agree? We won't say a word." Everybody nods. "We would hate to destroy your reputation, Jackson."

Ed gives him the number. Jackson calls. "Your brother thinks I might have upset you. You're Edie? I'm sorry. Everything will be fine."

"Who is this?"

"This is Jackson, Lady." Jackson does it again. Raises his voice and hangs up the phone. He says, "Okay, I did it."

"Yeah, okay, Jackson." It was the best I could hope for.

THE RADIO REVOLUTION

Jackson smiled. *This has got to be bullshit. A black senator from Kentucky.*

The five of us signed Gregory's handwritten contract dependent on monies' verifications and the corporation's commitment to follow through if the money appeared. I estimated we would generate about sixty thousand dollars, less twenty thousand in monthly expenses for ballot computations, retrievals, tower rents, and cable cost and telephone lines. Jackson signed with a flourish.

Ed starts driving us back to Edie's. I tell Gregory, "We've got a problem. Jackson is sure to check on your father. You shouldn't have bullshitted like that."

Mandy is in the backseat with Bradley and Juan and she speaks up loudly. "Danny, stop it, you trust us. We're not stupid. Gregory's father is really a state Senator of Kentucky. And Bradley and Juan can hack monies off from offshore accounts, at least for 36 hours if he does it on a weekend and, he'll come up with the notarized bank statement for you. I know your wife has tied up all the money. Talk about bullshitting."

I smile. "You gotta trust me, too, guys. I made a bet with Las Vegas, Costa Rica and Malta that Hawaii would win by at least 42 points. At 50 to one odds. Less the ten thousand I used on my credit cards, I got 490,000 and it will be in the First Hawaiian Bank a week from Monday."

I could feel it. It was destiny. It was really going to happen.

Ed in shock, "Is that where the money is coming from?"

I smile. "Yes."

He pulls the car over on to the shoulder and turns around. We're going to Keoki's again, guys. To celebrate!"

I say, "You better call Edie and reassure her. Jackson's apology wasn't too convincing."

Mandy screams. "Yes, the Radio Revolution is about to happen. She hugs Bradley. Then she hugs Juan. Then she hugs Bradley, again, looks into his eyes, and tears appear. Bradley smiles. "Your wish has come true, love."

12

THE CALL

Next afternoon the kids are in Edie's living room, Mandy sitting on top of Juan, Bradley asking Gregory, "I didn't know about your father."

"I know. My father, mother, older brothers and sister are all lawyers. Just me - different. I haven't seen or talked to my family in three years."

Mandy pipes in. "Sad. If I had family growing up..." she puts on that distant look of hers. "Gregory, why aren't you staying in contact, especially with your sister? You guys were so close."

"Space and time, I guess, and my father, he is so disappointed in me. He had high hopes. I don't know why; I just couldn't jump into that world. Dad told me, 'You're always welcome.' I don't know what is wrong with me."

Juan says, "Gregory, you are so lucky having a family growing up. You oughta at least call him."

Bradley says, "Hey, we do need a lawyer; maybe it's time you two get back together.'"

Gregory says, "I don't know. He might not be too much help, his specialty is anti-trust."

Mandy says, "Gregory. Call Ida."

Bradly says, "You heard the boss."

"It's long distance. Can't do it here. And she's a constitutional lawyer in Washington DC, working for lobbyists. But you're right; hun, I should call her. Just say hi, and let her know what I'm doing now that I have a new family."

Edie, overhearing the conversation, says, "If it's alright with Danny, you can call from here."

Mandy says, "It's Monday evening in Washington DC. She's probably home." Mandy leaps up and goes into the yard where Danny is playing with Edie's four and seven-year-old girls, who, playing doctors, find it necessary to operate on Danny's stomach.

"No, No! I'm not pregnant, I swear." The girls are squealing, the youngest saying, "Well, still, we can check you out. Something's bad in there." The oldest says, "You need a big pain killer."

Mandy says, "Still having troubles with women, huh?"

Danny shakes his head, smiles, "Oh no, Girls! No knives, okay?" The girls giggle.

"Girls, I hate to disturb your operation, but your mom needs Danny's approval for Gregory to call long distance to Washington DC, his sister."

The oldest girl says, "Approved." Danny nods obediently.

Mandy goes back inside, nods to Gregory, "Call."

Excited talking from both ends of the phone could be heard by everybody in the room. Gregory's end of the conversation: "Yeah, we were on tour in Miami and I met this girl and I left the band. We've been travelin' across the country, met this Brazilian guy in Santa Fe who's pretty creative with cheap travel and we ended up in San Francisco for four months, but too cold, now I'm on Kaua'i. Climate a lot like Jamaica but less muggy, and even the music has some similarities. It's been a wild four years I'll remember forever. And Ida, you won't believe this, but I'm getting real political now, like Dad and you. I've seen a lot of sadness along the way, a lot of people left out in the cold for no reason of their own, and on Kaua'i I met this incredible guy who has a way to change America for the best. He's got a plan and I am part of it, and we are gonna try and take over a chain of radio stations here in Hawaii. We were in a seven hour conversation with one of these radio chains, and it looks like he is going to get a contract to take over these radio stations for a test period of six months. Ida, you won't believe this. I really think we are gonna change America. Danny has a plan to eliminate big businesses' control over government and a lot, lot more. We are supposed to sign the final contracts in nine days. I know it sounds crazy. I'd love you to listen to his plan."

"Gregory, don't get your hopes up too high; it sounds impossible, you have no idea how bad it is in Washington. I scream every night in frustration." Ida adds, "I've seen the machine and it *is* white."

She continued, tears forcing a sloppy, crackling voice over the telephone. "Sometimes I wonder why I even try. I love you, and you have a heart of gold, and even if it is hopeless, if this is what you want, I'll help you any way I can.

"I'll call you back with my arrival time. Give me your phone number."

Gregory says, "Arrival time?" Gregory gets the phone number from Edie. Ida takes it and clicks off. Gregory hangs up the phone. "She's coming."

Tears form in his eyes. Mandy looks stunned. Tears moist her cheeks, too. "Oh my God, this is more wonderful than I can believe."

Ten people in a two-bedroom house with one and half bathrooms. It's getting a bit tight. Edie is so cool. She never mentions anything. But I see the problem and we are moving the family to the three-star hotel in Kapa'a, the Marriott. I contact Jackson and tell him where we are.

Four days before the contract is to be signed, Ida arrives. I have a meeting in the bar with her and unlike Gregory, she has no problem with alcohol.

I explain my strategy. I start with my sermon. "Radio is not like TV or the internet. If it opens the door to all kinds of music, all views, people start listening to be a part of the world. If it allows all

THE RADIO REVOLUTION

to participate in the music played, people of different cultures, sexes and ages share their combined music taste with others. And the world finds common communicators, songs that bridge the genre spectrum, and people begin to feel togetherness sharing their musical tastes with others. Radio is powerful because it unites the common mind of man through music and in a stimulating and imaginative way. That combination, stimulation and imagination together, with everybody sharing the listening at once, is a miracle when it is done with realness and honesty. It penetrates our universal minds and allows us, for moments, to think as one. It is like no other medium. Internet and TV is you and a screen, you are choosing from a plethora of choices. Radio, when it is open, is sharing choices."

Ida says, "You're saying radio is sharing your choices with others?"

"Yes, In the fifties and sixties, top 40 radio stations played all genres, country, foreign language, jazz, soul, blues, easy listening, gospel, rock n roll, if it was selling they played it, no concern for the sound nor the genre. Now radio lies dormant, lifeless in the hands of big business conglomerates who are intent on super serving listeners with smaller and smaller tastes. This contract is to take over radio across the islands and bring it back to life, stir the people, make them feel a part of the world around them whether they participate or they just identify with the people who do participate."

Ida starts wondering. "How?" She questions.

"We are going to turn the music programming over to the people. We are going to be playing all kinds of music back to back, with no restriction to genres. So we are going to have to take over radio stations all across the country and implement this system. Gregory and Mandy just understand innately. They see what has to be done. Bradley is a computer genius, and Juan is a natural DJ that can make the world sing, and he comes from utter poverty so his heart is stone fired, welded to the common people, and his voice will scream across the country when we up this mission into political awareness."

Ida takes a huge gulp of wine, almost choking on it.

I could already tell she thought I was mad.

She adds, "You think people will like all kinds of music? You think you can control music stations all across the country? You think everybody will just love this? Not possible."

Ida takes another swallow and adds, "And on top of that - so give this to me again, you plan to bring radio to life by allowing the people to program the music played, and when super popular across the nation, introduce a political agenda? They'll buy that?"

She obviously didn't understand radio. At least not consciously. But I could tell by her response that I had unnerved her. I reinforced my statement. "And through radio, the most stimulating media there is, ignite a fire underneath complacent America to bring change, with a simple amendment to the constitution."

Ida shakes her head, "You can't make Congress, which caused the problem, vote in the solution, Danny."

"We go around them. In the US constitution, amendments can be generated by the state legislatures."

"What? Danny, you can't get around it. Granted state legislatures, if two thirds demand a constitutional convention they can force congress to create a constitutional convention, but state legislatures are little microcosms of the US congress."

"Ida, we know Article V of the US constitution allows for a constitutional convention. You know in the Federation Papers James Madison says that he was leaving the fifth article vague to allow ways in the future to implement amendments, and even the constitutional conventions are vague in Article V. How to form them? Though it is mentioned in the Federalist Papers, US congress must stay out of it, if initiated by the states."

Ida smiles. "Sorry Danny. When Ohio tried to get the people to ratify an amendment to the constitution - Hawke vs Smith - the Supreme Court turned it down as a route to ratification, saying states cannot exercise federal powers."

Danny shakes his head. "That's insane. The states have the right to ratify an amendment to the constitution anyway they want. Article V doesn't specifically say how a constitutional convention can be formed. And the 10th Amendment says those rights not specifically prescribed to the constitution for the Federal Government, automatically goes to the states, or even directly to the people, for God's sake. When did the Supreme Court do that?"

Ida says, "Wow! Jesus, you're a real rebel." She shakes her head. "It happened in the twenties. But that was concerning an amendment generated by Congress, but you are suggesting a constitutional convention. That is a little different, a constitutional convention generated by the states. Still, this has to be generated by the state legislatures, not the people directly." She laughs, then continues.

"And then there is Coleman vs Miller, which said Congress should have final authority over ratification confusion. And doing a constitutional convention would qualify to be confusion because it is not specifically stated how it would be formed in the constitution." She laughs. "You have no idea how many special interest groups approach me with the amendment process. I'm a bit of a specialist in this. And now a radio guy." Ida shakes her head. "My world is crazy."

I say, "What about the Federalist Papers? Madison, the father of the constitution, admitting constitutional conventions are vague and in time they need to be worked out in form? And that amendments need to be fully deliberated and be the overall will of the people?

"This is one possible way of implementing the amendment. Have a constitutional convention in all of the states, and in that convention elect activist candidates to a temporary party whose only platform is to petition congress for this specific amendment to the constitution, maybe even convince some of the state and senate representatives of other parties to put this amendment on their own platform to gather votes.

"Then we get a large segment of these activists' candidates elected to the state legislatures and have these elected candidates petition Congress for only this one amendment to the constitution.

"We can use democratic radio stations to generate popular sentiment to this amendment.

"The plan is to get two thirds of the states to force congress into having a constitutional convention for solely this amendment.

"And then with that momentum we get three quarters of the states' legislatures to ratify this amendment.

"That is full deliberation and the overall agreement of the country. Right? Radio can do that. No other media can. We will create momentum, turn America alive, call this new party the Democracy Party. It would be hard to stop. And it would be attractive to state candidates of both the Republican and the Democratic Parties. And what elected official wants to go through the hassle of spending their own money and hassle others for donations. And once this democracy party gets this amendment into the constitution, never again would there be a need for parties, period. Parties are for funding elections."

Ida stares at Danny like in shock. Stays silent for a moment then says, "Well, you're right about using the Federalist papers. The Supreme Court historically likes to apply the 'spirit' of these papers to their decisions when the constitution is not clear on such matters. I agree. But a constitutional convention needs two thirds of state legislatures to ask for it. Then there would be a formal national constitutional convention. But congress would try to usurp it. When they see a state constitutional convention looming, they would decide to take it on in Congress, then vote it down, and that would be it."

Ida continues, "By design, the amendment process requires extensive deliberation and ensures that amendments are the settled opinion of the American people. That's a quote from Madison. I can see the Supreme Court divorcing the Congress from participation if such a scenario is presented to it. No guarantee, but quite possible".

Ida took another gulp of wine. "But this is outlandish, bizarre. I can't visualize it.".

I caught the waitress as she was passing and put up two fingers.

I just kept building, like a beaver. "Visualize this. People choosing the music, all the great unexposed bands making it to the airways, people knowing this is their radio station, everyone can participate, the youth welding together in a voicing strength, especially the 18-24s. Then this group of people will see the difference between radio controlled by the major record companies and the radio conglomerates, and real radio, where the people control what gets played. People will *feel a part of the real world* and their imaginations will expand, and they'll see What Can Be, and how it can be. Imagine seeing ballot boxes everywhere. Imagine saying, 'Why not,' and vote. Imagine listening and hearing a song you voted for, a song that never has been on radio before. Imagine that. Imagine being in a local band, and hearing your song on the radio. Imagine a ballot being read over the air, the songs somebody likes, the ones somebody doesn't like, and you like some of them, and then playing a song you would never hear on radio, like 'Bach's Fugue' as requested on the ballot. Imagine a Saturday Show where you play the 36 songs most wanted to be heard songs by the ballots over radio. And those songs will be so, so different from what radio is playing now. Radio can be that powerful. We can put out surveys, list every vote counted, both positive and negative votes and people can see what is popular and what isn't. It will tap into the common mind of all of us as we come together as one. TV can't do that. Internet can't do that." The popularity will be huge."

Ida looks at the strange white man before her, with his messy, wavy, black and grey hair, tattered jeans, a gifted, almost spiritual light in his eyes. The man that her brother idolizes.

Ida's body is a bit soft and a bit round but her eyes are dark brown daggers and there is fire in those eyes now. "If you are successful, Danny, which is pretty close to impossible to imagine, if you are, and you succeed, you have no idea what hell you will unleash."

"Ida, it has *got to be tried*. And the rage you are talking about is merely the exhaust out of a diesel engine that is fuming noxious elements into the air. It explodes from nowhere and its gasses dissipate into thin air. And you are underestimating the power of radio. Way too much. Radio can set this country afire, despite the complacent state it is in now. There's a nerve; hit it and the world will scream, not only America. Mankind will scream for this. Even if they don't like the music the radio is playing. Everybody will cry to emulate it in their own special cultures and places."

Where is he coming from? Some Alien planet? "What's the nerve, Danny?"

"We have been a free enterprise country, basically, creating value in the market by creatively filling the demand. Create value in economics and the economy booms. But in the last twenty-five-years capitalism has gone on runaway. Once big business gets a certain size, it can't be stopped. And it cares little about creating additional value in the market place. Instead, it concentrates on controlling the market, and one of the ways it does this is by going to congress for help. Congress helps and free enterprise gets tied down, unable to create value, and that puts a stranglehold on the economy. So the solution is to demonstrate what non-conglomerate radio can do, like with this format; demonstrate and explain to America how the new capitalism of today is strangling free enterprise, make the word "conglomerate" as nasty sounding as "communism" is now. Remember, both the conglomerates and communism are obsessed with controlling the market. Then, introduce a new amendment to the constitution that stops runaway capitalism. We show what a democracy can be over radio, compared with Big Business way of running radio, and people will awaken, and help us turn this ship around."

Ida says, "You are an amazing dreamer. But dream this is. The amendment you are suggesting to put a halt to this madness would have to be longer than the constitution itself. You would have to write a whole new constitution and that won't happen in this political arena. You are talking revolution. War. Further madness."

Danny smiles at Ida's conscious mind. "No Ida, it can be done with a very brief but effective amendment to the constitution.

"It's simple." Danny smiles. "Government pays for all election campaigns. No one can use their own money or other people's money. Each candidate that qualifies gets equal funds. Money never goes to the candidates directly; it goes to who they assign job orders to.

"It's the end of parties. People join parties to get their campaigns financed.

THE RADIO REVOLUTION

"It's the end of big business having control over congress, end of big business controlling the market as the new congress will assign restraints on big business.

"Each person running for a legislative office will receive equal pay based on the medium salary of all in America including the poverty stricken. The legislative branch, all congress, equal pay. There will be no pension. Thus the poor people will be more prone to run than the rich, who will make less if they run, and people who are service minded will likely be the ones running.

"And when America becomes aware that big business is running the government, and that it can now be controlled by congress and the President, then the people running for congress will do well to listen to the people, instead of outside interest. They will put controls on conglomeration of businesses, make big business pay fair taxes, restrict excessive weapons to the public, open up the door to discuss the practicality of welfare reform, eliminate the insurance companies and make health care free like parts of Europe, and the common people will at last have a say in America."

Ida's conscious mind and subconscious suddenly weld together.

"Well, you have set up an amazing series of events. First, getting a radio station, then turning on the populace, then getting more and more radio stations, and turning on the populace, then have everybody wanting to share their music with each other and not listen to what they use to, then rallying them around a never before done thing, creating a party with only one purpose, this amendment stimulated by state constitutional conventions, and do this while suppressing the powerful money controllers of this country, and have 2/3rds of the state legislature request a constitutional convention, and find a way to keep Congress out of the picture. Then have three quarters of the states ratify it. What a long shot!" Oh yeah - and force this constitutional convention to only handle one amendment, this one. Whew."

Ida rests back on her chair. "Danny, you are plum crazy."

101

"Remember: everyone who doesn't want special interest groups and big business controlling congress will like this. Republicans and Democrats both. It should be accepted by over 90% of the masses."

"You try this, Danny, and there will be so much money campaigning against you that people will be brainwashed into voting against it."

I say, "Let me ask you something. If we get that far, if two thirds of the states vote for a constitutional convention, and congress tries to usurp it, will you go and fight for us in the Supreme Court?"

"You really believe you can generate America out of its insane complacency?"

"It can be done. They just have to know how this will turn America upside down. Then a great swell of momentum will rise and a tidal wave will crash upon Washington DC."

"Well, if you do, of course, I'll fight for you."

I smile. "That's the plan. We were given a democracy, why not use it."

Ida weighs that on her mind. *We were given a democracy, why not use it?*

"Well not exactly. We were given a republic, then maybe. Why not use it," says Ida.

I say, "That will be our slogan. That will be our battle cry. "We were given a democracy, why not use it."

"I can't see it happening. It seems impossible. But I will say this. If it does work, and the amendment does get passed, even if this is an amazingly small possibility, but if it does happen, then it is worth the effort. Even one in a thousand chance. It's worth a try. Why? It would turn America upside down. And even if it didn't work, it might get far enough to wake up America. That amendment, simple as it is, would turn America into a democracy. I see what you are saying now."

I didn't say anything. I just let her think. We were silent a minute or two. She sipped her wine.

"Danny, once people know what is happening, that big business is running the government, that the people really don't have a say except with the vote, and the system is so polluted most don't want to vote, and you bring forth a democratic radio station, a real democratic radio station, with no tampering, oh my God! I see a sliver of light."

Ida suddenly can't stop. "Danny. I know people with money that can help us. Environmentalists. Women for Women. They have big backers, dedicated contributors but the backers and the contributors don't know how their money can really help so they give little. If they know they can turn government upside down, they will give everything they can."

I smile and say, "That's it. One little amendment, if passed, can turn America upside down. Even if they hate the sound of the station in the beginning, when they realize it just takes one little amendment to turn this country around, and they understand what that really means, they will begin to like the format. Their imagination will expand because the sound alone medium ignites the imagination. And radio will set off an incredible force on the common mind."

"So the kids know this?"

"Gregory and Mandy know, they just know. Mandy sees the future. Mandy is downright psychic, in fact. She sees everything before it is everything. Bradley is a computer genius; he doesn't know, but he will be a big help. Juan, despite his bitterness, is full of love, and he will ignite America when the time comes to do it, but he doesn't know now. And none of them but Mandy, including you, know what will happen when we turn on the light to this radio format. I and Mandy know. It will be incredible."

"And Gregory?"

"To me, it is Gregory and Mandy who got me off my ass to finally quit complaining and really do this. And your brother is a pure soul that given room to blossom can turn America on. He can relate to people. He talks, they listen. I talk, they think I'm mad."

Ida laughs. "You really need Gregory. I can see that. And you are right; he is pure, and a straight arrow mind.

"Danny, I can't believe this. At least you have a plan. And taking over four radio stations for six months is a start. I know of no one else who has a plan. We are simply spinning are wheels in frustration, day by day."

"Democracy is written into the constitution. It's written into the Declaration of Independence. It is written into the Federalist papers. We have to find a way to use it, dig deep to uncover it. In this case we need to find the inner secrets of the constitution and apply them. This is the plan to use the constitution. But don't tell a soul. Not yet," I said.

"Why tell me?"

"Cause Gregory and I are doing the planning on this end. I'm hoping you could do planning on the other end."

I add, "Neither one of us can reveal what we are really doing."

"Why do you trust me?"

"Because I trust Gregory. The son. The son your father thought he lost might do more for America than even his father. Sometimes a beautiful soul has this purity that sings to you, and with such clarity, it lights a fire inside you. That's what Mandy and Gregory do for me. Without them I wouldn't have had the courage to try."

Ida is caught in thought. "Yes, that is Gregory."

I go on. "You want what I want. You need what I want. You're screaming in hopelessness in politics. I don't want to lose you. I want you to know the plan so you can be patient and endure the mind bogging bullshit until the time comes. That's why I'm talking to you. And when the time comes, you will be a goldmine to me. Ida, life is strange. You work so hard, you try to do things, but you're frustrated, even fired for trying. Yet you keep trying and in the process you are building a great goldmine of value, and that goldmine will come to use when you least suspect it. Be patient, but persevere. Never give up, never bend. The time will come when that goldmine of value will flower. Then you and the world will sing."

Ida just looks at me.

I smile and say, "Mandy was so excited when Gregory said you would come, she knows things upfront. She's magical. And I didn't know what she was so excited about then, but now I know."

"So Mandy is the girl Gregory found in Miami?"

"Good choice, yeah?"

Ida replies, "I guess so."

I go on. "I told Gregory I'm a mathematician first. We are the most complex mathematical forces on earth now. Math demands balance. Conglomeration is imbalance. And math has a strange way of balancing the imbalance even when the odds are seemingly impossible. Even when things are on a runaway. In fact, that is what causes the sudden changes in evolution, I believe."

Ida says, "Yah, I heard. "You predicted the impossible, even risked running naked if the impossible didn't happen. Gregory told me."

"I'm a scientist. I experiment. It worked. It will likely work again. It is most certainly worth a try."

I couldn't tell her part of the reason it worked was because I introduced it over radio to the common mind, and when a chunk of the common mind believes it might happen, it has a better chance of happening. I couldn't tell her my strategy was part of the reason for the rout over BYU.

Ida smiles. "I hope it isn't the wine believing this." She laughs.

Secretly, I was hoping the same thing.

Jackson brought the corporation's lawyer, we brought Ida Stefan, a constitution lawyer working for the environmental lobbyist in Washington DC.

Ida had us put the corporation in Mandy Pang's name. She wanted a non-white as owner. It would be to our advantage later. Mandy was a combination of Chinese, Samoan, and Negroid. I was the President. Bradley was the vice president, Gregory secretary, and Ida treasurer. Juan couldn't have his name on the corporation's documents because he was residing in America as an illegal alien. But once Juan got his papers, Ida would turn the treasurer title over to him. Juan was fine with that. Our secret pact which we all signed and had notarized had all five of us (Mandy, Bradley, Gregory, me, and Juan) with equal shares and equal pay from the enterprise. We all got equal amounts whether we needed it or not. And Ida was our lawyer, Ed our operations' manager, and Rabbit our engineer. They would be our first paid workers.

Rabbit found a way to microwave from the Kaua'i mountains to Oahu mountains, to Maui mountains to Kailua-Kona on the Big Island for the Saturday Show. We were going to have to make a separate agreement with Hilo on the Big Island and use one of our vans to go up Maunakea and beam a microwave from Kona to Hilo for the Saturday Morning Show. And getting a signal for Hilo still had to be negotiated.

Ida proved to be a brutal negotiator when the corporation tried to find loopholes so they could choose some of the music that was to be played. She knew FCC rules, knew what conglomerates could and couldn't do. She made it clear if you were selling the idea over radio that the people were programming the music of a station, you were liable if you cheated on the music played.

The conglomerate lawyer was belligerent, and Ida had to pull out the regulation. "False representation and Government will force compliance or closure." And she made it quite clear that tampering with the music would be asking for a class action suit. "You can't sell something over radio you are not delivering." The corporate lawyer said, "Everybody lies in the media. That's ridiculous."

Ida responded. "You'll see how ridiculous it is when we sue for damages. Every person who could hear your radio station in your area, and this will be for all million people in Hawaii, will get money in a class action suit." Ida didn't tell the lawyer she would have an uphill fight to get that verdict, but he could tell by her eyes she would try.

The corporation lawyer said, "Well, we'll fix that clause, the people controlling the music, and take that innocuous statement out of this contract."

Ida's eyes turned into a laser beam. She began pacing. "You have made a tentative agreement, signed by your General Manager, then you come here and do a flip flop, and I'll take this to arbitration. We are investing a great sum of money into a democratic representation and you want the court to side with you? Good luck. The Radio Revolution has acquired these funds on that premise. If we take it to arbitration with the initial handwritten agreement made more than ten days ago, your corporation will spend more money in litigation than your station will want, or even afford." She stopped pacing. "Oh yeah, the way it's written, you'll be lucky if you even get a tooth pick extra out of the arbitration agreement. My brother knew what he was doing when he wrote out that agreement. He's from a family of five lawyers."

The lawyer said, "You can't make a tentative agreement stand."

"It was signed by the head of this radio chain, Jackson, contingent on the money being present. The money is there. You'll have a hard time telling that to a judge. You certainly can't speak for the head of the corporation."

Jackson gulped. He had done his homework. He knew Ida Stefan was a lawyer to be reckoned with, initiating scores of environmental suits that were decided favorably, or still pending, as well as a case in front of the Kentucky Supreme Court over abortion availability in Kentucky. Jackson cautioned the corporation lawyer in his ever so tactful voice.

"Twerp, shut up. Corporation lawyers don't run the corporation; they are paperwork flunkies and only do what the corporation ask them to do. Lawyers are mopper-uppers, not changers."

The corporation lawyer eyes intensified. "Jackson, are you mad? You are going to let the people run rough shod over the music programming?"

"Damn right. I'm mad. At you. I got enough twerps overthinking for me."

I add fuel to the flames, "Oh my God, what if we played what the people really wanted to hear---collectively. Oh my God! Oh my God! It would be the end of the world. How could we do that!"

I didn't expect that out of Jackson. Maybe he did have a heart under that massive flab and that loud machine gun mouth. I know radio. No corporation would allow the people to program a radio station. But Jackson carried a lot of weight in more ways than one, and I knew he believed in me. I'm lucky. Maybe I should give him some action in our company after it is successful. But my hands weren't open too wide; I knew Jackson would try to tamper with what I was doing. Jackson, like all radio giants, had his own idea of how things should be run. I knew those ideas were dead wrong, but still, they had to be dealt with as success came to this revolutionary format. But that was in the future. This was now.

The corporation lawyer stormed out of the room, Jackson shouting after him with more sensitive talk. "I'm damned stupid I paid for your ticket. I'm glad you are out of here."

With the corporation lawyer gone, Ida was allowed to enter some security clauses and the agreement was signed by we five and Jackson, and witnessed by Ida. The agreement began with the starting date January 25th (opening of the radio billing cycle), 1990.

We had three months to get ready for take-off.

13

TAKE-OFF

Three months wasn't much time. The first step was building five hundred ballot boxes. They were wooden, chained, eighteen by eighteen inches with a sliding board that stood ten inches above the ballot box with the sign "Declare your Radio Freedom. Vote."

We used Jackson's corporate radio stations to solicit carpenter volunteers to build the boxes on the six islands with the cry, "Become part of the Radio Revolution, build ballot boxes." Adding, "On January 25th, 1990 at 9:12AM, the Radio Revolution Begins."

Hundreds, mostly teens, showed up to help build on various locations in Hawaii. I went to every island to orchestrate the construction. We used local lumber yards and their saws and live remotes on Oahu to generate volunteers. We had the five hundred ballot boxes within a week.

The second step was securing computer design shop locations with Bradley making the computer program and synchronizing the computers through the state. Again, over radio, we solicited volunteers, and Bradley put them through one test after another to secure their loyalty, honesty, and efficiency in tabulating the ballots. He had actual seminars on ballot counting procedures with a sheet, four pages long, on how to proceed with each ballot counted, and when to disqualify a ballot. What do you do with same handwriting and same songs from one ballot location? Volunteer monitors were hired to random check the ballot counters integrity. What do you do with illegible handwriting? Etc.

I did settle with the landlord, and we used my rented place to organize our campaigns on Oahu, and I got my massive music library back from years of hounding garage sales and collecting radio promotion copies. So many of the songs requested I had never heard of though, and at times I was at a loss as to where to find them. For those, we called the balloteer and they would furnish the song for airplay. Volunteers were no problem; we even had a list of substitute ballot counters.

Mandy and Gregory established ballot locations at retail stores on Oahu. They got two volunteers to retrieve ballots. We bought four used Arrow Vans from an old radio supporter of mine for a song. They said, "Declare Your Radio Freedom." Three of them had micro-wave dishes on the roof so as to bounce radio waves across the Hawaiian Islands during the Saturday countdown show. One enthusiastic limo driver joined the team on the Big Island for picking up ballots and soliciting advertising. We stuck a micro-wave on top of his limo, and he drove up Maunakea Volcanic Mountain every Saturday morning to rebound micro-waves to the south side of Maui, the island of Lanai, and Hilo.

Rabbit secured micro-wave towers on Sleepy Giant Mountain in Kaua'i, to beam the waves to the Koolaus on Oahu (Honolulu), to Maui, then to Kailua-Kona on the Big Island so the Hawaiian Island Music Report could be heard state wide on Saturday Morning. One of the mobile vans that normally picked ballots on Kaua'i was moved to the North Shore during the Saturday Morning Music Report. That micro-wave was directed to a boat volunteered by a supporter in line of sight of Kapalau Valley and the top of Waimea Canyon on Kaua'i.

We negotiated a deal to use the Hilo signal only ten days before we began airing the Radio Revolution. They were quite hesitant to allowing their music to be controlled by the ballots but when they noticed the hysteria we were causing across the state they finally

THE RADIO REVOLUTION

submitted to the deal. Ida flew to Hilo to be sure the station understood there would be no messing with the music played for six months. Juan along with Jackson organized the high school and college ballot locations across the state.

Ed, the perfectionist, wanted the Saturday Morning countdown show taped like Casey Kasem. I said, "Perfection is not needed, Ed. Live, vibrant, listeners participating over the air and through the ballot system is what we need. Live Radio is essential."

Ed wanted to keep easy transitions between songs. He didn't like the idea of a Rap song followed by a heavy metal song, followed by Frank Sinatra, etc. I knew all the DJs would want to do the same thing, "mix" the music with easy transitions so Bradley brought in some contraption he invented to program the music playlist so the DJs on the islands had no say on what and when to play a certain song. I was having DJ meetings in the islands and the DJs were downright hostile. We were breaking endless amounts of taboos in radio. Jackson was worried. He had no idea that putting people in charge of music would upset radio that much. He kept telling them it was only for six months. But I knew he was worried. Ida stayed on his ass, reminding him of the contract 24-7. Jackson felt he had made a mistake. He brought me in the office one day, with his worries.

"We've got to tone this down, Danny.".

"I told you I wanted to change radio. And for the best. This will work, it will blow radio into a new dimension of reality. You need to trust me, stand behind me, for this to work."

"Danny, everybody's panicking. There's a mutiny in the wind."

"Don't worry, you're good at firing. If they don't want to go along with this I'll bring in DJs from college radio. They'll do what I say without question. And I need an evening slot for Juan on Oahu and a morning slot for Mandy on Oahu, anyway. And those two, you won't have to pay their salaries. They are on my payroll. And who told me DJs are a dime a dozen? If they complain, fire em."

"Why Mandy, an amateur, on the morning show? Is it gonna be you and Mandy in the morning?"

"Nope. It's just Mandy, solo, on the morning show."

Jackson was in shock. "I thought *you* would do the morning show, and who's ever heard of a woman being the solo morning DJ? And young, too. How old is she? Why aren't you on the Morning Show, Danny?"

"You want me to get up at 4am, prepare a show, then monitor five stations during a day, prepare skits, do commercials, tutor DJs, manage the ballot collectors' advertising... well, some of those things I will end up sucking at. Let me do the most important things: monitor the sound and prepare creative entertainment with the other DJs, and monitor the small time advertising. I can't do everything, Jackson. Saturday 10-2 with Ed Kanoi, that is it. And you won't have to pay Ed."

"Why are you putting an amateur young female DJ on prime time, Danny? It's unheard of."

"I started as an amateur. I know talent. Trust me. She's gonna be as popular as I was. I didn't even know how to run the board. She knows. And Ed is the best producer around and experienced with the morning show, he is going to produce her show with my help for entertainment. It will work, Jackson. Big time."

"The corporation is freaking out, Danny. My job is on the line here. If I didn't have an expensive Out clause, I would be gone."

"Who's complaining to the corporation?"

"DJs don't even know how to contact the corporation, but they complain to the sales staff, and the sales staff has some bad seeds that love to complain to the higher ups."

I said, "Look. I've got people going into every ballot location. Arm them with a sales pitch and an advertising program for small retailers, and Radiotron ratings will bring you huge money."

"You don't understand, Danny. Radiotron is here to make money. How do they do it? They ask for big bucks to get high ratings, no matter how much they deny it."

"Okay, I'll throw in fifty grand."

"Really. I thought you hated them."

"Jackson, do you have any idea how popular we will be?"

THE RADIO REVOLUTION

"Danny, you throw money around like it doesn't count. I heard what you are doing. It is beyond expensive, your obsession of hitting every location across the Hawaiian Islands." It's over forty thousand a month at least, and the set up cost over two hundred thousand. And having an 800 request line across the islands is a massive expense."

"It's expensive, yeah, but I got friends, and a creative engineer. It's under eighty- thousand set up cost. I got a lot of volunteers for pretty much everything. And with the exception of a few loose ends, the monthly expenses to maintain the ballot system, plus the micro-wave rentals and the micro-wave trucks, it will be under eight thousand a month, and that includes the 800 phone line."

I went on. "What's paramount important, is your ratings will soar. That will get corporation off your back and if the fifty grand helps, it is worth far, far more."

Jackson didn't look convinced.

I continued, "You were around in the fifties. Remember 1960, the first year Hawaii could vote for a President. You brought Huckleberry Hound campaigning for President. When he got off the plane there were thousands of people cheering. There were homemade signs and crowds along Nimitz Highway yelling, "Huckleberry Hound for President." You got in trouble with the FCC. Remember? Because air flights had to be delayed because of the Huckleberry Hound hysteria for President brought traffic to a stall on Nimitz highway. Remember? Remember Independence day top 300 and Tom Rounds actually counting those ballots. Even today, people hold on to that survey here in Hawaii trying to collect those songs. Remember the DJ go cart races at the civic, and two thousand people on hand? I'm bringing this back, Jackson. I'm bringin' it back. Have faith. And remember you had a 55 percent share of the entire radio audience on Oahu, then. I'm bringing that giant audience back to you, Jackson."

"Times have changed, Danny."

"Times don't change, Jackson. We change the times."

Jackson wasn't the only problem. I already knew what the number one song was gonna be by an overwhelming vote: "Fuck the Police"

113

by NWA. Every male 10-17 had it on his ballot, pretty much, and the song was two minutes and forty-six seconds and we had to take out the 'fucks' and the 'niggers,' That cut the playtime down to under two minutes. Yeah there was almost a minute of 'fucks' and 'niggers.' When that song reached the air in high rotation, there was no question in my mind, Jackson would pull the plug. If not him, his boss. So after that brutal conversation with Jackson I knew what I needed: Mandy.

Jackson would stay on the phone until eleven at night sometimes, with no consideration that the other party was off the clock. Mandy opened his office door at 9pm on a Thursday night.

"Shut everything down, Jackson. Everything. Kill the phone. Pull the plug, Turn off your computers. Turn off the lights. What I say and how you take it will either change the world or put it back in the middle ages." She used my spiel. "Radio is sound alone, Jackson, and sound alone excites the imagination. Turn your fuckin' contraptions off. Be blind; imagine and listen."

Mandy waited. Jackson turned off one computer, turned and looked at her. He was aghast at her confident presence. No one had ever approached him like that. And she was gorgeous. Mandy went behind his desk, yanked the phone plug out, then turned another laptop off by closing it. Then she spun around, went to the wall, and turned off the lights in the room. It was dark except the lights from the city in the window. She pulled the curtains closed. Utter darkness.

"You're too beautiful to turn off the lights."

Her shadow moved directly to his desk.

"Beauty isn't me, Jackson. The beauty is people expressing their frustrations, artist expressing their frustrations through beauty, and in a world where artists have been suffocated." Mandy abruptly sat on Jackson's desk. Papers jostled, a few fell to the floor. She continued. "You opened the lines to the heart of the people, people crying, people desperately looking for identity in this world, you do that," her voice raised its volume, "Then you *can't* shut it down. Danny is concerned. The number one song this week will be 'Fuck the Police.' It's getting overwhelming votes."

THE RADIO REVOLUTION

"Fuck the what?" Jackson came unglued. "Get Out! I'm shutting this thing down! Now!" He fumbled to open his computer.

In utter darkness he kept fumbling.

Mandy bent closer to Jackson. Jackson got a whiff of a subtle pikake perfume. Her shadowy presence still sat on his desk. "Relax, Jackson. You can't do that anyway. The street is turned on. The populace has plunged over the cliff. You want the populace with you, you got to jump over the cliff, too. Are we gonna reach the people or are we gonna lead them to insurrection and devastation? Let 'Fuck the Police' sing in the hearts of Hawaii. Let it, and you will be the most popular radio station in America. It's that simple. That number one voted song is just the tip of the iceberg. There is a revolution out there. I gotta be in it." Mandy did a sweep of papers off the desk in the dark, and sprung from the desk.

Jackson started thinking. What had he done? He was committed to this by contract, and a psycho lawyer. As Mandy slipped off his desk, Jackson said, "Honey, this is just entertainment. My bosses will shut this down if you do it. So its very simple. Ax that song." No way we can use the word, 'Fuck.'

Mandy seemed unfazed by his threats. Where was she coming from? Why did she seem so confident? *No one talks to me like this.*

She jumped back on his desk on her knees, now. She loomed over him. "Entertainment! Radio is being in a world and a part of it. The 'fucks' and 'niggers,' and the other bad words are out of the song. They have been spliced out. This is the biggest selling album in America since 2 Live Crew, which radio did play. Remember 'We Want Pussy?' And on the survey we are gonna call it "FCC the Police." You've got nothing to worry about. It's just another angry song identifying with the youth of today. It's beautiful, when you really think about it."

Jackson rebounded, "Think all you want, as long as the world don't hear it over radio."

Mandy came unglued. Her stately presence morphed into rage. She leaped off the desk, started pacing. "You are in a precious moment. Danny is reaching the people. This is what they want to say. Shut this down and you will regret it the rest of your life." She walked around and stood over him. Even in the dark Jackson could sense the threat.

She jumped on the desk. "You know what Danny says radio is for?" She turned looking directly in Jackson's direction. "You are in radio. You should know this. Radio is to bring the unaccepted into acceptance, to widen the circle, to make the world bigger than it is, to make the unaccepted beautiful among the whole. Look what rock and roll on radio has done. It has allowed the misfits, the degenerates, the minorities a bigger voice in the world. Please. Please. Jackson, the world sucks, you know that. Let's unsuck it. Danny can do that if you support him. You know what Danny told me? He said, 'Look for security, and you can never change the world.' What did he mean? You never capture the beauty of the world if you spend your energy looking for security. This is your chance Jackson, fight for us, and you may be awarded more than you expect. You may be awarded, 'beauty' and a singing heart."

Jackson was silent. He tried every way he could, but he couldn't think of a rebounding statement. He suddenly remembered the way he was in his youth. He was a misfit. Didn't even graduate from high school. And even as a teen he was massively overweight. Yet he had become a legend in radio. The machine gun mouth paused. He couldn't believe it. He was moved. "You're right Mandy. Radio did play the edited 2 Live Crew. We've done it once, we might get away with it again. I'll think about it. But I got to do more than think. I got to trick the power to be."

Mandy moved around the desk and slithered closer to him. She opened the curtains a smidge. Her shadowy figure was now completely revealed in a squeak of light. He saw her rich black hair swish with a quick turn of her head. She kissed him on the forehead. Her cleavage was right next to his face. He was still sitting down. She said, "Hold me, I want to feel your heart."

Jackson was uncomfortable at first. But then it just came out. Tears slipped down his cheeks. *What am I doing? How did I get into this?* Mandy kept hugging him tightly. Over two minutes she gripped him. She whispered in his ear, "Jackson, you're beautiful. You will be a legend when this is over." She kept holding him. "Thank You, Jackson. Thank you."

Jackson was gripping her as well. But he had only one thing on his mind. *What's Danny doing to me?*

Mandy felt his thoughts and his heart. She slipped back off the desk, turned on the light, picked up the papers on the floor, put them on the desk with a smile, and went over and kissed him on the forehead, again. She smiled. Again she said, "Thank you." Despite her unraveled hair, her white jeans, a cleavage showing blue t-shirt saying "Declare Your Radio Freedom," she had an amazingly stately presence as she turned, looked back, and left the room.

Jackson had new confidence she would be a killer morning DJ, despite being female. *Shit, she was gonna be the first solo, morning female DJ in the world.* He thought, Danny had a lot of savvy, he did know who to hire.

Outside the room, Mandy leaned against the wall. She was shaking. She dropped the duplicate projected playlist on the floor and started crying. She didn't know what was coming over her, but she was glad. *I stood up to him, and he got the message. I can do this.* Tears kept flowing. *I gotta get out of here.*

"God dammit, Danny," Jackson said it out loud to himself.

He started calling. He found out I was in Kailua with voting boxes. Finally, he called Chuck's Restaurant in Lanikai.

I was sipping beer with Bradley checking on the first ballot run. Already 2,000 ballots are tabulated and another four thousand are being tabulated as we are speaking. Looking at the first print out, an attentive waitress came up to me saying, "You have a phone call." I knew it was Jackson. Who else would have chased me down here.

I made a throat slitting gesture, and Bradley went to the phone.

Even before Jackson spoke Bradley said, "Sorry Jackson, he's off island."

"Don't give me any bullshit, the whole world knows where that tramp is, and right now he's been spotted with you in the lanai."

"Not now, Jackson. He's off island."

"How do you get off island in five minutes?"

Bradley said, "He's out there swimming to Rabbit Island to mediate with the seagulls. He'll call you when he can."

Jackson flipped out. "He's swimming at night, now? Get that tramp on the phone, now!"

"Jackson, you are in Hawaii. Duh. Nothing wrong with meditating with the seagulls at night."

Jackson slammed down the phone.

I knew I had a problem. I had to stay on the air a week to wake up the corporation to the success we were going to have. I kept looking at the print out of votes. I was utterly shocked. I didn't expect this. There were already seventeen hundred songs voted for and the top thirty-six vote getters except for three, had never been on the radio before. *I had expected a little of this in the beginning with it gradually ascending to less and less of the music played on radio now. But this playlist is gonna hit Hawaii like a shock wave. There has been so much suppression in the last fifteen years, this is going to be a volcanic explosion of music to reach the common mind.* Bradley is already wondering if we could doctor the votes a bit so it was more in line with contemporary radio. "Maybe count contemporary played songs three votes each." He said, "I mean they are on radio, the mass listeners are accustomed to them," Bradley said.

But I knew that was not an alternative. We had to let it happen and see where it would take us. The most likely route was off the radio in a day. Jackson was the key. He could buffer the anti-corporate sentiment if he knew the score and knew what to expect. I had to show him the list, play the music for him, get him ready for the onslaught and convince him everything was going to be sensational. *Yeah, right, convince machine gun mouth in the midst of a verbose out-spray.*

THE RADIO REVOLUTION

I told Bradley I needed a few more drinks, wondering what the easiest way to deal with the situation was. I said, "Pull out the negative votes and see what comes up." He fiddled with his laptop and in a minute showed me the proposed playlist without the negative votes. Nineteen songs that were currently being played showed up in the top 36. So it was the negative votes that were divorcing the playlist from what radio currently was playing.

He said, "Are we gonna kill the negative votes?"

"Can't," I say. "But it is good to know the problem and find a way to make it an asset."

The waitress came back, smiling. I could tell she liked me. "I did what you asked; he called you again and I said you left in your swim trucks toward the beach."

I noticed she was in her twenties, maybe early thirties. I said, "Brenda, I need help. I've got a radio station going live on corporate radio but I'm afraid the corporation can't handle it. Could you?"

"I don't listen to radio anymore. I might not be a help."

I showed her the votes.

"You gonna play this? Impossible!"

"Nine days, and yes, the top 36 in high rotation."

She smiles. "Then I will listen. And I'll tell all my friends. Everybody will listen."

"So you know these songs?"

"Most yes, and my favorite is the 'All I wanted was a Pepsi' song."

Bradley was questioning, "That's not on the list."

"Bradley, it's the Suicidal Tendencies Song, 'Institutionalized.' A teen anthem."

Bradley says, "A teen anthem? That song is only #31."

I say, "It's not just #31. Out of the 1700 songs voted for, it is in the top 2% of the songs most wanted to be heard on radio. It is the thirty first most wanted to be heard song on Hawaiian Radio. And by the first real research ever done on radio. That position is real!" Brenda looked shocked.

Brenda said, "Danny, you are the first radio person who ever really listened to the people. I knew that about you even when you were playing all that old music. I'll tell everybody. I'll go out and bang on doors when you play this! This is the most wonderful thing. It's beautiful, and Danny you are beautiful. I always knew you weren't like anybody else in radio! I'm so excited."

"Oh, you listened to me?"

"Yeah, I listened to all those old fart songs you were playing a few years ago and the way you made everybody seem special. But I never expected this."

Bradley was quiet. I think he was stunned. It was the first time he realized accuracy was going to erupt in mindless, public, hysterical sentiment.

"Brenda, I'm gonna dedicate the first show to you. Why? 'Cause you kept my heart straight as an arrow when everybody else was screaming. Girl, you are special. You have kept the flame burning."

Brenda says, "Stand up, Danny," Her voice had a demanding tone. She hugged me. I hugged her. She said in my ear, "I'm so happy, I see hope. I see a new world. I see a torch burning to change things."

Cerebral Bradley was in shock. When Brenda went back to other customers Bradley said, "You really know what you're doing. You're bringing the people alive. I can't believe it."

"Bradley, radio is being honest. That's why we can't tamper. We've got to do it the way it comes." I knew this purity couldn't last forever, especially when we had a sensational impact, but it was needed now. It was the flame that would ignite a new world. Like a baby in this world, the innocence would dissipate with time. But Brenda had armed me with how to deal with Jackson.

I went to Jackson's house. "We gotta talk in private. The world is changing. Jackson. And radio isn't listening."

"Who's talking? You never listen. Danny don't give me your shit. Last I heard, 'The world's not changing, we change the world,' and now this flip flop, 'The world is changing.' How can I ever talk to you? You don't have a word of sense in your vocabulary. Now Mandy,

THE RADIO REVOLUTION

that woman can at least make sense. You? You are like a fire bomb in a water tank. Just little bubbles and then puff, your words are gone. And nuthin' gets heard. You gotta start listening. You can't turn radio upside down in a single day. The Earthquake would be devastating. You the first casualty. You can't. It's just that; bloody, simple."

I said, "That's what is going to happen a week from Saturday at 9:12am. Neither you nor I can change that. I'm here. Why? What are we going to do when it happens?"

Jackson shook his head. "You're right for once, Danny. What in the fuck can we do? Kiss radio goodbye?"

Jackson continued. "You think we're scared, Danny. You have absolutely no idea what the other radio stations are thinking. They're talking sabotage. You're making so much noise out on the street, they're panicking. That tells me that you are on to something. That's what I'm telling corporate. We are getting a giant bonanza of free advertising, plus our expenses are being reduced, and the other stations are scared. Some of our competitors are talkin' about changin' format. They don't know what's gonna come down; they have no idea what is happening, but we *are* getting such a massive jolt of publicity that they're scared, for that reason only. For God's sake, our station was on the news last night, five solid minutes. Radio is a small community. All the stations are playing in a little pond. Make too much noise, splash around too much, and the others are afraid of drowning. They'll panic. They can't afford that. They're gonna get treacherous. And we gotta be prepared for that. But when they hear the playlist Mandy dropped on my desk their fear is gonna be gone. They're gonna be laughing and think we're doomed. And so will corporate."

I was silent.

"Thank God. This is the first time you have shut up and listened," said Jackson.

Jackson continued. "It's January, the slowest quarter in radio. I've invited the President of the corporation and his "thing" down in Georgia, to a vacation in Jamaica with my family. We will be away three weeks. I'm coming back 17th of February. I'll let him know what is really going on. He trusts me. I just don't trust, myself. He's got eighty stations, so if four go poof, it is no big deal to him. And if this goes big, better believe, he will want to be in on the action nationwide. By time I get back in three weeks, things better be damn stable here, Danny. And this Monday, I'm firing those seven DJs that are making most of the noise. You better have those college kids ready, and prepared to move to various stations in the chain. Plus, Mandy and Juan better be ready day one. You say three of those college Djs are great? Well, all five of them better be. And you're gonna have to pay their expenses for relocation; that's all I can do on short notice. And Pep has that small retail advertising package you suggested. We are going on the premise that if you have but one location, you get a reduced rate for advertising. It's the first quarter which is always slow, so we'll have plenty of room for advertising, and if you are a small retailer, we don't have to pass it on to the big agencies. I've got sixty packages ready for you to pick-up Monday. Brief the ballot collectors this week how to sell it, and they better sell it. When I come back I want advertising booked up on the stations with all those complaining sales reps getting the message. You swing that, and we'll make it through the first six months. And I need the fifty grand for Radiotron Monday. And by the way. you are the General Manager while I'm gone, though that does piss off Pep.

"So, you better make Pep happy, and if anything goes wrong, you're gonna pay for it. Got it? I don't like meetings. Especially private ones. That's it."

I smile. *What in hell did Mandy do?* I used one word since Jackson liked brevity. "Done."

He nodded. I left.

14

POOR LITTLE PIPER

9:12am, January 25, 1990

We open the station with a skit where the entire station is owned by a bunch of monkeys. One monkey wants to be boss, but the other monkeys don't want anything to do with that nonsense. No arguing, no complaining. They just push that monkey out of the tree, saying "Oops." Then there is a splat on the pavement. The monkeys screech, "Poor little boss."

They start to wonder how do you run a radio station, and in the skit they start listening to excerpts from other radio stations for ideas. To their shock they hear the same song being played on every station. And minutes later it gets played again.

After much confab the monkeys decide they need a big human with a giant sledge hammer to annihilate the music they are hearing.

I notice this dead monkey on the cement. I look up. "Okay, I say. I'll do it." I just seem to know what they are saying. Of course there are a few hints. There's this dead monkey on the pavement with a boss sign on his mangled body, and there is another monkey struggling to lift up a giant sledgehammer. The monkeys give me a rather long title to my name, "Sheriff Danny, here to eradicate all air hogs from ever scouring the eardrums and the airways of Hawaii---ever again." My job is to execute the criminal songs that are disturbing the masses. I tell them they have to be fair so it will be up to the masses to decide who the criminals are. They agree. I am given the giant sledgehammer that is hard for even me to lift, and with a lot of squealing they shout, "Pound! Pound, so we never may hear that again." We play snippets of "Opposites Attract" by Paula Abdul and "How Am I Supposed To Live Without You" by Michael Bolton, currently one and two on the radio. I tell them fine, but let's think about the positive first and play the 36 most wanted to be heard songs over Hawaiian Radio. They squeal in delight and I start the radio countdown presentation.

"You are about to hear radio history, the first time radio has gone to the streets and asked three simple questions. One: what are the songs I want to hear on the radio the most? Two: what are the songs I want radio to stop playing the most? And three: is there a song I think will become a hit if radio played it?

"During the past month over eight thousand people have gone out to ballot locations across the state and cast their ballots. You are about to hear the results. We call it the Hawaiian Island Music Report. And it is, indeed, an honor for me, Danny Fall, and," Ed's voice says, "And I, Ed Kanoi, to be your hosts on this the first presentation of the Hawaiian Island Music Report.

"And it is a shocking report. For fifteen years music has been so suppressed so little has reached the radio. But this is the radio revolution, and today, right now, we will hear the thirty-six most wanted to be heard songs in the state of Hawaii by the most extensive music research campaign ever conducted.

"And may I dedicate this first report to Brenda Sedorai, who was the first to see this list when I was in Kailua last week. She lightened my heart, telling me this was a fantastic list of music crying to be heard on radio. So most of the songs today you will never have heard on the radio before. Yet when eight thousand people, all volunteers, who saw our ballot boxes across the state and took the trouble to fill out a ballot and say what they really wanted to hear, this is the list they came up with. Actually, they voted for 2,617 different songs, and this 36 are the cream of the crop. We start at #36. 'Dear Prudence' by Siouxsie and the Banshees."

There are people shouting on the first note. Cars are blaring Dear Prudence.

Before we play the top ten songs, the monkeys start squealing with squeaky sounds: "Pound pound pound," and I interrupt the show. "It seems our owners, the Monkeys, can't wait for us to annihilate the least wanted to be heard song on radio, so that it can never be heard again.

"This week, adding the positive votes and negative votes, many of the songs ended up in the negative. One particular song has scoured the eardrums of the masses far too long, and when the final count came in, this criminal song got a net total of 1017 negative votes." I brought out the sledgehammer and Ed screamed, "Oh my God, you are gonna annihilate the number one song on all the other radio stations. It got a Grammy!" Ed says, "Wait, I gotta get my goggles."

I don't wait. "Bye bye, Paula Abdul!" I swing the sledge hammer, and it comes down on "Opposites Attract."

Splinters of plastic fly as I scream, "Kill, kill, kill!" The CD shatters, pieces get ground into the floor. The rug tears. A hole in the wooden floor appears. I keep screaming and pounding. The monkeys are squealing with delight. Then there is silence on the air. I think Ed in fear, is hiding under the radio panel and actually broadcasts what we call Dead Air - a first for Ed.

For twenty seconds I keep pounding. I stop. Heavy breathing. Otherwise dead air. "You can come out from under the panel, Ed. And don't worry; you will never hear 'Opposites Attract' again."

"Oh, are you sure?" Ed carefully raises his head. Ed describes the damage to the floor, the plastic splinters, one big splinter stuck into the ceiling, and the sweat on my face. Ed says, "We've been in an earthquake. Damn Danny, the name of that song should be Opposites Attack!" We both grin at each other. It was a great radio skit but we didn't fake anything. There is really a plastic splinter in the ceiling. There is really a hole in the floor.

The monkeys keep squealing, and we proceed with the countdown of the ten most wanted to be heard songs over Hawaiian radio.

The first week Rabbit sets up a remote to Pink's Garage, and the next Saturday evening, just one week later, two thousand people show up to "Dance Floor Democracy." Dance floor democracy is done live over the radio, with people voting for songs they want to dance to, and radio 10PM to 2AM every Saturday night is live from Pink's Garage. Outer island kids pay for flights to Honolulu to go to Dance Floor Democracy. Every week more and more line up to get in, and hundreds wait outside hours so to get in.

It's hysteria. I am utterly shocked. Dance Floor Democracy becomes a cash cow as we take half the door and monthly our station grosses 20,000 dollars from the event.

The vans drive up to the key locations so the Dance Hall Democracy can be heard all across the islands. The van drivers are utterly dedicated. Whenever we have a special event besides the Saturday Countdown they nevertheless take their micro dishes to key points so the special event can be heard live over radio across the islands. It is a thrill to me, to see so many people turned on and sacrificing their time so we can do what is so needed to be done.

Ballots start coming in at a clip of two thousand a week. Jackson would be shocked. Dance Floor Democracy plus the Beer companies splurging twenty thousand a month to stay with the kids, and the ballot retrievers bringing in another seventeen thousand the first month had us well on the way to the biggest sales month the stations ever had.

Mandy rallied the masses out of bed each morning with skits, games, political commentary on a morning show called "This is your world, this is your music." She was outraged that kids had to get up in the dark, walk to school in the dark, while facing the morning traffic of adults going to work. So Mandy introduced a new school time called Moonlight Savings Time. Kids needed to push the clock back four hours so that when six am Moonlight Savings Time came, the time the kids were normally forced to get up, it was ten o'clock Hawaiian Time. Then kids could go to school in daylight, after their parents were at work and they would have free time without the parents hanging around. High School kids especially liked the idea. If they had a curfew of midnight, now with moonlight savings time they could come home at 4AM and in moonlight savings time it would only be midnight. Kids started to turn in petitions for Moonlight Savings Time to the principals. The education system complained to the FCC. But the petitions made the night news and Mandy's show snowballed into the number one morning show 12 to 35 years-olds by a landslide.

One morning in the seven o'clock hour, Mandy read a ballot and played a listener's song discovery. It was a twenty-two-minute song, Rhapsody in Blue by Oscar Levant played during prime drive time. It got so much attention it made the evening news show with the anchor saying, guess what, Radio will never be the same. The radio revolution is here." More people, curious, started listening.

Everything was happening, with industrial music like Nine Inch Nails, Ministry, KMFDM, plus a host of eighties heavy metal bands like Anthrax, Slayer, Metallica, new wave like Blondie, Tears for Fears, Depeche Mode, the Smiths, New Order, reggae like Alpha Blondy, Bob Marley, Lucky Dube, rap like Public Enemy, Naughty by Nature, and NWA, ska like Dance Hall Crashers, Hepcat, Bad Manners, Madness and the Specials, Hawaiian like, Teresa Bright, Makaha Sons of Ni'ihau, and Butch Helamano, rock like Pearl Jam, Stone Temple Pilots and Jane's Addiction, rockabilly like Blasters, Red Devils, and Stray Cats and all being played side by side. There were even oldies like "Beyond the Sea," by Bobby Darin that made the countdown. The town was coming alive, and we started having concert after concert come to the islands organized by Gregory which brought another 20,000 dollars to the coffers that first six weeks. Then came a Gregory Isaac concert, which brought a hundred thousand dollars to the station with two shows at the Blaisdell Arena.

It was a major coup. Gregory Isaacs wasn't allowed in America because of a drug charge. Our Gregory flew back to Boston and talked to a sponsor to get Gregory Isaac into the country. Then our Gregory went to Jamaica and got a personal commitment from Gregory Isaacs to show up.

Gregory Isaacs was then flown to Boston, but he ditched his sponsor, probably because of a mandatory drug test, and flew to Hawaii for the concert. His sponsor turned him in to the INS and the INS broke into the concert an hour early to apprehend Gregory Isaacs before the two night sell out concert. Mandy and a host of girls in the promotion department dressed Gregory Isaacs as a girl and slipped him into the audience. Bradley got security to bring the INS into the Blaisdell office to get permission from the officials, who were always coming but never came, and Gregory Isaacs was ushered to the dressing room and came on stage performing an incredible concert to a standing crowd of 8,000 people. The next night the INS, in rage at being detained, finally snuck into the concert saw the incredible jubilation and waited until Gregory was in the dressing room preparing for his encore. He was arrested. I called Jackson who was in Atlanta with the head of the Corporation. Jackson got Mr. Isaacs an INS lawyer who managed to thwart Gregory Isaacs's arrest, pending a hearing in Boston. Gregory Isaacs then snuck back to New Orleans and got a boat to Jamaica to avoid arrest.

Revenues during a slow quarter for radio had broken all-time records for the entire chain, and we were in only a medium radio market.

It was astounding. We five had gotten back our cash outlay in the first quarter. By the time Radiotron had come up with its trends in March we had an 18 share, dominant number one by a landslide. Number two, the previous perennial number one station in the market, dropped to two with just a 6 share. Radio stations started scrambling to get back their ratings before the next book.

It was crazy. In April, another radio station changed format in Hawaii and started playing the songs we were playing, less the "crazy" hard metal, industrial, local punk, Hawaiian, easy listening and rap.

Jackson told us to settle down. Play for the common market. The real listeners don't vote.

I told Jackson it couldn't be helped; youth jumps stations to hear their favorite songs, but we still have them most of the time.

THE RADIO REVOLUTION

Other stations were making fun of Mandy as the only solo female jockey on prime time in America. They even suggested she must be sleeping with somebody important to get the morning gig. Mandy was beyond pissed. She demanded a women's weekend. Screw male dominated radio! So in May, Rabbit set up a simulcast with every station in the chain and from 2PM Saturday, after the countdown, through Monday morning 'til six am, only female voices were on the air, and only female voices were on the request lines, and only female songs were played on the radio, and talking on air was about female suppression in society.

It was a big feat to simulcast for such a long time with van drivers parking for the entire weekend so it could be heard-island-wide. Mandy had stirred up a hornets' nest, so much, the radio airing the Wild Women's Weekend, made the top story in the entertainment page of the Honolulu Advertiser on Sunday morning while it was still on air. And Saturday night news cast with a female anchor spotlighted the Wild Women's Weekend, in her news show.

Jackson had flown back to Atlanta ten times in the first three months. His boss, owner of Dead Duck Enterprises, a chain of eighty radio stations across America, wanted weekly updates in person. His name was Piper Zweigolf and he was obsessed to do this format in twenty-three other markets. He didn't want to wait, thinking other stations might steal the format before he got it operating. And he was oboisessed with finding short cuts so he could get the format on all his radio markets instantaneously.

Jackson had warned him that each market would have a radically different sound, and putting it on satellite from Hawaii, nationally, wouldn't work. But Piper wouldn't listen. He said to Jackson, "Hawaii Calls had been on radio in the forties and fifties and nationally and it was a money bonanza. This is mainland music. It will be even bigger.".

Piper was upfront with Jackson. "I want to own the format, and do away with this Danny guy who is breaking every rule radio has ever invented, as you say."

129

Jackson suggested he come talk to Danny, that the man was a radio genius and the last thing he would recommend is getting rid of Danny.

Jackson countered with the suggestion that they, Piper, Jackson and Danny, form a three-way partnership for national distribution.

Piper told Jackson. "We can shut down the contract now. And do it ourselves. We don't need that radio rebel." Piper, in a rage, said, "When you find gold, you take it." He pounded his fist on his desk. "Simple. That's how I got here. That's how I operate."

Piper was standing up now, red vested with a bright orange tie, and in a black, glossy silk suit, a young no-nonsense executive, and eyes spewing out some strange substance.

Jackson couldn't believe it. It looked like tears.

Jackson rebounded, "The gold is Danny, not the format."

Piper stared down Jackson. "Listen! You have no idea what I have done to get where I am. It was hell. But I did it. Jackson, I'm going to tell you. I haven't told a soul. But it is best you know how I operate when I see gold. 'Cause it's damn pertinent now."

Piper waited until he had Jackson's full attention. "I was just four years old, finally getting a bit mobile and in the kitchen lower cabinets my mother had these glass jars stuffed with silver dollars, half dollars and silver quarters, a hundred and twenty-one heavy jars stuffed."

Jackson laughed, "You counted them—at four years old?"

"Later, yeah. We had a compost pile in the back yard, one that just kept growing. No one ever used it. It was behind the duck pond. My mother was a wanna be gardener but she just clipped and watered.

"I was thinking if I could get those jars out of the house and drag them through the duck pond and pass that mean duck, I could hide them in the compost pile 'til I got older and then spend them. Problem was each jar was so heavy. I tried rolling them but they got stuck in the pond, and the mean duck kept attacking me." Tears, or something, were forming in Piper's eyes.

"So I had to put them back. Imagine, a four-year-old with a mean duck snapping at his little legs while he was rolling them through the

THE RADIO REVOLUTION

mud and the duck shit, then when they got stuck, rolling them back and lifting those heavy jars back in those bottom kitchen drawers. And I was in a panic, I had to get them back before I got caught.

"I was thinking I could get my older brother to lug them there, but then I would have to share them with him later on, and I didn't like that."

"You were thinking like that at four years old?" Jackson suddenly realized. Piper wasn't going to go into a partnership with anybody.

"Yeah. Your Danny might be a radio prodigy, but I am a money prodigy. So, I had to improvise. We had this Collie named 'Horse,' and my mother had this harness she used on me when we walked in the market. So, for months when my mom was in the bathroom and my brother was in school I would try to put a jar in the harness and wrap it around the Collie's neck so he could drag it to the compost pile. And when the shower stopped in the bathroom I had to push the jar with all my might back in the kitchen cabinet. I was a mess with duck bites, mud, duck shit and my mother would get furious and spank me almost to death."

Piper paused. "It was horrible. I had welts. I was an abused kid." something shiny seeped out of his eyes.

Jackson wondered. Were those tears... or nitro glycerin?

"After maybe three months or so I finally figured how to tie a jar to Horse so it wouldn't fall off. Then I got some milk bones and threaded across the pond using a hammer to shoo away that mean duck and put the milk bone right next to the compost pile. I still have scars from that mean duck."

Piper reached back and held the back of his left thigh. Were those tears??

Maybe he had an eye infection.

"The dog, dragging the jar, would have to go across the pond for the milk bone. Horse didn't have a problem with the duck. The duck was scared of Horse. And I would be on the other side waving the milk bone in the air, giving it to Horse, and taking the jar that Horse brought and burying it in the compost pile. I had to wait until my mom took a shower to do it and she would become violent each time she got out, and spank the devil out of me. And after I started to bury those jars in the compost pile I was not only muddy but smelly. I mean duck shit is bad. But compost is worse. My mom was shouting, 'I'm gonna put you in reform school if you go in that pond one more time.'

"Can you imagine your mother telling you, a little four-year-old, she didn't want you, you belong in reform school? Finally, desperate, she started locking me in my room when she showered. And she would leave me in there all day sometimes until supper. I was a prisoner, a little kid, a prisoner. I cried and cried all day. Still she wouldn't unlock the door!"

Jackson was trying to control his laughter. It looked like more substance was seeping out of this hardnose-executive's eyes. Jackson had to pretend to look sympathetic, muffling his laugh.

"Then I had to go to school when I was five. So I started doing it in the middle of the night when everybody was asleep and then hosing myself off in the yard in the freezing weather, sometimes. And to hide what I was doing from my mom, I did it naked. I couldn't dare let her catch me with dirty clothes that were obviously caused by my trips through the pond. And I had to hide my wounds from the bites of that mean duck. Yeah, each time I succeeded, I counted it by making a mark on the inside of my closet and by age six, with hundreds of trips through the pond that were futile because of that mean duck, or Horse being uncooperative, I, nevertheless, had taken 114 jars and they were safe, stuffed in the bottom of that compost pile.

"When silver prices started rising my father went looking for those jars. When he looked, there was just seven left. He was furious! He thought my mother had stolen them or used them.

"He called the police. He was going to send my mother to jail. But the cops told him there was nothing they could do. She was his wife and his money and hers were the same.

"They ended up getting a divorce but I kept quiet. I didn't want to go to jail, or for a kid maybe it was reform school. I wasn't sure. And I was happy realizing I had pulled a coup. I had gold, in this case silver, and it was nowhere anyone would dare touch.

"You have no idea how terrible it is when your parents start fighting and getting a divorce. A whole year they were shouting at each other. Me, my brother and my mother were poor." Piper swallowed a lump in his throat, and another glistening drop, or at least a watery substance, seeped out of his eyes.

"That's the way I do business. I see gold, I take it. Understand. I have got to have that format. It's gold."

What a tall story, Jackson thought. " What happened to those smelly jars?" Jackson laughed. Jackson, looking at Piper's eyes, suddenly realized, he had made a mistake.

"Don't laugh, Jackson. Silver kept rising from three dollars to thirty dollars and in 1979, at age sixteen I hauled them on the bus, fifteen or twenty pounds each into Deak Perera, one at a time, like five a week and got cash worth a total of almost, almost a million dollars. Silver had become forty, even for a few weeks fifty times more valuable, and later in that year, during the summer, it crashed. I cashed it in just in time. Though the last few jars had already crashed to about twenty-five times their May value of fifty times.

"There was an electrical valve in the ground in the patio, and nobody opened it because it was full of cockroaches, so I put the money in plastic bags I found in the kitchen and let cockroaches crawl over my arms until it was well hidden deep in the ground. Piper shivered, shrunk his shoulders, and those strange tears emerged again. "It was horrible, some of those cockroaches actually climbed up my neck and into my hair and even on my face, and I didn't know. Cockroaches bite.

"Then at eighteen I bought my first radio station with it. The station was in Albany. They wanted 750,000 dollars for it. I shocked them at eighteen. I just walked in with three lawyers and dumped the cash on the table, but only 680,000. Take the cash and give me the station or I'll take the cash back. That's how I got started."

Jackson thought, the way Piper told the story you would think it really happened. Poor Little Piper. But it was still fishy. "You are telling me the money exchange gave you, at sixteen years old, almost a million dollars?"

"Yeah, as long as it was under ten thousand dollars at a time, it didn't need to be reported to the IRS, and kids in those days didn't have to have social security numbers, so they just figured my parents were having me do it to avoid notice by the IRS. It averaged about seven thousand a trip and the total was 810,612 dollars, all from being a determined little kid that was forced to go through hell to get it. And sometimes I had to wait a day or two to get the cash 'cause they didn't have enough cash in their vault. I couldn't cash a check then. I finally killed that duck. My parents looked at the mauled duck and thought Horse killed it, but it was sorta my revenge. It had put me through hell when I was little and helpless. You couldn't even tell it was a duck anymore. But they found the feathers floating in the pond and the duck was missing."

Jackson was on the verge of believing it. The name of Piper's company had that weird name, "Dead Duck Enterprises." Piper, a young stud-looking executive seemed a bit sincere, like he at least believed it. "Your family has no idea you stole all that money from them."

"No idea. And I'll tell you bluntly. When I see gold, you better help me. We'll go to Honolulu tomorrow, and I will get that format, and your little prodigy will be out of the picture."

Jackson was about to declare Piper mad. But he cooled his words, "The contract is for another a month."

"If Danny isn't completely cooperative, I'll get my lawyers to break the contract." I can't wait a month. Some other chain might start doing it."

Jackson stared at Piper, half in shock. "You got a problem. Danny has a lawyer that attacks the juggler vein. Your whole company might be in jeopardy if you try that. At least wait another month."

"And have another chain take away my gold. Hell no. I saw the contract. It is hand written. You gotta be kidding. It has to be easy to break."

"Well, at least, talk to your lawyers first. Get their advice. And be careful, his lawyer cuts through crap like a cyclone."

Piper said, "You signed a handwritten contract that let one man control the music played. You know Fledge, he is my chief program director for the chain. He flipped out when he saw that contract. He makes almost two million a year for my company by playing ball with the record companies. And with Hawaii not cooperating with the music programming, Fledge is getting flack from the record companies. I should fire you for that alone."

"Jackson laughed. "If I hadn't signed that piece of paper, you wouldn't have any gold."

Piper laughed, too. "Your story is about as good as mine, I guess. Tell me why on Earth you signed it."

"I told you. Danny is a radio genius. And a sensational DJ Honolulu loves. But he can't work with anybody. He knows what is needed, but no one well listen. I shut him out of Honolulu waiting for him to get the message, with the intention of hiring him when he was willing to be more cooperative. And then out the blue, he makes the front page of morning paper saying he is gonna start a radio station state-wide for the 'people.' I had to stop that Piper, I'd rather him doing his thing causing all that trouble, than let him loose on Radio without our corporation getting the gravy. And Danny being Danny, he demands to call all the shots. And it is working."

Piper says, "This is not a corporation. I own it completely. That's why I call the shots."

Jackson was shocked. "You are personally liable?"

"Hell no, it's an LLC."

"Then who are all those national sales managers and accountants I have to deal with daily?"

"That's a service I hired. I let them do my dirty work. Hell, they are a corporation. but all eighty radio stations are mine. I own it all, Jackson."

Jackson starred at Piper. Piper just shook his head. Piper said, "Jackson, you're a gambler, but I won big time with this format."

Piper, along with his three attorneys, his head program director Fledge, and Jackson, got on his private jet plane Saturday night in Atlanta, and landed in Honolulu at 2:30 PM Sunday.

Jackson wasn't even in a position to warn Danny. Piper and his lawyers were in heated discussions through most of the flight. They told Piper the contract was air tight. Their only hope was to kick Danny and his team off of radio, and nevertheless, pay his commission through next month. There was nothing in the contract that said Danny had to be in control. The contract said simply Danny's corporation controlled the music played. The lawyers said Piper's best out was to kick Danny off air, along with his employees, allow him to adjust the music from outside of the station till his contract ends in a month. They expected Danny would probably refuse to control the music if he was fired from the inside. Then start Piper's satellite broadcast across the US. Then Fledge could be in Danny's place and the Hawaiian Island Music Report with Fledge, could be simulcast across the nation. Piper then wouldn't have to breach the contract which could cause a law suit. Of course, he would need to change the name of the report unless Danny hadn't registered it with the state.

Fledge suggested if the name wasn't available they could change the name of the Hawaiian Island Music Report, to the Official Music Report. Drop the Hawaiian and it could be aired across the country. And gradually they could get votes from the other stations. It would be ten times bigger than Casey Kasem's Top 40. And he would take Danny's place as the DJ. Fledge's job was mostly getting money for playing the music of the stations. Fledge was thinking of the incredible power he would have over the record companies. And sure, who would know if a song was voted in properly or not.

The lawyers insisted it was very wise to still pay Danny his commission through the end of the contract. But once the contract was finished just eliminate Danny completely.

The lawyers were outraged that the contract was signed by Jackson and recommended Piper fire Jackson for incompetence and sue him for damages caused with his loss of control of the music. They didn't like the idea that Jackson had fired the lawyer, one of their associates, during the negotiation and Jackson should be liable for the act of negligence.

Jackson wasn't being docile. He knew shit when he saw it. That's how he had gotten ahead all these years. But he still couldn't see a way out of this. He curled up in a blanket on the plane listening to the outraged lawyers trying to fire him. For the first time in his life, he was beginning to believe Danny. Conglomerates trying to control the market lead to disaster. *Damn Danny.*

15

TAKE-OVER

Everybody rushed off the plane and waited in the cargo area for their bags. Jackson thought, screw my bags. He needed to get to a phone unnoticed. He was about to call Danny, then thought wisely and elected to call Ida instead. Ida picked up the phone on the second ring.

"I got one minute. Listen. Dead Duck Enterprises is taking over the format and kicking Danny out of his contract. I'd give that radio revolution just one more hour on the air. Piper is obsessed with taking over the format."

Jackson expected outrage or non-believeability from Ida. Ida said, "Jackson?"

Jackson replied, "Yeah, Jackson."

Ida said, "Thank You." She added three more words after a pause. "Don't tell Danny." Jackson answered, "I haven't." Ida said, "Good," and hung up the phone.

It was Sunday evening in Washington DC, but Ida knew the committee chairman of the FCC, George Hanson. They had crossed paths a few times in Washington DC. She sat in her home starring at the ceiling. Should she call George, now? *Too late. Sunday night. Not cool. I've got to think of what I will say.* Her mind kept ticking.

THE RADIO REVOLUTION

The Piper six, including the three lawyers, Jackson and Fledge, crammed into a town rent-a-car. It was a tight fit, Jackson took up the space for two people. Fledge was sardined on Jackson's left and a lawyer on his right. Piper had a lawyer in the front seat flip on the radio to 102.7FM. Jackson didn't want them to notice he'd made a phone call so he was forced to sacrifice his bags, at least for now. On the radio Mandy was proposing to read a poem from a female listener. It sounded like a mob of girls were in the studio with her, some giggling.

Piper said, "Poetry, on the radio? What the fuck is that shit!"

Fledge, a bit of a brown-noser said, "I can't believe it. Poetry on a music station. What, have we gone non-profit, public radio?"

Piper turned his head to Fledge in the back seat. "I don't need an echo chamber."

On the radio, Mandy started the poem: She started in a desperate tone.

> *Radio listeners were enslaved,*
> *By lack of quality and choice.*

Then her voice jumped into a rejoicing tone.

> *Now we have been saved,*
> *Since freedom found a voice*

There were female voices cheering in the background.

> *Instead of corporate product,*
> *And safe commercial stuff*
> *People fill out a ballot to say*
> *When enough IS enough*

More noise from the female studio audience and a few squeals from monkeys' sound effects. Her voice turns into a preacher struggling to bring life to her following.

This is the radio revolution,
We the people chose the song
It's the end of music tyranny,
Now that Radio Freedom is on
She toned it down.
With crazy in-house ads,
DJs that are cool and real
Exploring genres, artists and fads,
Variety helps us live and feel

One minute ska, hardcore or classical,
Next rap, folk, reggae or funk
Then rock, progressive or dancehall,
But if it gets old, out with the junk
We are here, it's worth the wait
We programmers can't be second guessed
Our freedom is found, to hell with fate,
The people's music can't be suppressed.

There were high pitched screams from the studio audience.

Then Mandy said to the girls in the studio, "Let's hear it!"

They screamed, "The Radio Revolution 102.7 rages on!"

And Mandy shouted, "And the Wild Women's Weekend raves on!"

There was a jumble of voices, slaps, shouts and incoherent talk in the background.

Mandy said, "Let's hear it again girls!" and they all shouted, "The Wild Women's Weekend raves on!"

Mandy kept pumping. "We have now played 176 songs by female artists in a row, listened to females on the phone lines only, talked about women's rights, wolf whistled at the stubborn boys who called trying to disrupt the wild women's weekend, applied furniture and nails to front door to prevent male intrusion, and now what? We've still got thirteen more hours to go. What do you ladies want to do next?"

THE RADIO REVOLUTION

There was ten seconds of silence. Mandy said, "I know, I know what boys like. They like us."

There were cheers in the studio. She played the Waitresses song "I Know What Boys Like,"

After the first chorus she stopped the song. "I got an idea. It seems boys don't think it is wrong to mess around, but their girlfriend? Oh she needs to be a goody, goody. But boys are always drooling over girls. They think we are hot. Why shouldn't we share our stuff. I mean they want us more than we want their self-destructive, possessive nature."

"Yeah, Yeah," came the cry from the studio audience.

Mandy continued, "So many boys want us, but they get creepy and say they want us to be with only them, while other boys are lookin' us over all the time. We should share ourselves. Sure we like sex, but with one guy only?"

"Yuck, Yuck," came from the mob of girls. Mandy continued. "If they can't handle us with lots of sexual partners, we don't need them, there is more than one boy out there."

"Right. Right," screamed the female chorus.

Piper didn't ask the lawyer in the front seat to turn off the radio. He slammed the radio shut, himself. He turned to the back seat facing Jackson. "What in the hell is going on?"

"You're listening, Piper. What do you think is going on?"

Fledge piped in, "Total politically incorrect chaos, that's what's going on. And you can't play two female artists in row, and how can you play a metal song followed by a rap song, these bratty girls are defying radio itself. Who is that Mandy?"

Piper answered while turning to the back seat again and staring at Jackson. "Mandy is the morning drive DJ. What's she doing on the weekend show, Jackson?"

Jackson didn't know. "Hey, I was in Atlanta. I don't know."

Fledge said, "She sounds like a kid, who is she teamed up with in the morning?"

Piper turned to the back seat and starred at Jackson once again, saying, "She is the solo morning drive DJ. But she is gone, don't worry,

Fledge. This is her last show and it ain't gonna last another thirteen hours."

※

Ida was thinking. *How do I destroy Dead Duck Enterprises.* She laughed. What a name. It should be easy. Well, first off, possession is 99% of the law. Ida called Mandy at Danny's home. No answer. She called the Honolulu hotline. To her shock, not knowing about the Wild Women's Weekend, Mandy answered.

Ida said, "Get all the music carts, all the LPs and all the CDs and all the stations liners, everything connected to the radio revolution, out of the studio now. Then leave the building. Vamooze. After you leave call the other stations and do the same. Dead Duck is usurping the contract. Don't say a word to Danny or anybody. Just do it. Take the station's stuff to Danny's house and stand guard over it. If someone tries to raid, call the police." She added, and you don't have much time, a half an hour at best. "Viva the Revolution."

I'm talking too strong. I gotta slow down.

Mandy was brief. "Will do."

Ida thought, shit, Danny was right. Mandy knew before it occurred. "And call that Big Island limo driver and tell him to get your ballot collectors in Hilo and raid the Hilo station and take all the carts, music and liners. Take everything connected to the Radio Revolution and tell them to hide it. Tell Bradley to confiscate the computers and take them to Danny's house. And the computers on the Maui, Kauai and Big Island, have them vanish into secret hiding places. Got it."

Mandy said, "Ida, can I tell Gregory?"

"Yeah, but don't say a word to Danny. They might be grilling him, and it's best he doesn't know our little sabotage."

"What about the ballot boxes?"

"Yeah, have the ballot collectors pick them up at least the ones you can get Sunday night. Take them to Danny's house. After the

THE RADIO REVOLUTION

take-over is official I'll have you call a press conference at the house I'll tell you what to say after I talk to the FCC tomorrow."

"They can help?" Mandy asked.

"Good chance," responded Ida.

Mandy said. "I'm on it." She hung up the phone.

⁂

The Piper six arrived at the Likelike Drive-In, a block away from the Honolulu Station, to organize the take-over. One of the lawyers got a paper. They were seated at a large table. He passed the sports section to another lawyer. Fledge, in shock, caught a glimpse of the giant headline in the entertainment section: WILD WOMEN'S WEEKEND. Fledge grabbed it and said, "What's this?".

It was an article written by Sarah Toast who had an astrological column in the Entertainment section. But this was the leading story in this section with a giant headline and an article to follow. Fledge started reading. In the middle, he stopped. "Listen to this, guys." Fledge decided to read the article out loud.

Fledge began reading. "On the eves of the pending tetrad blood moon, lunar eclipse, smack dab in the middle of Mercury retrograde in Gemini, I am noticing the Radio Revolution, that Gemini rising station. And lo. It's the Wild Women's Weekend. Astrology doesn't lie.

"We all know the islands are a seductive sandy oasis, isolated in the beauty blues of the Pacific Ocean. All serenaded by Hawaii's mild mannered commercial radio with its farthest reachings, consisting of, yes, those live call-ins from drunken DJ's, sputtering about beach side bikini contests. Then along comes the Radio Revolution."

Five faces stared at Fledge. He shook his head and read on.

"Zigzagging music verging on lyrical chaos, free range shock DJ's, controversial outrages, scandalous concerts, rule breaking commercial content and sledge hammering madness of the Radio Revolution has brought on a multilevel revolution statewide. Fledge looked up.

Piper said, "That's in the newspaper?"

Fledge turned the page towards Piper showing the giant headline "Wild Women's Weekend."

Fledge turned the paper back and read on. "But this weekend the Radio Revolution has gone beyond the beyond and opened up a Wild Women's Weekend." Piper said, "Like Hell."

Fledge continued. Piper's eyes were enlarging.

"Neurons are bouncing around in female minds, and in unfamiliar places, as thoughts of those listening are primed for a whole new way of processing life. While Deeelite is gettin her groove into the heart...grinding gears are going from Sweet Leilani to Chemical Imbalance to Bjork, while other female voices cry out their rage. Males gut out spastic moans. It is a major twist to the mind and oh, did you want the red pill or the blue pill? The Radio Revolution brings poetic justice, rantings, ravings and outspoken words from depthful females and unorthodox female DJ's, on a deep mission called WILD WOMEN'S WEEKEND.

"Public Response? Reactions, oh my! And the ballots started it. Along with the phone calls and personal visits to the station from concerned listeners. Complaints and rumors arose that some of the programming, entertainment features and DJ's at the station were sexist, male dominated, downgraded women, and or were not offering true empowerment to women. So the promotions department, headed by women...wild women and the craziest female DJ of the world simply known by the simple name "Mandy Blossom," decided to hand the airwaves over to "the women" for this weekend. The Radio Revolution had an offer on their ballot for women's weekend, and it won! It is only right to let the female listeners vote for the programming they want to hear and host the programming the way they want to present.

Fledge looked up. "Do you want me to read on?"

Piper's face looked like a statue. "There's more?"

Fledge read on.

"Some have focused time on women's issues in the community, positive accomplishments, intelligent discussions,"

Piper went ballistic. He shouted. "Intelligent what? Intelligent blasphemies. That cunt is finished."

The patrons of the restaurant looked at Piper. A woman manager rushed to the table. "One more outburst like that, and you will have to leave."

Piper looked around. Everybody was looking at him. "He nodded, "I'm sorry."

Fledge said, "Do you want me to continue?"

Piper nodded.

Fledge continued. "And more awareness to lift up the sisters. Then, there were some who are expressing the wild side or completely silly side until Monday morning at 6AM, when Mandy Blossom once again will do her "normal" morning show. I went to the street and here are some of the comments.

"Enough," said Piper. His eyes were staring at Jackson. Finally, at the end of a long stare, Piper said, "I don't understand a single word said. "What is this cunt saying?"

He said it loudly. The lawyers frantically motioned him to talk softer.

Fledge responded. "It's a female uprising, bent on destroying radio."

Piper said, "Exactly." He pointed at Jackson. "You are fired!"

One of the lawyers added, "For incompetence."

Another lawyer said, "You don't get a cent any more. Expect a lawsuit for damages."

The last lawyer said, "You lost control of the music. You lost control of the stations. We are going to call it deliberate sabotage. You are going to jail, Jackson."

The voices were still loud. The female manager reminded them to tone it down.

Jackson just got up and turned to Piper, who was still stewing. "Now, I know why you got three lawyers. They got such pea brains, it takes all three of them to say I am fired."

Jackson didn't wait for a response. He left. He thought about getting a taxi and go back to the airport for his bags. But he called Ida first.

"Ida, just want to let you know. I've been fired. Danny is being kicked out, but to save a suit, he will get paid until the end of the contract next month. Piper plans to take it national probably next week. Or very soon."

Ida replied, "Go to Danny's house and wait till further notice. Go now. Timing is important. Mandy should be there, or very soon. She'll tell you what to do."

Jackson laughed, and said yes to Ida. *Maybe Mandy will be my new boss.*

He left his bags at the airport. *Probably they are back on that stupid jet.*

Jackson got a taxi. Told the driver to turn on the station. There was dead air. He got to Danny's house before Mandy. No one was there. He sat on the porch thinking about his bags. *Damn that Danny.*

I got a call from Piper. "Meet us at the Likelike Drive-In."

"When?"

"Now."

"Let me talk to Jackson."

"Your little savior isn't here."

What is Piper doing in town? Where is Jackson? What does he mean, "us?" My stomach cramped. *This is not right.* I arrived, my mind racing. *Piper is in Honolulu.*

I enter. There are two rooms of diners. I see four suits and a polo shirt in a booth. It's gotta be them. *Who wears a suit in Hawaii, and four of them, plus a polo shirt?* I approach. The one doing the talking looks up. He is young, wide head, slender body, dressed in a shimmering black suit with a purple and orange tie. I want to laugh because he looks like a clown on a neon sign. His face is so white he doesn't need powder.

"You Danny?"

I nodded.

"Well, little rebel, you are finished. We are taking over the format and controlling the ballot counting from now on. This is Fledge, my chief programmer." The clown indicated the Polo shirt with a pimpled, smug face. "Your little contract doesn't detail who needs to be in control of the station. So Fledge is gonna take it over. And your money ends next month anyway. So you can go collect your funds and there is nothing else you can do about it. We don't need you anymore, and you have fucked over the populace and your contract with this stupid Wild Women's Weekend shit. So you are being fired due to incompetence. Just thank me for being nice and letting you collect revenues for this month and next, to fill out your contract."

Piper was loud. The whole room was listening. The manager had her hand over her mouth.

I'm used to raving lunacy of radio executives so I just brushed it off, and laughed. And something just came out of my mouth that even I didn't expect. "You're finished, Piper. Your corporation is falling into a pit. Your next stop, jail. My next step, turning America alive. Fuck you. You deserve it!"

Piper smiles. "Little rebel, your world is finished; not mine."

I just shook my head. "You lost it. And now I'm bent on you losing everything. I don't want you on the planet. Understand." I couldn't even believe the fire of hate that was burning inside of me. He wasn't attacking me, he was attacking my whole family and the dreams of the state.

Piper's eyes enlarge. I add, "Bye bye Piper,"

Another suit and tie says, "He's threatening your life, Piper."

I reply, "He doesn't have a life to lose."

Another suit and tie says, "That's good enough ground to dump the contract."

The third suit and tie says, "And put his ass in Jail."

I add. "Poor little Piper. Having a little temper tantrum 'cause he can't get what he wants."

Piper's eyes come unglued. He tries to tip the table. It doesn't budge. Then he grabs a saucer. Doesn't hesitate. He flings it at me. There is a loud shatter.

I stumble back, there is a crack sound in my ear. White light appears. Fires start in my forehead. Sharp, stinging pain. I am bleeding. Blood gets in my eye. Blurry vision. I smile. "Assault and battery. I think Piper is going to jail before me." I reiterated, "Poor little Piper."

No one messes with the family.

Piper leaps out of the booth. He's tall, maybe six feet five. He rushes me. I take another couple of steps back.

One of the suits grabs Piper's leg and gets dragged out of the booth, struggling to hold on. Another suit leaps up and grabs Piper's waist. The last suit gets between me and Piper.

I say, "Um, now I see why you need three goons with you. To control you."

The woman manager is standing there watching. I look. She stares in shock. Blood drips down my face and much of the shattered saucer is in my clothes and on my shoulders. I can feel the warmth of the blood. I don't try to stop it. I'm throbbing, stinging, in burning pain. *Shit, Let it drip..*

I smile. "I think I need to fill out an assault charge on this man over here in the clown suit. Can you call the Police?"

The woman manager says, "Yeah, but all of you, except Danny, go outside and wait for the police."

A suit says, "Danny just threatened this man's life. He pointed to the clown suit." Piper smiles.

The manager just smiles, too. "Nevertheless, this man is injured and none of you are. You all go outside and wait for the police." A lawyer showed a credit card to pay.

Becky said, "We don't take credit cards."

Piper said, "Then fuck, you don't get paid." The five left without paying. Piper gets corralled by the lawyers and coaxed outside.

The manager picks up a napkin and applies it to my cut. "You sit down, lean your head back. No, better - lay down in this booth on your back, and apply pressure to the wound. Did any pieces get in your eyes?"

I shake my head. "Just the blood. Maybe some water to rinse it out."

She smiles. "You must have a pretty hard head to shatter a saucer. If the blood doesn't stop, I'll call an ambulance. I'm gonna round up some witnesses and hold them over until the police come. Danny, what's going on?"

I smile, "Welcome to radio 101. Thanks, what's your name?"

She smiles. "Becky."

"Thanks, Becky."

A waiter hands Becky a glass of water. She gives it to me. I touch a wet napkin to my left eye.

I'm thinking. No one knows how hard it is to deal with radio people. No one knows what I have to go through. If they did, they would call me a hero. Yeah, they call me a hero, but they have no idea what I have to go through. They have no idea how mindless and totally insensitive radio is, to the people. I'm so proud I got this far.

16

A REVOLVING REEL TO REEL

I'm still lying down, trying to stop the bleeding and the shock of the saucer hitting my forehead. Suddenly, it hits me. I need to go to the station. Becky took off the napkin at my request. "It's looking better; the bleeding seems to have stalled. Rise to a sitting position, and see if it's stable," she says.

I rise. I feel a little off center. I say to Becky, "They're trying to take over the station and destroy the Radio Revolution. I got to get to the station."

She seems to notice my urgency. She hesitates, then nods and gives me her hand, helping me to stand up. She notices me staggering a bit and puts my arm over her shoulder helping me reach the street, me still holding the napkin to my forehead. Piper and his gang are gone. They haven't waited for the police.

I'm bewildered, but then it hits me. "Oh my God, they've gone to the station!"

Three police cars speed into the parking lot, one behind the other. Becky rushes up to one car and says, "The suspect is probably at the radio station around the corner with four other guys. He's a tall ha'ole in a silk suit and an orange and purple tie." I give them the address. One car takes off for the station.

The other three officers are told about the assault. Becky says, "Danny's pressing charges." An officer calls it in. "The suspect is a tall

Caucasian between six three and six six, in a shiny black suit with an orange and purple tie."

"Color of hair, sir?"

"Don't know, but don't worry, dispatcher. There can't be more than one shiny black suit with an orange and purple tie in Honolulu."

※

Piper and the gang didn't wait outside for the Police. They got a taxi, not knowing exactly where the radio station was, but the taxi driver knew. It was only one block away. Fledge, Piper's national program director, was the only one with any cash. Grudgingly, he paid the five-dollar-fee.

※

The three police officers arrived at the radio station, on the fourth floor of a ten-story building. They saw the four suits while another guy in a polo shirt was pounding on the door.

One of the police officers called for back-up. Another asked, "Which one of you is Piper?" There was silence from the group.

The third officer pointed, "I believe that one, the one in the glossy spoof suit."

"Hands up. All of you," said the first officer.

The one in the Polo shirt starts to raise his hands, then, looking around, puts them down. No hands go up. One of the lawyers says, "Officer, you can put your hands up. This is a citizen's arrest. This is the owner. He is being locked out of his own radio station. We are three lawyers taking notes of everything you say, to put forth our case to the Prosecuting Attorney. I repeat: put your hands up."

The officers look at each other, and two of them start laughing. The other smirks. "An owner without a key and lawyers without note pads?"

The second lawyer says, "Danny Fall has breached the contract and threatened this man's life. You arrest us, you'll have a civil suit that'll take your sorry asses off the police force. You should be arresting Danny!"

The officers, all who like Danny Fall the DJ, just smile. "Danny Fall says that this guy in the clown suit assaulted him with a," he laughs, "A flying saucer. Mr. Piper is going to jail right now to straighten this thing out. We understand Danny is in an ambulance, and he is pressing charges. Mr. Piper can worry about 'his' radio station if the Judge feels he is fit to get out, and *he* can convince the judge it is really his station."

Still no hands have gone up.

The third lawyer says, "Do you know who you are talking to? He owns eighty radio stations, and if he is arrested, if anyone is gonna be in trouble, it's you guys. You are talking to three lawyers."

One of the officers looks at the other two. "I think we need to add another charge to the charge of assault. Let's see." He put his hand to his chin while his other hand rests on his holster. "Let's add attempted breaking and entering and refusing to cooperate with the police. Better yet, resisting arrest."

Henry smiles. "Creating a substantial risk of causing bodily injury to the law enforcement officer or another, *is* resisting arrest. You're good with numbers, Al."

"Yes, Henry. Statute 710-1026 1b."

Officer Henry laughs, "Gentlemen, you don't raise your hands, you are risking the safety of every police officer here. I'll ask you one more time, Get your hands up. All of you. You're all going to jail." Four more officers rush out of the elevator. The back-up.

Still no hands go up.

Officer Henry says, to all the six other policemen on the floor. "Draw your guns, officers. "Handcuff these five. They are refusing to raise their hands. If one makes a false move, shoot em." Henry adds, "Any movement whatsoever, shoot em, even if they are just scratching an itch. We have no idea if it is an itch or a gun."

"You'll pay for this," says one of the lawyers.

Officer Henry says, "You won't have a problem if you just raise your hands. You're all under arrest until we can sort this out." *Or before I shoot your dumb asses.*

Then comes the typical privileged white man scenario. Piper yells. "You can't do this. Do you have any idea who you are talking to. I'm gonna put you all in jail."

Officer Henry laughs, "Well, you first, Mr. Piper."

✢

Witnesses come forth. After twenty minutes, and at my insistence, Becky drives me to the station in her Chevy. In the car she checks for the station on the radio. Just dead air. Still in her manager's uniform, she seems to forget about her job. She is petite, short haired, and, I am realizing, fearless.

We arrive at the radio station in the four o'clock hour on Sunday afternoon. There should be a few cars in the parking lot. On a Sunday afternoon seven or eight cars could be noticed normally, and this being the Wild Women's Weekend? Instead, there are no cars. I think it strange. Even Piper isn't there and the police must have left, maybe because he didn't show up. I take out my key and open the door. Becky insists on going with me inside and to my surprise the studio is completely empty. Not only no people, but no LPs, CDs, carts, or promos are inside. Even the advertising carts are gone.

It is too much for me to assimilate. I sit down on a bench in the studio. I close my eyes.

✢

Ed Kanoi was on Kaua'i. His sister Edie drove over to Ed's newly made studio with the news the Wild Woman's Weekend had been off air for more than a half an hour. Ed, who demanded not to be disturbed when he was in his studio working on the morning show for Mandy, got disturbed anyway, and called the hotline in Honolulu.

༄

I let it ring. Finally, I motion Becky to answer the phone.

She answers, then motions me to the phone. "It's Ed Kanoi."

My head is still blurry, but I say, "Ed. It's a corporate take-over. Piper must have taken the music and promos. I've been fired. Don't know where Jackson is. No one's here."

I have this sickening feeling, like my dream to change the world had just vanished, and instead I'm putting these kids in torment.

Ed just says. "Nail yourself in."

"What?"

"Like DJs use to do in the fifties. Nail down the doors to the office and the studio, put the couch, filling cabinets, anything between you and the doors. Then go on the air and tell the listeners what's happening. I'm getting on the plane as fast as I can. I'll call the studio here on Kaua'i and have them evacuate the music and the radio promos and shut down the radio. I'll call Rabbit and see if we can simulcast you across all the Hawaiian Islands. Where's Mandy and the girls from the Wild Weekend?"

"I don't know."

"Danny, are you alright?"

There is silence. "Danny, Danny, let me talk to that girl who answered the phone."

I, listless, just hand the phone over to Becky.

Becky appraises Ed of the situation. The flying saucer, the bleeding head, Piper screaming in the restaurant calling Mandy a cunt, firing Jackson. Then Piper firing Danny, the bare studio, and Danny looking like he is in shock.

Ed told Becky, "I'm on Kaua'i. This is an emergency. You gotta be me for a while. Nail down that front door. The fire escape door can only open from the inside and it is five inches of solid steel. Don't worry about it. Nail yourselves in. Then stick as much furniture between the door and the office as you can. There's some super glue in the maintenance room. Put it on the furniture next to door so it is harder to push the door open. Use the whole damn tube. Then nail down the studio as well. The long nails are in the recreation room next to the window sill. Then get Danny on the mic and tell him what to say."

Becky writes down the words Ed tells her to tell me to say. I just stare at the phone for long minutes as Becky writes down words.

I overhear. I say, "Jackson fired, too?"

Becky nods as she is writing.

I am motionless.

Becky hangs up the phone, stirs me. "Let's take action and make a blockade!"

"A what?" Becky motions me to follow, I don't move. She takes my arm and throws it over her shoulder.

Just outside the door of the studio there are two hammers and a bunch of nails, and two filling cabinets. Mandy's gang had really nailed in the outside door and then someone had pried it open. I help Becky nail down the office door. Becky motions me to move an office desk to the door. The two of us lift another desk and put it on top of the first desk, upside down. For being so small Becky seems to have super human strength. We lift the desk with the drawers full, on top of each other. The strain makes me dizzy, and I get a series of cramps in my stomach while lifting. It takes three attempts for us to get it on top of the other desk.

I don't know why I am doing this. It is an act of desperation with no purpose. Maybe Ed doesn't understand.

Becky then runs back to the utility closet and gets some super glue and applies it to the legs of the bottom office desk. She has me lift the top desk, now upside down, up a bit, so she can super glue in between. Then we shove the filing cabinets behind the desk. She wants them on top, but I stop that. They are far too heavy to lift six feet in the air. At least for me. Even when we take out the files first.

She uses the last of the superglue and glues the filing cabinets to the floor after we put the filling shelves back in the cabinet.

We try to nail down the studio door but the wood is too thick and the nails not long enough. I just sit back down on the studio bench, exhausted. I'm a little dizzy too, plus I have a dull headache. Becky goes into the production room, and I hear noise like a bulldozer is annihilating the production room. But I am too tired to move.

The noise goes on. I am about ready to get up and see what is happening when this petite little woman slides into the studio a giant one-foot-deep, splintered production table. I help get it through the door, and then we sit down on the floor together, sweat soaking her brown Likelike Drive-In Uniform.

I don't expect Becky to move, but she just says, "Wait here." She leaps up and leaves. I don't hear any more destruction so I wilt into a half sleep. When I wake Becky has returned from the break room with pizza, a gallon jar of water, and a six pack of Coronas. She is sipping one. I look at the giant production table laying against the double glassed studio and say, "Thank God I got a construction worker helping me."

Becky smiles, "Now get on the radio, Danny, and let 'em have it." She looks for Ed's message but then says, "Forget it. Danny, get on air and let the listeners know what is happening."

I get up, walk to the DJ chair, splice the reel to reel and sit down, and go live on the radio.

Something happens to me when I face the mic. Adrenalin flows.

"The Radio Revolution is being ambushed as I speak. Corporate radio has gone crazy. We have a contract, but they're breaking it. They've raided the studio and taken all the music. I'm on the air because I've nailed down the doors, and I've put tons of furniture between the doors and me. Anyone who has a cassette tape recorder, record this and take it to the news stations. We will be back, and the Radio Revolution will continue. Becky, rewind the reel to reel and play this message over and over."

THE RADIO REVOLUTION

Becky yells from across the studio, "Viva the Revolution!"

She says, "Danny, that was wonderful. Better than what Ed told me."

We sit down, smiling at each other. She gives me a Corona, we clink bottles. We listen to the message repeating over and over and over again.

※

Mandy arrived at Danny's house in a pick-up truck and two Radio Free Hawaii Vans filled with screaming girls. They started hauling in the music, liners, surveys and ballot boxes.

Mandy was a bit alarmed to see Jackson, unsure which side he was on.

Jackson said, "Ida sent me here. I guess you're my new boss, since Piper fired me,"

Mandy hugged Jackson and kissed him on the cheek. She told Jackson that Danny was at the radio station with a looping message broadcasting. "They haven't broken in, yet." Mandy was hoping the ten o'clock news would cover the story. She told Jackson, "Ida says the FCC can help."

Jackson just shook his head, saying, "That agency is way too laid back to do anything except when there are complaints of intercepting signals."

Mandy just smiled. "Jackson, you don't know Ida. You've been on the wrong end. Trust me."

※

Over three hundred people showed up to the news stations with cassette recordings of Danny's repeating message. Danny's message was aired on all three networks during the late news.

※

Mandy called Ida appraising her of the situation. Ida called the hotline and talked to Danny. By this time, with the help of Rabbit and the Radio Free Hawaii devotees, Danny's message was being aired on all five radio stations.

Ida seemed concerned. Danny wasn't himself. It was like he'd gone into a cave. She said, "Let me talk to Becky."

Becky got on the phone and explained what had happened in the restaurant and that Danny was shaken from finding out Piper had taken the music and promos.

Ida explained to Becky that she had Mandy take all the music and promos in all the stations to prevent the company from using the music to maintain programming. Ida added, "Let Danny know. The music programming, even the ballot boxes and the ballot computers, have been hidden from the corporation. Tell Danny we're gonna stop this madness, but he needs to clear his head."

Becky turns to me and tells me the good news.

I, overjoyed the studio's music and promos had been confiscated by Mandy not Piper, see hope. I say, "Let me have the phone."

Ida tells me what to do. I go back on the radio. "The corporation has fired me and the General Manager of four of these stations. They want to take over the programming of the radio revolution. There will be a press conference near 346 Black Sand avenue, next to Kapiolani Park at 9pm tomorrow night. The conference will take place at the east end of Kapiolani Park. We're gonna need your help to resume the Radio Revolution. Please come if you can. This is a revolving message that will stay on as long as the corporation can't break in to this studio." The message was added to the previous message. Both messages are put on loop.

Becky goes back and reheats the pizza in the micro-wave and brings two cups of coffee. We had finished the beers, me four, her two. I smile, "Still working?"

She laughs, "Yeah, I think I'd better call work. They can't fire you, can they, if you are being held captive by a mad DJ?"

I say, "I think that's a valid excuse, but maybe check the manual."

THE RADIO REVOLUTION

We laugh. I say, "Thank you, thank you. I couldn't get this far without you."

Becky says, "Danny, everybody I know is on your side. Viva the Revolution." She holds up her coffee cup. We click. I say, "Viva the Revolution." I could start seeing a way out of this dilemma. I feel better. Having a few beers helps.

※

The five in the Piper Gang were booked at the Honolulu Police Station. Piper for second degree assault, the others for attempted breaking and entering. The other four bail amounts were 300 dollars for attempted breaking in and resisting the arrest. There was no way on Sunday to get proof Piper owned the station, and no one had enough cash to be bailed out, and with the exception of Jackson, none of them knew anybody in town to call. The Police, siding with Danny, didn't allow Piper long distance service. If you don't have the money, you can't call. All their belongings were put in a locker. Piper and the gang spent the night in jail shouting out threats of civil suit. It took a few fellow inmates to convince them to shut-up.

Danny and Becky spent the night in the studio.

Mandy, Jackson, Gregory, Bradley, Juan and later Ed Kanoi spent the night at Danny's place just outside of Waikiki.

Ida had a sleepless night in Washington DC writing up a complaint to talk to the committee chairman of the FCC Monday morning.

Rabbit had a sleepless night as well along with his volunteers, protecting the radio towers. The morning headline in the Honolulu Advertiser in giant print: "Radio Revolution Shut Down."

※

Ida was at the door of the FCC at nine am. She asked to talk to George, who had a bit of a wishful agenda towards her. George wasn't there. The job wasn't much of a full time enterprise, she guessed. Well, she needed to wake up the agency. She plopped a complaint for Dead Duck Enterprises on the counter--all eighty stations. She said, "Give this directly to George Hanson."

The attendee said, "Complaints don't go directly to Mr. Hanson." Aware of the possibility, Ida said, "Well here is a second copy; give this one to George."

The Hawaii stations weren't up for renewal until September of the following year. But nine other stations in Dead Duck Enterprises were up in one to three months. She submitted a request to the FCC to disallow their license renewals.

The attendee read over the complaint. Ida stood there as she read.

No one ever had made such a complaint for this reason, that these radio stations were "misleading" the community. Nor were they performing "in the interest of the community." Furthermore there was now no one directly monitoring the four radio stations in Hawaii to insure the corporation was performing for the interest of the community. The owner had no partners, no secretary or treasurer, and operated as a 100% owner of a LLC, and resided in Atlanta Georgia; thus this owner would find it difficult to control the day to day operations of his other stations across the United States. All these stations were being conducted without adequate supervision. His chief programmer lived in Atlanta, Georgia. How could he, as a sole proprietor, prevent misleading the listenership and be receptive to the community needs of all of his eighty radio stations (Yeah, Ida put in the explanation mark)! "There is a concern in his four radio stations in the Hawaiian market, five thousand miles away, that he is literally outraging well over a hundred thousand listeners. Request no renewal of any of his eighty radio stations. Petitions from thousands of concerned listeners coming forth within the week."

The attendee said, "Well this is a novel complaint. The company making the complaint is what, The Radio Revolution?"

Ida's razor sharp eyes bore into her. "I'm their lawyer. An outrageous act has just occurred. Be sure George gets this."

"Well. It has to go through the proper channels first."

"Your office is going to be flooded with thousands of letters and maybe 20,000 people on signed petitions within a week! It is going to be national news. You want George and the rest of the committee to find out about this from the news?"

The attendee asked, "Do you know George personally?"

"Tell him Ida Stephan came here."

The attendee looked shaken. "Yes, Ms. Stephan."

Ida stormed out. Slammed the door.

17

NEWS CONFERENCE

Next morning Piper Zweigolf and his gang were released from jail. The charges on Fledge and the lawyers were dropped. Piper was forced to stay in Honolulu for a hearing the following morning on a second degree assault charge. He got a local criminal lawyer to defend him. His three lawyers were busily writing and filing a civil suit against the city of Honolulu.

Piper was released on two-thousand-dollars bail. Along with Fledge, his head radio programmer for the chain and two police officers, the four went to the studio. They were given the key to open the door by the management of the building. A nailed door finally got pried open only to face two desks, one upside down on top of the other, with the legs super glued to the floor and the top desk super glued to the bottom one. It was too much to budge, even with four men pushing in unison.

Piper was furious. "They're gonna pay for this," he said.

The police got the fire department, and after looking over the plans, the fire department opted to pry open the fire exit door.

Becky was sleeping on Danny's shoulder till she heard the front door being assaulted. She waited. Would they be able to get in? Half an hour later, she heard the fire door being pried open. Alarmed, she prepared to fight. Danny didn't seem to wake-up, even jostled and shouted at. Becky was concerned. When they finally broke in, she told the fire department Danny needed an ambulance. Even with Becky off his shoulder, and the commotion in the office, and Piper in a rage screaming, "What have they done to my production room?" Danny was still asleep on the bench 'til his body, without Becky's support, slumped itself into a prone position. Even hearing the ambulance siren and attendants rushing in with a gurney, Danny responded by just staring at the ceiling. The ambulance took Danny to the hospital.

Piper, Fledge, and Becky stayed in the studio. Becky decided the revolution needed a witness. Fledge turned off the repeating reel to reel message, and replaced it with his live voice, "This is The Radio Revolution. We are back!"

Piper, looking at the ransacked studio, suddenly screamed, "Theft! My Station has been robbed!"

Becky, defiant, yelled, "Screw you, this is the people's radio station!"

Piper, infuriated, lunged at her, grabbing Becky's arm, and yanked her toward him. Then realizing what he was doing, let her go. Becky lost balance and fell back, slamming against the wall. The police officers heard a ruckus but were in the other room making a report of the damages.

Piper shouted, "Get out, bitch!"

Becky looked at the bruise on her arm from his tight grip. She screamed, "You're nuthin'!" while struggling to get erect.

Piper became enraged. Looking at her defiant face, he kicked her in the crotch. "Bitch!"

The police rushed into the room.

Becky folded over and fell to her knees. Gasping, like it was her last breath, she said it again, "Nuthin'."

Piper raised his right leg, but a police officer intercepted his thrust, and threw Piper to the ground while the other police officer handcuffed him in the back.

Piper yelled, "Arrest that thief!"

Fledge was on the radio in the midst of explaining that the radio station's music, promos, and advertisements had been stolen and there would be another delay until they got the station in order.

Piper was shouting even while being handcuffed, "Arrest her!"

A lot of listeners had kept the repeating message on, waiting to see what would come next, and they heard the ruckus. First Fledge's "This is the radio revolution, we are back," then a Piper's voice, "Theft! my station has been robbed!" then Becky's voice, "Screw you, this is the people's radio station!" Then the noise, like a fight, Becky hitting the wall. Then a man shouting and Becky's voice saying, "You're nuthin'." Then a snap, followed by a cracking sound, and Piper saying, "Bitch." Then, again, "Nuthin," in a gasping female voice. Then more sounds as Piper tumbled to the floor, screaming, "Arrest that thief!" as a policeman tackled him and thrust him to the floor. Then again, the sound "Arrest her!" Followed by dead air as Fledge finally had enough sense to go off air.

A listener was testing his reel to reel in his home when he heard the radio say, "This is The Radio Revolution, we are back." He quickly turned on Record and taped the dialogue. Amazed, he rushed to a news station. The six o'clock news played part of the dialogue and Becky's response, "Screw you, this is the people's radio station!"

The news further reported that Piper Zwiegolf, the owner of the radio station, had been arrested on two second degree assault charges. His bail had gone up from two to five thousand dollars within 24 hours, and when the judge was informed that two policemen had prevented further injury to a woman, and the second assault and third attempted assault were within 24 hours of the first, and both victims were in the hospital, one in ICU, the judge raised the bail to one hundred thousand dollars. A reporter at the hearing said the Judge said, "One more violation, even a verbal threat, and you will be in jail a long, long, time." It was a special report on TV in the afternoon, on Monday. They also reported Danny Fall was in ICU, under observation, and Becky Chu was assailed by Piper and in the hospital, suffering possible internal bleeding.

THE RADIO REVOLUTION

I enter the hospital on a gurney. I figured after the CT scan I'd be free to leave. I feel better. I just need some sleep.

The doctor disagrees. He tells me I have a contusion in my brain in the center of my forehead, and a lesser bruise in the back of my brain. I laugh and say, "Yeah, there must be a lot of space in my head for my brain to jingle around that much. I'm a real airhead."

The doctor doesn't appreciate my humor. He puts me in a wheel chair. I know the routine. You can't leave the hospital except in a wheel chair. Liability. A nurse takes me to the elevator, and to my shock, the elevator goes up. "Where are we going?" I ask.

"You're staying for observation."

"Wait a minute, I feel fine. I gotta go. There's a radio revolution out there."

"Not for you. It's time to be a spectator."

I'm stripped down to my underpants and put in one of those wimpy pieces of cloth that looks like a painter's smock. It's really weird having a female nurse undress you, as if I couldn't do that on my own. She even wants me to piss in a bottle. I laugh. "I can use the bathroom." She got a male nurse to help me. But even he gave me a bottle.

God, I hope I have clean underwear on. Almost as embarrassing as running naked down a street. My God, this can't be.

It takes two nurses to coax me into bed. The male nurse looks on with my piss in his bottle, smiling. *What does he think? He's looking at my piss as if it is gold.*

I ask to turn on the TV for the news. I want to know what's going on.

Instead, some lady wants my blood pressure. Another nurse is attaching an IV to my hand, while another is sticking wires into my skin above my heart and on my scalp, while a doctor is finally dressing the cut on my forehead. *How can they move in this room? There are so many nurses and doctors.*

This is not good. I'm sitting down on the bed thinking. Suddenly I can't remember what I was thinking about. A male nurse approaches me with a smile. "Mr. Heinzwaffle, I'm here for your blood. Which arm do you want me to use?"

I shout, "Nobody calls me Heinzwaffle! You can call me Danny Fall."

The nurse looks at his board. "It says here you are Danny Boy Heinzwaffle."

"Well dammit, call me Danny."

When they at last all leave, I move all the wires and the contraptions that are attached to me along with the IV and the monitor to the TV. and turn it on. I am so anxious to see the TV, I don't notice the remote. No news yet. I have to wait. I'm drifting off a little bit, feeling a little sleepy. I gradually set myself on the floor. The IV stand topples over. The floor seems comfortable. I lay down on the floor and rest. I feel peaceful.

A nurse screams. Two male attendants rush in my room. I don't feel so peaceful anymore. They lift me on to the bed. The nurse starts taking my blood pressure again.

"You already did that!"

"Mr. Heinzwaffle, you need to relax."

I shake my head, "Hospitals!" *They sure don't keep track of what they are doing with their patients, do they? I already had the blood pressure test. I already told them my name was Danny, not Mr. Heinzwaffle.*

※

Ida had got Robert Zayes, a Washington Post reporter, to go to Hawaii. She said, "Something is looming in Hawaii. The nation needs to know what is happening."

Robert Zayes had covered many of Ida's crusades which had made print in the Washington Post, so despite the long trip the Post funded it.

He was from Puerto Rico, with wild black hair that seemed to stand up on its own, and a straggly beard. He felt she was doing something positive for America and he desperately wanted to be a part of it. But at the moment he was in a stressful situation. He had constant

THE RADIO REVOLUTION

reprimands from the editor; he felt his job was in danger. His wife was pregnant with their fifth child. Editor George Talbot told him he was too emotional. So he landed in the islands with a desperate need to be objective.

Ida didn't help. She called the news stations in Hawaii and told them a Washington Post Reporter was coming in on the Delta 7pm plane from Chicago for emergency coverage of this event.

※

Piper was headed for jail again. Becky herself earned an ambulance when her breathing became irregular. The policemen had finished their report of the incident and had just left.

So Fledge, the national program director for the stations, was in the studio alone with no music to play for the revolution. Only the carts the station used before the radio revolution were in the studio. And they were in boxes, disorganized. Fledge needed to resume the radio revolution, but he didn't know what to play. Even the contraption Bradley used to program the music hour by hour had disappeared. He was tempted to call Jackson for help, but he didn't even know Jackson's last name... or was Jackson his last name? And he needed to find the DJs.

Fledge went on the air and posted a looped message with his voice, "The Radio Revolution will continue shortly."

He checked the office for radio personnel but found nothing there. Mandy and her gang had done a thorough job of eliminating all evidence that the radio revolution even existed. Fledge decided to go to Tower Records and ask around.

He entered this massive music store and the first thing he saw was a giant banner: "Declare your Radio Freedom. Vote." But there was no ballot box. Fledge did notice a few surveys from the station on the floor. Well, nobody seemed interested in this station. *They discard the surveys on the floor?* What were they playing? Looking at the list he began to wonder. *I never heard of most of these, are they selling?*

167

Fledge, puzzled, asked for the manager. The clerk told him the manager wasn't on the floor, but the assistance manager was.

"Give me the manager, now. I control the music of Tower Records and the stuff it reports nationally, to Billboard. I'm Fledge Granston! He'd better know who I am."

The manager came out and cordially met Fledge. He said, "That station plays mostly independent records that are hard to get and even harder to keep in stock. Tower's buyers don't really have ties to these distributors."

The clerk interrupted. He pointed to the number one song. "That's been number one for the past four weeks and Tower's buyers won't let us buy more than five at a time. It's classical. "Pachelbel's Canon in D by the Julian String Quartet."

"Number one for four weeks?" Fledge shook his head. "You can't be serious."

The manager smiled. "I don't like that station, but they don't call it The Radio Revolution for nothing."

Fledge asks, "Why don't you like that station?"

The manager laughed. "They got a crazy night guy, called Don Juan with the Magic Wand. I mean you either love him or hate him. No in between. He's always interrupting things, playing songs a little bit, then changing to other songs, somethin' he calls, 'going bananas,' with monkeys screeching in the background, and damn he's political, I don't mean a socialist, a full blown communist at least, feels the poor people should run the Earth, as if they could do a better job, maybe not even a communist, maybe more like an anarchist. And he keeps waving that stupid wand around and stupid girls squeal and their squeals come blaring over the music while its playing, its irritating as hell. And his accent is so bad you can't even understand him half the time. I gotta put up with it, my girl thinks he's God. I hate that station."

"What about the music?"

"You won't believe this. The first week on, they literally sledgehammered a single by Paula Abdul, a Grammy winner, and promised

THE RADIO REVOLUTION

never to play it again. You believe that? The voters are wacko. An R&B song gets voted on to their stupid survey one week, and it gets sledge hammered the next, never to be played again. They're nuts. They rather vote in pure noise. Those kinds of records never get sledgehammered. It's horrible."

Fledge looked over the list. "I'll tell you what, give me whatever is on this list." The manager hailed a clerk who went about pulling the music. He didn't have Nine Inch Nails' "Head like a Hole," Operation Ivy's "Take Warning," Dance Hall Crashers' "He Wants Me Back," NWA's "Fuck the Police," Public Enemy/Anthrax's "Bring the Noise," Suicidal Tendencies' "Institutionalized," Gregory Isaacs' "Red Roses for Gregory," Yellowman's "Bedroom Mazuka," They Might Be Giants' "Ana Ng," Fugazi's "Waiting Room," My Life With the Thrill Kill Cult's "Sex on Wheels," Dead Milkman's "Bitchin' Camaro," Siouxsie and the Banshees' "Cities In Dust;" Aswad's "Best of My Love," Bobby Darin's "Beyond the Sea," Teresa Bright's "Polihale," Hepcat's "Same Old Song," Ministry's "Thieves," Rage Against The Machine's "Wake Up Wake up," Violet Femmes' "Blister In The Sun," Butch Helemano's "Wave Rider," Bob Marley's "Redemption Song," Pearl Jam's "Yellow Ledbetter," Smashing Pumpkins,' "Rhinoceros nor Pachelbel's Canon in D.

Tower Records only had thirteen of the thirty-six songs on the list in stock. There was not a single song on the Billboard top 100 on the Radio Revolution Chart. The manager explained, "A lot of the Radio Revolution's songs are from independent record companies and don't have very good distribution. Independent companies have to file elaborate forms to get into Tower Records. A lot of them don't know the procedure. And our mainland buyers are shy about bringing in large quantities, like Pachelbel's Canon. But when they do come in, they are gone that day."

Fledge asked the clerk pulling the music, "Do you like the station?"

The clerk stammers, "Well, a lot of people love it."

The manager laughed, "It does have its supporters, but it is a huge minority."

Fledge was in shock. *This list is a disaster. It'll never make it on the mainland. This is a foreign country. I have to tell Piper it isn't going to work. No simulcast from Hawaii. Maybe we can take in the votes in Atlanta and simulcast it from Atlanta, Georgia.* That would make at least the charted songs sane.

Three reporters, sweating with excitement, met Robert Zayes from the Washington Post at the airport.

"Well, well, well, I'm just here to access the situation. It is peculiar."

"Are you writing a story for the Washington Post?"

"Well, well, that is really not my decision. I'll apprise the Editor. It's his call. I'm just neutral here. Investigating. Give me a few hours to get adjusted to this event, please."

The interview with the Washington Post reporter was aired on all three news stations in Hawaii.

People who turned on the radio only heard a buzz sound. Rabbit had turned off the signal on all the stations but Hilo.

Fledge thought. *We've got to get out of this country.*

Ida demanded a news conference meeting at nine pm, Monday. She had Danny announce it on the reel to reel Sunday night. and then coverage of it was hyped on the six pm news this Monday night. Bradley had a giant spotlight erected with flood lights and a stage for the meeting in Kapiolani Park.

THE RADIO REVOLUTION

At nine pm Mandy went on stage. There were over two thousand listeners in the audience as well as a flock of reporters. More were coming. Parking was a huge problem in the park.

She started. "We are here to bring back The Radio Revolution. A fire was lit in Hawaii, and now someone is trying to douse it.

"The owner had a contract approved by his General Manager, and now he intends to usurp the contract and take over the radio revolution for himself so he can broadcast it across the nation with his other seventy-six stations.

"The owner doesn't want Danny Fall, the father of The Radio Revolution, connected with his station anymore. His exact words at the Likelike Drive Inn were..." Mandy looked at a piece of paper. "'Well, little rebel you are finished. We are taking over the format and controlling the ballot counting from now on. This is Fledge, my chief programmer.'"

"That was followed with Piper throwing a saucer into Danny' forehead, causing a concussion." The audience was silent. Murmurs here and there.

There were signs waving. "Long Live The Radio Revolution," and Becky's now famous words on signs everywhere, "Screw you, this is the people's radio station!"

Mandy paused. Then shouted, "This Radio Revolution is not for one man, Piper Zweigolf! No, It is for the people!" The audience started screaming and cheering.

"How are we gonna get it back? One, Danny was misinformed with his speech last night on the repeating reel to reel. Piper didn't confiscate the music, nor the ballot boxes, nor the surveys. I did! They are secure as I speak. And they are NOT coming back until Piper and his posse go back to Atlanta!"

More cheers from the audience.

"But we need to do more than send Piper back to Atlanta. We need to get Piper out of radio period!"

Fledge was in the audience. *Madness. They're insane.*

Even louder cheers.

Robert Zayes from the Washington Post was in the audience. *Oh my God, my deadline was an hour ago. It'll have to wait a day.*

Jackson was on stage. *Is Mandy crazy? Get rid of Piper totally - totally out of radio?*

Mandy continues, "This is how we're gonna do it. We are passing out petitions to you now. Get as many signatures as you can between now and twelve midnight Wednesday. You have fifty hours to get as many signatures as possible. Bring them back here. There will be people here to retrieve them and mail them to the FCC.

"The petition says, "We want Piper Zweigolf out of radio. He is a threat to the community. We want the Radio Revolution back on the air with Danny Fall as its director!

"There is an affidavit on the back of the petition saying, this is my only signing of this petition. And this is my address and phone number. So everybody needs to fill out both sides. And please, no one sign more than one petition. That is very important. The state will verify all the signatures. So write legibly. And don't mail them directly to the FCC. Bring them to us so the state can send them together.

"Even if you have but one name on the petition, the petition needs to be returned this Wednesday night by midnight.

"But that is not enough! Each one of you needs to write a personal letter to the FCC with your own personal reasons why you want the radio revolution back on the air with Danny Fall directing it. On the bottom of the petition is the FCC address. Also we have fliers here for you to give the address to your friends.

"This is what is necessary to bring The Radio Revolution back with Danny Fall! Are you willing to do it?"

Mad waving, screams, cheers.

"*Are you willing to do it?*" Louder cheers.

As the crowd gradually dispersed and picked up petitions and the flyers, Robert Zayes approached Mandy. There were reporters, DJs, office personnel and listeners surrounding her. People were rapidly firing questions. Mandy, however, wasn't answering. She was looking around. She waved to Robert and shouted, "Come with me, we'll talk in the house."

She pushed through the crowd to him. "Ida told me about you, I so appreciate your coming."

Robert was looking at the most beautiful girl he had ever seen. Her deep, near black eyes were as warm as a bonfire on a cold night. He couldn't help but stare. *And I've got to be objective? Oh boy!*

"Hi, Mandy, is Danny okay?"

"They're afraid of possible brain damage, and they're looking for possible brain clots, but he seems fine so far. The impact was centered on one small spot on his forehead. It caused a contusion. He has some bleeding, they say minor, and no swelling." She stops. Then adds, "I don't know how minor bleeding in the brain can be, but they don't seem worried about that. At least they don't see a need for surgery.

"And he is a bit rebellious. Gregory is at the hospital. Ida's brother. He says they said he's calming down with the meds."

Robert notices Mandy is shaking.

"Does Ida know?"

"Yes, Robert. I talk to her most every hour. She says you are a very caring individual. I can see that already."

18

THE MYSTERY GROWS

Danny's house has seven bedrooms; a den which includes a library, a giant garden in the back that was a bit overgrown and wilted without Dorothy, a small but well equipped "listening room," a basement recording studio, and a room for ballot counting on nine computers. In the back of the garden he has his "football" room, a shed filled with football stats for every 1A football team in college football, all 89, stretching a twenty-year span. But now that room is stuffed with what Mandy was instructed to take from the Honolulu radio station, including the LPs, CDs, music carts, advertising carts, ballot boxes, Brad's contraption, and personnel records.

Mandy has Robert wait in the living room. She goes to the kitchen and calls the hospital.

She asks for Gregory. As they talk she breaks down in tears. She drops the phone and Bradley hugs her. Bradley says, "He's going to be alright."

She says, "Doctors aren't that confident. Gregory says he isn't even conscious, and the doctors keep giving him CTs. Gregory is staying overnight. Even Gregory seems worried. Doctors say there could be long term depression, or even a change in personality due to the blow. I had such a wonderful family. How could this happen?"

Bradley hugs Mandy tightly. "You do have a wonderful family. We all would give our lives up to help you. We're inseparable. But Danny loves you and he needs you to fulfil his dream. He's strong, determined, he'll pull through. I promise."

Juan witnesses this and hugs them both. "Mandy, he'll be all right. I feel it. I know head injuries, and he sounds like he only needs rest. I've seen kids with horrific blows to the head, and they pulled through. Doctors are paranoid. They always overreact to head injuries. I'll talk to Robert for you. Bradley needs to stay with you tonight."

Mandy, realizing Juan finally understands, hugs him fiercely. "Oh Juan, thank you. Thank you."

Mandy never knew her parents. She was raised by the elders of an ancient Vedic religion who believed Mandy to be a sacred soul. She spent her childhood in nomad communes that traveled from Indonesia, to China, to North East India. Like Bob Marley, she was a fortuneteller at age five. Mandy was the circle of attention in communal life. As she got into her teens she began feeling uncomfortable with the intense adoration of the master guru of her sect. At fifteen she met Bradley, a tourist from Massachusetts, who had come to India for spiritual guidance. Eschewing the constant expectations of the elders, lack of freedom, and a feeling that she was being used, she ran away with Bradley to America. Bradley promised her a happy family. That's what Mandy was missing or so she thought at the time.

In Florida Mandy met Gregory, who taught her voice and dancing, and the family became a threesome. In New Mexico, Mandy met Juan in a library, both bonding trying to self-learn, unable to go to school, Juan because he got into the country illegally with no papers. Mandy, being a free spirit, who couldn't handle the regiment of schooling.

Then came Danny, and she suddenly started changing. Before Danny she'd stayed away from middle aged men. After Danny, she suddenly saw a purpose for life. She felt more dependent upon him than the others. Suddenly she wanted to show her worth to the world. And even more than that, she wanted to help Danny show his worth to this world. Tonight Bradley held her in his arms patiently, let her weep, told her what she had made: this wonderful family, a family that would never part and will do anything so she can be whoever she wants to be because she is more than special. Mandy cries. "I need you so much, Bradley, so much."

Bradley smiles, "You need all of us. We all need you."

※

Juan meets Robert in the living room. "I guess I'm the chosen one for the interview tonight."

"What happened to Mandy?"

"She's on the phone with the hospital. Danny is still in the ICU, and Gregory, Ida's brother, is in the hospital standing guard, our correspondent."

The commotion of the night had died down. Both are seated in lounge chairs facing the open sliding glass windows where still outside people are picking up petitions beneath the Cook Pines, as the trade winds and the night air cool them down.

"The news - not good?"

"Danny will pull through, head injuries, just needs rest. Mandy just needs Danny to be here, now. She's been brave and tough, but after the news conference, she just had a bit of a let-down. Bradley is with her now."

"Bradley - is that her boyfriend?"

Juan ignored the question. He said, "There are five of us running this radio revolution. Mandy is the morning DJ. Bradley is the computer master who tabulates all the weekly votes, programs the music, handles the Honolulu traffic for the station, and does the books. Gregory orchestrates the concerts, and I'm the evening DJ. People vote weekly for what they want to hear and what they don't want to hear, and Danny runs the countdown show every Saturday morning. We take our orders from Danny, our President."

"How does Jackson fit into this?"

"Jackson is a trip. He's General Manager of four of the five stations, and the guy we signed the now broken contract with. Jackson got fired, too. Mandy says the owner of the stations, the one that put

THE RADIO REVOLUTION

Danny in the hospital, wants to take over the station and satellite it across the nation. Ida is trying to stop that."

"How did Ida get involved with this?"

"Ida is Gregory's sister. She's our lawyer."

Robert had his note pad out writing down the five names. He was aware of Ida's two brothers, all lawyers, like her father, but Gregory?

"Is Gregory a lawyer?"

Juan smiles, he remembers Ida saying Gregory was in a home with five lawyers.

"You seem to know Ida's family better than me. But no. Before he got involved with the Radio Revolution, Gregory was a musician in a reggae band, the 'Jamlins.'"

"So Ida is involved because of her brother?"

"Danny is the one that got her involved. Her brother just introduced them to each other. Ida got completely crazed at what we were doing after talking to Danny. Then she became our lawyer when we signed the initial contract last November."

Robert was thinking. There must be something political going on here for Ida to take such an interest. "Dead Duck Enterprises. I looked it up. No listing. Is that a dba for something else?"

Juan looks surprised. "I don't know. We signed the agreement with Dead Duck Enterprises LLC."

"He owns eighty stations and he is only an LLC. He must have a flock of financial partners. Does he own 51%?"

Juan stands up walks toward the patio, voice rising. "Jackson says he doesn't share anything. He has no partners. He ain't an LLC, he's an idiot and a bastard. Anybody that hurts Danny and upsets Mandy is asking for it. The pussy kicked a little Chinese girl in the stomach, she is in the hospital, too. If he even touched Mandy, I'd do away with him myself. And he's pissed off thousands and thousands of people by kicking Danny off the station. If he gets out of this town alive, I'll be surprised. Jail isn't even safe. The inmates would do him in. He sure isn't staying."

Robert is shocked at Juan's anger. He stands up, too. "You've only been on the air five months, and the town is that upset?"

"We are the revolution. We are here to change things. And the people love it!"

Robert says, "Say that again." He writes it down. Both are on the patio facing the park. Tall pine trees' outlines emerge in the darkness.

"Are you guys a corporation?"

"Yes, it is called the Radio Revolution."

"Ida set it up?"

Juan nods.

"And your backers?"

"We five. Mandy is the owner."

"How old is Mandy?"

"She turned twenty in February."

"Who has the money?" Robert couldn't believe these young people had the money.

Juan didn't like the question. He hesitated. "We five. I think that is all now. You can talk to the other four later. Bradley's helping Mandy hold it together. Gregory's at the hospital. And I'm damn tired. It has been a hell of a day." Juan didn't want to say anymore without Mandy's approval.

Robert says, "I bet. I got a lot of people to talk to anyway. Where is Jackson?"

"He hasn't been home in ten days. Hasn't had much sleep either. He's probably gone home. He'll be here tomorrow."

Robert goes to get his car and go to the hospital. There's a tow truck and a police cruiser; his rental car is just about to get hoisted. He runs. "That's my car, officer!"

The officer, pen poised over his ticket pad, points to the sign. "No parking anytime."

"Everybody was parking here. I didn't see the sign."

The officer considers, then tells the tow truck driver to wait. "Why were you parking here?"

"I was at the news conference for the radio revolution."

"We let the radio revolution fans park here, so many, and no parking. But the last ones left a half an hour ago."

THE RADIO REVOLUTION

Robert pulls out his Washington Post Reporter Pass. "I was interviewing Juan and Mandy after the conference."

The officer flips the cover slip back down on his ticket pad. "Ok. You were the guy on the news."

Robert is shocked and gratified.

"Robert, just so you know. This town wants The Radio Revolution back on the air." He calls the tow truck driver over. "This is Robert Zayes."

"From the Washington Post?"

Robert is shocked. "Take care of us, good man. The radio revolution is the best radio station, ever."

The officer voids the parking ticket. "Never done that before, guess it is a first."

Robert asks the way to Queens Hospital. The officer says, "Follow me." The siren blares.

※

Gregory is posted in a fold out chair near the nurses' station, eyes closed, possibly asleep. Robert introduces himself, says, "Ida says hello."

Gregory perks up. "You're Robert?"

"It seems this town knows me, and I've only been here three hours."

"How did it go, the news conference?"

"Big crowd, maybe 1500, took petitions, seemed intent on getting them filled out. A lot of cheering, concern for Danny, poster-wavings Becky's, 'Screw you, this is the people's radio station.' But Mandy, the owner of the format, said something strange: the Petition is to get Piper Zweigolf out of radio, and return Danny to heading The Radio Revolution. I thought it was a bit unrealistic; I mean, how do you get an owner of 80 radio stations out of radio? The FCC can do that at kind of thing? I doubt it. He owns this station. Bizarre statement. But it sure rallied the crowd." Robert waited for Gregory's response.

179

"Mandy wouldn't say that, unless Danny- oh, wait a minute. Danny was out of it. It must have been Ida to tell her to say that."

Robert dismissed that. "Couldn't be Ida. Perhaps Mandy said that on her own, in the heat of the moment?"

"No way. In the family, we take orders from Mandy, and in The Radio Revolution, we take orders from Danny. But he's out of it now. Ida would take over for Danny. It must be my sister who told Mandy that. Ida is our lawyer."

Robert looks around. The nurses' station seems busy. "Why don't we talk in the lounge?"

Gregory nods and they move to a couch in the lounge. Robert says, "She's your lawyer, and second in command when it comes to The Radio Revolution Corporation?

"Yes, Danny and her work together on the Radio Revolution."

Mandy did say to me she is on the phone with Ida hourly. But Robert couldn't believe that Ida, a very careful lawyer, would tell Mandy to say such an outlandish thing. But this was the second time the word "family" had come up.

Robert said, "Tell me about the family."

Gregory said, "We're a team. We started the radio revolution as a team. We five. All credits, all properties between us, remain in the team. All five take credit, or all five take the responsibility for whatever is done. There is no one more special than another in the team. Though when it comes to the radio revolution, we follow Danny, and when we follow our family relationships we take our guidance from Mandy. But now, with Danny in the hospital, Ida is directing Mandy. I'm sure."

"Gregory, your sister is great force for the common people as a constitutional lawyer in Washington DC. I'm sorry, but she wouldn't make such an outlandish statement. She wouldn't."

Gregory looked haggard. After a few seconds, he said, "You can ask Mandy."

"So what's the word on Danny?"

When he is awake he seems to be his old self. He's trying to get out of bed a lot. They're using drugs on his brain and right now he isn't very coherent. I'm kind of pissed about that. He had some bleeding in the brain, but it has stopped. They were afraid of swelling, but it seems it was a false alarm. But they don't want him to move for 24 hours. The doctors are getting optimistic, but brain damage? They don't know. He has a contusion on the center of his forehead in the brain, and a smaller one on the back of his skull. They don't think he would have bled but he did a lot of physical stuff after he was hit, and they think that was what started the bleeding. And it might have been aggravated when he fell or slipped to the floor in the hospital. They aren't sure. So they want to keep him still."

Robert is moved. "Damn, that must have been some hit."

"His doctor says it impacted such a small area with a large force, kinda like flinging a blunt needle on to the brain causing his brain to jiggle, and bounce around in his skull."

Ida is committed to this radio revolution. Something big is happening here, but what?

She had given Robert no clue when she said, "You might want to cover a little radio station in the middle of the Pacific. There might be a big story looming." She had given him so many important stories in the past, and her name was enough for the Washington Post to give him travel vouchers to go to Hawaii. But he knew his editor. He needed to get both sides of the story. Piper was in Jail, and probably a hostile witness. At the news conference he heard that his national program director was in town. He needed to find Fledge.

"Do you know Fledge, Piper's national program director?"

Gregory says, "No. I heard he was in town from Mandy, but that is it."

"You don't know his last name?"

"He was in jail last night, you probably can get it at the police station."

"Gregory, thank you for your time. You ought to stay here, sleep awhile."

Gregory smiles.

Robert starts thinking. This is stranger than strange. Why is Ida so invested in this radio format? And why is she so close mouthed about it, to me? And why does the owner want to take over the format for more of his stations? *I'm gonna be working all night. Screw jetlag.*

Robert got Fledge's last name and photo at the police station and started calling the local hotels around the radio station. First he called the Pagoda Hotel, a short block away from the radio station. Fledge was registered. Robert rang the room; no answer. He went up to the room and banged on the door; no answer. Fledge was probably at a nearby bar. Robert went on foot; there were scores of bars in the area, mostly strip and hostess bars. Entering the seventh bar called Saigon Passion, in the top story of a dilapidated building with a creaky staircase, he saw a man that looked a little like Fledge in his mug shot. He was at a table nursing a drink.

"You need a girl, young man?"

"What are you a pimp?"

"Just joking, but I need a seat."

"Hey, I'm straight."

Robert laughed, "Me, too. But I want to get crooked and sit, Okay?"

The music was blaring, not much chance for comfortable talking, and the man's attention was on the stripper twirling naked around the pole. The man didn't answer.

Robert hailed a waitress and asked for two more of whatever the man was drinking.

The dancer finished, rushed off stage as if embarrassed, and the lights came on. The music stopped. Robert was shocked when he gave the waitress a twenty and she gave back no change. Then he sipped the concoction. It was double shot of whiskey and something horribly sweet.

Robert passed the new drink to the man and said, "You like Amy?"

"That's her name?"

"Yeah."

"Yeah, sorta. Small tits though. I'm surprised they let her dance."

Robert said, "I'm Robert; what's your name?"

"Fledge Granston, from Atlanta, Georgia."
"So, Mr. Granston, here on vacation?"
"I wish. Hey, you from here?"
Robert nodded.

Fledge said, "Do you know The Radio Revolution, do you listen to that?"

Robert shook his head. "Nah, I don't listen to that shit."

"It seems people either love it or hate it."

Robert tips his glass to Fledge, "Yeah, whatever."

The evening passed to closing, Robert buying most of the drinks. Fledge paid for one round. Not much talk. Too noisy. Fledge didn't want to go to sleep, and the waitress mentioned there was an all-night Korean Restaurant around the corner. Robert and Fledge took off together.

"Shit, I got a day tomorrow. My boss is in jail; might be out now on bail, I don't know, and he wants to take over that radio station here, that Radio Revolution, and simulcast it nationally. He's crazed. I mean this is a foreign country, that kind of music will never go over on the mainland, but shit, I don't know how I'm gonna tell him that. It'll probably cost me my job."

"How can you take over a radio station?"

"He owns it. But it was on lease to those Radio Revolution guys."

"Why is he so hot about taking it over?"

"It's a huge cash cow. I mean, this is a medium market, and even during the slow first quarter, it broke the sales record for the entire chain ever, even for our number one station in Cleveland during a booming fourth quarter. We've never seen sales anything like that. And he thinks if he can get it in his twenty-three other markets, simulcasting it, it will lower expenses and make him a killing.

"Boy, is he wrong. If he simulcasts this music on the mainland, I doubt he'll have a single listener. The voters are strange. I was at Tower and the manager said, "Shit they sledge hammered a Grammy winner's single on the air.' None of their songs are even on the top 100 of billboard."

Robert laughed, "Seems like a rebel format."

"Psycho format is a better name for it. No way we can simulcast this shit on the mainland. This is like another country."

"So why is he in Jail?"

"My boss? Some stupid assault charge, hell, that charge had me in jail last night for no reason, all five us, his three lawyers and me. That's why I'm partying now. Damn, jail sucks."

"So you are what to him?"

"I'm his national program director and he wanted me to take over a slot here in Hawaii and simulcast the station nationally. I was gonna, but not now, after I saw what they are playing."

"So how are you gonna tell him?"

"That's why I'm drinking," Fledge laughed.

"Does that station have any political overtones?"

"Funny, you ask. I was at Tower today and the manager said the night DJ was beyond communist, more like an anarchist. Why did you ask?"

"I just heard some rumblings, - people talkin,' that's all, couldn't make much out of it."

Robert hit the sack at four, set the alarm for eight am. Screw Jet lag, this story is too big, His adrenalin was flowing. *What's Ida up to now. Shit, I forgot to call my wife.*

He calls her. It's nine in the morning in Washington DC. At the end he says, "Better get your mother to help you with the kids. Looks like I'm here a while. This story might be really big. I'm gonna be longer than I expected."

19

A SKYHOOK FOR THE NEW AMERICA

Robert is at McDonalds at nine a.m. planning his day and going about asking locals, puberty to forty, what they think of the Radio Revolution. One out of three love it, another third is indifferent or hates it, and one out of three never bothered to listen to it. Though in the sample of twenty people only one had never heard of it.

Robert's plan included getting enough information to encourage his editor to send a photographer to Hawaii or line up a photographer for him here in the islands. He had decided he was going to hold off pushing the story until it is full blown and rounded.

He made a note to interview Tower Records and other record stores, Piper and his lawyers, Jackson, Mandy, Bradley and as many people as possible who would discuss The Radio Revolution with him. Then make his "balance" report to his editor. And he knew by five o'clock he would need to talk to his editor, who most likely was expecting a story. He didn't put Danny on his list to interview, only to check on his availability.

Ida is waking up in Washington DC. canceling her regular work load to concentrate on the Radio Revolution.

Ed is posted with a troupe of Wild Weekend Girls at Danny's house to protect the Radio Revolution stuff. He is in his element.

Jackson is home with his three kids and wife, taking a much needed day off.

Mandy, Bradley, Juan are at the hospital talking to Gregory who is now at Danny's bedside. The doctors have at last agreed to allow Gregory to watch over Danny.

Danny is still asleep. The family isn't talking much. Just going in and out of the room mostly due to restlessness.

Piper is at the Hilton with his three lawyers discussing the hearing the FCC is asking for him to attend. There is a complaint. In order to renew his license of nine of his radio stations a hearing is demanded. He waits for the complaint to be faxed over from Washington DC. Last evening, he ended up paying 140,000 dollars to the bail bondsman so he could sleep in a nice cozy room for 370 dollars a night.

Fledge is asleep at the Pagoda, possible hangover looming.

༄

I awake. I look. It looks like I am at a meeting with the family. "Hey, you guys are gonna have to make room for all those doctors and nurses hounding me. Better yet. Build a blockade. Where's my blockade builder, Becky?"

Mandy almost jumps out of her chair. Standing she says, "Danny!" She smiles. "Ah, you've got a new girlfriend?"

I say, "Nah, I need more love tutoring before I can grab another girl." Smiles everywhere.

Gregory says, "I hate to break it to you Danny, but Becky got a foot in the stomach from Piper, and she's in the hospital too, maybe being released today."

Juan says, "Piper was on the air saying, 'My Station, it's been robbed.' Becky responded, 'Screw you, this is the people's radio station!' He then kicked her in the stomach. It was on the air, live. At the conference people were carrying signs with Becky's words on them."

I question, "Becky? Oh my God." Then it hit me. "The conference! It was last night?"

Mandy says, "Yeah, they got the petitions and were asked to write letters to the FCC. Two or three thousand were there, but not all at once since there was a parking problem."

Danny says, "I'm glad I told that asshole he was going to jail; his company sinking, and me turnin' on the world. I don't know what happened. It just came out of me. Out of the blue. He gave a smug remark. I was so pissed. He was messin' with the family. I remember shouting, 'Fuck you. You deserve it!'

"You kids know I live by my words. Then he knocked me senseless, and I lost direction for a while, but now I'm back. He's going down. We are going on, and stronger than before."

All smile. "I'm so glad you are back," says Gregory.

Juan says, "Yeah, he is already in Jail, but if he was in the fevela he'd be tortured, cigarette burns all over, and everybody pounding his bones, leaving his skull free to think of his pain, then throwing him in an outhouse and let him suffer until death, with a sign on the door, 'Traitors Only.' And nobody would use that outhouse ever again."

Juan makes a fist with his right hand. "No one messes with the family!"

Mandy squeezes Juan's left hand in support.

Gregory winces. Bradley is silent.

But I understand where Juan is coming from. "That's why I said what I said to Piper." I, too, hold up my fist. "No one messes with the family."

Bradley and Gregory are taken aback by my own venom.

I say, "Look. What do we do when somebody decides to evaporate us from the planet? The station is us. It is living through us. The listeners are living it, too. It is a living thing. No one can mess with a living thing. That's murder! He's attempting to murder us, without getting in trouble from it. We annihilate murderers. Do you realize he is trying to destroy America? Granted, unknowingly, but we can't allow that. We need to obliterate his presence from Earth. We can't have one man, or an institution thwarting the new America that will make the people sing. We can't allow that. Too much is at stake.

"This little episode with an idiot named Piper is gonna be easy to put down. And Juan is right. He needs to suffer. We need to keep him from ever owning anything, ever again. And we will do that. No question. But there will be bigger and bigger obstacles along the way from much more intelligent and treacherous people, people with almost unlimited power. So this little skirmish is a good preparation."

The faces in the room were suddenly intense. Danny was back, at last, giving directions. I continue, "Taking care of Piper and getting back on the air is something me and Ida will do. Your guys' job is to walk the streets, talk to people, tell them to sign the petitions. Get all the devotees to get petitions. The more the merrier. We need to make enough noise that we hit the papers nationally. We are The Radio Revolution. Revolutions are people suffering, crying for their rights, and yeah, in the face of hell. In our case, Piper hell."

Gregory says, "A lot of the bands want to do a benefit for us. But that's not gonna help too much, yeah?"

"Hey, exposure counts. Rallying more people to help put us back on air with letters and petitions can't hurt. Keeping the fight alive is important."

Gregory interrupts. "But didn't you say you want to make national news? Playing here in Hawaii won't help much. What if I get the bands to do a demonstration in front of the FCC in Washington D.C? Play their music. Encourage them to write songs about the Radio Revolution, do it on July 4th. Rabbit has those killer sound guys who can do open air concerts, and then we can make a record for national distribution entitled 'The Radio Revolution at the FCC Washington D.C.' Have a ceremony and all the band members laying their letters and petitions on the doorsteps of the FCC. Then get guards to stay that night and put 'em in the door the following day with coverage from the papers because of the concert the night before. Have Robert Zayes mention it in the Washington Post. Bet we'd have a crowd, especially if we get those Compton Guys to participate. Ida can get us space to do it on the July 4th holiday, get us a permit right smack on Maryland Street. If we get the NWA guys, they oughta do it, we are the only ones playing their music on radio and 90% of Washington D.C. is black. Getting whites and blacks together on the street, it will cause quite a stir. And our listeners who want to support us, if they can get the funds, for sure will show up.

"Should make the national papers big time. Could put us on the map nationally, in fact. And all the bands, so many need national exposure, and a big selling record or CD, live at the FCC, including their music, is good publicity even if no one else plays them. And in the album we can state our mission, which Danny is about to say, right?"

"Gregory, that is utterly brilliant. Damn, we'll do it. We'll cover travel and lodging expenses. Get Pearl Jam, Dance Hall Crashers, Hepcat, Nine Inch Nails, Butch Helemano, the Toasters, Tantra Monsters, Cocteau Twins, Alpha Blondy, Rage Against the Machine - all of them, and we'll have a crowd, alright."

Gregory smiles. "Should make a lot of noise, for sure."

Mandy says, "The record companies should be happy to follow our lead, not try to muffle it."

I say, "Love, not gonna happen. They are obsessed with only one thing: control. They need to control the market so they can orchestrate anything they want on to it. And what they end up doing is making loads of money without producing value. You want to depress the economy, try to control it. Creating value like the new exciting music of the day is how the economy expands. Control shrinks the economy, and that means it shrinks the income of the masses while they, those obsessed with control, get richer and richer. They love that. They don't want to see it go, and they got all the money they need to thwart what we are doing."

Bradley says, "Damn Danny, you sound like it is hopeless."

Gregory smiles again. "Like beating BYU by 40 points?"

I respond, "Well, we'll need to introduce a new political agenda to overcome them."

Gregory raises his hands. "Here it comes, I can feel it."

Bradley says, "The world is so jaded with politics. How are they gonna fight for us, with us doing another political trip on them? Most won't buy it."

"Bradley, people have a set mind. They use it to search for their own personal identity. Part of it is music, part of it is religion, part of it is politics, part of it is their sports team, part of it is their personal prejudices... that's their sky hook, their way to live in this chaos. We are gonna create a new skyhook; a skyhook that the suppressed and angry can grab. It's this: 'We were given a democracy, why not use it!'

"They can keep their religions, their politics, their prejudices, and their musical identity, we are just gonna add one more, 'We were all given a democracy, why not use it!' When they say they are Christian, we'll say, 'Yeah.' When they say they are Republican, we'll say, 'Yeah.' When they say they hate reggae, will say, 'That's your choice.' When they say they hate blacks, we'll say that is your choice. When they say they are upset with the world, we'll say, 'Yeah! We all are. But we were all given a democracy, why aren't we using it!' That is our battle cry. That is what we are gonna concentrate on. Don't worry how stupid their skyhooks are to us, respect them, but always add, 'We were all given a democracy, why not use it!' And of course, you can add, 'Just like the radio revolution, the first radio station that *is* a democracy.'"

There was silence in the room.

Juan finally says, "Oh, my God. This might work. And Danny's right; there will be a huge desperate fight to suffocate us."

Mandy hugs Gregory. "See, you, the lost son might do more for America than your father could even imagine."

Bradley grips her, "See what you've started."

Juan adds, "We are gonna need protection. People will be out to kill us."

I smile. "Juan's right. "I bet you know some good radio guys."

Juan's eyes bulge. He looks shocked. "You know the favela? I was mostly a specialist, making fake documents, raping bank accounts, capturing passwords, pick pocketing here and there. Yeah, I worked at a militia, and I was fluent in four languages and did some translating for them. I kind of was free from daily wars. I was only in a few when I was in the wrong spot at the wrong time. I know the good radio guys. Yeah, but the grags aren't likely to give up any of the good ones."

Mandy, noticing Gregory and Bradley's bewildered faces, says, "Radio guys are the lookouts. Juan says they are incredibly alert, they can hear slight movements a hundred feet away, even in between the noise of gunfire. He says they sleep awake. Eyes sometimes, even open. They even know their individual enemies' walk. They give the warning when an ambush is looming. If you got a good radio guy, they don't even ambush you until they are sure he is not around. That's what Danny thinks will make good protection for us."

Robert gets Piper's contact information from the bondsman. He arrives to the Hilton at ten forty. Not in his room. Robert tracks Piper down in the hotel lobby with his three lawyers, staring at a fax.

Piper is yelling. "What a bunch of bullshit. I can't believe it!"

One of his lawyers says, "They do have a precedent. Some guy in Ohio was living two hours away from his station, and the FCC refused renewing his license because he wasn't hands on. That was four years ago. He still owns the station and its operating, but it is pending the result of an appeal."

"But I have managers. They are hands on."

The second lawyer says, "Who do they work for? You or your accounting/management firm that is handling your day to day operation. Your payroll only shows Fledge as a salary worker."

The third lawyer says, "Piper, you might need to sell your stations. I would love for you to appeal since I'd make a personal fortune from the legal fees, but I'll tell you straight: you are gonna lose this one. We can only delay the forced sale."

"God damn it, you're fired. I don't need losers on my team."

There was silence.

Piper shouts, "Why are you standing there? Get out of here. I will win!"

The third lawyer turned, with a smile, looking at the two lawyers left, he said, "I wish you boys luck," as he turned and walked out of the lobby.

Robert stared at Piper and the lawyers. He was shocked.

"Creep, what are you looking at."

Robert smiled. "Sorry sir, but you were a bit loud. I'll leave you alone."

THE RADIO REVOLUTION

Ida must have lodged a complaint with the FCC. Gregory is right. Ida told Mandy to put it on the petition, to get Piper out of radio. That is one crafty lady. When I talk to my editor tonight I'll have him get a copy of the complaint. That'll let him keep me here, maybe get a photographer as well.

Robert shows up to Tower and asks for the manager. It's 11:05, the store opens at nine and the woman clerk says the manager is at lunch.

Robert shows her his Washington Post reporter pass. "When do you think he will be back?"

The clerk gulps. "I, I, I don't know. I think he had an emergency. He might not be back today."

"Who's in charge?"

She laughs nervously. I'm sorry, sir. In order to talk to the media, we need special authorization from the head office."

"You realize, I'm gonna report this in the Washington Post. Tower Records doesn't take interviews from the media concerning the radio revolution."

"You don't understand, sir. We don't take interviews from anybody without approval. We are a huge company. We have a whole media staff that answers questions. I'll give you their number in Sacramento."

"Well as far as the Washington Post is concerned, you don't take interviews about The Radio Revolution 'cause that is all the Washington Post cares about. We could give a shit about your stupid operation." *Shit, I gotta cool it. Why is she making me so mad?*

"Well mister, we are the music scene. No one else is in our league."

"And I take it you don't like The Radio Revolution."

She smirks. "It was a travesty. Thank God it's gone."

Robert leaves. Thank God he had his recorder on. His boss would never believe it otherwise.

He checks the phone book, calls around. Asks people on the street where they shop for CDs and cassettes. More than half say the name Jelly's. He goes. The front is baseball cards, and comics, then rows and rows of books, then records, then in the back cassettes and

CDs. It's noon on a Monday and the store is huge, and packed with customers. He asks for the owner. A heavy set Chinese lady, possibly in her late thirties, comes out of the comic department. She smiles, "Well hello, Robert Zayes. Everybody is talking about you. I'm Cindy, what can I do for you?"

He shows her his press pass. Cindy smiles. "A long trip, huh? How do you like Hawaii?"

Robert laughs. "Well if I wasn't so tired, I think I'd really like it here. Especially meeting you in this place. Your store has a warm feel to it."

"Yeah, to the kids it is almost like home. I wish I had room to feed them in here. It's horrible, you know, the kids are so depressed with the shut-down. You got kids?"

"Yeah four - 10, 8, 6 and 4, and one coming in December."

"Good! They're close enough; they all help and take care of each other."

Robert smiles, "Yeah, but they do need a lot of attention, I hope my wife's mother is there to help. This is an unexpected trip."

"Well, we all hope you can help put the radio back on. There have been suicide watches at some of the private high schools after the shut-down. The kids just don't understand how this could be."

"So after being on only four months, the kids are dependent upon it?"

"Yeah, it's a lifeline to some of them. They live by each note. Kids are constantly getting shut down nowadays; it is not like when we grew up. Their paintings - some are in rage, their graffiti angry, their poetry necrophilia. They have concerts and police shut them down because of noise complaints. We just supported a 'No Place to Play Concert' on the strip stage at the Club Hubba in the slums of Honolulu. So many kids showed up, half had to stay outside because it was a fire hazard, and the fourteen and fifteen year olds were out past curfew. Gregory from The Radio Revolution organized it with those great promotion girls who cooled the police concerns of teens out past curfew. All the local bands got a chance to play fifteen minute sets. It started at four on Sunday, and after having to oust half the crowd to the street because of a fire hazard, a lot of kids had to wait until the first crowd exited. But the kids didn't mind. They loved it."

"So this is a kid station?"

"It's more than that. It's a music lover station, too. Everyday our three stores get at least a hundred ballots, and a lot of older people vote too. It's not just kids."

Cindy took Robert to Sideway Inn, a cafeteria style plate lunch joint. After two hours Robert wasn't sure who was interviewing who. Cindy managed to get him to confess his life story how and why he moved to America, the trouble he was having with his editor, why he loved what Ida was doing, and his experience at Tower Records. He had his first taste of saimin and a plate lunch and left exhausted, stuffed, but exhilarated at the same time.

He got in the car. He closed his eyes. He awoke, sweating and looked at his clock. It was 5pm. He had slept two hours and needed to get back to his hotel room to talk to his boss.

Nine days later, on the Washington Post's front page, left hand column, June 8th, 1990, below the picture:

Above is a photo in a room of the Federal Communication Commission here in Washington DC. The picture includes an estimate of three thousand letters complaining about the shutting down of The Radio Revolution, a radio station format that has been airing on five radio stations in Hawaii.

Not shown in the picture is a petition with 63,000 signatures (5% of the entire population of Hawaii) on a petition asking the owner of four of these radio stations to be ousted completely from ever owning another radio station (he owns 80 radio stations) and to instead bring The Radio Revolution back with the originator of the format, Danny Fall. The signatures are currently being verified by the secretary of state office in Hawaii.

What is The Radio Revolution?

It is a music format that utilizes a weekly ballot system allowing the listeners to vote for what they want to hear, what they don't want to hear, and a song they think will become a hit if, radio played it. Five hundred ballot boxes are in retail stores and schools and retrieved weekly, tabulated on computers at an enormous expense. On Saturday, there is a countdown of the 36 most wanted to be heard songs on radio, and those songs go into immediate rotation. The least wanted to be heard song, the song with the most negative votes, after subtracting the positive from the negative, gets sledge hammered off radio "forever." During the first week on the air, the Grammy Award Winner "Opposites Attract" by Paula Abdul met the sledge hammer, never again to be played on the Radio Revolution.

It is odd, but most of the songs voted for are not on the radio charts anywhere. When asked why, Danny Fall, the most popular DJ in Honolulu, and orchestrator of this format, said, "I don't know. You want me to guess? Musical tastes have been suffocated by major record companies. How? I can only speculate. And my speculations are not worth being in print. To me it is simply astounding!"

Fledge Granston, the national program director for all 80 stations in the chain, says, "It's because Hawaii is a foreign country. This music would never go over on the US mainland."

So why is it off the air?

Fledge Granston says it is because it is making so much money; breaking records for the whole chain even though it is in a medium market, and the owner wants to take it over and satellite broadcast it in his other 23 markets. He believes he can cut down his staff in other markets, which will pay for the huge satellite costs. Piper Zweigolf, the owner, doesn't consider it a foreign country, and he is willing to dispose of his formats in 24 US markets and run this satellite format instead.

Oddly, the radio revolution had only a six-month lease, but after four months Mr. Zweigolf couldn't wait to take over the format. He felt he had to usurp the contract immediately.

THE RADIO REVOLUTION

But when he got to Honolulu, Hawaii, someone warned the station, and all the music, promos, even advertisements and liners disappeared. He wasn't in the position to run the Radio Revolution. Thus for twelve days, it has been off air.

The format has been on the air only four months, yet in the Radiotron's first quarter report in early May, the listenership had more than doubled, almost overnight. And in the Allison Poll, listenership of the five stations maintaining the format tripled. But to give an idea of the impact of this format, just after six days on the air, I repeat: after only six days on the air, 2,000 people showed up to a night club for Dance Floor Democracy, where the listeners can vote for what they want to dance to. And major concerts, mostly with bands only this radio station is playing, have had attendance reaching 15,000 people per show. What's odd, only a few of these artists are on the top 100 charts of the nation. When radio is turned over to the people, their music taste for what they really want to hear is vastly different than what is being played on radio nationally. The Honolulu evening DJ on the Radio Revolution, known as Don Juan with the Magic Wand, said it this way: "We are the revolution. We are here to change things. And the people love it!" And he followed that statement with the thrust of a fist.

Is radio buying into a payola scheme from the major record companies? Or as Fledge Granston, the national radio programmer for the chain owner says, is Hawaii "a foreign country?"

No word on when, or if, it will return. The complaint from the lawyer representing the Radio Revolution, Ida Stephan, is to have FCC force the owner, Piper Zweigolf, into a forced sale of his eighty stations because he is living in Atlanta, Georgia and mismanaging 80 stations across the country without adequate supervision. Zweigolf has responded by buying out a management/accounting organization.

Cindy Lau, owner of one of the major record store chains in Hawaii, Jelly's Comics and Book's, says, "The youth of Hawaii have gotten depressed. There have been suicide watches at some of the private schools. Kids just don't understand how this can be." She is referring to the Radio Revolution being shut down. The Tower chain of stores in Hawaii has refused to comment regarding The Radio Revolution.

There is no comment from the Federal Communication Commission or its committee, which is authorized to apply force to non-compliance of the Federal Communications Act of 1934.

But this coming July 4th, in front of FCC here in Washington DC, there is a demonstration concert for the Radio Revolution featuring many of the bands that are charted on these Hawaiian Radio Stations. They plan to play their music and lay their own personal petition on the steps of the FCC in Washington DC.

The last countdown of the top 36 songs voted by the people of Hawaii is listed on page A6.

20

WE WERE ALL GIVEN A DEMOCRACY, WHY NOT USE IT

George Hanson, the committee chairmen of the FCC, read the article in the Washington Post. He didn't know what to do. He wanted to call Ida but wondered if it was appropriate. He decided it would be better to wait until she called him and asked for a meeting.

Leonard Silver, president of Coldbolt Records, one of the big five record conglomerates in America, was at his desk in his plush office. Among the paintings and gold records on the wall, was a giant tank, twelve feet long loaded with big fish eating little fish, and above, a giant head of an endangered Rhinoceros from Mr. Silver's game park safaris. In a soft red-leather couch, under the rhinoceros and the fish tank, was the head promotion director of the Coldbolt music division, a scrawny guy with a bit of fuzz on his chin. He was holding a blow-up of the Robert Zayes article in the Washington Post, so Lee couldn't see his face.

Lee sipped a bourbon, then stared at the rhinoceros. "I love that horn."

He continued. "What's going on? Look at that chart, Tomlin. Unbelievable. Thirteen of those top 36 songs are on independent record labels. And the other twenty-three are songs none of the major record companies are pushing. We got only two songs on that list. How did they get those ratings?"

Tomlin turned from watching a giant fish scare a little fish, laid down the paper, eyed Lee, and said, "They gave Radiotron 120,000 dollars, I'm sure that helped."

Lee asked, "Who's working with these stations?"

Tomlin said, "Sonny Tom, but since the Radio Revolution came on, they aren't cooperative, don't even ask for promos anymore. I let it go. They are in Hawaii, in medium and small markets, but now I can see I should have paid more attention. Incredible. In four months, they turned the populace on. But they are off the air now."

Lee said, "There are two possibilities. One, they might get back on the air. But if they stay off the air, some other radio station will get their greedy eyes on this story and try to do the same thing."

"I don't think they'll try," said Tomlin. "We're tight with Radiotron and radio stations know it, big time."

"What about the Allison Rating service?" Lee asked.

"We've been putting the squeeze on them. I think they're ready to be bought out by Radiotron."

Lee inhaled the aroma and took another sip. "I shouldn't ask this, but how are we tight with Radiotron?"

Tomlin looked around, and hesitated. "Hush, hush this. I never said this. I'll swear on a stack of Bibles, if confronted."

He paused, swallowed, looked again at the fish tank, smiled, as a big fish was chewing on a small fish. The little fish was still squirming.

Lee, bending toward Tomlin, had his full attention. Tomlin turning his head back to Lee said, "Radiotron gets the bulk of their monies from the radio stations they survey. We can't mess with that. Too obvious, too dangerous, but they do get smaller monies from ad agencies."

Tomlin smiles. "Every quarter ad agencies pay two thousand dollars for Radiotron's service. And Radiotron knows we coop those fees with the ad agencies. We give these add agencies a thousand dollars per quarter and pass it on through middle men, the independent promoters. The ad agencies, of course, then have to follow Radiotron ratings to the letter or we stop helping them with their subscription cost. Kind of tricky," Tomlin smiled. "That's why the Allison Rating Service is suffering now. We're making Radiotron the big cheese."

Tomlin continued. "Devious way to stay undercover, even though we never talk to Radiotron about their ratings. It's magic. It's underground intimidation without really intimidating. And even if the money we give to indie promoters for ad agencies gets observed, we always can say we are advertising our artists. In fact, ad agencies give the independent promoters actual invoices for advertising that never gets placed, to cover the money we give for their Radiotron subscription cost. It would be extremely hard for anybody to trace these funds, and if they do, they would only be for advertising our artists. So no payola problems either. It's beautiful."

Lee smiled. "The things I don't know."

Tomlin smiled and continued, "Ad agencies are 90% of radio's revenue. After that article in the Washington Post I just suggested to the independent promoters to call Radiotron and have Radiotron take them off the survey because they are closed. I just got word back that Radiotron put a new clause in their bylaws. If a station is not on the air after the survey is completed, or they suddenly change their format at the close of the survey, the new bylaws demand they are eliminated from the survey just like the non-commercial stations."

Lee gulped, the whiskey burning down his throat. "And Radiotron will drop them, even if they lose 120,000 dollars?"

Tomlin smiled. "Radiotron already got the 120,000 dollars. It will just demand those funds for the stations that rise to the top of their new ratings. That's the way they work. You get high ratings, you need to pay big bucks or your ratings will go down in the next book. The

Radio Revolution, if they do get back on the air, will be hurting for sure."

Lee smiled. "I can't believe they got away with it. We let things loose for four months, and this. Stay on it Tomlin. This and the internet downloading. The world is getting crazy."

※

The BBC organization, reading the Robert Zayes article, did send reporters and photographers to Hawaii to interview Danny Fall.

※

The Rollingstone Magazine's readership poll voted the Radio Revolution in Honolulu, Hawaii in the top 3 nationally in Medium markets, and the Maui Station number 4 in small markets. And noted they got that rating from readers of Rollingstone Magazine while only being on the air three months.

※

Three M in Australia, a chain of radio stations in Brisbane, Perth, Sydney and Melbourne came to Honolulu looking for a way to up their popularity and grab the name "The Radio Revolution."

※

The editor of the Washington Post advised Robert Zayes not to mention the legal problems of Piper Zweigolf in his article. It could affect the proceedings and if it was something they couldn't verify it could possibly make them liable.

Being accused of two counts of second degree assault, one count of attempted assault, and with two people in the hospital, one in the ICU, Piper was facing court action and a possible jail sentence. At

THE RADIO REVOLUTION

the encouragement of his criminal lawyer, a Mr. Thompson, Piper elected to have a jury trial.

His lawyer warned him to be sure to hold his temper at the trial, not make any faces or jests or anything that would indicate he had a temper. Just sit, calmly, no matter what. Mr. Thompson gave Piper earplugs.

To the Judge, Mr. Thompson argued, "A fair trial cannot be held in Hawaii because of the publicity of this case. This is an incredible publicity issue. Some listeners heard the conflict over radio, and the media replayed it on the news. We request a neutral site. Radio is always pretending, yet a lot of Hawaii is sympathetic to the Radio Revolution and possibly took this playacting on radio serious."

Judge Kanahele said, "Well, if you think that, recommend your client waive a jury trial. Or do you think a Judge, like myself, can't be impartial?"

Piper's lawyer said, "We could at least bring jurors from out of state."

Judge Kanahele stared with an incredulous look. "Yeah, we can do a lot of things. We could hold court on Rabbit Island if you want. But I don't think seagulls will be considered by the court as a community of peers."

The judge bends his head over the podium. "Mr. Zweigolf is to be tried by his community of peers. Hawaii's laws don't allow extradition to another state and I am sure they could make a case for not transporting jurors from other states."

The Judge intensifies his stare. "Surely you can find twelve unbiased jurors amongst 800,000 people on this island. Go to another island and you will have the same situation. It stays in Honolulu, judged by Mr. Zweigolf's community of peers."

Mr. Thompson was insistent. "Bring jurors from out of state or I will demand a mistrial before it even starts. Piper Zweigolf is from Georgia; his peers are from there."

"Mr. Thompson, you are out of order. You can't demand anything, Mr. Thompson. You are at the mercy of the court. If you appeal I'm sure another Judge will understand the word 'community of peers.' The defendant is entitled to a jury trial of the community of his peers. Unless you can argue successfully with the appeal court that you think the people of Hawaii are too primitive or retarded to qualify as peers to Mr. Zweigolf? Do you think you can do that, Mr. Thompson? Do you think the people of Hawaii are mentally equal to pidgeons?"

"No sir, I wouldn't suggest that."

"Then Monday the selection of jurors begins."

Danny, Becky, witnesses at the Likelike Drive-in, and the two policemen who witnessed the double assault on Becky were called to the stand to testify. Doctors were called to testify regarding the injuries, and the hospital bills for both defendants were submitted.

Mr. Thompson brought Piper's two lawyers to explain that Danny had actually threatened his life, but the jurors did not have a problem with Danny's assault charge; it was verbal, even if it existed, and non-violent. Piper was not being threatened with bodily harm at the moment he threw the saucer. And later Piper tried to rush Danny. And all the jurors agreed Becky being grabbed, kicked in the groin, and Piper's attempt to kick her in the face when she was on her knees qualified as second degree assault charges.

The ear plugs apparently didn't work. Seven days later, after several Piper Zweigolf's temper tantrums in the court room, including a futile attack on the Judge and disparaging language to the jurors, the Judge sentenced Piper Zweigolf to two years in prison with no parole and asked the bail monies be withheld until personal damage suits of Danny and Becky had been settled.

Mr. Thompson tried to appeal. But in the meantime, Piper went to Jail.

When Ida reported the verdict to the FCC, the FCC demanded the closing or sale of nine of Piper's radio stations that were immediately

THE RADIO REVOLUTION

up for renewal. His lawyers suggested he sell all his radio stations in a package deal to avoid upcoming renewal problems.

※

Fledge got hired by 3M stations in Australia to conduct the Radio Revolution. He explained he was specialist at this.

※

Piper's purchase of his accounting/management firm was on the rocks when the wealth of his radio stations were in immediate danger. His radio stations were going into chaos as the accounting/management firm syphoned off large amounts of funds do to the dilemma. Personnel of his radio stations were fleeing to other radio stations. Piper was struggling to sell his eighty stations that were fast becoming vacant. Even his two lawyers bailed out when they saw the handwriting on the wall. They hadn't been paid since they got on the plane. All three lawyers, of course, sued Piper for their "rightful" pay, immediately.

Piper, a loud mouth ha'ole, did not do well in jail. Inmates were able to discourage his mouth, and guards weren't sure he was safe, anywhere. The prisoner they partnered with him was an eighty-old-black gentlemen named Sasafrass, in for life on a 1924 drug charge where seven people died within a gunfight while he was the guy watching the door at age 14. Sasafrass didn't listen or talk to the six-five-foot Piper, despite Piper's constant verbiage. Instead he asked for library duty and KP duty and stumbled into bed long after Piper was asleep.

※

On the ninth day of being off the air, Ida informed Jackson it was imperative to let the FCC know the reason the station was not operating and to mention it was lacking direction from its owner and no one was getting paid.

On the thirtieth day off air Ida asked for an extension of three months before resuming and had Danny pay the electrical bill for the solo radio towers, so they would not be a threat to low flying aircraft.

On the fortieth day Jackson went to the prison, explained the situation to Piper, including the fact he was being ripped off by his accounting firm, and let him know that if he wanted any money he'd better let The Radio Revolution back on the air. It was a bad day for Piper, who had just got word his appeal was denied. Piper agreed to a two year lease to run the radio revolution with Jackson as its General Manager. The lease gave Piper 50,000 a month and put the expense of the rents, electricity, payroll and maintenance on the Radio Revolution. In lieu of this. Danny released any suit for damages and Becky was promised 2,000 monthly for two years, which would be taken out of Piper's 50,000. This released the million-dollar bond, the money which Piper would have had to come up with after ninety days.

Piper agreed. It seemed the only alternative in the situation.

Jackson talked to Ida. He mentioned he could line up backers to buy Piper's company and then set up the format in Piper's other 23 markets.

Ida said, "Never. Danny wants Piper totally out of the picture. Let the signals go to waste. By law no one can take over for a year, anyway. And as renewals come up the stations will go silent. A year silent and Piper loses the signals. And Piper will be fined and fined."

Jackson asked, "Can't he sell them?"

"No. Not with my complaint and his lack of satisfactory response to his ability to maintain the stations. He is not on the premises. The FCC will not allow the sale. As far as they are concerned, the Radio Act of 1934 demands owners to have hands on all their radio stations or they don't really own them. I will put a hold on any sale until he can go to the hearing which he can't, while in jail. Then there will be a mandatory wait of one year, before such silent radio signals can be put on the market for sale by the FCC. And Piper will get nothing. I don't want those signals available to anybody right now, anyway. If they were we would have to bid over people who want us off the air at all cost."

"He could lease his radio stations?"

"Only crazy people like us lease," Ida laughed. "Finance backing demands owning. And even if he did lease, he would still need an employee at the station as a hands on owner. Piper is paying you 8,000 a month to be hands on, Jackson. So he's really only getting 38,000 a month. Remember, Becky is getting two thousand dollars a month."

"So why did Danny agree to give him so much money?"

"Because all the money we're giving him is just bait. Granted, I don't see how Danny can pay Piper 50,000 dollars a month and all the other expenses of the station, but that's Danny. When Piper is faced with paying the electric bills of his towers that are not coopted with other radio stations, or fulfilling the lease of those towers being fined by the FCC for not keeping them lighted, all the money he's getting will disappear. And all the suits will come in from the landlords, lawyers, tower owners and his tax liabilities. By the time he gets out of jail he'll have nothing and be forced into Chapter 7."

Jackson says, "So he'll be penniless, and after one year of his radio stations being silent, he'll lose his signals."

Ida smiled. "No, he'll be in debt up to his eyeballs with scores of settlement demands for leases of property he was paying rent on, and wages and federal withholding tax not paid by his accounting firm. That firm, in this chaos, will find a way to bankrupt him and put all his liabilities in his camp. They'll extract huge funds for interest and non-payment from his revenues of the other radio stations until there is nothing left. All he'll have left is the four stations in Hawaii. And he'll be personally liable for wages, withholding taxes of his other radio stations, and the federal government will eject the funds he has in the bank and put a lien on his Hawaii stations so big he won't be able to sell them."

Jackson shook his head. "Danny really does want to evaporate him from this planet."

Ida nodded. "Danny says, 'It is necessary for the morale of the family.'"

Jackson shook his head. "But if he could take over Piper's stations, he could continue his agenda to change America."

"Sorry, Jackson. Putting Piper away is more important to Danny and the family."

Jackson shakes his head. "Sounds like the mafia. Everybody thinks Danny is loveable, friendly, nice boy. Boy, what they don't know."

Ida says, "There is a thin line between love and hate." She smiles.

At four o' clock on July 4th, 1990, on 12th Avenue SW in Washington DC, between Maryland and Maine avenues, in front of the FCC building, a block party with fourteen restaurant booths, three ice cream stands, two hot dog stands, two water trucks furnished by the Radio Revolution, giant tents stretching two long blocks, forty speakers on ten foot stands, fourteen giant fans, and a high rise stage coalesced in front of the FCC building. The cost of the set-up was over twenty-grand.

Six thousand people, eighty policemen, more people coming, and more cops probably coming as the crowd amasses. Eighty percent are black and wanting to see NWA perform including the song "Fuck the Police." Tension is mounting in the sweltering heat.

I get on stage. I shout, "The water trucks are free to everybody including the police, paid for by the Radio Revolution. Each truck has 20 faucets."

The murmurs of the crowd continue. Some yell, where's the beer.

I have to get their attention. I yell, "What does the word Fuck mean?"

The crowd starts yelling, "Fuck!" Some say, "Fuck means fuck."

THE RADIO REVOLUTION

I shout, "It has another meaning. Try. Go up to the President of the United States and say 'Fuck you.' What will happen? You'll end up in jail. Why? Because the President represents the establishment and 'fuck' is an antiestablishment word!

"Fuck is not blasphemous!

"Fuck is not crude.

"Fuck is a razor sharp statement" I shout it. "I don't want any unnecessary controls over my life."

The crowd shouts. "Fuck!"

"Today is a momentous day that will probably be in the history books in the years to come. We are bringing a real democracy to America. It is The Radio Revolution, the radio station that allows the listeners to program the music played. The bands you hear today were voted by the people of Hawaii on to radio. Most of the bands you hear today are not on any other radio station in America.

"Their songs are loaded with 'fucks.' Why? Because we, the people of America, have been suppressed by the establishment. 'Crushed' is a better word."

Cheers from the audience.

I go on. "I didn't know how much we had been crushed, until we turned over the music programming to the people. So the word 'fuck' today is an expression of America's frustration over the state of affairs controlled by the establishment."

More cheers. Some shout it, "Fuck!"

I shout, "You want to be here today?"

Screams from the crowd. "Yeah." And "Fuck yes."

"Well, the police don't want to be here. They are here because that is their job. They don't want to stand in their hot black uniforms and turn into statues while people jeer at them as their families are at home barbequing. So let's allow them to have an enjoyable time. Buy them a coke. If you can, try to dance with them. But no moshing with the police, alright?"

Some laughter.

209

"Try to allow the police to be a part of this monumental, historic event. It's a holiday. The birth of a new America. I've passed out food vouchers so the police can eat and drink free, courtesy of the Radio Revolution. If the line is long, allow an officer in front of you, today. Make it a day of peace, for we all are in the same oppression, police and attendees alike, yet looking at our oppression through different eyes.

"Maybe I need to repeat that. We are all being suppressed, police and us, alike. Our only difference, we are looking at it through different eyes."

There was silence.

"Are you crazy, motherfucker?" A boy in the audience calls out.

I shout, "Hey, if your boss called you and said you had to work July 4th and sit in the hot sun and listen to a bunch of people call you names, would you like it? There is a lot of anger and resentment here, we know that!"

"Yeah, if I could get a job, yeah, a job that means something," the boy screamed

The crowd cheers.

I let the voices continue. The voices rise in volume. Noise increases. Incoherent words. Voices, all talking at once. I shout loudly, "My apology. I didn't know. And in our Capitol." I shout "Fuck!"

"Fuck yes," screamed a multitude of voices."

More voices shout, "Yes, Fuck Yes, Hell Yes."

"How would you know? You're white!" Came a voice on a megaphone.

Mandy had rushed into the crowd looking for the man who burst out "Are you crazy, motherfucker."

Gregory steps to the mic. "If you see someone start to lose it, help the police by holding them back. The police are in the same position we are. They are dealing with this suppressed society like we are. And they too have frustrations that if aggravated today could ruin this concert. So I ask the police, too, if one of you begins to lose it, have the others corral and try to calm him down."

I went back on the mic. "But to display anger now, at a time when we are on the verge of changing America, oh my God, what a waste.

THE RADIO REVOLUTION

It could destroy our chances. We were all given a democracy by our forefathers. Why......don't....we..... use it!"

I raised my hand in a fist. I was expecting cheers. Wrong. There was silence. *Of course, most of this crowd doesn't know me.*

I continue. "The Radio Revolution will show you how to do it. And step one is having a democratic radio station where the listeners choose the music. So let us lift your spirits today with the music and begin showing you the way to change America. I repeat: we were all given a democracy; why aren't we using it?

"Did anybody hear me. We were all given a democracy. Why not use it?"

A voice shouts, "How? How do you change fuckin' America?" More people start screaming, "How?" Some start laughing.

I don't want to go there. I don't want to alert the powers to be, right now. *But what can I do?*

I say it. "How? How? Our forefathers left a way to change America. The constitution allows it. An amendment. It's in the fifth article of the Constitution. We initiate a constitutional convention in every state. We don't go to congress, we don't go to state legislatures at first, we go to the people. We look for activists, people who have the time. They call for a constitutional convention in every state. A constitutional convention for one single amendment. There we elect candidates for every position in the state's legislature. We call it the Peoples party's candidates. Get these candidates elected to legislature. Use radio to generate support for them, then have the states petition Congress for a constitutional convention for simply this amendment. When it is ratified it will turn America upside down. The politicians will no longer listen to conglomerates, big business and special interest groups, because if they want to get reelected they will have to listen to the people. The amendment? To take money out of the political system. The amendment is this. Only the government can pay for election campaigns, not the wealthy, not big business. We were all given a democracy; why not use it,' that is what I mean. We can change America with an amendment to the constitution that takes money out of the political system. The people can do it. We simply need to vote it in. I pause. Silence. I repeat. "We can change America with an amendment to the constitution," I start shouting. "THAT TAKES THE MONEY OUT OF THE POLITICAL SYSTEM."

There is still silence in the audience.

I continue, "What is the amendment? It evaporates money from the political system."

I pause. I have to let them respond.

There is silence. Still no boos. Or yeahs.

Later Gregory said, "They were in shock, Danny. That's why they didn't respond."

Gregory jumps back on the mic. "So with no money to fuck up the voting process, the people running are doing it to serve the people, and if they want to get reelected they better pay attention to what the people want, not what the big corporations want. There will be no more need for parties; parties are used to fund campaigns, big business lobbies will become futile, and those running will begin to put curbs on big business, break it down into smaller units, and make it pay its fair share of the taxes. And free enterprise will once again flourish, and runaway capitalism which has led to insensitive conglomerations with companies that want to control the market, not produce value in the market, will be halted. Value in the market place will increase, and the economy will bloom. And you, sir, will have a job that means something to you. A simple amendment all the country can get behind. And we have turned America upside down. Gregory takes his hands, raises them high, then puts them down on the ground. "Upside down. No longer will money rule. The people will rule. We were all given a democracy, why not use it!"

More silence. *Why aren't they responding.*

Gregory repeats it. "That's what Danny means when he says, 'We were all given a democracy, why…..not…. use….. it!'"

Gregory repeats it, "We were all given a democracy, why not use it!" He puts a hand behind his left ear. "I can't hear it." His right hand was on my shoulder. He shouts. "No longer will money rule. We, the people, will rule!"

There were mumblings, some say it.

Gregory shouts, "We were all given a democracy, why don't we use it!"

The crowd in unison, at last, says it. Gregory prompts them to say it again, and again.

Gregory says, "So remember, Fuck is not a crude word, nor is it blasphemous. It is a word to vent the frustrations of our suppression. May I now introduce you to Rage Against the Machine, a band from Los Angeles, California, voted as one of the most popular bands on the Radio revolution in Hawaii. Let expression flow. Let the people rule!"

The crowd cheers.

The band members of Rage Against the Machine raise their fists, and thrust it forth, shouting, "FUCK!" They thrash out a chord. "Fuck." Thrash again. "Fuck." Thrash again. "Fuck." The concert begins. The crowd goes wild.

The lead singer sings:

> *Yeah!*
> *Yeah, back in this...*
> *Wit' poetry, my mind I flex*
> *Flip like Wilson, vocals never lackin' dat finesse*
> *Whadda I got to, whadda I got to do to wake ya up*
> *To shake0 ya up, to break the structure up*
> *'Cause blood still flows in the gutter*
> *I'm like takin' photos*
> *Mad boy kicks open the shutter*
> *Set the groove*
> *Then stick and move like I was Cassius*
> *Rep the stutter step*
> *Then bomb a left upon the fascists*
> *Yea, the several federal men*

Who pulled schemes on the dream
And put it to an end
Ya better beware
Of retribution with mind war
20/20 visions and murals with metaphors
Networks at work, keepin' people calm
Ya know they murdered X
And tried to blame it on Islam
He turned the power to the have-nots
And then came the shot

Uggh!
What was the price on his head?
What was the price on his head!

I think I heard a shot
I think I heard a shot
I think I heard a shot
I think I heard a shot
I think I heard a shot
I think I heard, I think I heard a shot

'He may be a real contender for this position should he abandon his supposed obedience to white liberal doctrine of non-violence…and embrace black nationalism'
'Through counter-intelligence it should be possible to pinpoint potential trouble-makers…And neutralize them, neutralize them, neutralize them'

Wake up! Wake up! Wake up! Wake up!
Wake up! Wake up! Wake up! Wake up!

How long? Not long, cause what you reap is what you sow!"

THE RADIO REVOLUTION

Bradley plowed through the crowd to the Captain of the police. "This so important. Do what you can to control your officers' anger. We're really trying to bring everybody together. And Danny will lead the people that direction today. Help him. He's a force, but he needs help."

The officer said, "What is going on here? We were told it was 'a small demonstration' in front of the FCC. We don't have enough officers for this."

Bradley said, "You have plenty, and if all goes well, you all can join the party."

The officer said, "They're still coming. Look at that - the count might reach ten thousand."

Bradley answered, "When NWA comes tonight, the crowd might be double. If you think you need more, wait. Don't overreact. We've got two free water trucks, fourteen restaurants serving food, forty speakers in a two block radius so everybody can hear the concert even if they can't see it, and Danny as an emcee. You are in secure ground. And no booze, unless they bring it. But if they do bring it, let it go. It is simply a party, granted, with an agenda, but an agenda that only wants to respect the police and wake America to a real democracy."

Mandy brings the guy voicing dissent to the captain. "Sir, this is Russel. He wants to make an apology."

Russel hesitates. Mandy holds his hand. He stutters, "Sir, Sir, Sir, I'm sorry for my outburst. I really am. Today is not the day to aggravate the rift we have with the police department, or to grieve over our loses."

Mandy hugs the outspoken one. She is crying. She turns to the captain. "I can't believe this is happening. Danny is right. We are all suppressed, yet looking through different eyes."

The captain looks at Mandy. "My name is Captain Boyle. That man on stage might be right. This concert might make it to the history books. I'll tell my crew. We'll try to be supportive."

Robert Zayes was present. He listened to the amazing speech. *So this is so Ida. This is political to the max, A new America, my God.*

Ida had a date, George Hanson, head of the committee of the FCC. "Well George, you've got a thousand employees, and half are here tonight, most likely to support the 1934 radio act where the people have a say in radio programming before Nixon eliminated the preamble to this radio act for the people in 1969 after the Woodstock Concert. Can you imagine somebody eliminating the Declaration of Independence? The preamble of the 1934 Radio act is similar. Still, the law suggests radio is to serve the public; an imperative. And now you have a man who wants to use radio the way it was meant to be. What are you going to do?"

George smiles, "If I knew how to dance to this stuff, I'd ask you to dance."

"I'm a bit out of shape to mosh," Ida laughs. Her eyes sparkle with mirth.

George grins.

21

THE RADIOTRON CONSPIRACY

Washington Post July 6, 1990. Again on the front page
BENEFIT CONCERT AT FCC FOR THE RADIO REVOLUTION
By Robert Zayes

This last July 4th the Radio Revolution of Hawaii had a benefit concert right on the steps of the FCC in Washington DC.

The Radio Revolution, a listener programmed music format of five radio stations, was shut down by the owner of the stations May 27th. An estimated nine to twenty thousand at any given time showed up for the demonstration-turned-concert. The concert lasted six hours and included a host of bands that had become popular on the Radio Revolution in Hawaii. Most of these bands are not even on the top 100 on Billboard Magazine and most receive no airplay except in Hawaii on the Radio Revolution format.

It was like a wild block party, with scores of restaurants represented, along with rows of speakers over two long blocks. The emcee, Danny Fall, the originator of the radio format, shouted out a political agenda including, "We were all given a democracy; why not use it." The crowd cheered, the majority of who were residents of Washington DC.

Rage Against The Machine, yes, that is the name of the band, the name coming from a 'zine in Los Angeles, opened the concert to a wild frantic audience moshing (slam dancing). The show's closing act was NWA, which band currently has a multi-million selling album that gets no radio play anywhere else in the country but on The Radio Revolution.

Danny Fall said the concert was recorded and is going to be released on his own label called "A New America" within the next month. Despite the station still being off the air, there were screams for A New America from Danny Fall and Gregory Stephan. Danny Fall was advocating on stage to use the Article V of the constitution of the United States in an unorthodox way. He called for constitutional conventions in all the states to be held for a single amendment to the constitution. This amendment would promote representatives to be elected to state assemblies and state senates for one purpose: to petition the US Congress to have a states constitutional convention. This amendment would take money out of the political campaigns by allowing only the government to pay for campaigns.

Gregory Stephan of the Radio Revolution screamed on stage: "Do you want big business running the government and those who can throw around the most money? Or do you want the people finally getting what they need. We were all given a democracy; why not use it. Let's evaporate money out of the political system. And let the people finally run the government. We'll make this amendment to the constitution. And America will sing. The peoples' voices will at last be heard."

To Gregory's rant the crowd cheered.

Danny Fall offered the police free food and drink and even suggested the attendees to treat the police to a coke. Jarring between the police and the attendees was, surprisingly, kept to a minimum, despite the last song played was called 'Fuck the Police.'

The bands left their grievances regarding the station in Hawaii being shut down on the door steps of the FCC. This only adds to thousands of letters now piling up in the FCC, plus petitions from the populace of Hawaii that have reached 60,000 signatures, a full 5% of the total population of the state, now verified by the Secretary of the State of Hawaii.

No response yet from the FCC, though the committee chairman of the FCC, George Hanson, and hundreds of FCC employees were attendees to the benefit demonstration.

Piper Zweigolf, the owner of four of the five stations that was airing the Radio Revolution format, and the man who took it off the air, has just been incarcerated in Honolulu Hawaii, being convicted of two counts of second degree assault and one account of attempted assault.

Danny Fall believes that now it is just a matter of time before the Radio Revolution returns to the airways.

Jackson calls me to his home. "Shit's happening, we got to talk."

When I arrive I expect the talk at the door or on the porch, but Jackson ushers me through his house to his exercise room with a walking machine attached to a movie screen and a small children's desk in the corner. The wallpaper is filled with balloons, flying angels, and in the middle of the room is a four-sided pyramid staircase leading to a pile of toys and above on the ceiling there are pretty pink clouds in the shape of goats, dogs, unicorns, cats and a Mickey Mouse design.

This is the first time I've been beyond the porch of Jackson's house. It looks like a rainbow colored nursery.

"This is your kid's nursery, when they were younger?"

Jackson, exasperated, shakes his head. "No, it's my wife's idea to calm my blood pressure. Jessa thinks it will actually lower my blood pressure and it is laid out in some Feng Shui pattern crap. If you ever mention this to a soul, you're dead. She told me to bring you here, today, to 'lower' my blood pressure. I used to have a desk over there, now it's a little desk for a child. Jessa says it'll bring me back to my happy childhood, which shit, if I could only remember it being happy. Maybe the ice cream truck? Take a seat."

Jackson's massive weight makes the little chair squeak, then rumble like it is going to shatter. It is supported by a thick cushion. I aim my ass into a tiny seat, too, without a cushion. Plop, I look to the ceiling filled with pretty little pink and blue angels. My knees are just as high as my shoulders.

I look across the table to Jackson who looks like a Humpty Dumpty with a scowl on his face. "Something is up, Danny. Radiotron has dropped you from the rating service."

"What, you didn't give them the money?"

"Damn Danny, don't insult me. You know I'm honorable."

"I'm sorry. I know that of you, at least."

"They claim it's because you're off the air. But that's bullshit. You get a dip in the ratings being off the radio five days on their survey, but dropping you entirely from their survey means somebody superseded our 120,000 dollar donation to those bastards."

"Who?"

"I'm not a fuckin' detective. Who knows. But somebody for sure."

"Well, we still got the Allison Ratings."

"I checked. They're negotiating to be bought out by Radiotron, but Radiotron is holding back until Allison goes to their knees."

"What does that mean?"

"It means our 120,000 dollars is not enough to please Radiotron. Now, with Allison almost out of the picture, Radiotron controls ninety billion dollars of revenues from radio stations across America. And they don't want you to have any of it. That's what it means. Ad agencies are welded to Radiotron now. In the last year they don't even look at Allison's ratings. Most quit subscribing. If you are not on Radiotron in the top 5 in any demographic category, then you don't get a dime from the ad agencies."

I shake with anger. "They know we are incredibly effective. They know!"

"If you're not in their system, you could have every listener on Earth and they won't give your radio station a cent. Danny, you're an idiot. You gave Piper fifty grand a month, plus took on all the expenses of the stations, even his back payables, and now you are going to be completely shut off from the advertising agencies. And what did that 'benefit' concert cost you?"

THE RADIO REVOLUTION

"I don't care how much it cost; it was essential to the hope of America."

Jackson just shook his head. "Well it looks to me like your hope for America just had its last hurrah."

"Shit, I only need a 120,000 dollars a month to cover expenses? Maybe 110,000 dollars if I dump all the sales representatives servicing the ad agencies. I still got the beer companies, the concerts, the small independent stores, Dance Floor Democracy. That's between sixty and eighty grand a month."

Jackson sighs in disgust. "I don't know Danny, I could get backers, but what backer is going to invest in a company losing fifty thousand dollars a month with no hope in sight?"

"Don't worry, Jackson - this radio format is on a runaway train now, it can't be stopped by anything."

"Running away money, maybe."

"You know me, Jackson. I'll find a way."

"Well, time is ticking. If you are going back on the air next Saturday, how are you gonna last, even three months? How much money do you have now?"

"Maybe about three hundred and fifty thousand counting receivables. See that staircase to toy heaven over there?" Danny points to the four staircases reaching almost to the ceiling. "Look at all the routes to toy heaven. There are a lot of ways and we'll find one."

Jackson says, "That's a staircase to the clouds. You're in the clouds, Danny. You always come up with the stupidest shit. It's making me stupid, too."

Jackson looks at the ceiling, then eyes the toys on top of the pyramid staircase, then the ceiling above the toys.

Jackson settles his eyes on Danny. "Jessa told me to do this. I want to puke. Jessa actually likes you, and what you are doing. She told me to give you my salary I'm getting from Piper for the next three months if, I repeat if, if, you can come up with a plan I can approve, to keep the Radio Revolution afloat for the next two years."

"Jackson, we must be in an alternate universe, let's have more meetings in this happy land. thank you."

"Damn you, Danny, I'm just trying to keep a happy marriage." Jackson shakes his head. "You're constantly sticking your head in one hornets nest after another. This Article V stuff, if you start pushin' it, you'll be ejected off Earth into an undisclosed trajectory toward outer space. There is no place for even a grave on Earth for that shit."

I say, "We'll figure something out. I'll talk to you Friday night with the plan. Jackson, you helping us like this, we so appreciate. The kids are gonna be in a shock when I tell them, and that will boost their morale. Jackson, this is wonderful. Tell Jessa thank you, too. Mandy says you're gonna be famous. I now see why."

"I don't need an eulogy, Danny."

I see Jessa standing at the door, smiling. I walk to her and say, "You married a great radio man. And thanks for the help."

"Danny, Jackson loves you, he talks about you all the time, like you are a radio God. I'm glad he is finally full on with this Radio Revolution stuff."

Jackson is behind me.

"Damn Danny, I can't believe I'm in this situation. Friday night, and it better make sense."

※

I call a family meeting. We meet in the living room of our home. We are still pumped from the concert and Gregory's great ploy for us to go national. It is a praise party for Gregory, basically. They don't know about the bomb I'm gonna drop at the party. Everybody is happy, and we are a few days from going back on the air.

We're all sipping expensive wines except Gregory. I told Gregory, "Remember when I told you I was looking for your help, and you said to me, 'You're crazy. You're the one with all the answers,' you said that to me. Remember?"

Gregory smiles.

I toss him the newspapers from New York, Chicago, San Francisco and New Orleans with the stories underlined. "We got fantastic national coverage of the concert, pretty much every big city covered it on the UPI and AP. Your idea to have the concert at the FCC in Washington DC was brilliant. Then you implemented the concert flawlessly and finally you helped me keep the crowd with us. That's the biggest help I've ever had, maybe in my life."

Gregory says, "Well maybe you and Mandy are in the same league with this fortune stuff. I'm sure not. But just for the record I was scared shitless."

We all smile. "Me too," I say, and raise a toast. "Everybody, a toast to Gregory." We clink glasses. Gregory clinks an empty glass."

Bradley lit some weed, takes a hit, and passes it to Gregory. "Take three; it's your party, man."

I let the happiness permeate.

Mandy is talking about the worldwide interest in the Radio Revolution and her BBC interview last night. She says, "The whole world is now conscious of a possible amendment to the constitution. They're actually reading the US constitution."

Then ten minutes later I break the news. "I've just been talking to Jackson. We've got a problem: Radiotron took us off the survey because we were off the air. Bullshit, but that's the reason they gave. We were only off the air five days in their survey. We still would have been number one. Jackson says when Radiotron takes you off the survey, the ad agencies will not spend a cent on our radio station. It doesn't make sense but that is the way it is. We were getting 80 to 100 grand every month from the ad agencies. Not anymore."

Bradley said, "Not quite. Most are so slow paying. It takes 90 to 120 days to get our monies. There is about 260,000 out there now, and our sales reps don't like trying to collect it. They're busy selling more advertising to the agencies instead of collecting the old balances. We really need to do something about that. And those receivables go to Piper's company. And we get only 12% of that.

"Well, we don't have to worry about that anymore. I'm gonna drop most of the sales staff. And no more 12% on the ad agencies. I signed a two-year lease with Piper, paying him 50,000 a month, and we get all the outstanding receivables."

Juan says, "That bastard is getting fifty thousand a month?"

I smile. "It was bait. He'll never see the money. But I didn't expect this Radiotron disaster. The monies go into his bank account, and in jail, he won't see it. Yep, he's in jail, his empire is collapsing, and when his signals are silent for a year, he will lose those too. By the time he gets out of jail he'll be bankrupt, owing millions to landlords, FCC fines, electricity for seventy-six stations and payroll taxes. He'll have an IRS lien on our stations too, so high, he'll never be able to sell them. Ida has blocked his ability to sell any of his stations. He's finished, but he doesn't know it, and that's why he took the bait, because his accounting/management firm is raping his shrinking revenues into nothing."

Bradley says, "I can't believe you gave Piper that, Danny."

Juan says, "I thought you were family."

Mandy stands up. "Come on guys, mistakes happen. Hell, how would he have leased the radio stations with a smaller deal?"

Gregory says, "Mandy's right. We didn't know the ad agencies would dump us, how could Danny have even guessed that as a long shot?"

Juan thinks about it for a second, puts up his hand and says, "Hey, one of us makes a mistake, we all make a mistake, but we are strong, we're family. We can overcome any mistake."

Mandy grabs Juan's hands and yanks him off the couch. She puts her head on his shoulder. "Thank you."

I say, "Juan, thanks man. The way I see it, we'll be short fifty grand a month. So we're short 50,000, and if we come up with a plan Jackson can accept, he'll forfeit his eight grand a month salary for three months. Piper is forced to have an employee on the premises, and Piper is paying Jackson eight thousand a month to manage the stations.

Bradley says, "What?"

"I know it is a shocker. But I think Jackson finally realizes big corporations are not the way to go, though he is far from being onboard with Article V of the Constitution. We can thank Piper for giving Jackson a wake-up call."

Gregory says, "Maybe he heard Wake Up Wake Up by the Rage Against the Machine. What about the CD and record, 'The Radio Revolution at the FCC.' That can bring a lot of revenue, can't it?"

I say, "It's a good advertising vehicle, but we have no national distribution, and if we give it to independent distributors across the mainland, likely we won't get paid soon enough to even cover our pressing cost, especially if it escalates in popularity. Our only choice for revenues is excessive advertising and doing it through mail order on the mainland. We could use interns to ship the orders. It could help. Not sure how much. In Hawaii alone though, it could make 100,000 dollars if we sell and get paid for 25,000 copies. And distribution is not a problem here. We can deliver it to the key music ballot locations. Would be another source of income, help some and we could sell it at the concerts. It would cover one or two months of our monthly deficit. But we need to cover two years."

Mandy says, "Wait, by the next book of Radiotron, they will have to put us back in the ratings, yeah? We just have to cover three months."

"Don't count on it. We gave Radiotron 120,000 dollars for the entire year. And suddenly they take us off the ratings after the first book. Jackson says it means somebody paid them more to get us off. And we are not going to have any money to give them anyway. And even if we did, I'm not sure it would help. We've been divorced from Radiotron. It's all out war now."

Mandy says, "What if we start our own agency? It doesn't even have to be connected to us publicly. We could guarantee results if we approve their advertising plan. If it doesn't work to their satisfaction, we'll do another equal exposure absolutely free. And part of the plan would be tie their name to our concerts and advertise on our radio stations. A lot of retailers and manufactures might jump over and give us a try. Especially if their current agency can't advertise on our radio stations."

"Remember," I say, "A small part of ad agency's business is radio, they spend a lot of their client's funds on TV and print ads."

Bradley says, "The computer design shops that calculate the ballots have great artists. Print not a problem. They'll do it free if they see the need. TV is the only problem."

Mandy says, "I know who to get. She was on the wild women's weekend. Toni is an independent TV production company. She does TV commercials for a slew of clients. We'll have to pay her, she's really busy, but she loves the station. She'll do it. And we can charge her fee to the advertiser.

I ask, "What do we call the ad agency?"

Juan says, "Fuckatron."

Laughter. Gregory says, "We'll call it the **BBRB** Agency. Breezing By Radiotron's Bullshit. We don't have to tell them what the initials stand for."

I say, "That can help, but that is not the cure. It'll take time for retailers to change their ad agencies, and there is sure to be a backlash attempt to stop us."

It went on for three hours. Bradley took out his pencil and began projecting the budget and the cost of establishing a new advertising agency. Finally, Bradley says, "You want a long shot way to make it? Get 380,000 dollars in funding, and if the record is a success nationally selling a half million copies and the independent distributors pay off within a year, we can retrieve 260,000 dollars in receivables, the ad agency can recoup 30,000 a month from the other ad agencies, and we get 10% interest rate, we got a chance to make it for two years. But will Jackson go for a long shot way? I'm assuming his gift of 22,000 dollar wages after withholding taxes is in this budget. And where do we get 380,000 dollars for a long shot idea?"

"We'll get it," I smile. "Draw it up as a business plan tomorrow and I'll get it."

THE RADIO REVOLUTION

Ida calls a meeting with funders for a Progressive America. She has a copy of Bradley's business plan, articles from across the nation of the Radio Revolution Concert, and a letter from Danny Fall describing the long term aim for a "New America" with a simple amendment to the constitution of the United States. She is asking for a 380,000 dollar loan for two years at ten percent interest.

Shockingly, the funders are excited with the news articles and the commotion on the streets, not only in Hawaii, but worldwide. They want to give more, and they want to start the amendment party and line up activists nationally to initiate the People's Party and constitutional conventions in every state.

Ida tells them, "No. Not yet. We need a far stronger presence on national radio, and Danny is in the process of setting that up before we even consider starting the People's Party. And it'll take a few years of legal work to get in a strong position to initiate a constitutional convention. This is a ten-year plan, she tells them. Just the loan for now. They agree, but insist on charging just 3% interest.

Ida calls Bradley. Bradley is shocked. "You got somebody to give us 380,000 dollars and at only 3% interest?" Bradley tells her where to wire the funds.

Ida doesn't mention where the money came from. She just tells Bradley payments are to be made to the Elizabeth Fowler Corporation at a post box number in Ontario, Canada.

It's the first clue, a New America has been impregnated. Exciting chills run up Ida's spine. *My God, they're excited. Danny might do it.*

Kentucky State congress is out in summer session. Ida calls her dad at home. "Dad, we gotta talk. I need your help."

22

IDA'S PLAN

Ida calls me. We are on the phone a few minutes giving each other praises, then Ida drops the bomb on me. "Keep bugging the advertising agencies for advertising. Send them proposals. Show up in person and tape the conversations. Ask them why the sudden change and the refusal to advertise with us. We gotta test the waters Danny, see how resolved they are to stay with Radiotron."

I tell her, "Jackson is convinced they won't budge. It's just a waste of time."

"Well that's hearsay. We need proof."

"Damn." I forgot I'm talking to a lawyer. I respond, jokingly. "What? We can sue the ad agencies for not advertising with us?"

Ida's tone is somber, "Danny, I don't want to prejudice you with the purpose of this. Just do it. Keep exact records of your confrontations with the ad agencies. Send me a weekly report. Go to the biggest ones first. Keep going back over and over again with new proposals. Just keep hounding them. Even look desperate, like the station will fall apart if you don't get them. And do it personally. Don't send anybody else. Every day set an appointment with a major ad agency. If they won't give you an appointment, record their refusal, and show up anyway.

"That's not all. Have your interns do your own telephone surveys. Like you are a rating service. And show the results to the ad agencies.

And even offer 2,000 dollars to these agencies, if they conduct the same survey, regardless of the results. Offer them that option."

"You think that will work," I question.

"You, yourself told me you're a scientist. Call it an experiment. Let's see if they break down and advertise with us."

"That's a lot of expense, and a lot of time."

"Danny, its important."

"You think we won't make it without them?"

"Trust me. And the expense is nominal. It's just a little extra work every day, visiting or interrupting an ad agency. Stick to the biggest ones, first. I'll tell you when to go after the small ones. And it is a little extra work for Bradley. He can be in charge of conducting the surveys."

"Ida, I don't know if you know how busy Bradley is. He does the books. He does the receivables for four stations. He does the traffic, which is a job in itself for the Honolulu station. He supervises the ballot collection and tabulations. The guy's insanely busy."

"Danny, Bradley is the only guy I can trust to do this right. You take part of his work load, or have somebody else do it. Just be sure he lays out the procedures exactly, encourages the interns to be honest, no fudging, and have him call random numbers, make the survey like the Allison's rating service does it, and of course break it down demographically by sex and age."

I ask, "What questions do you want the interns to ask?"

"Make it quick and simple. 'One, what is your preferred radio stations in order of preference? In other words, which ones would you turn on to listen to radio, tomorrow? And in order of preference. Two, which stations did you hear today whether you like them or not. Three, what is your age,' and write down sex or ask, if questionable. That's it."

I say, "I don't see how this will help."

"Mr. Scientist, I can't tell you how this will help because that will prejudice this little experiment. Have interns call three times a day, morning, mid-day, and evening. I know you won't get much of a response in the morning, but it needs to be balanced, the phone calling. And only call random numbers; don't use the phone book. Find out from the phone company how many phone numbers are in each prefix, so you can call a balance of prefixes. Have Bradley note the exact procedures you use. And list the phone calls who refuse to participate, and their reason if they give one. Once you've logged in 2000 responsive phone calls, have Bradley send me the raw data with his exact procedures he used. I'll have a political poll compile the results for an accurate sample. Then have Bradley start again with another survey. And when you get back the results with the political poll stamp on it, it will make it look very official, and political polls will show how they complied the results of the raw data, then you visit each ad agency personally, show the results, and try to get them to buy a flight with you. Or, at least, offer to give them two thousand dollars if they do the survey themselves. And tape record their response."

Ida is intense. I can feel it. I could imagine those spears in her eyes as she says this. "Okay, now I am a spy, secretly taping conversations. Call me secret agent 1027." The Honolulu Station is 102.7 on the dial. "How long?"

"Until I tell you to stop. Each week send me the tapes of your conversations, which agencies you approached, and how you approached them, and if you gave them a proposal, and the proposal itself. Everything, mail it to me weekly. Get a very efficient intern to put everything together each week. Give me the name, I'll stay in contact with her or him, okay?"

"What? Are we going to court or something?"

"Secrets, Mr. Scientist, but you'll never guess, even in your wildest imagination. And don't tell anybody I told you to do it. Let them think it is your wild eccentric idea. If they ask me, I'll tell them I don't know why in the hell you are doing it. Got it?"

"Man, I'm a spy, undercover."

"Danny, this isn't a joking matter, okay?"

"Like I and Bradley don't have enough to do with the station going back on the air?"

"Thanks, Danny."

Time to get a few beers. I haul my beer partner Bradley with me and we walk to the Pagoda bar.

I tell him about the survey. He shakes his head. "Easy to do. Two thousand dollars? If those agencies had any sense, what agency wouldn't do that! They got big offices, plenty of phones, they just need someone to work nights for a week and hire minimum wage workers. Could do it for eight hundred to twelve hundred dollars. Get it done in five to eight days." Bradley's money machine was ticking. Maybe ten days calling random numbers. "Two thousand responses! They'll make an extra thousand doing it. But they won't. You must know that, Danny."

I'm thinking the same thing. "Well then we won't be out two thousand dollars per ad agency. It has got to be done to the letter. And once we have the procedures down, I'll get a political poll service to okay the procedures. The only prejudice in this survey is who answers the phone? If a certain type of person is more prone to answer the phones it could distort the results, though I don't think that is a big problem providing we get a big enough sample in each age/sex bracket.

"Bradley asks, "When the interns call, do they talk to the whole family on the phone?"

"No. Only talk to who answers the phone. Put that in your procedures. Certainly, Radiotron's diary system is probably more prejudiced that way. In their system, who'd take the time to carry a diary with them and write down what radio stations they are listening to at each particular time? A lot of people will balk at that. And Radiotron insists giving it to the entire family without getting individual approval from each person in the family. That's the problem with their survey. They want such detailed information, like what you are listening to hour by hour, demographic by demographic, and they have to bribe 18-24s with money, to get a decent sample from that group, and they still don't get it with that diary system. They are asking for too much information from such a small sample. We are using a bigger sample, and just asking who did you listen to today and who are you likely to listen to tomorrow (your favorite stations), a bigger sample, with lesser information. It is far more accurate for a general overview of relative listenership in radio. Radiotron wants to count exactly how many people listen at exactly what time. Impossible with such an itty-bitty sample, even forgetting the diary problem."

Bradley smiles, "Yes Mr. Scientist. But will the ad agencies dump their bullshit survey for ours?"

"That's why we experiment." I paused. "Plus, it gives us an indication of what we are doing, are we increasing listenership or decreasing listenership?"

"I'll do it, for your last reason only. Ad agencies are hopeless, and they are shitty payers. You get a high rating, they don't care what you charge, they pay whatever Radiotron tells them to pay, no matter if it is double your normal rate. I've actually offered them a lower rate. They say, 'know we got to pay this much.' We pay by points. Then you fight for months to get paid. Stupid. No hope. Your experiment is futile."

"Bradley, in science, an experiment very often reveals shocking things. Just do it."

Bradley shakes his head, takes a last gulp of his beer, "Get me another."

I didn't believe what I was saying either. I needed another one, too. *Damn, at least somebody can drink with me.*

Bradley asks, "Why can't we ask other people in the same house the same questions? It would make it easier."

"Because it drastically reduces the sample. Radiotron might get three or four people from the same household, but that only lowers the individual sample size So when you only talk to one person in a household you are spreading the sample to two thousand, but if you get 1200 diaries from people in seven hundred households, you are restricting the sample drastically. So even if Radiotron gets 2000 diaries, their sample is far smaller than ours, because they are only reaching eight hundred to twelve hundred families whose samples are connected to each other. And that is even smaller if you expect those people to tell you how many people are actually listening to a particular radio station at one moment in time!"

Bradley takes a gulp of his new beer. "So this is all out war on Radiotron. I sure hope we can make it. I'd love to shove real ratings in their face."

I smile. "You got it Bradley, make it or not, if we do make it, it will scare the shit out of Radiotron. That's why doing this survey is so important. Not just checking our popularity ups and downs, but making them aware radio stations don't need their bullshit. Trust me. There isn't a radio station who doesn't feel they are being extorted by Radiotron. We show them a way out, they'll love us, much as they hate us now."

Bradley shakes his head, "You know that 260,000 dollars in receivables from ad agencies that is in my business plan? I didn't think of this before. It's gonna be harder to collect it now. We can't count on getting all that money back now that Radiotron has disavowed us. I forgot about that when I made the plan. And this little project is gonna make it worse trying to collect those receivables of a quarter million dollars."

"We gotta do it and take one battle at a time. Do you need me to get help for you, for some of your other work, so you got time to do this?"

"I can handle. Only for you, Danny, only for you."

We tank beers, have an early dinner talking statistics, and balance approaches, killing one stat with another to balance the sample and make it more stable. Then we write out our procedures for the ones that would be conducting the survey. We decide to do it in 500 phone call blocks. Total the results. Then add another 500 to see the difference in the sample. Then add another 500 and check for additional differences. Then add the final 500, and see what the differences are. By the last 500 it should tell us if the sample is big enough if the differences between 1500 and 2000 is less than one percent. If there is wider divergence, then we'll need to expand the sample to more phone callers or adjust our procedures. We decide to put all five hundred blocks of calls into the survey to show ad agencies that the sample is adequate. That means each 500 block of calls must have equal calls each day of the week, and each morning, afternoon, and evening, and at the proper ratio of the prefixes contacted. It means we have to discard phone calls in a sex/age demographic once that demographic is filled. Discarding demographic responses trying to fill up other demographic responses might take an extra week or so. But Bradley won't budge. He says, "If we are doing an honest survey, it needs to be done right." I see why Ida insisted on Bradley doing it.

I fax Ida with the procedures and a sample result. We are on it.

※

Once we are on the air, Jackson calls all our old advertisers. Says he isn't part of the Radio Revolution anymore, (a lie); he is the general manager as far as the FCC is concerned, but he says he is starting a new ad agency.

"Come give the BBRB agency a try. We guarantee if you are not pleased with the results, we'll run another flight of equal exposure, absolutely free."

The war is on.

Our guns are blazing.

23

WHY AREN'T WE ALL USING IT?

The editing of the concert and the approval of the bands took longer than expected. We were forced into 98 minutes of music to meet the demands of the artists who were giving us the full royalties for the CD and LP. That made for a three record set and a two CD set.

Below the title on the cover, "Why Aren't We All Using It," was the short paragraph that was Article V of the US constitution, the shortest Article and the only one with just one paragraph. And in large caps, "OR BY CONVENTIONS IN THREE FORTHS OF THEREOF."

Article V, Of the Constitution of the United States.
"The Congress, whenever two thirds of both houses shall deem it necessary, shall propose amendments to this Constitution, or, on the application of the legislatures of two thirds of the several states, shall call a convention for proposing amendments, which, in either case, shall be valid to all intents and purposes, as part of this Constitution, when ratified by the legislatures of three fourths of the several states OR BY CONVENTIONS IN THREE FOURTHS (OF THE STATES) THEREOF as the one or the other mode of ratification may be proposed by the Congress; provided that no amendment which may be made prior to the year one thousand eight hundred and eight shall in any manner affect the first and fourth clauses in the ninth section

of the first article; and that no state, without its consent, shall be deprived of its equal suffrage in the Senate."

The CD was done in a long box with a sixty page-pamphlet on how to initiate a constitutional convention in each different state, predictions on what might happen to America if money is taken out of political campaigns, excerpts from the Federalist papers concerning Article V of the US constitution, and a printed copy of the speeches both Danny and Gregory gave in between the bands' performances at the FCC concert. One of those speeches, Danny Fall had given before the last act, NWA, went on stage, is as follows.

"The constitution was written by astoundingly brilliant men. Brilliant in that they thought through their objectives, brilliant in that they had no problem discussing diversifying opinions and considering such diverse opinions from others. Brilliant in that they actually studied what worked in history and what didn't work. Brilliant in the need to compromise for the most affectual results.

"They were blessed men in knowing no poverty, and where their position was surmised sufficient to discuss such important matters. And above all, they believed in deliberation, for such deliberation was gentlemanly, and looked upon favorably, and was considered only proper for such serious matters as governing a people.

"They didn't know what would occur in the world, though they speculated heavily. Yet they would have been astonished to know that a free society could be destroyed by a new rich class, who didn't take responsibility for the people, while dwelling in a privileged position. For in those days you were born into wealth and mindful to be dutiful to the people of lesser rank. And it was these men, who through deliberation and respect for each other, created the Constitution of the United States of America.

"There were some parts of this constitution that were deliberately vague to allow a flexibility to the constitution as well as not forcing the convention to harp on minor points.

"One of the vaguest articles in the constitution was the Article V, the amendment article. For congress to initiate an amendment it was precise. But for the states to initiate an amendment is was a bit foggy. And for the people to initiate an amendment to the constitution, a door was left open, through Article V and the tenth amendment, but absolutely no procedures to enhance the process were discussed.

"Judges often went to outside letters from these brilliant men who had a habit of writing such elaborate letters, and from the Federalist Papers, letters written to the public campaigning for the constitution, and answering all suggested concerns.

"These men were not like American politicians today. They actually entertained all possibilities, suggested the value and the negatives of each governing concept. And when words were spoken inappropriately, or spoken in too general terms, without giving exact situations, these men showed the shallowness of those words, seeking a solution, and dispelling unfounded words. And others listened. And judges through the years have sought for the spirit of those words to make key decisions in the courts.

"Today we are just spoiled citizens, basking in the glory of America, not considering what damages we may be initiating, nor considering how distant we have become from the spirit of these men who introduced a new form of government to the world that made a genuine effort for all people to be equal.

"Most know. We all are not equal in opportunity today though the match toward equalization was lit in 1789 with our constitution. And the harder driven do have a better, but not sure chance, of greater opportunity. And of course not all of us seek happiness by gaining money, many of us have different motivations. Some want to be leaders or are thrown into that position accidentally. Some want to be supporters of the leaders yearning for a better life, some want to utilize their creative expression. Some have special talents that bring them and others joy and/or mankind progress. We need them all, and no one should look upon another with less respect than he does upon himself. We, together, are strong. Fighting for prominence over others only weakens and sickens us.

"It is wise to read these Federalist Papers, written when the constitution was forming, if only to notice the great respect given to each person, and the succinct words used to obliterate unsubstantiated rhetoric.

"It is now our turn to consider all possible avenues and consider where they might lead.

"But today, in order to have an effective political atmosphere like our fore fathers had, we need to obliterate the party system that just flings one generalization after another upon the other party, and has no means to discuss important decisions seriously, and whose generalizations seem to have totally forgotten how America came to be.

"How do we eliminate the party system? People join parties for funding. We ratify an amendment to the constitution that says only government pays for campaigns. Every candidate gets equal funding for the job they are soliciting, and the moneys go directly to those whose services they request. No funds go directly to them. They can't use their own moneys, or anybody else's moneys. Then we can begin to deliberate, consider the possible alternatives, take in deep thoughts and argue them concertedly and make an America governed by the people, for the people.

"Right now the 'for the people' is missing. Right now our government is for big business, conglomerates and special interest groups, who don't give a flying fuck what the people want. They are the new wealth with no concern for those of lesser moneys, or the environment, or the will of the people, or even simple grace. A new, short amendment to the constitution will change that! With one little amendment, America can move toward a real democracy.

"Imagine a politician who, if he wants to get reelected, needs to listen to the people, not big business, conglomerates, and special interest groups. Imagine big corporations being forced to pay their fair share of taxes, imagine big companies who seek control of the market instead of creating economic value in the market, find their endeavors suddenly being halted. Imagine a country without insurance companies, where the government deals directly with hospitals

THE RADIO REVOLUTION

and drug companies, and where medical services are paid out of our taxes at far less cost by eliminating the middle man, the insurance companies, like in Europe. Imagine a country that has a flat tax, rich and poor pay the same percentage, and no deductions whatsoever, and the percentage is far less than today because all are participating equally. Imagine a country where stricter control on weapons reduces mass killings. Imagine where the people have the power over irrational police behavior. Questionable actions are referred to a community of peers, and the people decide the judgement. Like a real court hearing with people not involved in police enforcement being the judges. Imagine thwarting runaway capitalism that is more concerned with controlling the market than producing value in the market, and where free enterprise can once again flourish, and with it, a giant increase of value in the market place that will make the economy bloom. Imagine real estate giving a section of its wealth to each individual in the country, thereby giving a minimum income to each individual, regardless of work. Then when you work, you do it not out desperation, but for what you want, or enjoy. Imagine open debates on entitlements where we consider ways to get people off welfare, remembering all people want to free themselves of welfare if there is an alternative, and give themselves an opportunity to find themselves in the booming new economy. And to people working full time but in poverty, working on a way through real estate's additional income to get a respectable income. Imagine the power of radio, all of us uniting as one, sharing our diverse musical taste with each other, breaking down racism in the process, making us feel more together as a nation.

"Imagine! These are all things the mass majority of America wants, but have no hope of getting, without this simple amendment to the constitution.

"Tonight's concert is to begin this amendment with imagination. In the coming months we will show how the people can make this amendment a reality. So tonight imagine. The more of you who can imagine, a great flood of energy will stir even more to imagine. Start thinking what would really happen if only the government paid for elections? Think seriously. What problems might occur, what change would occur, what has more value, a government run by big business, conglomerates and special interest groups, or a government run by the people? Do what our fore fathers did. Think of all possibilities. Look at history. What worked, what didn't. And that imagination will shortly manifest into reality.

"Tonight you screamed, "How, how can we change fuckin' America?" When I heard that, I cried. We've totally forgotten. Today, we are so caught up in the rhetoric of the day, so brainwashed in believing we have no way out of this quagmire, we don't realize, we were all given something so precious, we were given the key to a democracy. That's why I screamed back in rage. "We Were All Given a Democracy." And yelled to you, 'Why Aren't We Using It?'"

24

OKAY, STOP

Tuesday morning, July 17th, 1990 the Radio Revolution returned to the airways. It began with a song that we five, plus Ed, did live as we reopened the station statewide. Music was by Gregory Stephan, Lyrics by us five.

> Grab your pen, get out to vote
> Don't you want, that radio jolt
> Yeah Yeah Yeahyeah….radio freedom's back da dum da dum da dum
> Raise your feet, and dance to the beat
> Now's da place for genres to meet
> Yeah Yeah Yeahyeah….radio freedom's back da dum da dum da dum
> Dah aah air is sweet
> Dah aah DJs neat
> If you have something to say, they're there to greet
> Grab your board, up on the rack
> Don't you worry 'bout us comin' back
> Yeah Yeah Yeahyeah radio freedom's back…da dum da dum da dum
> Radio Freedom's back da dum da dum da dum
> Ray-dee-o-free-dom's back! (high pitch ending).

Mandy sang lead vocal. Juan on bass guitar, Gregory on guitar, both Juan and Gregory doin' the harmony, and me doin' the "da dum da dum da dum." I was hammering out the rhythm with a hammer and a tire iron upon an upside down tin pot, while stomping on an empty file cabinet drawer. Bradley got in the act doin' the "yeah yeah yeahyeahs." Ed did the one liner in a low bass voice "If you have something to say, they're there to greet."

It was rather spontaneous, composed an hour before we went on the air, but we got sufficient response to make it the top of the hour ID for the first day back on the Honolulu Station. The song even got voted into rotation for a week, a month later, after it had been off the air for three weeks including the miscues and laughing that went on when Bradley missed a "yeah" in the "yeah yeah yeahyeah." This caused a pause in the song as we waited for the last "yeah," then Mandy added the last "yeaaahhh." I kind of cheated and told Bradley to keep the rotation light when it got voted on the survey. I was afraid if it got played too much, it might get sledgehammered.

Juan kept airing Gregory's speeches he did at the concert, and taking phone calls about what the people thought of the speeches at the convention. His favorite was Gregory's "Out of hand" speech.

It went like this. "And as Alexander Hamilton said in the convention, 'There must be a way for the people to have a say, if the government gets out of hand.'"

Gregory continued, "Has the government got out of hand? Is the government doing what the majority of the people request? 70% polled want more restrictions on fire arms. 93% polled want big business to pay their fair share of taxes, 80% want police to answer to the people not to the police departments. 70% want additional environmental controls and a mass majority want free health care like Europe has. And what does congress do, they thwart any effort to listen to the majority of people. All of the above can't even be discussed in congress, even put up to a vote, much less passed! Government is out of hand, not responsive to the people. This amendment to the constitution can change that."

I ask Juan, "Why do you like Gregory's speeches better than mine." I am honestly just curious.

Juan smiles. "Gregory gets right to the heart of the matter. I worry that if they listen to your speeches, they'll fall asleep." He plays me another classic Gregory speech. He calls it the "Or" speech.

"Let us remember the tenth amendment to the constitution. "The powers not delegated to the United States by the Constitution, nor prohibited by it to the States, are reserved to the States respectively, or….to….. the….. people." He repeats loudly, "OR TO THE PEOPLE! If we the people of America want a change in government where the Federal Government has no say, we can, by this statement alone. And it is further emphasized in Article V of the constitution. OR A CONSTITUTIONAL CONVENTION IN THREE FORTHS (OF THE STATES) THEREOF. There is an 'OR' in the constitution. It is time to use that 'OR' and make America more responsive to the people."

I smile. "Well, at least play my speeches every once in a while. People need to see different points of view. *I couldn't believe he wouldn't play my forefather speech.* "I do give a wider perspective. Try it. See what response you get."

Juan shakes his head. "Danny, you don't understand. Gregory's words ignite the kids' interest in the constitution. They debate our pamphlets in the CD and LP in classroom here in Hawaii, and likely in other states. And there is this outrage from the politicians who are saying it is impossible to happen, and then they hear Gregory, and the kids get excited. And they don't even talk about your speeches. Hey, even stuffy history teachers like Gregory's speeches. They even discuss them in class, and kids get extra points critiquing my radio show each night. Kids have a short attention span. I'm afraid to use your long-winded speeches. The kids would probably fall asleep and get no extra credit. And Gregory's speeches make the kids read the constitution and the Federalist Papers. Really read it. Interested even. Kids probably would just fall asleep and not even finish their regular homework if I put your speeches on."

"If kids read the Federalist Papers with all those old-style wordings, they sure as hell can listen to my speeches. Dammit, Juan! My speeches are more in depth. Kids can study those, too. Plus, if you don't do my speeches, I might come on your show every night and talk to the kids myself."

"Sensitive, we are." Juan laughs. "Okay boss, I'll do it the next time I need a long bathroom break."

We survived the first year, partly with Jackson's BBRB. ad agency, but mostly with the phenomenal sales we got from the concert CD and LP. And the pressing cost I was so worried about paying before we got the money back from the independent distributors, wasn't a problem at all. There was no record of the 380,000 we acquired on the secret loan, so the banks, not knowing we had that loan, funded the pressing cost for the LP and CD at 9% interest. And we were lucky enough to win a suit in Australia against the Three M Radio Chain using our name, the Radio Revolution. Fledge had lied and said Dead Duck Enterprises owned the name and format.

Australian Courts are a trip. The lawyer can't talk to the judge, he is forced to use a middle man to talk to the judge, and that man called the bannister had no idea what The Radio Revolution was about, and when the Judge asked him questions about The Radio Revolution, his answers were completely erroneous and embarrassing and I couldn't say a damn word. I was forced to cringe, restrain, and contain myself from bursting out in court with the truth. Luckily, I didn't. And we won a huge settlement, anyway.

The radio revolution roared on even after most of the ad agencies did what appeared to be a concerted effort not to pay us the back bills. We were stiffed 180,000 dollars and Ida told me not to push it, least it is an excuse for them not to advertise with us now. Bradley was right, once you were off Radiotron, the big ad agencies felt no need to pay you what they owed you when you were on Radiotron.

THE RADIO REVOLUTION

Do to President Trenton's Clemency act for illegal immigrants, Juan got his papers. Ida took her name off and put Juan's on the Radio Revolution Corporation as an officer, the Treasure. And with Juan's new stature, he didn't agree or do what I suggested half the time. It was okay. The boy deserved a voice. Besides, if it was really important I could always go through Mandy and he would bend. Funny. His position as an official officer worked to bond us closer. It was actually easier to deal with Juan when he saw himself as an equal.

※

In the following surveys, Radiotron kept listing us as number six in all the demographics, and the major ad agencies kept refusing to buy from us. There was one exception. A big surf retail chain literally demanded the ad agency to advertise with us. They were a huge account. The ad agency asked the retailer to do a focal group, which meant taking a survey of what radio stations you listen to when customers walk into their shops. The chain did, and we, of course, came in number one. The ad agency, not believing the results, did their own focal group of the same chain, and, oddly, the results were very different, but we still came in number two. They told the chain that they were obligated to buy only from the number one station on the focal group. They said it was "corporate policy."

But when the big surf company lawyer said that was good enough reason to break the five-year contract, and go with the BBRB Agency, the ad agency did buy a small ad package from us, but just once. I told Ida about this in my weekly reports. Ida wanted the name of the lawyer and the President of that surf company.

"Ida, when is all this gonna stop? I'm tired at beating my head against a wall approaching ad agencies every week." I had been doing this for the past ten months, Bradley was moaning as well. He was working 72 to 80 hour a week including monitoring the in-house surveys.

Ida says, "Okay, stop."

I stutter. "I... I don't have to do this anymore?"

"Yes," she says.

I call Bradley, "It's over."

We hit the bar.

We both are laughing. Bradley has this somber tone to him that normally prevents laughter. But he was cracking up when he heard me being called "the plague" by the ad agencies.

"You know, this wasn't my idea," I say.

I thought you were crazy, Danny. Juan thought you had really lost your mind. Why is it over? Did you get your mind back?"

"It wasn't my idea."

"Oh, were you a channel for some strange alien being?"

I have been doing a special Monday afternoon show I call "The History of Rock n Roll for Extraterrestrials, figuring the kids were so far removed from the fifties and sixties, they might as well be extraterrestrials. And a lot of rock singers in the sixties talked about extraterrestrials like they were real, like Jimi Hendrix, Axis Bold as Love and Pink Floyd's Saucer Full of Secrets and in the seventies George Clinton and Parliament whole show was about extraterrestrials. They actually had a spaceship landing in the show.

We both laugh. "No. Ida made me do it. I couldn't tell anybody. She told me to tell everybody it was my crazy idea."

"Ida is the crazy one?"

"Yeah."

Bradley laughs. "You were crazy enough to listen."

"Hey, if Ida told you to do it, would you do it?"

"Wait a minute. Yeah, I would. She's a killer lawyer. Why did she ask you to do it?"

"She said if she told me why to do it, it would prejudice the experiment. That's what she called it. An experiment."

"Did you keep a diary of this experiment?"

"You have no idea. Every contact, every word spoken to agencies, their responses - I taped them. Every proposal - I was writing one proposal after another, and I had Terri, the intern, put the dialogues, the proposals, and your surveys in a Fed Ex package and sent them to her weekly. That job was so fuckin' time consuming, and then being called the 'plague' by the ad agencies, I think I had a harder time with this than you did, kid."

"Why did she ask you to stop?"

"Not sure, maybe because we finally got a flight from the Gadson Agency, that small surf buy, maybe, I don't know."

"I feel better. Ida's a cracker jack lawyer. She put you up to this. We're going to court or getting a settlement, from somebody, maybe Radiotron."

I started laughing. "I'd sure love to put a squeeze on Radiotron."

We might have had ten beers, I don't know. We're solid drinkers, never a hangover, but we sort of hung on to each other in order to walk, too drunk to even consider driving. We took a taxi home that night. Still laughing, we fell asleep on the grass outside of the house until Mandy came outside at 5am heading for the Morning Show and almost tripped over us.

That afternoon, Juan asked me how many did I drank. I gradually remembered. We had switched to wine after ten beers and I did have a dull headache until about 5pm that day. I wouldn't call it a hangover, though.

I answer Juan, "Yeah maybe fourteen, ten beers and four or so wines."

Juan shakes his head. "That's sure stupid, you the focal point of the revolution and all. You can't afford to do that anymore, Danny. And Ida called for you four times today, but I couldn't even wake you.".

Shit, she's changed her mind.

I called her with rocks in my stomach. No answer. Strange. It was evening in Washington DC. Shouldn't she be home?

25

DEPARTMENT OF JUSTICE

It is near midnight. Bradley and I are sipping beers in the living room, listening to Juan's closing of the night show. He always says, "And now my love, I'm coming home to you." I think he does that because all the girls are throwing themselves on to him, and he is true blue to Mandy. Mandy brings us another round, and says she needs to get a few hours of sleep, but we know she is with Gregory and pot on the back porch. It is Gregory's night anyway. There is no real schedule but Mandy seems to hint during the day if she wants to sleep with one of us that night. They seem to get more attention during the day.

Oh, there are surprises. I remember the nights when Mandy would just sneak in my bed, and we cuddle and talk, almost all night. Sometimes sex, sometimes not. I love those nights the most. I loved to talk deeply, and introspectively, and she would clutch me sometimes in tears, with what I said. I felt like we were one mind. I don't know why. We were both dancers, challenging the world in our own way, avoiding one obstacle after another. No one ever had come close to the communion I felt with her, though I suspect she had a different communion with the others. Mandy was our family. It is beautiful. We help her, she helps the whole group of us. And together we are helping the world. That's what we believe.

THE RADIO REVOLUTION

The doorbell rings. Bradley struggles to get up in his inebriated state. He slowly opens the door, thinking it is some crazy person at this hour. "My God!" He shouts. "Ida."

"Can I come in, Bradley?" Bradley steps aside, and motions her in. Then picks up her bags at the door steps and brings them into the living room.

After Juan told me in the afternoon that Ida called four times, I tried to call her four more times. No answer. No wonder. She was on a plane from Washington DC, how could she answer?

She flops on a lounge chair. "Well, I did it. Get the family together. We need to talk. When is Juan off?".

Bradley was already on the hotline telling Juan to hurry home. "Ida is here."

I went to get Mandy and Gregory. They'd heard the commotion and we ran into each other in the kitchen. Ida was saying to Bradley, "And get me somewhere to sleep, I'm exhausted."

Mandy overhears from the kitchen and shouts, "You can use my room."

Ida nods. I fetch her a glass of wine.

I'm excited. I feel good news is coming. Ida is smiling as her brother lifts her up for a hug. She says to Gregory, "Dad is so proud of you. I played him your speeches from the concert. He had tears in his eyes. He so wants to talk to you. He's coming later this week."

Small talk for a while, then Juan bursts in the door, saying hello. "Thanks Ida, I'm now a citizen."

Ida gets up. "Juan, that is so wonderful. You must have killed the test."

"I was teaching a lot of the people about America that were there to get their citizenship. But I didn't know some of the stupid questions on the test, like where did the Statue of Liberty come from?

"But you passed with flying colors, yes?"

"Yeah, I got the best score. That's what the examiner said."

"Juan, you are so amazing, and so balanced, I know you are helping Mandy, Gregory, and Danny, though Danny doesn't probably appreciate it."

I say, "Wrong, Juan is an incredible help to me, and he gets me grounded a bit, when I'm ready to fly."

Ida says, "Now that I got you all together, here's what's happening. I showed the Radiotron complaint to my father last week. He made a few changes then told me it was solid. Then I filed it as an anti-trust case early today.

An anti-trust case? Was that what the paper work and hounding ad agencies was about?

"Dad worked for the Department of Justice as an anti-trust lawyer before he went into politics. He made a call and I got an appointment for a preliminary hearing. They told me there are more important priorities right now, but they will consider a hearing in due time. I don't know what 'due' time means.

"The reason I'm here tonight is because Radiotron will get an immediate notice that we are talking to the Justice Department about taking on our complaint. They will get everything I submitted in my complaint. Radiotron's behavior in the next couple of weeks is unknown. The Justice Department will take their feedback before they allow a hearing.

"My suspicion is they will accuse us of trying to sabotage their survey by bad mouthing their results, for which they will get support from 'experts,' and that our allegations are unfounded. I deliberately withheld a lot of information in my complaint, so they can't prepare for us, before we have an official hearing at the Department of Justice. So no bad mouthing Radiotron, okay?

"We know Danny has already bad mouthed Radiotron to ad agencies, but I didn't put those conversations into my complaint. So, unless somebody taped your conversations, Danny, you don't have to admit anything. You just don't say anything, like nothing is happening.

THE RADIO REVOLUTION

"A lot of you might get a call. You are all officers and Mandy is the owner on record. If they call one officer and they don't get what they want, they'll call another looking for a weak link in the corporation. The ad agencies will probably be interviewed, also. Don't say anything if they contact you. If they push you to say something. Say I don't know anything. If they get ballistic, direct them to me. Don't even admit there is an anti-trust case looming. Why? Because nothing is looming until the Department of Justice makes an informal inquiry

"Radiotron should be freaked out. I don't know what they will do. We'll see their response and the Department of Justice's response, probably next week or Radiotron will try to put in some delay tactics before they make a response. They might want to probe all of you, and the ad agencies. They might not have time to do that, but they might try. If anybody contacts you on this issue, don't say anything. Remember saying anything about a possible anti-trust litigation could get us sued for defamatory rhetoric if the Department of Justice doesn't proceed.

We nod. I am excited. We all join a circle. Mandy calls it the power circle, and Ida is now in the center.

Ida says, "Don't get too excited, guys. This can be a very long, irritating, disturbing process."

Mandy starts the aummmm" We all join in, a full forty second of aummmm."

Then I break the sound, "Ida, you don't understand. Radiotron thinks they can't be touched. Today you touched them. We're ecstatic. Yeah, the punches come later and finally the blow to the balls. But it is started. They know now: they got to answer to somebody."

A lot of changes were happening in the programming of the station, all of which were being stimulated by comments on the back of ballots. The comments were a riot, maybe chaotic, with people complaining about this and that, from rotation, to personal hatreds about songs, or DJs, to demands for specialty shows, to ideas for programming, to complaints on how we tabulated the ballots (our weighing system) and of course a great many ballots were raves for this or that, that the station was doing.

The Radio Revolution was a listener programmed station, but how could we absorb all these conflicting comments on the back of the ballots. Thus came Gregory's idea to have an open forum on the back of the ballots where we would take the most bulk of sentiments from the ballots and put it to vote on a ballot in the upcoming weeks. The first overwhelming issue was the rotation. I, treating the station like a typical top 40 programmer, had the top thirty-six songs in two, three and four-hour rotation. But the listener comments on the back of the ballots were screaming for a slower rotation. We put it to a vote, first going from five to six to eight-hour rotation, then finally back to five-hour rotation, settling with the top thirty-six all going in five-hour rotation, so you never heard the same song in any particular radio show.

But still there were constant complaints of hearing the same songs too much. So I added a rule to the voting. The new rule was that an entire artist could make the top 36. And when the artist came up to be played, we could play different songs that were voted for by that artist, instead of just the same song every time.

One open forum suggestion was that we have the listeners as guest DJs for a half an hour each day with them choosing their favorite songs to be showcased on the radio. It got voted in 3 to 1. That further watered down our rotation plays each week.

Then came the icing on the cake. One day to my shock, somebody suggested on the back of the ballot that every seventh week, we would have what they called a Dark Horse week. On that week we would play the songs that got votes, but not enough to make the survey. In other words, we would play the bubbling under songs. And put these smaller vote getters, all 36, into the weekly rotation instead of the bigger vote getters of the week.

I thought it was an insane idea, but Juan insisted we put it to a vote. To my shock it was voted in seven to one. And Dark Horse week turned into an insanely popular week at our station.

Can you imagine a station that has a rotation and suddenly, every seventh week, that entire rotation is dropped, and songs never heard on radio go into rotation for a whole week? Radio programmers worldwide would rather jump off a cliff than hear their radio station do that! The Radio Revolution was indeed, well named! What's amazing, the response was tremendous. Listeners couldn't wait for that seventh week!

So there was this trend. Because of all the high rotation on the other stations, and so unlike the fifties when we loved to hear our favorites over and over again, this new listenership of the nineties wanted desperately a far wider selection of music over radio. And radio stations of the nineties were all going the opposite direction, less selection, more familiarity, and I suspected that was because of Radiotron's diary system. Radiotron's diary system seemed to be supporting listeners who would prefer familiarity over a wide open music selection.

I'm mentioning this because when I would go to ad agencies badgering them for advertising, they blamed are low ratings with us playing too diverse a musical selection. Of course, when we did our own survey, we were still number one or occasionally number two behind the main R&B station. We did lose a little ground with other stations competing with us in the market, playing some of the music our listeners had discovered, in higher rotation.

One station, a typically formatted station of the day, started not only playing some of our music, but they were trying to identify with our listeners so bad, they started calling themselves the Radio Rebellion, instead of the Radio Revolution. And of course, Radiotron had them number two in the market and us number eleven (overall) in the market.

To the ad agencies it was simple. Our genre jumping and wider selection of music was costing us listeners. Even though the number one ad agency had lots of their employees filling out ballots each week and obviously listening to us, I, too, actually believed it for a while. It was the diary system, not sabotage that was causing our poor showing in Radiotron. But what could I do? The Radio Revolution was controlled by listener input. And they were ferocious about wider music selections.

It had been six months since Ida had sent in a complaint to the Department of Justice. Senator Stephan said Radiotron finally filed a response after much prodding. But they seemed to be silent, not contacting us, or for what we could tell, contacting ad agencies. Why was the Department of the Justice sitting on the request this long? Just before we decided to approach the Attorney General of Hawaii instead, they asked for a hearing. I am headed on a plane to Washington DC.

Last night Mandy snuck in my bed about 2am. She seemed worried about my emotional state, now mostly concerning Radiotron. Of course, that was between us. To the outside world I didn't say anything.

"Honey, don't think like that. Your rage just clouds things up. Don't let them distract you for what you need to get done. One thing at a time. Remember: when you go to court, one thing at a time. Don't let them trap you into taking on everything at once. Forget about the sabotages, the record companies, the Amendment, just concentrate on Radiotron. The Department of Justice has no idea where you are coming from. They just want to follow the rules. Heart, blood, soul, sacrifice, they don't care about that. Don't say a word about that."

"You really think they'll try to trap me at this court proceeding?"

"I'm sure of it." Mandy says. "No outburst, okay? You can do that in speeches and on the radio to people, but don't try that in court. Listen to Ida. You have a habit of not listening to anybody."

"I listen to you, you know that."

She hugged me. I kissed her cheek. She said, "Yeah, maybe, through a distorted ear. But this time really, really listen to me. Promise?"

"I promise." I knew she was psychic. She'd probably had a dream of me botching the interview.

※

December 2, 1991. I am at the Department of Justice with Ida and her father, state senator of Kentucky, Gerald Stephan, who had worked with the Department of Justice when he was younger as an anti-trust lawyer. The hearing is for ten am but it has been moved to the afternoon an hour after our arrival. Senator Stephan doesn't like that. He had never heard of such a delay. He looks concerned.

The room is big. I feel like I am in a Senate hearing, except there isn't a mob of reporters, lawyers and secretaries there, just us seven. Three men, probable lawyers sit on platforms like judges while Ida, her father and I, are sitting in chairs next to a small table about ten feet away. A female recorder is sitting at our left. It is almost an hour into the interview. I am on the mic saying. "Ad agencies are a strange breed."

The recorder was transcribing. I continue. "They buy advertisements for their clients by adding points. Radiotron determines which station gets what points for each demographic. For example, if you are number one in the female 25-34 age bracket, you get the most points, 'cause they are the best consumers in Radiotron's mind. Then Radiotron goes one step further. It tells agencies how much to pay for each point based on the size of the market. The station may have a standard rate, and Radiotron might ask to pay the station more based on the points. And the ad agency will insist on paying the higher rate. Because why? That's the Radiotron rate. I mean the ad agency could get a much lower price but they insist on paying the Radiotron higher rate.

A man on the panel interrupts. "Why is that?"

"Possibly because they get a commission from their client, and if a client has to pay more, they get a bigger commission. I really don't know. I can only speculate."

"Radiotron now has a monopoly controlling 90 billion dollars in advertising per year. They bought out the last of their competition three months ago."

Another man on the panel asks me, "How do you know this?"

"Allison closed down their rating service three months ago. They sent back the 1200 dollars I sent them for this quarter's subscription, and they referred me to Radiotron, saying they are encouraging their clients to go to Radiotron."

"Did you bring the letter?"

I turned to Ida. She was already walking to the panelist with the letter.

"Did you subscribe to Radiotron?"

"Our station gave Radiotron 120,000 dollars, our rate for the entire year and they omitted us completely from the survey in the second book, even though we were number one in the first book, saying the reason was because we were off the air for a week in the second book. We were off the air for five days in their second book survey, but we still should have been number one or two in the second book, not zero listenership. So we didn't re-subscribe. We had already paid for the entire year. And then with us totally out of the top 5 in every demographic, for the following books, we felt no need to subscribe again. Allison, on the other hand, had us number one."

"So you relate not paying with not getting a fair rating?"

"Sorry, we paid, yet we were off the survey. Completely."

"And the next book, were you off the survey?"

"No, in the next book we came in number six in every demographic 12-35. Which is the same as being off the survey, because ad agencies only buy five deep in any demographic. And thereafter, in every book, we were off the survey, and number six in the demographics 12-35."

I added, "There was one case where we were the only station playing a band that is in concert, and we got 15, 000 people to the concert. But did the major record companies who have these bands allow

THE RADIO REVOLUTION

us to be the presenter, and pay for advertising for us to promote the bands? No. They went to the station that was closest to us in programming, but wasn't playing these bands, and advertised the concert with them because they were on Radiotron (in the top 5 in concert demographics) and we were not. Then this radio station showed up to the concert with their banners. We were the station that made many of these bands popular in the first place. Furthermore, we are the promoter of the concert, yet our banner must hang with theirs. That is documented in our report."

One of the panel members says, "So the listener's choices are not affected by this? They have choices who to listen to, correct?"

I was taken aback by the question. "Not if we are off the air. How do you stay on the air if you can't get ad dollars to keep yourself on the air?"

The panel member says, "But you seem to do fine, you are still on the air."

I was in shock. I didn't know what to say.

I look at Ida. I look at Senator Stephan. Apparently they weren't about to say anything.

I flounder for what to say. I had been briefed that, amongst other things, we had to show that value in the market would be increased if Radiotron was not controlling the advertising dollars clients spent. Of course, Ida's documentation made a strong case for Radiotron controlling the advertising dollars, but it didn't make a case that the value of radio would increase if Radiotron wasn't in the market.

There was silence. I was thinking, thinking of what Mandy said to me.

"You have no response. Indicate no response," said one of the panelist nodding to the secretary, recording."

I say, "I have a response. You don't realize what we have done to be on air. So many people believe in us. Bands have donated their rights to their own music to keep us on the air.

"We won a suit for a huge sum of money from an Australian radio chain that tried to use our name and format without permission.

"We've generated a huge sum of money from concerts that we conducted, even though another station got the advertising and presenter credit for the concert one time. We've done a million things that the other stations couldn't do because we are that popular! That's how we survived despite the fact 99% of ad agencies dollars were blocked by Radiotron, since the ad agencies apply their ad dollars exactly as Radiotron suggests.

"And there is now no other survey we can use. Radiotron is a monopoly. We have been voted two years in a row one of the top 5 stations in America by the readers of the Rolling Stone Magazine in the medium markets for the entire nation, and still Radiotron claims we don't have enough listeners in any demographic for the ad agencies to buy advertising from us. The other Rolling Stone Magazine Radio Stations voted in the top 5 are all number one or two in 18-35 year olds by Radiotron.

The panel person said, "Still you have survived. And still you have had a voice to propagate your political agenda."

A rage explodes in me. "My political agenda has nothing to do with this complaint. We do have free speech, don't we, or don't we?"

Another voice on the panel says, "What the distinguished panelist is saying is if the value in the market place is still available to the listeners then we have no recourse to apply restraint on Radiotron."

I look at Ida. She looks at her father.

I swallow a lump in my throat. I feel I've been before this committee all day, though it is probably just an hour and a half. I gulp. "How many radio stations who offered alternative programming have survived? Maybe public non-profit stations, but how many have survived in the commercial world? All the stations now sound the same. Different formats, but all the formats mold to what they think Radiotron favors. So to increase the value in the radio market, to introduce alternative programming to aid the value of radio overall, Radiotron needs to go. I am survivor; there are thousands of radio stations that struggled to create value in the market place, but now

THE RADIO REVOLUTION

they are gone. Because of Radiotron. And I am here today because we are not that sure to survive either."

I look at Ida. She smiles.

Senator Stephan told me not to mention the closing of the radio station and the huge response we got upon its closure. I so wanted to tell that panelist that, but I shut my mouth. Why shouldn't I tell them? I wondered. I just couldn't believe the panelist's audacity. But Mandy had coached me to stay calm and on the point. I remember her telling me, "They have no idea where you are coming from. They just want to follow the rules. Heart, blood, soul, sacrifice, they don't care about that. Don't say a word about that." I stopped talking.

There were murmurs between the panelist. Finally, one said to us, "Please wait in the lobby. There may be more questions."

I look at Ida. She looks perplexed. We are ushered out. I leave upset. *They don't have a clue what I've gone through to make my point.*

We are in the lobby. Senator Stephan places a gentle hand over mine as we sit side by side. Ida is on my left. "You did well, son." They should make a decision soon to take or not take this case."

Senator Stephan turns to Ida. "And hon, those reports were quite thorough. I don't think they have ever gotten such a thorough complaint. Certainly not when I was here."

I'm thinking. The most thorough report they ever got, but still, more questions. And it took us six months just to get a hearing. *Something's wrong.*

I try to talk to Ida about that. She shakes her head. We wait.

Twenty minutes later, a lady enters the lobby. "The panel wants to see Mr. Heinzwaffle, again."

We get up, Ida looks at her father. Senator Stephan's eyes show concern.

Oh no, what now.

We walk through the wide marble hallway. I can hear my heart echoing, bouncing against one wall then the other. I enter the hearing room. I take a chair. Ida and her father are on my left. The three panelists are perched high seemingly scrutinizing me. Their first new question totally floors me.

"The record companies are supporting new creative expression. Why are you fighting it?"

I'm about to lose it. *I'm fighting creative expression? Calm down. Think.* How do you answer such an absurd question? You don't.

Then I got an idea. "The question, your Honors, is which record companies are supporting new creative expression? And which ones are not?" You are asking me for a very subjective answer.

"But, now that you asked me, I'll tell you how I perceive it. The major record companies tend not to introduce the new exciting music of the day, they wait until it has been supported by independent record companies first, or by international sales that get strong import sales in America, or a huge response in concert goers. Then they still don't support it until they bring it into their net. On the other hand, independent record companies are always experimenting with new sounds, but because the charts seem to be controlled by the major record companies, or at least a great bias toward favoring major recording releases, the new exciting music of the day does get thwarted from being aired over radio. When we turned the programming over to the people, far more independent records made our chart than were on the national charts. What I find myself fighting, is the major record companies' efforts to control the market. I didn't intend to do that. It just surfaced through the listeners participating in the programming."

"What you are saying here, Mr. Heinzwaffle, and what your documents that have been submitted aren't saying, is the flamboyant statement, a conspiracy no less, of the major record companies controlling the music played on radio. These are serious and unsubstantiated, claims."

I remembered what Mandy told me. Don't let them change the subject. Stick to the documentation. They'll try to trap you, be smart. Don't let them.

She was right. I should have been quiet, or made the panelist articulate better the question. I was about to say, *The major record companies rigged the charts. Major record companies make concerted efforts to have particular songs on the radio in all markets simultaneously. That's attempting to control the market. Ask any top 40 radio station.*

But remembering what Mandy said, I didn't.

Instead I said, "You asked me, I gave you my opinion."

"You don't have any proof of this?"

He set me off again. "You don't have to know how it is happening, to know it is happening." Then I cooled. "Besides that shouldn't be the issue here. This is about our radio station being shut out from giant quantities of advertising because of a monopoly rating service, and that service is thwarting innovation on radio."

The man in the center says, "We don't take personal complaints, unless it is something all radio stations can benefit from."

I look to Ida. Those eyes. Darts were flying from them.

He continues. "And you have no proof of any of this. This is just your impression. Right?" *My God, why is he pushing this.*

I get pissed. "The disadvantage you have sir, is not being there. If you were there, it would be blatantly obvious. Ask any radio station in America playing major record companies' music. But again that is not specifically our complaint today. That is something you would have to pry into separate of our complaint."

Another panelist says, "Yes, we definitely will!"

What's going on?

"You're excused."

We three walk down the long marble hallway out through the heavy hinged doors into the dusk of the early evening. *My God, we had been there all d*ay.

Ida and her father don't say anything to me. I've got rocks in my stomach.

Senator. Stephan at last says, "Why don't we get some coffee?"

I smile. "I would prefer a beer."

"Yeah, maybe you are right," smiles Ida.

We enter a lounge where everybody is wearing a tie and the waitresses are streaking about taking orders. There's a moose head on a wall staring at me. *What is a fuckin' moose doin'in a bar?* I noticed Ida and her father are the only black people here. I now know why Senator. Stephan suggested coffee, not drinks in what Ida calls Washington DC, "I saw the machine, and it is white."

We are feeling uncomfortable, then Ida adds to it. "Damn Danny, emotion goes nowhere in this type of hearings."

"I showed emotion?"

"Yes, you sure did, son. But I would call it controlled emotion. It was more in the tone of the voice than the words. I actually thought you did okay. But they did seem to have another agenda. And I did detect a bit of hostility towards you as well. I don't know what's going on. I'll try to find out."

"Drinks?" A waitress is upon us. "Any light beer," I say. Ida orders a house red, Mr. Stephan requests some drink I couldn't understand amongst the voices in the bar.

Senator Stephan goes on, "It might mean they are going after a bigger fish than Radiotron. Maybe there is a complaint against the major record companies and they don't want to take up their precious time with a smaller fish. I don't know. It seems this hearing is for something else than what was on our complaint."

I say, thinking of what Mandy told me, "They were trying to trick us, they weren't neutral at all. We could go to the Federal Trade Commission, couldn't we?"

Senator. Stephan smiles. "Not really. If the Department of Justice turns us down, the Federal Trade Commission would call it a done deal. The Department of Justice handles overseeing communication, not the Federal Trade Commission. If they don't take the case, we'll have to make it a private case. I might start with the Hawaii State court system. It would be easier than taking on the whole nation."

"Dad, are you willing to help us, if we have to go private?"

"Yes, honey. Gregory gave me an earful. I'm beginning to believe this is a very important matter to the whole nation. A dream of the people having a say. I'll stay with you on this."

I say, "So why couldn't I tell them about the huge response we got from listeners when the station was shut down? That would prove our value in the market place, wouldn't it?"

Senator Stephan shakes his head. "We got unlucky. We got the two judges on the panel that are the most conservative. If we brought up the FCC concert, and the reaction of your listenership, they would listen to the tape hear all those "fucks" and all those screams and see it as a threat to America. You heard the comment from Judge Henry commenting on your political agenda. By the way, your response, Danny, was great, reminding him of free speech and the irrelevance of a political agenda in this case."

He continues, "We want them to stick to the law. They like doing that, in fact, yet the law in this case is a bit subjective and gets molded this way and that way in cases. But bringing out the populace sentiment in this case, I feel could backfire. That's why I told you not to mention it. Let's just let them concentrate on past cases, and the law itself. That's our best hope.

"If they do take the case, trust me, Radiotron will be in a vice. And if Radiotron bought out the Allison rating service, or squeezed them out, their only competition, they are in trouble anyway. By law they have to report to the Federal Trade Commission the buyout, and get approval, and they haven't. And I'm sure if there is a possibility of a squeeze out, there will be an investigation. Especially considering they have bought out two other rating services in the past five years. Even if the Department of Justice doesn't take our case, I'm pretty sure they'll investigate Radiotron."

"So those were judges asking the questions?"

"Two were, and the one in the center was a lawyer representing the Department of Justice."

I'm so tense I realize I still have three fourths of a beer. "When will they tell us?"

"We expected an answer in a few days. It seems like an airtight case and your answers only helped us. Technically they've got ninety days to make a decision, and after their comment about the record companies, and calling in interviews from other radio stations, it might, now, take a full ninety days for their decision. Hell, it took us six months just to get this hearing."

"Well thank you, guys, for all your hard work. And Ida, tell Mandy about my interview. She was worried I'd blow it."

"We all were Danny. You're such an emotional sparkplug," she laughs. "And my father told me they hate it when an interviewer confides with his lawyers before he speaks. So there were more rocks in my stomach than in yours, not knowing what would come out of your mouth next."

"But you did better than most, Danny," Senator Stephan shakes my hand. "It is really great what you are doing. I'm proud of you and Gregory, and of course, you, too, Ida. And... I thank you for bringing my son back to me."

The lights in the room are dim but I think I detect tears in Senator Stephan's eyes.

26

MONKEY TRAIN

Our radio station had rules. Like a constitution, there were things we could do and things we couldn't do. There were the sledgehammer rules for destroying the least wanted to be heard song over Hawaiian Radio, so it could never be played again. There were voting rules, weighing rules, rules to open an open forum question, and how to allow listeners to alter the music programing rotation.

Then, there was the Monkey Train rules. This was a strange event. It was time when listener phone calls totally controlled the music that got played.

Once an hour a listener was allowed to ask for the Monkey Train. And twenty-four hours a day, somebody always did. But when they asked, which was done over the air, they would need to get seven consecutive phone callers over the air to agree to get aboard the Monkey Train. That was hard. It was only successful two or three times a month.

When seven agreed, we would replay the skit of opening day where the monkey boss would be pushed out of the tree, splat. And the DJ would call out "All aboard the Monkey Train, destination unknown."

The seventh phone caller would then choose an artist, and the station would play three songs from that artist in a row.

Then we would open up the phones again and ask if listeners wanted to continue the monkey train with this artist or not, and take up to seven more phone callers who either said yes or no. So the fourth no or yes would make the decision. If yes, the same artist would continue another three songs. If no, the listener had the choice to shut down the monkey train or change the artist.

When the Monkey Train did get started up, normally it lasted an hour or so but there were a few times it was hard to stop, sometimes going six, eight, and once fourteen hours, and making the late-night news. It was amazing but the lights on our four phone lines were constantly blinking even at 3 and 4 in the morning.

There were a few Saturday mornings I woke up and heard the Monkey Train still rolling through town and feared it would blast through my Saturday Morning Hawaiian Island Music Report Show where we announced the new top 36 for the week. But to my relief, someone would stop it before the show.

The lack of control, the fact that anything might happen anytime on the Radio Revolution, was causing trouble with our Hilo station, the only station we didn't have total control of, and they decided to end the contract. But given the opportunity of another station in Hilo taking on the format, they reconsidered.

For example, one day the band Sublime was in Maui on vacation listening to the Radio Revolution. Bradley Nowell, the lead singer and songwriter for the band, was in shock. Hearing the first notes, he said, "Who's ripping us off, sampling our songs?" Then he realized, "Oh my God, some radio station is really playing our music." Then he heard the DJ say, "The most wanted to be heard song in the state of Hawaii this week, 'Waiting for My Ruca' by Sublime."

"Yeah," went the band Sublime. Bradley Nowell called the Maui station. They told him it was a live broadcast from the Honolulu Station.

THE RADIO REVOLUTION

Bradley Nowell calls. Ed answers the request line. "We're Sublime, the band. What's going on?" I had just finished the show, but Ed got me outside on the steps and says "You won't believe who is on the phone."

"Well, tell me."

"Bradley Nowell."

I tell Ed "Find out where Gregory is, let's get him to get Sublime to do a concert. Get their number."

"I told them about you, and Bradley wants to talk to you---only."

I hate getting involved with artists directly, but I say, "What the hell." I answer.

Bradley Nowell says, "You know anything about ska, rock steady, and early reggae?"

I say, "Shit, you got something to say about music, come to the station, we'll give you a free hour."

"Not at fuckin' midnight!"

"Well, if you can get up by three o'clock in the afternoon, come on down."

"Fuck no, not on Sunday." (Today was Saturday).

Cool your jets. Monday at 3pm, I'll have our morning DJ cover the show and put it live on the other four stations in the Hawaiian Market."

"I don't need no fuckin' DJ."

"Then don't show up."

"Bradley Nowell, laughs, "Okay, 3pm, Monday."

3pm Monday, Rabbit and his devotees have set up a live one hour simulcast throughout all Hawaii.

> Sublime arrives to the studio on time. Bradley, Eric and Bud slowly creaked the studio door open. Then, abruptly, catapult themselves inside. Bradley yelling "What's up Sister? What'cha fuckin gonna play? let US do the DJ…ing."

He moves around the long desk and comes behind Mandy who is facing the mic.

Mandy says," A little ditty, a sublime moment in the universe, right here on 102.7FM"

Bradley yells, "FM's for radio programmers. Stands for Fuckin' Morons. We are Sublime. We'll sing any fuckin' thing especially if it isn't on your playlist!"

Eric laughs, "DJ Mandy, you don't have to work so hard, Bradley loves singing. Just give 'em the mic and the playlist. No problema."

Mandy, somewhat rattled with the hurricane strength of their entrance, forgets she is on air. Then realizing the mic, it is on, she points to the mic. She gulps, "On!"

Bradley steps back. Mandy spins the seventeen-minute version of Iron Butterfly's "In-a-gadda-da-vida" to mentally organize her thoughts for the interview already spiraling out of control. She leaves the mic on, so not to disrupt the flow.

Eric starts yanking CDs out of the wall racks, tossing them on the table, "Play these," he says.

Bradley Yells, "Bud, see if you can find Eric Monty Morris."

Bud says, "Shit, they got Black Flag. Let's play that."

As the intro to "In-a-gadda-da-vida" continues, Mandy announces over the seventies epic hit, "In the studio right now we have three of the supreme 18-27 males, as defiant as hell at this world and the muck it dwells within. The group SUBLIME."

Bradley starts singing along to In-a-gadda-da-vida.

"In-a-gadda-da-vida HONEY,
Don'tcha know that I love you?
In-a-gadda-da-vida BABY,
Don'tcha know that I'll always be true?
Oh won'tcha come with me,
And take my hand?
Oh won'tcha come with me."

As the first vocal stanza whines down, Mandy lowers the volume on the music and turns up the ambient studio mic to 100% volume. "And you are hearing it all LIVE on 102.7." (She purposely leaves the "FM" out). "Bradley Nowell singing love songs. Gee Bradley, you sing it all don't you!"

I'm in the office listening, sinking lower and lower in my chair looking at the ceiling, wondering when will it fall in. I calm myself. It'll be okay, Mandy can handle anything. I hope. Thank GOD I had her do this interview. Interview? Hell, it sounds like an invasion. or is it a take-over.

Twelve more minutes of In-a-gadda-di-vida, and no *live* mics during the long instrumentals that are playing. *Whew*. I figure she has settled them down.

The song ends, the mics go on, and Mandy says, "Well, what do you guys want to pass on to the Hawaii listeners? Bud says, "KROQ sucks. They only play pulp over and over. The Radio Revolution Rules."

"And you Bradley?"

Bradley says, "The greatest song ever made comes from Hawaii. We've covered it because we felt it needed to be played to let the world know it exists." He starts singing,

> "I smoke two joints in the morning
> I smoke two joint at night"
> "Bud and Eric join in, "I smoke two joint in the afternoon
> It makes me feel alright
> I smoke two joints in time of peace
> And two in time of war
> I smoke two joints before I smoke two joints
> And then I smoke two more."

Mandy pulls out Sublime's version of the song, but Bradley stops her.

"Play the original. We just recorded it to let the world know the greatest recording ever recorded is out there and it comes from HAWAII."

Mandy whips out the twelve inch from under the table, puts it on the turntable, and cues the Toys' version of "Smoke Two Joints."

The whole band screams, "Aloha Hawaii," Eric adds, "The only place in America that has got it straight."

Mandy says, "Those leis on the guest mics are for you guys!"

Bradley says, "Something's missing. Isn't a wahine with no top supposed to put it on me, and give me a kiss?"

Sorry Bradley, not since Captain Cook, the no top, and you know what happen to him, but a kiss? "Okay guys, Bud, Aloha." Mandy kisses him on the lips and places the lei around his neck. And smiles, "The greatest and most creative drummer I've ever heard."

"Eric Aloha." She follows through with the kiss. You can hear their lips smack on the radio.

"Bradley, Aloha." She delays. "Ummm. Alright." She kisses his lips and places the lei around his neck.

"Sublime, Welcome to Hawaii," she gasps, as Bradley clutches her a bit too tight.

He finally lets up saying, "That's better. You got another lei?"

Mandy says, "We'll be right back with the Toys, "Smoke Two Joints," the greatest song ever recorded as proclaimed by Bradley Nowell of Sublime, after a few commercials.

All three band members suddenly yell in unison, "Listener Alert. Turn your radio down."

Mandy says, "No. Money alert. We need money. It cost 110,000 dollars a month to keep the Radio Revolution on the air. Listen to the sponsors and support them."

Bradley belts it out. "No way. You want to be shoved into doing things for somebody's pocket book, you want to be yanked and pulled about until you can't conceive a damn thought on your own, you want that, then listen to fuckin' commercials!"

In the office, I sink deeper in my chair.

Mandy says, "My Bradley. You don't want to know what is out there. Don't you want to sort out what others say, and decide what is good for you and what isn't? That's not leading you, that's offering you an additional opportunity. And because the sponsors are paying for it, it's a no-lose situation. It keeps your songs playing to the masses."

Bud says, "Ah, finally someone, givin' it back to Bradley. Mandy, you want to join the band?"

Bradley laughs, "You're hired. You just gotta stand there on stage. That's an attraction unto itself."

Mandy puts in an advertising cart called: Highway Robbery.

COMMERCIAL
Sound effects: loud growling monster truck shakes the studio walls, a rumbling sound as the truck comes to a screeching halt.

Voice one: "Juan, Oh no! The cheesecakes fell."

Juan: "Damn, (Bleep) Oh what the hell." Juan smacks his lips.

Voice one: "Our last delivery. Eight Cheesecakes. Take it easy MAN! "

Juan: "Damn this Traffic Jam! Well, they're wasting away…look at that one, completely ruined."

Voice one: "Juan, oh no, No! No!! Dude what are you DOING!? Stop puttin' your paws in cakes man! What is UP with you?

Juan:(With a mouth full of cheese cake, talking), "Hey, I got no utensils brau."

Horns blaring. Truck rumbles, starts up again.

A voice yells, "Pay Attention to the road, you FAKA."

Breaks Screech.

Voice one: "Well, Juan, are you the one to bust out the news at Jelly's Piikoi. No Otto Cheesecakes today?"

Juan" (Talking with a mouth full of cheese cake). "Yeah, traffic jam, Got 'em all kapakai."

Voice one: "Maybe we better say there was this un unreal accident." (As wheels screech, making a turn in the road trying to make up time).

Juan: "yea….accidente.." (Still talking with a mouth full of cheese cake).

Breaks screech. Truck rumbles to a stop.

Voice one: "Go tell Cindy the news brotha man Juan."

Cindy: "What the FUCK(bleep). "What!? You WEARING Cheesecakes or what!? Don't give me that bull. ACCIDENT! SHIT (Bleep), My OTTO Cheesecakes are RUINED and you been grinding on em.. ALL PAU!? FUCK(bleep)THAT.

(Three beeps squeak on the phone, 911 answers the phone).

Cindy: "IT'S HIGHWAY ROBBERY. This fuckin' (bleep) thief is here at Jellys Piikoi. JAIL EM' NOW! He ate all EIGHT of my OTTO Cheesecakes. Supposed to be for da kids.. not that FUCKER (bleep)!

Mandy looks at Bradley. "You know, how you can use your mouth better, here's a slice of Otto's lemon coconut cheese cake." She pushes the slice into his mouth.

There is a deep silence, then munching and slurping sounds over the air.

"Why Bradley, you, a did, a commercial! Was that a good choice? Guess so. Cause it broke your mouth."

Eric and Bud are laughing. Bradley trying to swallow the last bite.

With a quick push of the cart button Mandy seques into the next advertiser commercial called Etoen Ice Coffee.

COMMERICAL
Juan screaming, "I CAN'T BELIEVE IT. HOW HOW HOW!"
Mandy exasperated, "How, What?"
Rapid pounding sounds like a thousand tap dancers in a frenzy.

Juan: "Those Japanese pizza dough makers. Look at em, slamming, whamming, pounding harder and harder…harder and FASTER than the Americans. Mandy. harder than EVEN the Italians, harder than the Chinese. DO THEY EVEN SLEEP? Can you imagine a JAPANESE pizza "And they don't even eat Pizza in Japan!. We're finished! Our workers will never catch up.. THE JAPANESE are winning the Hawaii pizza war. JAPANESE PIZZA! HOW HOW HOW!"

Mandy: You know they drink Etoen Ice Coffee by the gallons. Makes them work faster, think harder.

Juan: Then order a SEMI of Etoen Ice Coffee NOW! Put on the SIRENS. GET IT HERE YESTERDAY. THIS IS AN EMERGENCY! We need to save Hawaii or we will be eating JAPANESE PIZZAS, FOREVER!

Mandy: Yumming. "Umm, Etoen Ice Coffee, the original and the only canned ice coffee produced in Hawaii. No preservatives, specially blended with the finest ingredients for superior smooth taste, with no artificial flavors. Safe, healthy, well-designed and delicious." She is smiling away in apparent bliss.

Juan: Slamming and whamming the table. "Get Etoen Ice Coffee on the phone NOW. We'll be slapping, slamming, whamming harder than the Japanese in no time." Manic laughing. Juan's voice fading, "Ha ha ha we're gonna get em with MORE MORE MORE MORE Etoen Ice Coffee."

COMMERCIAL FINISHES.
Mandy says, "Here Bradley, Etoen Ice Coffee. Coffee break. Hot days in Hawaii need an ICE coffee break. Yeah?"

Mandy waits for a Bradley's swallow. So now Bradley, look at you, you are very talented at commercials. You could make a million dollars representing Advertisers."

Bradley answers, "If I had a million dollars I spend it in a week and give the rest away to charity."

Mandy replies, "Then what would you have?"

"I'd have a lot. What I got, is love."

Bud says, "Hey Mandy, those are all lyrics in Bradley's new songs."

Mandy says, "He sings away his life? Gives everything away?"

Bradley says, "I don't own anything."

Eric says, "He doesn't even own that stinking van."

Bradley says, "All my flesh and blood is put into things that end up in the pawn shops. Then the monies I get from the pawn shops. Flow down the river. Immerse into the abyss of the ocean. And in the morning. I wake up and wonder, where all the money has gone. Just doin' time. Here on Earth."

Bradley starts singing, "Summertime and the living is easy. Fish our jumpin,' As I'm twistin' my strings. Mandy's good lookin' and the breeze just kissin,' the sweat from my face, no fret, no cry. 'Cause LOVE, is what I got. And love, IS a lot."

Bud says, "I think Bradley's at it, song writing again."

Bradley starts singing, "Can't resists, the need for resistance. Can't resist the desires of the kids Can't resist the need for assistance. CAN, CAN resist those crushing lids." As Bradley's voice goes way low on 'those crushing lids.'

Mandy says, "You sing your way through life, Bradley?"

Nah, "We just put our rage into the beauty of rhythm and melody. Smells better that way."

Eric says, "And how."

※

That night I talk to Mandy. "What happened in the studio? You let them on air for three and half hours. I think I counted seventy-three fucks, shits and their derivatives.

Our own Bradley was there and laughs, "You like my name because of him? Well, Mandy met another sparkplug spewing, Danny. I thought you were the only one. Now you got competition."

"I would never talk like that," I say. "Especially on Radio."

Mandy and Bradley look at each other. Mandy says, "No, just in front of twenty thousand people and half the world when the press expounded on your words, worldwide."

"Come on guys, I'm not like that."

"You need to look in the mirror, Danny," says Bradley.

I was feeling volatile, edgy like. It had been twenty-six days. No word about Radiotron. I called Ida. It was past midnight in Washington D.C.

"They'll probably do something after the holidays." Ida says over the phone. "My father says they're waiting for more information, and Radiotron is not submitting even a request for a delay. It's like they are not even paying attention to the complaint."

"Well, what happens if they don't reply?"

"That's uncharted territory. My father says he never has heard of them not responding. They had two weeks, max, and ten days have pass since the deadline, just silence. Maybe they think they can use the holidays for a delay. Any commotion on your end?"

I say, "It's weird, it seems like the ad agencies don't know. No prying into us either."

Ida goes on, "My father says there is a payola case pending with Coldbolt Records conducted by the Federal Trade Commission, but no information forth coming. And somehow the Department of Justice is getting involved. The two departments are trading information. Something is going on but it's weird."

I'm thinking. Coldbolt records might be telling Radiotron not to make a move, pending some strategy planning. I always felt the major record companies were in bed with Radiotron. Just had no idea how.

"Fuck, dammit. It smells like collusion. Can't you guys make a, a complaint? Or something? Radiotron can break the law? Like no one else? They are immune to everything? Money protects them?"

Mandy yanks the phone from me. "Ida, sorry. Danny is just frustrated. Had a bad day. He'll be fine tomorrow."

I don't like to embarrass Mandy, but I guess I have.

Bradley knows better than to say anything, and leaves the room.

"I'm sorry, hon. It just drives me crazy, the way Radiotron thinks it owns the world and goes on doing anything it wants."

Mandy zeroes in on me. "You know Ida feels responsible. You know she is doing everything that can be done. Trust her. And don't upset her. She deals with this kind of stuff daily. You get a little frustrated having to deal with it for one day, and then you take it out on her? Tomorrow call her, and apologize. Okay?"

I think about it. Start calling back.

Mandy takes away the phone, "Damn Danny, she was probably sleeping. Tomorrow, okay?".

I nod.

27

TELECOMMUNICATION ACT

November 14, 1993

We had survived almost three years, selling a million and half copies of the CD and vinyl record of, "We Were All Given a Democracy; Why Not Use it?"

The BRBB Agency, with Jackson heading it, was now the third largest advertising agency in Honolulu.

And tonight there was a great celebration with Ida, her father, us five, Jackson and others. Why? The Department of Justice had finally made a decree, and Radiotron had to support two other companies' set-up costs, and allow them to compete in the market. We seemed to have won one front of the war.

We were celebrating in front of the house at the edge of the park amongst the pine trees with two local bands, the reggae band Dread Ashanti and the ska band, the Tantra Monsters, local bands that were big vote getters on the Radio Revolution.

Despite the carpet of pine cones and needles, Mandy was dancing barefoot with just about everybody at the party, being tossed here and there as she frolicked about like a school girl.

Ida, her father and Gregory were in a family confab, probably giving kudus to each other for their part in the Department of Justice's final decision. Ed was out there dancing, oblivious to his dead leg, and Mandy had dragged Jackson away from his wife for a twirl or two.

A bit winded after a few twirls with Mandy, Jackson came over to me and said, "We gotta talk."

Talks with Jackson were bad news generally so I laughed it off, and said, "Hey, we'll talk tomorrow."

Jackson grabbed my hand and started dragging me back into the house.

He plunked his body on to the couch, sweating. Let out a few short breaths like he was winded. I said, "I'll get a few beers," even though I had a half of one in my hand.

Bradley, the only somber one at the party, even when he is drunk, didn't help. He brought in the beer chest. No chance to get away now.

"Danny, I got a real interesting call today."

I relaxed. The first words weren't a death sentence. "So tell me," as I guzzled a big vacancy in my beer can.

He said, the caller was calling from Radiotron, but the phone number was from Los Angeles, and Radiotron is in New Jersey.

"Could be a representative. Radiotron has representatives in every market," I say.

"But this is the kind of phone call you would expect from the central office."

Shit, this might be another death sentence. "What did he say?"

"He asked if I would like four thousand dollars put in my personal account. I said, no, but you can send a check. No way I'm giving my bank information.

"He said, 'Radiotron doesn't write checks for this kind of stuff. However, I could get a middle party to write you a check. Radiotron would prefer to drop the money in a personal account every quarter I'm in business. And they would reduce my Radiotron subscription's payment to zero.'"

Jackson says, "So I asked, why the generosity?" If I choose to go along with this, I would save twenty-four thousand dollars extra, every year.

"He replied, 'A simple request. Buy your advertising using the Radiotron formula. You pay whatever Radiotron formula tells you to

THE RADIO REVOLUTION

pay, whether it is less or more of what the radio station is asking in dollars.'"

"My God." I was floored. I looked at Bradley. He shook his head. "So Radiotron is bribing the ad agencies so they can get big bucks from the Radio Stations. And even if there are other competitors in the market now, Radiotron will rule. It is like there is no way to stop corruption. It just gets more creative."

I say, "So Radiotron doesn't know the BBRB Agency is connected to the Radio Revolution?"

"No, but they know we do a lot of advertising with the Radio Revolution, I think they just want to stop that."

"Have you told Ida?"

"No, I thought you should know before I do anything."

"We'll set up a meeting tomorrow."

I got Ida and Jackson together the following day. Jackson, working with Ida, found a way to document the solicitation and two weeks later Ida sent the bribe solicitation to the Department of Justice."

Ida instructed Jackson to go along with the bribe but not follow Radiotron's formula.

April 6th 1995.

It was now seventeen months later. Ida's complaint had opened a huge can of worms. Investigations proved that independent promoters had given out millions of dollars to ad agencies, as well as promotion prizes to radio stations, and even straight out cash to radio stations. The conglomerate radio stations were hijacking the major record companies to play their records. No record got played without favors and monies directly paid to the radio station. The independent promoters were the go between, receiving the monies from the major record companies and transferring them to radio stations to get songs played.

The FCC and the Justice Department instituted huge fines on the major record companies and in light of Radiotron's coercion, and huge fines on Radiotron as well. This forced Radiotron into bankruptcy, and a group of political surveyors became the rating services for radio stations.

It was an earthquake in the radio and the record industry. Gone were the independent promoters. Gone was Radiotron. And fines were being considered for the conglomerate radio stations that were hijacking the record companies for favors, promotional prizes and outright cash.

Piper was out of the picture. After his other seventy-six stations were off the air for a year, they went up for sale and sold to various radio entrepreneurs. Piper's debt for all his other stations including fines, his electrical bills' debt, combined with the IRS liens for not paying payroll taxes to employees for his other seventy-six radio stations, had accumulated, and now manifested into two giant liens on Piper's last four owned radio stations - our stations. With penalties and interest, these liens had risen to seventy-five million dollars, and no one was that obsessed to get us off the air for that kind of money.

After the first two years The Radio Revolution was on the air, our contract was over with Piper, so we just continued without paying him a cent. There was nothing he could do. He tried suing us, but couldn't keep a lawyer to do it. Last I heard, he was in Australia with Fledge who had been his national program director.

Political surveying companies started using electronic ease dropping systems so one could tell how many listeners were broadcasting a signal at a time in any market. Radiotron had refused to use electronic ease dropping technology, probably because, they wanted to manipulate the results, though demographics were still handled by phones calls with the political surveyors.

The Radiotron diary system was dismissed as being absurd by political surveyors' analysts.

Radio stations across America now paid a set fee to the new rating services depending on the size of market. So if you didn't subscribe to a service, you were not listed at all. There was no more of Radiotron's policy. If you got high ratings you had to pay more to keep it.

The FCC Concert CD and LP was approaching three million in paid sales after another year and half. It was steady sales, non-stop, but not escalating. It just kept selling at a steady pace but we found out it was being bootlegged a lot by pressing plants that were selling bogus copies. As long as they bootlegged the booklet and artwork as well, we let it go. It was more important to get it out there and make America conscious of the Amendment to the constitution.

When something works, radio stations are great imitators and a lot of independent radio stations were starting to follow our example. We even had a yearly radio conference on beautiful Kauai where we explained in detail what we were doing and how we were doing it. And we had a thousand radio stations across the country who periodically came to these conferences. Our format became the darling of small and medium market radio stations but because of the enormous cost of ballot distribution in larger markets it became harder to do. But the internet was gradually turning into a way to do the ballots in larger markets and even major markets were running some of our concepts through ballot internet participation.

During the conferences, I made my speech. "Radio should never try and super serve a particular preference, it should be adding variety allowing more and more people to feel a part of the radio station. Once people believed all could express their views and tastes in music, people will feel your radio station is real, and they are a part of it, and in the sound alone medium, their imaginations will be stirred, as they hear *themselves* within the real world."

It was revolutionary thought, and radio programmers had a hard time mixing genres and allowing anything to happen if it was choices generated by the populace of their listeners. So tutoring an industry that had been doing pretty much the opposite for so long was an uphill battle, and many big chains balked at the Radio Revolution concept. But with our incredible success, owning a twenty-seven percentage of the population that listened to us, in Hawaii and being the number one radio station in medium markets on the Rolling Stone Magazine readership poll, they had to consider my philosophy.

Music wise though, even the big chains were following us. We were breaking all kinds of new music out; we were trend setters. It was the end of the major record companies' outright manipulation of the music played. Of course it wasn't us. It was listeners' ballots that were setting the trends.

One band, Reel Big Fish, came to one of our Big Meles, an open air concert with 15,000 or so attendees, and gave away five hundred of their CDs hoping the attendees would vote for their music on the Radio Revolution. And six months later, due to the accumulation system, their music did finally make it to the survey's rotation, and eventually their "Beer" song went to number one.

With that success, more bands having trouble getting airplay started campaigning to our listeners. Most radio stations across the country paid attention to our charts, even though our charts, unlike mainland radio charts, were in constant flux. What was number one on a weekly chart, could be off the survey the next week. This was caused by the negative vote counting and our accumulation method, where once you accumulated enough votes to get on the survey, the next week you started at zero.

So a lot of songs would go in and out of rotation, something radio programmers had a hard time dealing with even after it had proven to be so successful.

Nor did our charts reflect songs gradually rising and then gradually descending. There was a lot of jumping around week to week. Though, there were a few steady songs that remained on the chart for long periods. They were songs that didn't accumulate negative votes from overplay. Songs like Pachelbel's Cannon in D by the Juilliard String Quartet a song discovery from our listener, Reed Ota. It spent seven weeks at number one; Sublime's Santeria was eight weeks at number one, Pearl Jam's Yellow Ledbetter four weeks, and Bob Marley was the artist who almost never left the top 36 survey.

The neat thing was that now across the country each market had its own individual sound with many local artists doing extremely well in one market and not being played anywhere else. Like the fifties.

Rotation of music included more variety, even in major markets. And independent and import record companies began to dominate the charts once again.

By 1994 we had started to syndicate some of our specialty shows like Dance Hall Democracy, Juan's late night talk show, and even my oldies radio show, called the History of Rock N Roll for Extraterrestrials. It was a show that told the history of rock n' roll to kids who were just as informed as extraterrestrials were, to what had happened to rock n' roll, and the history of radio, and how it had come to suck.

There was underground payola still, unnoticed by the Federal Trade Commission. But it was not controlling the whole nation's market like the major record companies had done in the seventies, eighties and the early nineties. The songs that had gotten on radio purely through favors were quickly dropped if they weren't selling or being requested. Before, major record companies had been able to keep songs on the radio for lengthy periods of time, even though they had no requests and few sales. It was so bad, the top 40 songs of the entire year by Billboard in the 80s were rarely selling half as well as the popular bands *not* on the radio. Now with the major record companies not manipulating the charts to their favor, a good band could find instant popularity and become a hit overnight as thousands of independent record companies returned to the charts with regional hits.

Our amendment campaign was not doing as well. It had momentum for a little while, talked about on some news channels, laughed at on other news channels, nixed on others. The sum of money needed to fund all political campaigns in the nation could escalate to twelve even twenty-billion-dollars a year, some said. And you could have hundreds of people running for office in one race. There were giant logistic problems in qualifying, and couldn't you use your own money, or other peoples' monies to get enough signatures to qualify to run. And what was there to stop special interest groups from campaigning without using a candidate's name?

It appeared to make this work we were going to have to have a lot of rules, and every new rule would make it harder to get the amendment passed. I figured, get it started anyway. Down the road, we could augment necessary rules only when they became an obvious deterrent to the spirit and effectiveness of the amendment.

Besides, there were those who felt skeptical; no matter how many controls you put out there, representatives and senators would find a way to break the rules making it impossible to enforce it. Cheating was so common in Congress with congressmen getting illegal paybacks, no matter how free candidates were to make a choice for the people, they would still find a way to take care of lobbyists. It was a realistic problem. But it was a problem that might only arise. Worry about the amendment first. Worry about the problems later if they appeared. Action was first needed. Get the rudder of the nation moving in the that direction first. At least political parties would be dissolved. That, in itself, would change the fabric of politics.

Ida had held me back for four years pushing the amendment proposal in order for us to wait for the Department of Justice and the Federal Trade Commission to bring down Radiotron and the payola scams.

I became nervous, almost psychotic. But as the news came in that things were really happening I settled down and waited. Mandy was good at cooling my jets with our love, the conduit to hold me at bay.

But in the last six months we had started talking aggressively on the morning show about the amendment, and had rallied other stations using ours or part of our radio democracy concepts, to push for it.

Ida and the Progressive supporters set up The People's Party nationally. The Peoples' Party didn't care about one person's political beliefs. You could be a Republican, Democrat, Libertarian, whatever - you joined the party for one purpose: to push for this amendment and to force a states' constitutional convention for this one amendment only.

This amendment, alone, would open the door for a Congress to be more responsive to the people. Then other bills and amendments could be initiated once this amendment was law. So it was paramount this was the first amendment and all other amendments were not to be discussed until this amendment was ratified.

Then Congress would be free to listen to the people. And as candidates made it from the Peoples' Party into state legislatures, they started campaigning with other legislatures to have each state, demand a constitutional convention. And because most politicians spent near half their time begging to get monies for their campaigns, the amendment didn't seem too negative to other state legislatures.

Juan was such a great advocate of the amendment, and had such a passionate following for it, we switched Juan to the morning show, and put Mandy on the evening slot, trying to get an older demographic interested in the Peoples' Party campaign for the amendment.

Then Mandy between eight and nine on week nights started a radio show inside her room.

She would stop being a DJ and be in her virtual bedroom as a high school teenager. The show started with a recording by her father of the rules. She had to keep the bedroom door slightly ajar and have at least one leg on the floor if she was on her bed, have her homework finished by eight-thirty, and at a nine o'clock every night, lights out. Of course when the lights went out, Mandy would be under her covers listening to her transistor radio. And her regular show would resume. Once a month on Friday nights she would have a slumber party from eight to midnight and girl listeners who had won prizes were invited to her bedroom and they would talk and play songs tell midnight.

It was a completely relaxed show. "Oh hum, now, let's see. I think I'll play this Pixies' song, it reminds me of that cute boy at school." Homework problems, Mandy hated her math teacher, and she would wait for a listener to help her with her math homework. And of course, there was political science and history homework, and this new amendment to the constitution was discussed and the history of amendments were talked about, especially the negroes having a vote and women's suffrage. Mandy mused, it seems the amendments in general were efforts to make America more of a Democracy, and wasn't that true of this new amendment proposal?

Jackson loved the show, believe it or not, and he managed to get it syndicated across the United States with the help of the Hawaii Visitors Bureau. After a short six months, fourteen hundred radio stations, mostly in medium and small markets, had Mandy's recorded Bedroom Show playing between eight and nine each week night. Mandy started adding talk about the beach areas and surfing and what she was planning to do on the weekends in beautiful Hawaii because of the Hawaii Visitor Bureau's sponsorship.

She would talk about the great concerts coming to the islands, generated from popularity on ballots of the Radio Revolution. We were having two or three concerts each week as well as Dance Floor Democracy.

Juan's morning show was aimed at how the new amendment would change America. He invited legislators from both the State House of Representatives and Senate to guest on his show, and if they refused, he made a big deal about their refusal. He discussed the feasibility of a constitutional convention, asked the representatives what they were concerned about that they might not vote for this amendment, and then found pukas in state representatives' defenses.

Then he would open the phone lines and let the listeners ask these legislators their questions. There were some wild morning dialogues with enraged listeners letting their representatives have a piece of their mind. But Juan always redirected the questions to the amendment, and made it clear that if you called to complain to representative about anything else, Juan would cut you off. It was like his musical bananas show in the evening when he would change the song in midstream upon a listener's demand. The phones were so active in the morning that he would shut off one listener after another, as the lines were on fire from six twenty to eight forty every Friday morning with calls to the representative he was interviewing in the studio. And not a single song would get played until after eight forty AM on Fridays.

THE RADIO REVOLUTION

There were lots of complaints, but when Juan's show was put in the open forum, it was voted to be continued three to two. Juan was so emotional and so intense, and people loved to hear their representatives in the hot seat, so the show became a giant success. Legislators who refused to come on the show began reconsidering, when voting time came around. Juan would list every Friday morning each representative who so far had refused to come on his show. That included every attempt Juan tried to contact them, as recorded on the reel to reel tape recorder, and there no answering, or refusing to come to the station, or even the lies where they said they would come but never solidified the appointment. Juan was merciless, and the listeners, as a majority, loved it.

So, the People's Party started six months ago, had no concern to elect a President of the United States of America, or United States Representatives to Congress or the Senate. It was restricted to getting representatives elected to the state legislatures for one purpose: to generate a national constitutional convention of the states for this single amendment to take the money out of the political system, and make the government pay for elections.

So, making America aware of what this amendment would really mean, despite the dissenters and big money trying to confuse the people - that was our quest now, nationally. I mean it was so simple. If you want a radio station that plays what the masses want to hear, you set up a voting system. Duh. If you want big money and special interest not tampering with the government, you don't let their money effect elections. Duh. It was such a simple thing to fix with this new amendment to the constitution. Juan started calling it the "Duh" amendment. "If you don't want them tampering with government, don't let them effect campaign elections. Duh."

Gregory, now traveling with the bands around the country presenting concert after concert, always found a way to give speeches in the concerts making people aware of what this amendment really means. The name, "Radio Revolution Concert" was enough to bring people, even if they had never heard of the bands before.

And Gregory was now in the national news as the face of this new amendment, and on CNN and talk shows both with Republican and Democratic bias. Still the parties fought the idea. They didn't want to be obliterated with the government taking over their function of funding campaigns. We were getting a bigger and bigger segment of America aware of what this simple amendment would really do.

Then it happened.

Ida called. "We got a problem, Danny. There is an aggressive lobbyist in Washington DC pushing for a bill that would allow conglomerate radio stations to have five FM signals and three AM signals in every medium and major market across the entire United States. If it goes through, they can buy out all the small radio stations using our format, and with Piper still the owner, even our stations will be in jeopardy. Then they can consolidate all their stations under one roof, to save expenses, and have an even better edge in the market. It's being billed as being more competitive, which is total bull, and it includes the internet which is a sore point with the major record companies, but they got the monies to sway congress. Record companies started it but now the most powerful lobbyist in Washington, the media, is behind it to the max. I'm coming next week. We need to cut our losses the best we can. It is going through. I'm sure of it. I'm bringing two of the officers of Progressive America and the head of the People's Party with me. I sent Gregory back to Honolulu for the meeting. He should be there at eight tonight, on a direct flight from Chicago, three days before I can assemble my crew to come to Hawaii."

"You think the major record companies are doing this to shut us down?"

"Damn right. You and the internet. The major record companies are the ones initiating this and they were big supporters of the Trenton campaign. And even if he does veto it, the overwhelming majority will put it through anyway. Right now, there are only six senators and representatives against it.

"Where's the bill now?"

"It's in the House committee on communications and scheduled for subcommittee in two weeks. But believe it or not, the subcommittee is refusing to schedule a hearing with us. They say we need to prove how we are relative to their decision on this bill even to be heard by the subcommittee. And there is an even bigger push in the Senate. It's bipartisan. And they are actually excited to make this bill clear. If they do, someone will talk to the tax department, get a lower fine on Piper's radio stations, and buy out your radio station from Piper, and shut you down. Danny, I'm frightened. I'll tell you straight up. They are obsessed with this bill. It is the highlight of the session. We could rally the people to fight it, but congress doesn't listen to the people at all; you know that. Nor do we have time. And this bill will eliminate competition. Only conglomerates will be running all the radio stations of America in medium and large markets henceforth. It's that bad."

"Relax kid. It's just one more hurdle. We'll figure it out."

"Danny, you piss me off, calling me a 'kid' all-the-time. Optimist is too good a word. You are in lala land. I warned you we'd get the heat. What a creative and crafty way for congress to sabotage us. It's a master stroke, and you better know it, we are in trouble, deep."

I said, "Don't forget we've got a lot of things going for us now. Radio is coming out of its coma and it is the most powerful media there is."

"Danny, it is going to happen. We can't stop it. Meet us at the airport, Delta flight 3543 landing at 750 pm Sunday night. Get us three rooms at the Pagoda, Okay? We got to find a way to cut losses, even if it means losing all our kind of radio stations, and somehow get this amendment ratified. that's all."

"Ida, you stay with us, not the Pagoda. Okay. Calm down. Don't bring in the other parties until we all settle on what to do."

"Danny, you don't understand."

"I understand. You need to be with us alone, first. Then we'll talk to the other parties."

After that shocking phone call, I started investigating. The word was getting around at radio stations about this new change to radio act of 1934. It was talked like it was done deal. I got more concerned and called a meeting.

The meeting was in our living room.

When I arrived, it was like our house was on fire. Gregory had scared everybody even before I arrived. Gregory, on the couch, said, "Ida thinks somebody will buy out Piper's lien. She says there is a lot of money out there that sees us as the biggest obstacle to their agenda. And the IRS will make a settlement on the seventy-five million, knowing they are not going to get any money any other way. Same with the FCC fines. She says if this goes through, there will be a big push to buy out all our sister stations that are using part of our format, too."

Bradley says, "Before we do anything, we need to cover our ass. We go to the IRS and the FCC, and negotiate a settlement. Get the Progressive America to put up the first lump payment, then we can pay off the rest, maybe sixty-thousand a month, in a ten-year agreement. That's close to eight million dollars and with a ten million first payment by the Progressive party, we have enough funds to put up a million of that ourselves; and considering the alternative of no money at all, the IRS will probably go along with it. That will ensure we are on the air at least ten years even if this bill becomes law. Then once we get the amendment into law, we can dump this bill, pretty easily, I would think."

Mandy said. "Are you crazy? If we clear the debt, Piper will sell the station to somebody else. Or somebody could offer IRS even more money to take care of the lien. The IRS only needs to bargain and sell it to the highest bidder, like in an auction. and they can throw in another million for Piper and buy the station. And what about the sister stations of ours in America. We need to stop them from being bought out, too."

I said, "We could buy the station from Piper, give him a million, and make a deal with the IRS and the FCC to pay the balance."

Everybody stares at me. Juan says, "No way. Piper gets nothing."

I say, "I don't know what I was thinking, sorry."

THE RADIO REVOLUTION

Gregory says, "No way, Piper will just look for a better deal. And that will open a new can of worms."

Mandy says, "Any offer to Piper will show our weakness, our concern, and he will start nosing around and the last thing that vengeful soul will do is go with our deal if he has an alternative. He's already tried to lease the stations to other parties. Ida stopped it, him not being present in America, and unable to get FCC approval because of the pending fines."

Mandy adds, "We simply have to stop that bill from happening. Put all our resources that direction."

"Wait a minute," says Bradley. "We could buy other radio stations in our markets now, close these stations, and then we'd be safe, and Piper would be left out, hanging.

I say "As soon as you propose to buy a station, it gets posted, and whoever wishes can make a claim to stop it. And of course the other radio stations can outbid us."

Bradley says, "Then we need to find a third party totally divorced of the progressive party and us, and have them buy signals in the five markets and then we will agree to lease the stations for a ten-year period, pending ownership."

Mandy says, "That's still dangerous. Plus, who can we trust to go along with that? They would have to be somebody we reach in secret and then have absolutely no association with us until they become the owner."

Mandy reiterates, "We need to stop the bill, period."

"But how?" says Bradley.

We join in the power circle. Mandy puts herself in the middle. We do the aummmm. Juan grabs my arm, hard. Gregory grabs the other, also with unusual pressure. We maintain the aummmm, breaking into a sweat, I don't know why. There is so much intensity. It lasts longer than usual. Then Mandy goes to her knees and says solemnly. "Thank you. We'll put it together. Keep thinking until we see Ida. There will be a way."

She adds, "We have come so close, and then this masterful coup by big business. We *must* stop this."

28

THE DESPERATE MOVE

The next two nights Mandy stays with me. Lying next to me, she says, "Danny, Ida can't help us here. We've got to do this ourselves."

Since this disastrous news, she knows how crazy I am becoming, and she is trying to keep me calm. I am reeling. I don't know how to handle this situation. And Ida, the Peoples' Party and the Progressive America are landing tomorrow night.

I tell her, "We've got to talk to this Bernie Sanders. Ida says he's the only one in Congress fighting this tooth and nail."

She says, "No. We need a rudder to change the momentum. A congressman can't move a rudder in a new direction. Only the President. We've got to get to the President."

"How? He's for this."

"No, he is the President. He's for the *people*, especially at election time. We've got to get to him and show him what's really happening."

I say, "He is committed to this because of campaign funds from the record industry."

"No, he is committed to the people. After this election, he can't be President anymore. Whatever funds they gave him, if he can show the world how bad this will be, he will be remembered as a great President, plus he loves music. He just doesn't know what they're really doing. We've got to explain it to him. No matter who the President

THE RADIO REVOLUTION

in this country is, he is not like Congress. An enormous responsibility consumes his mind. He wants to do right for the common people. The President's position is so special. I don't care who he is. He cares for the people, even if he never has before, but sometimes he gets misinformation. It surrounds him constantly, but if we give him the real information, he'll help us. We've got to get to the President."

"You want me to talk to him?"

Mandy's eyes get that mischievous look again. "I wonder what songs the President of the United States would put on his ballot?"

"The President filling out a ballot." I laugh.

Mandy muses, "While Congress rushes this bill to be signed by the President, we'll slip in the back door and sabotage the bill and all of Congress, and yeah. Maybe Ida can help a little, after all. I've got an idea."

"Well, what's the idea?"

"The immediate idea is you and I get some cozy sleep together. It's okay love; it's gonna work out."

I laugh. "And Ida thinks I'm the optimist living in lala land?" I kiss Mandy's forehead. She puts her head on my chest. She says, "I love you enough to have your baby."

I'm in shock.

She smiles. "But let's get this Amendment ratified, first. Danny, this is our destiny."

How can it be? I suddenly feel completely at peace, amidst this disaster. I fall asleep with her head still on my chest.

❧

Next morning, I talk to Mandy about her idea at the breakfast table. She smiles. And writes on a note pad:

> "It's complicated, Mr. President. You are the rudder of this nation. You are in the best position to move this nation one direction or another. But you get a lot of

misinformation; people telling you things for their own benefit. Sometimes it is wise to listen to innocence, simple people, who see the world so differently than people with an agenda. It can broaden your perspective and help you make wiser decisions. That's what I'm hoping for, sir. You, in the next four years, perhaps making many wise decisions. I know it sounds mysterious. But some things are not tangible, not precise, and yet they can help you see a better world. And frankly, they can make you cry with their simple beauty."

"This is for the President?" I ask.

Mandy smiles.

"What, a letter?"

Mandy shakes her head. "This is for Ida, but don't tell her it is written by me. Tell her you wrote it and want her to memorize it and say it to the President. The President will see Ida. He won't see you, very likely, you're merely famous for the 'Fuck' speech."

"So, Ida goes in and says this out of the blue? Won't work."

"No, she goes in to see the President and asks him to listen to my show on WBCC that night in Washington DC. Asks him to fly to Honolulu and visit Mandy's Room. Ida's very respected, and the President will listen to what she says. And when he's thinking her request is absurd, have her memorize this speech, and say it. Danny, he'll find a way to come. There's a good chance he will."

"And what is gonna happen when he comes?" I ask.

"He'll talk himself into helping us."

"You have a premonition?"

"Danny, I think it will work. But you've got to convince Ida to do it. She owes you a lot. She won't want to do it. It'll jeopardize her career, but she'll do it, because you will be insistent and she won't be able to refuse you, she owes you so much. She'll see the President, and he may come."

I say, "Is that what you mean when you say, 'Go in the back door?' Mandy's Room is the back door?"

"Our radio station is the back door."

"And, I'm gonna be able to convince Ida of stuff I don't even understand?"

"That Danny, you've got to do it!"

🍥

Ida Stephan is ushered into the President's Oval Office. The room is like a living room with a pink/rouge walls, four sets of couches around the room, and in the distance, barely visible, sits what must be President Trenton, guarded by two flags.

Ida is surprised at the immensity of the room. The President stands up and walks down the long room to her, "Well, what an honor, Ms. Stephan."

Ida is amused. "My, such a warm introduction, I may not be too warm, though. Half the radio industry has asked me to talk to you."

President Trenton, laughs. "Well, you certainly are *not* intimated by this office as much as other first-time visitors. Have you been here before?"

"No, but I hope to live here one day."

"Well, if a black woman makes it to the Presidency, the odds in this town say, you will be the first. Please, have a seat." He motions Ida to sit on a side couch. They sit down, side by side.

"So, this visit is about the Telecommunication Act?"

"You've been briefed?"

"No, but I do my homework, and with you, it didn't take much research to know I'm dealing with a deadly lawyer who fights for the common good, and who instigated the investigation into payola and bringing down the monopoly rating service. So I put two and two together. Am I right?"

"I'm not here to waste your time, Mr. President. The Telecommunication Act looks like a done deal. But I want you to experience something, I want you to see what live radio is really like, and it will very likely help your re-election campaign this fall."

President Trenton hesitates. "You know, I had a college radio show at Boston College. I know what live radio is like. I don't understand."

"Perhaps I said it wrong. I want you to experience listener driven radio."

"Oh, so this is about the amendment being pushed by that Radio Station in Hawaii?"

"No, I wouldn't waste your time with that. That amendment is only dedicated to get candidates voted into state legislatures so they can petition congress for a states' constitutional convention. That has nothing to do with you.

"No, I want you to come to Hawaii and go on the Honolulu Radio Revolution Station for one or two hours and get a taste for what listener driven radio is. And the show you will be on is syndicated to fourteen hundred radio stations across America. It's called 'Mandy's Room.'

"She is inviting you. You can listen to it tonight on WBCC from 8pm to 9pm. She is inviting you to go to Honolulu and be on her show. I realize it is an outlandish request, but it should help your re-election tremendously."

President Trenton just laughs. "Physically? On her show? A strange request from a crafty, ruthless lawyer. In person, in Honolulu? No phone calling. Or phone interviews?"

"Yes, Mr. President. And I may be ruthless but I'm on your side. I voted for you and I will do it again. This should help you tremendously in the future."

"And who else will it help?"

"The youth of America, who are so jaded with politics and doubt there is any room for them in this world."

"You are doing this for kids?"

"Precisely."

The President laughs. "And kids will help me get reelected?"

"Yes. They have mothers, fathers, grandparents. When word gets out you're gonna be in Mandy's Room, a full one or two percent of the entire nation will be listening. Listenership without you is over two million. It's the most popular radio show in America, not counting certain sports events."

"I'm not sure if this will assist certain parties campaigning against me more than the youth of America. You know I can't really discuss official matters in a girl's bedroom, even a figurative one. This is outlandish, what you are asking."

Ida smiles. "Then you'd better brush up on your algebra. Mandy's having trouble with her homework, she might ask for your help."

President Trenton laughs. "Well, that would be fine. Certain parties out there are terrible at math." He laughs, enjoying his own joke.

A man in uniform enters the room. "Mr. President, the Chief of Staff is waiting."

President Trenton nods. "Give us ten minutes."

Ida watches the man's eyes bulge. Then acquiescing he says, "Yes, Mr. President."

"Mister President, at least listen to the show tonight. Then make your decision."

"You're serious?"

Ida nods.

"Ms. Stephan, I have respect for you, so I'll listen. But this is an outlandish request."

The President uses his intercom and the Secretary rushes in. "Be sure I listen to...?"

Ida says, "870FM on the radio dial, tonight from 8 to 9pm,"

The President adds, "Don't allow any calls. Except for a raging emergency."

The secretary takes out a notebook and looks strangely at Ida. And repeats the President's and Ida's words as he writes them down. His eye brows rise when he says, "raging emergency."

The secretary says, "Sir, the Chief of Staff is waiting. He says it is urgent."

"Give me five minutes."

Ida defers. "I shouldn't keep you, sorry Mr. President."

"Wait. You haven't told me the whole story. What is really going on?"

Ida waited until the secretary departed from ear shot.

"I can't say it any clearer, Mr. President. America needs you, desperately needs you. And Mandy's Room is the perfect place for you to be."

"Ms. Stephan, you are a natural politician. You answer a question with a bigger question. Okay, I'll listen. I'll do that, at least. I'll call you tomorrow or maybe in a day or two. You're asking me to do the unbelievable with no rational reason, so don't get your hopes up. Leave your number with the Secretary."

Ida recites the message Danny asked her to memorize.

"It's complicated, Mr. President. You are the rudder of this nation. You are in the best position to move this nation one direction or another. But you get a lot of misinformation; people telling you things for their own benefit. Sometimes it is wise to listen to innocence, simple people, who see the world so differently than people with an agenda. It can broaden your perspective and help you make wiser decisions. That's what I'm hoping for, sir. You, in the next four years, perhaps making many wise decisions. I know it sounds mysterious. But some things are not tangible, not precise, and yet they can help you see a better world. And frankly, they can make you cry with their simple beauty."

The President seems distant. Thoughtful. *They can make you cry with their simple beauty.*

Ida stands up.

The President stands also. "I'll seriously consider a visit to Honolulu, Ms. Stephan, simply because you have asked. The logistical nightmare - overriding parts of my agenda - must be considered pragmatically. But I'll listen tonight. And respond to your request tomorrow, or maybe in a few days."

"Thank you, sir."

The President says, "You're a mysterious but brilliant lady." He smiles and shakes Ida's hand. Then walks back to his desk and turning, waves goodbye, maintaining his smile, "Until you make this house your home, goodbye."

Ida is in shock. *He's actually entertaining it. Didn't even bother over a phone interview.*

The uniformed man moved briskly into the office as Ida departed.

29

MANDY'S ROOM

Ida walks into Mandy's show as Mandy is saying goodnight to the listeners. Mandy looks up. She is shocked. "What are you doing here?"

"I've got to talk to you in private."

Mandy looks around. "The overnight crew is just outside."

Ida says, "Then meet me in the blue rent-a-car in the fourth slot in the parking lot."

Ida makes an abrupt turn and leaves.

The overnight crew looks at Ida as she bursts out of the building. "Who's that?"

Mandy lies, "My aunt."

One DJ says, "She looks pissed."

Mandy goes to the parking lot, looks around, gets in the car, shuts the door.

Mandy asks, "Is something wrong?"

"The President will be here in a week, on Thursday, June 23rd. He's on his way to China, but he will stop by for a few hours while his plane is being refueled. But the bad news, for security reasons, we can't say he is coming. You can't even say we have a very special guest coming and be sure to have your parents, grandparents and great grandparents all listening. We can't say anything, not even suggest that something important is coming. Nor can you tell anybody at

THE RADIO REVOLUTION

all. If word gets out he'll be forced to cancel the visit. The President is taking a helicopter from the Wheeler Air Force Base and landing right smack dab in the middle of Amana Street. The streets around the station will be closed off under cover of emergency construction. Everybody on Amana Street will be unable to go home for two or three hours, and they will get no warning. Don't tell Danny, don't make up a skit with your parents about the President's entrance. This will be a total surprise. Only secret service personnel will be blocking off the street. But after the event, we can advertise it on the other fourteen hundred stations, providing the President approves the rebroadcast. Don't tell Danny or anyone. Don't say a word to anybody, even the family. Let everybody be surprised. Better, shocked."

Mandy asks, "How do you evict everybody off the block? Is that necessary?"

"The President has to land in the middle of Amana Street, Mandy. The immediate area will be closed off. They tell me the secret security with FBI badges will clear out the area. People in the building will be escorted out; everybody but you."

"The whole block will just be me and the President?"

"And the helicopter pilots, plus his security entourage, and the Military man that carries the nuclear communication box."

"Mandy, you have no idea how many feathers you are ruffling by making him stop at a location in Hawaii, with limited security. Most of his security team is scoping out his China destination and he was forced to bring in last minute resources for this stop. So no word to anybody. I couldn't even call you on the phone. I had to fly here and talk to you personally. And I'll be frank. I'm scared you might blow it, and ruin my career."

It's dawning on Mandy that the President is really coming.

Ida asks, "Does anybody know that Danny asked for the President?"

"Well, I've mentioned it to Gregory. Bradley and Juan... I don't think I mentioned it to them. But Gregory and Danny might have said something to them."

Ida smiles, "I guess people can know Danny invited the President, but presumably you haven't gotten a response."

"I hate lying to the family."

"You can explain why you were forced to lie, after he comes. It is so important that only you and I know, and the secret service. Danny doesn't know I'm here. Don't say a word to him. Come to the show Thursday like normal. Everybody in the building and on the block will be ejected for a spell except you, so you'll probably have to run the board a little before seven o'clock when your show normally starts. So come in before six. And say nothing to whomever is there."

"So what does the President know?"

"He knows nothing of what you might ask him or the listeners. Danny had me memorize what to say to him if I thought the President wasn't coming. I thought Danny was being crazy. But it worked. The President was very moved with Danny's rudder analogy and the mystery of it all. Did you hear what Danny told me to say?"

Mandy smiles, "Yeah, I know." Mandy feels relieved. She's thinking, I know how to push his button, I can handle the President. But it is too early to celebrate.

"Actually, what are you going to do? Whatever, don't make him look bad. My neck is on the line. I can't believe he agreed."

"I know why he decided to come. The President is so bottled up. He is looking for a moment to be natural. He listened to my show, didn't he?"

It's past midnight. Cars are closing their doors, leaving. Mandy is trying to absorb Ida's intensity but the pressure is stifling. She never has seen Ida so intense.

Ida says, "Yes, Danny insisted I tell him to listen. And Danny made me memorize that rudder speech. Me, I can't believe it. I don't know why we got the President, Mandy. We got him. I just can't believe it. I don't know what good it will do, but we got him for two hours and twenty-seven minutes."

Mandy smiles. "It's just like convincing Jackson. I know how to do those things."

THE RADIO REVOLUTION

"You gonna convince the President of what?"

"I'm not gonna convince him of anything, just let him be natural for one or two hours. And he'll convince himself."

Ida says, "I've got an appointment with the President because of my accomplishments in DC. Danny told me to say some crazy things like this radio show has no agenda, just lighting up the kids, making them feel there is place for them in government. But I know Juan and you are constantly pumping the amendment. Don't mention it when he's here. Promise me. Danny drives me crazy. I hope he isn't misleading the President."

"Mandy smiles, "You're safe, Ida. It will work out okay."

※

Orchestrated by the secret service with FBI badges, a bomb scare was announced at 6:40 pm, June 23rd. Amana Street was cleared. People in the high rises were asked to leave and businesses were forced to close. The Honolulu Police Department shut down the streets around Amana street for everybody but residents and business.

At 7:50 pm the helicopter motor blade buzzes as it settles down with the President and four escorts. Mandy's hair is blowing in the wind, her black blouse flapping as the helicopter is winding down. The President steps out of the helicopter last. He greets Mandy with a smile. Shakes her hand as the propeller winds down. The six take the elevator up the four flights to the radio station's entrance.

Mandy says, "Mr. President, Can you think of us as in a play here live on the radio? Can you pretend to be seventeen again and be our class President instead of *The* President? And pretend I'm sixteen and you're my friend, just hanging out. My imaginary father has grudgingly approved and has allowed me to stay up till ten, or until we are finished with my homework, knowing I have a big test tomorrow."

President Trenton smiles. "Don't mind being seventeen again, and where is your cat, Mercedes?"

"Oh, so you've listened to my show! But this is an imaginary show. The leader of our format believes radio lives far better in the imagination, stirring the mind with the medium of sound for others to create their own pictures of what is going on. That's why this show is play-acting. So tonight, you might have fun, pretending."

President Trenton says, "Can we stay in the dining room tonight? It might not look too good being in your bedroom."

"Yes, my dad is in the living room tonight, while you are helping me with my homework on the dining room table. Ida had me set it up that way."

The President felt relieved. Ida was thinking of his situation as President in a girl's bedroom.

He looks at the studio as Mandy moves behind the long desk table. The walls are lined to the ceiling with a library of thousands of CDs. A record player has an assortment of vinyl records, and a few vinyl 45s in a small bookcase underneath the desk table.

The President is on the other side as Mandy punches in a cart as the radio starts voicing the imaginary father who begins to tell the rules for the night. "Now Mandy, be sure you concentrate on your homework with your helper, I'll turn off the TV so you guys can concentrate on your homework. You sure Bobby can help you?"

"Yes Dad, Bobby got an "A" from Mrs. Becker's class." End of tape.

Mandy turns on the mic. "Welcome Bobby, thank you so much for coming. I'm having a little trouble. I got a D on the midterm in government. And tomorrow is the final."

The President says, "Yeah, I had that teacher last year. Mrs. Becker kicked a lot of kids off the football team because of poor grades in her class. She's a tough grader."

Mandy smiles. The President is jumping right into playacting. "But you got an A."

"I'm not very smart, Mandy. But if I got a B, I might get in trouble at home. My stepdad got all 'As' in school, and takes my grades way too serious. I have to get As, or I might get kicked out. He is always telling me to be responsible, face life. It sucks. You are far luckier than me, having a caring and understanding dad."

"Wow, Bobby, he's that mean? I'm sorry." Mandy was honestly, stunned. She thought, there must be an element of truth in the President's statement.

She catches her breath. She whispers, "I think we can hold off homework awhile. Oh, the phone's ringing. I better pick it up before my father does, sorry."

Mandy talks over the air to the phone caller. "Oh hi, I got the class President with me. You want to talk to Bobby? it's a dollar a minute, nah, I'm joking. You can call him Mr. President 'cause this is the second year he has been voted Class President. Shush, Bobby Trenton is in my home."

"Bobby's your boyfriend?"

"No silly, He's helping me with my government final. He got an 'A' from Mrs. Becker. Dad is worried about my government grade."

President Robert Trenton smiles.

Mandy turns to Bobby. "Real smart people, if they are smart in school, play it down, so they can fit in with everybody else. I know what you're doing, trying to pretend you aren't smart. But you *are* smart," and in a whisper, "cute" and in a hush whisper that had a bit of an explanation point on it, "hot."

President Trent laughs. *It's fun being seventeen again.* He smiles, his eyes a bit watery-- possibly remembering a girl in his teen years.

Mandy puts in a cart and Dad says, "What's going on? Who's hot?"

"Dad, it's the popcorn popper; it's hot. We're just studying."

Mandy says, "Bobby, Mrs. Becker asked me on the midterm test to write an essay on what Government does. And I wrote three whole pages and she gave me an "F." What do you think government is for?"

President Trenton says, "Well Mrs. Becker is a purist; she wants you to recite what government is supposed to be. Government is everywhere. The guys picking up the trash on Mondays, the people, like Mrs. Becker, trying to help give kids an education, the highways running smoothly so we can get to work and school, all that is government. Did you mention that? Government is for the common good; that's what Mrs. Becker wants you to say."

"So big business, oil companies, bank conglomerates, Wall Street, are they government?'

"No, they're capitalism. They have special interests. They're not concerned with the common good."

"Is religion government?"

"No. The First Amendment, Freedom of Religion, states that Government must stay out of religious stuff. The people that made up the Constitution were deathly afraid of religion being a part of government. There was so much of that back in the seventeen-hundreds, and it caused all kinds of turmoil. When the constitution was taken around to the states the very first thing they demanded was freedom of speech, and second, religious freedom. The very first amendment to the constitution was concerned with your ability to voice your opinion and your right to religious freedom. A lot of their parents and grandparents had fled Europe to avoid religious persecution. For in that day, it was utterly revolutionary. People can say what they think? That was an entirely new concept in the 1700s. And religious freedom, that too, was unheard of then. Governments then, mostly had a state religion."

"Phones have been lighting up." Mandy smiles. "I think my friends want to talk to the high school student body president." Mandy airs the phone call over the radio. "Mandy, you're kidding, is that the President?"

"Where are you calling from? Are you studying for tomorrow's final?"

"I'm Melissa calling from Salt Lake."

"Oh Melissa, I've got a cute guy in my bedroom. You know, that cute guy, Bobby Trenton?"

The dad on tape says, "Mandy, stay off the phone. Concentrate on your homework."

Mandy goes on the mic, "No dad, the phone call is for Bobby."

President Robert Trenton laughs and picks up the phone.

The President asks, "Are you doing your government homework now, too, Melissa?"

"Not anymore."

Mandy grabs the phone from the President, "Well you know, Bobby is smart, He can help, if you want."

Melissa says, "Where's your house? I'm coming over. Now!"

Mandy says, "I got to talk to Dad, and because I got Bobby to help with my homework. I don't know, maybe he can help you on the phone. I think I'll take a break and play 'Rhinoceros' by the Smashing Pumpkins. You talk to Bobby. You like Smashing Pumpkins, Bobby?"

President Robert Trenton says, "I don't think I've ever done that."

Melissa is giggling. President Robert Trenton starts talking to Melissa, but not on the air. Rhinoceros by Smashing Pumpkins plays over the air.

"What are you studying in government?"

"The separation of power, stuff."

"Like the Judicial, legislative and Executive?"

"Yeah."

"Our forefathers were deathly afraid of dictators. Still, they needed a single leader. Mrs. Becker thinks today it might be best to have multiple leaders; one leader to take care of international affairs, one to take care of national affairs... the world is getting too small, and the job is too big nowadays for one man."

"Or a woman?"

"Right Melissa, or a woman, sorry."

The President continues, "So they separated the power into threes. Today, Mrs. Becker would prefer it be separated into fours with two separate Presidents."

"But can we change it to four?" Melissa asks.

"With an amendment to the constitution, possibly."

Mandy asks Bobby, "Is it alright if I air your conversation?"

"Sure, if it is alright with Melissa."

Melissa, says, "Oh my God, yes!"

President Robert Trenton is beginning to think. This is for teen kids. This is a masterful plan of Mandy's, to remind everybody what the constitution was about in the beginning. He finds himself feeling sentimental. And he is thoroughly impressed with Mandy.

Mandy says, "Oh hum, I might study better with a heavy metal song by Slayer." The song "Angel of Death" blares over the radio.

Off air the President says, "So this station is called The Radio Revolution? What's the name revolution for? To remind people about the American Revolution?"

"Well Bobby, revolutions are to make things more democratic, I think. We've got this voting system; did you fill out a ballot this week?"

"A ballot?"

"Here, I got an extra one. Vote for the ten songs you want to hear on radio the most. The three songs you want radio to stop playing the most, and a song you think will become a hit if radio played it. I'll put it in the school box in the cafeteria tomorrow for you."

"I don't know what you play."

"Vote for anything you want to hear on the radio, like right now."

"Stations don't have what I want to hear."

Mandy smiles. "Try me."

"Curtis Fuller?"

"Oh, that's right, you play trombone."

"You're familiar with Curtis Fuller?"

Mandy sweeps around the desk like a ballerina and plucks out a cd, barely even looking. The President steps aside. As she walks around the desk back to the mic she waves it proudly to the President, saying, "My ska friends who play the trombone love Curtis Fuller. He gets votes sometimes; I've heard it on the radio before. Here is that relaxing scaling sound now." As "Angel of Death" ends, she replays their conversation over the radio.

The instrumental begins, softly. Over the soft instrumental with the mic still open, the President says, "Mandy, I'm quite impressed. You really do know Curtis Fuller!"

"Of course, I listen to the radio all the time. I've learned a bit about music from the listener ballots on the Radio Revolution." Mandy smiles. "By request from Bobby Trenton, our class President, here is Curtis Fuller." She raises the volume.

The President says, off air, "This is novel. This station plays anything?"

"Yeah, whatever gets voted gets played. Be sure to fill out the whole ballot, okay? Everybody will be interested in what the school president wants to hear. And each time you fill out a ballot you get to be a program director. Program directors choose the music played on The Radio Revolution."

"Mandy why are we talking about the constitution?"

"Bobby, we are just playacting. Like a girl in a doll house, boys playing war games in the muddy dirt outside their house. We are just playing. Don't think about anything else; just play."

"But I have to be responsible for every word I say. My words are just fuel for the media sensationalists. I'm the President; always a media target."

Mandy stares at the President. "President, why are you here?

The President hesitates.

Mandy answers, "To play. Every other hour you're thinking this, thinking that, thinking what will happen with that? What will happen if I say this? You're worried. Understandable. But tonight, we are just play-acting, and by doing that, everybody will know you are just like everybody else, and they'll vote for you. So be yourself, and make everybody listening feel your magnificent presence. You are cute, You are loving. You are embarrassed. I see that. You are having fun and you play-act well. And you always can say we were just acting. But in the process, with my guidance, you will remind people what built America. The kids need to know. In fact, the whole country has seemed to have forgotten."

The President considers. *Who is this woman? So brazen, so confident.*

"Mr. President, there are no set ups here. Everything is live. Whoever calls, calls. Danny, our leader, demands that we just let things happen. That is the radio revolution. Let pure democracy happen, at least on radio.

"Are you up to that? If not, I can key the show down. The last thing I want to do is make The President feel uncomfortable."

President Trenton says, "I feel uncomfortable." He laughs. "But somehow I feel it is alright. Keep doing what you are doing. I'll try my best to play-act."

Mandy turns the mic back on as the Curtis Fuller song fades.

"So that's why I got an 'F' on the midterm test. Government is here for the common good, not for special interest."

The President responds, "Yes, Mandy. Mrs. Becker says that you can't put a limit on money for health issues, self-defense, justice, or Education. You can't put a limit on money for infrastructure; you can't. Whatever is needed for the common good has got to be done. The common good, the needs of the people to live and pursue happiness - that is beyond money."

Mandy says, "But those kinds of things cost lots of money?"

"They are needed. That is beyond money. Mrs. Becker says that government needs leaders who know that, and they must find a way to tax everybody equally to take care of those needs, and find the most efficient way to pay for those services that are really beyond money. Taxes hurt the economy if government doesn't do it efficiently and fairly. Government needs to do it equally. Then everybody doesn't feel bad sacrificing money to the government. and the government can't play God, all things need to be equally important, and it would be a disaster if government decided not to take care of all those things, each with equal importance."

Mandy says, "Um, I must have been asleep in class. How is it a disaster?"

"If our self-defense is not sufficient, that would be a disaster. We would be vulnerable to massive destruction. If health, education, infrastructure, and our overall welfare of the populace wasn't taken care of, it would plunge the economy into a recession and finally a depression. And if we didn't spend funds for justice, true justice, then it would cost us with riots and chaos. If you said that on your paper, Mrs. Becker, a purist, would have given you an A."

"So if you were the President, how would you do that?"

"That's Congress's job. We have separation of powers. The President can spur the country a certain direction and if Congress gives him bills that don't fairly take care of the needs of the common good, then the President can veto the bill, slow it down or stop it from happening. But that is really Congress's job, not the President's. Sure, the President controls the armed forces and he can exact ways to make the services more efficient and cost effective, but funding itself comes from Congress. The constitution is set up so that the President doesn't have control over those matters, though he can campaign Congress to take care of those matters. But Congress has the last say."

"So NRA, big business lobbies, special interest lobbies, they are not government, but they get their way with Congress. How can that not be government?"

"They have special interest yes, but they are such a big part of the economy, that their special interests, on most occasions, end up aiding America and the economy. Not always, but many do. And when they go international our Congress aids them in their endeavors, generally. But rarely do their interest internationally aid other countries. That's why with the world getting smaller and smaller, Mrs. Becker thinks what happens in the rest of the world ends up affecting us, and she thinks it is time we have an international President who works with the world and airs other countries grievances before Congress, and allows other countries to make their case in front of Congress and the Senate.

"Wow, so the world is getting so small we all, not just the nation, have to work together?"

Mandy, Mrs. Becker sees America in a privileged position. She has talked about that, yeah? She says we need to remember that, and that a great part of the World isn't in our position. But they are people like us. She says we need to help them, whether it helps us or not. She believes we just don't know how it is going to help us, until we do it. Sometimes, it just fills our heart, but we don't see the economic value, at least right away."

"Filling our heart? Mrs. Becker thinks like that?"

"Mrs. Becker will find a way to say it helps us. She'll rationalize it will help us. It might not. It might help. It is like helping the less fortunate opens a can of worms. We don't know what is going to happen. It might help. It might not. The point is it might help. And they need help. So give it a try. The economic thing is, if we do it for the common good, and not for special interest, even if it doesn't appear to work immediately, it costs the economy less because the government is doing it for the common good. Taking care of special interest in the government costs the economy. Taking care of the common good normally doesn't cost the economy a cent." President Trenton, laughs. "I figured that out all on my own in class. And when I told Mrs. Becker, she took back my homework, and wrote an A plus on it., Even though my homework wasn't completed. And she said, "The campaign for the world president would enlighten the populace of the troubles of the world. Not just US citizens' personal concerns."

Bobby, so that's how you got an "A?"

President Trenton smiles "Embarrassing, huh, I didn't do too much homework and the technical detail stuff on the tests, I, I, didn't do too well with that."

The show continues for another forty minutes.

Mandy says, "I'm surprised. Danny, our director, might like you to have a show on our station. We do a lot of political stuff for the common good. Do you have free time for that? I don't mean that. Sorry. You got to concentrate on your studies. Would your stepfather really kick you out of the house if you didn't get an A?"

Mandy puts on the cart. Her imaginary father says, "There's a lot talkin' going on in the dining room. Is the homework finished. It is after nine."

Mandy goes on the mike. "Dad, Bobby's being a big help, and yeah we are talking about how to get good grades from Mrs. Becker."

Mandy laughs and whispers, "I'm really learning how to be a teacher's pet. Thanks Bobby. My next test with Mrs. Becker is tomorrow. It is on government's role in the economy. The essay test is "'We are a free enterprise but do we need the government to get involved with helping the economy?"

"Well, I had the same essay last year but I was lucky because in history class my special project was President Franklin Roosevelt. And I wrote on that test this. 'When Franklin Roosevelt took over the economy in America during the giant depression, a great economist told him bluntly, 'You just got to put money into the nation. Just give it to them, every single man, give them money, or you'll never get out of this depression.' You've got to remember then, America was desperate. People were so desperate they wanted Roosevelt to become an emergency dictator. But the President resisted doing that.

"Roosevelt said, 'Americans are too proud to take money for nothing.'

"The economist rebounded, 'Well then, put the money in the ground everywhere, let them dig, let them sweat, looking for it,'

"The economist name was Keynes. He said government budget deficits are good. Providing the debt is going directly to the people for their common good. As long as your gross product of a nation is relatively high compared with other countries, you can maintain a large debt and America has the most gross product. America could even exceed its gross product with debt in times of emergency and still be fine. They did it in the second world war. The point is, going into debt for the common good will increase gross product and reduce debt. Throw money you don't have into the pot. Keynes was adamant. Do that, and the economy rectifies itself. And he was right. It has been proven. It works over and over again."

Mandy says "So the difference is, you put money you don't have into the common good, and that money actually doesn't cost you, it helps stir the economy?"

"It's deeper than that. It creates value. It promotes the well-being of individuals which in turn stirs the economy to grow. It creates new avenues for growth. It is like watering a tree. They need water desperately, or they wilt. You want them to grow new branches and soak up more sun. And as they grow they reduce debt through increase growth of gross product. The tree grows and grows, if you water it.

"It was like during World War 2, Keynes told Roosevelt when the war finishes, you are going to have a recession. You water for growth. And after the war Roosevelt's plan suggested by Keynes, gave GI loans for houses and education and saved our economy from slipping back into a recession. So it is imperative during a recession or depression, for government to spend money it doesn't have to reactivate the economy. In other words, to do it for the common good. So if you spend money on education, infrastructure, health care, all things for the common good, etc, you will rise out of the recession rapidly. That is what government has to do to prevent recessions and depressions. That's what Mrs. Becker wants you writing about."

Mandy says, "But if I spend money I don't have, I get in trouble. Even go bankrupt. Can't pay my bills which hurts the economy, even more. What's the difference?"

"You are over spending for your personal benefit. That's the difference.

"If Government spends money for the common good, that's different. The money they are spending is creating value in the marketplace. Better health care, better infrastructure, better environment controls, better education, better welfare, better self-defense, its different. So it's really not just spending money. It's also creating value in the market which booms the economy and then pays off the debt incurred. The debt is not important. Of course, if government is not spending properly, paying more heed to special interest and self-interest, than the common good, it hurts the economy. And starting wars is not for the welfare of anybody but special interest."

"But if somebody else starts a war with you, what do you do?"

"Then you are forced to fight back." But the world is so small now, with technology and everybody depending on everybody else for economic stability, that the one who starts the war always loses the war. In ancient times people could start and win wars. But for the past hundred years who ever starts the war loses it. Why, because the economic damage to the world escalates, and the other countries pull together and fight back in unison. Granted they are hesitant, no one wants to go to war except crazed leaders and special interests, but when the economic pain gets unbearable, and then starts hurting other countries' economies, they amass together and fight back. And yet it is funny, if a whole country feels it is good to fight, everybody pulls together, and magically it aids the economy despite the government going into deep debt, even including the death and destruction the war causes. Mandy the human spirit is what really decides who wins a war, no matter how powerful the enemy may be. Even two hundred years ago, think of America under British control. We fought insurmountable odds, and somehow won. So the people or dictator that tries to take over, always loses now that the world is getting smaller. Eventually the other countries gang together and the one getting invaded gets help to win the war."

Mandy says, "So war needs to be avoided, unless we are being attacked, or helping somebody else who is getting attacked. Right?"

The President says, "Yes."

Mandy says, "So helping people with free money who can't make it on their own. Is that part of the welfare you are talking about that is also for the common good?"

"The economist Keynes said bluntly. 'To get out of the depression, just give em money you don't have.'. But President Roosevelt said, 'I can't, they are too proud.'

"That killer dialogue is a mind blower. Roosevelt knew something that maybe Keynes didn't consider.

"The most driving force in a free enterprise state, *is self-worth*. If the economy blooms with government borrowing money it doesn't have, and people still have no self-worth, that blooming economy starts to wilt. So, the government really needs to put people to work and then give the money, hopefully based on the value of their performance.".

"I can see why you got an 'A' from Mrs. Becker. And I see why you got reelected class President."

President Trenton, laughs.

Mandy was conscious not to open the phones. She wanted the President not to be disturbed with his presentation. Nor did she want people questioning him, are you really the President? The phones could come on her next show Friday and Monday night. Then they can discuss what the President said. And she was impressed with this President. He was sticking his neck out with pretty revolutionary thinking and she didn't want him to have to defend his position. She put the phones on eternal busy. She knew Danny wouldn't like that. Danny thought open participation, no screening phone calls, was everything. She tells the President off the air as the Dance Hall Crashers play "Shelley," "I'm afraid to open the phone lines. I think it is best we close the show, I just want to know, do you want me to send this show to the other 1436 stations? They normally get my weekly shows the next week, this one next Thursday."

President Trenton hesitates then says. "This show has been wonderful. You have addressed things that my speech writers have stopped me from saying. I'm glad I said it. Yeah, I can always blame Mrs. Becker," the President laughs. "Sure, there will be turmoil that I said these words. But we have *started* to deal with what government is really here for. And I guess that is the rudder that Ida wanted me to start moving the right direction. She's a crafty lawyer."

Mandy smiles.

The President continues, "The last question I want you to ask me is, 'Is that all I need to write on Mrs. Becker's test tomorrow?' And I'll mention something else Mrs. Becker is looking to be found on your essay."

Mandy looks at the President. "God, thank you. Thank you, Mr. President."

"Thank you! I'm glad I came."

Mandy smiles, puts in another cart, "Mandy, it is getting awful late. Bobby has to go home,"

"I know Dad, we are almost finished."

"So is there anything else Mrs. Becker is looking for on tomorrow's essay?"

30

THE RUDDER MOVES

Bobby says, "So we know what Mrs. Becker is for: putting value into the common good. And she believes when we get comfortable, and people don't have to spend all their time just surviving, then some can get lazy and coast, or others get more active and try and get ahead of the next guy or learn more to be more productive in society. They have a choice. Some do. Some don't. But the ones who do? This creates innovation. And innovation increases demand. It can be a new technology, or a new easier way to reach the old demand like with convenience, or simply shortening time.

"But of course, if government pays heed to special interest groups, this depletes the economy instead. It does it two ways. First, the biggest businesses try to sway congress for better ways to improve their position in the world market, and government goes along with this, thinking it's helping America over its competition in the other countries.

"That's why Mrs. Becker thinks we need someone to work with other countries, to allow other countries to voice their concerns over this behavior. The world is getting too small, and if other countries hurt, it starts hurting us too, she says. And if we are all tied together using the American dollar as currency and possibly two thirds of our currency is in other countries, when recessions happen in one country, because we are catering to self interest in our country, it hurts the economy world-wide, maybe less here in the United States than elsewhere, but nevertheless it hurts.

"Also, Roosevelt's self-worth looms bigger as well. Helping giant businesses get bigger reduces the self-worth of each individual working in the big business. If you are in a small business, you can see your presence helping the business grow. Your self-worth grows. But when government is helping a big business get bigger, the people in the big companies see their self-worth diminishing. Big business goes after controlling the market while innovators trying to increase value in the market get muffled or fired. Suddenly you can't see the difference you are making to the overall picture in a big company. Reducing self-worth gives less incentive and productivity, therefore the economy, suffers. Didn't Mrs. Becker talk about that in class?"

Mandy says, "Yeah, sorta, I think. So there needs to be a way to get self-interest out of government and keep big business from getting bigger? Why doesn't government just do it?"

"You might get an 'A' in class if you mentioned that question to Mrs. Becker."

The President continues. "Congress is full of normal people, all of which need to balance their checkbook every day. So it is hard for them to realize taking care of the common good isn't the same as balancing your check book. And the pressure from big business to go on runaway and consume markets is so huge, they don't realize that is really crushing free enterprise and hurting the economy while it reduces self-worth. Mrs. Becker is always talking about runaway capitalism, even though her class isn't an economics class. Haven't you heard her talk about that?"

Mandy puts on a cart. "Mandy, Bobby has to leave right now. You are way past your bedtime, and your final is tomorrow. Bobby, time to say goodnight."

Mandy goes on the mic. "Yes, Dad. Sorry Bobby, I guess you gotta go. But wait, did you finish filling out your ballot? I'll turn it in to the cafeteria tomorrow."

"Well I haven't finished. I'll fill it out later and turn it into the cafeteria myself."

"Okay. Well Bobby, you have been a big help! I'm sure I'll do well on the test now. I thought Mrs. Becker was, well, you know - a bitch. But now I see what you mean: she is just trying to help us realize what government is really for. Thank you."

Mandy, in a haunting voice, says, "Bye Bobby."

The President smiles, fading from the mic, "Mandy it's been fun."

Still over the mic Mandy announces, "Time to get into my pajamas now." Twenty seconds later with a rustling sound, "Okay, now I'm gonna slip my head under the covers, turn off the light and where is my transistor radio? Oh, I see it."

There are twenty seconds of dead air as the covers rustle. Then her father says, "Goodnight love, good luck on your test tomorrow." And shuts the door. She pretends to be asleep and then turns on her transistor radio listening to the song "Hello Goodbye," by the Beatles.

In the studio Mandy says off air, "Mr. President, thank you so much. You have been a big help. Do you have time to fill out your ballot, no?"

"Well, I didn't fill it all the way. Maybe I should take it with me and put it in the box, myself."

"Okay Mr. President, thank you so much!"

The President leaves with his entourage. Mandy hears the helicopter propeller crank up.

She sits down and puts her face in her hands. "Oh my God, that was the President."

She lets a string of commercials she had held back for an hour and seventeen minutes begin to play. She heard the helicopter leaving. She calls Danny. "Did you hear?"

"Hear what?"

"My show."

"No, I was with Bradley."

"Drinking? Shit."

"I missed something?"

"No, it was just a bit political. You can go back to Bradley."

The phones are lit up the rest of the night. "Was that the President?" "Why didn't you talk about the amendment and the Telecommunication Act? You get the President and you don't even mention it?" Several listeners complained. The questions kept coming. Mandy just let them talk, didn't answer any question directly. She was still stunned. The President was alright. It might be safer to pretend he was an imposter, an actor for the show. She didn't tell the listeners it was one way or the other.

Ida showed up at the closing of the show.

"Mandy, you are a master! That was terrific! I liked this President, but now I *love* him. He really understands government. How did he take all this?"

Mandy smiles, "He was scared. Worried. But at the end he seemed to think it worked out."

"And you were so wise not to push our agenda on him. Did he okay airing this on the other stations next week?"

"Verbally, yes."

"But I think we need him to confirm it in writing," Ida says.

"No. Don't. I'm not sure I want this to go national. I've got to think about it. He said some pretty revolutionary stuff and I don't want him to get into trouble. I'm gonna tape an alternative show for next Thursday night, nationally."

"Well the show went way over an hour. We could edit it."

"Ida, Danny would never allow that. We don't distort words with editing. We either run it or not. If we do decide to run it, counting the station breaks, it will be a perfect one and half hour show.

"I didn't run the ads until after he left, so we can put them in if we and him decide to take this national. We'll figure that out later."

Ida says, "If we do run it on all the stations, then the President will have a pretty hard time not vetoing that bill. He pretty much said that making businesses bigger isn't good for the economy. Or, he might just ask Congress to make a few changes in the bill and delete stations having eight radio stations in one market. Still, we need approval in writing."

Mandy says, "We'll just see what happens. I'm not gonna ask him anything."

"Then we can't run this show on syndication."

"Ida, just let things happen."

The headlines four mornings later in the Honolulu Advertiser left no questions on the President's approval.

THE PRESIDENT VISITS THE RADIO REVOLUTION

The President's press secretary announced on Monday that the President made what he termed an emergency detour to The Radio Revolution in Honolulu, two nights ago, between eight and ten o'clock while traveling to China. The President says he had a very enlightening talk with Mandy Blossom, the host of the radio show called Mandy's Room. He mentioned Mandy's Room will rebroadcast the show over 1400 stations the following Thursday night at 8pm."

Fredrick Widgewater, Republican US Senator said, "The show demonstrates the President's idealistic teen dream vision of our somber political condition. Anybody who believes you can spend money for the common good and it doesn't cost anything, is in lala land. Shockingly, the President said exactly that. He is using this syndicated radio show to promote his reelection. It was an obvious ploy, a lollipop vision of our political scene, just to get votes. Utterly irresponsible."

The President rebutted Widgewater's comment while in China today. "Well, the show will be on 1400 stations across the country this coming Thursday night at 8pm, a full hour plus show, and I'm sure the listeners will understand my words more accurately than the criticism blurted out by an antagonistic voice from a party obsessed with putting me down.. Listen to the show and judge for yourself."

Mandy had goose bumps realizing the future of America. She could envision Danny's dream coming to fruition. *It is gonna happen. And I'm gonna have Danny's baby.*

An older gentleman in a suit came to the Punahou High School cafeteria the next day and dropped a ballot in the Radio Revolution ballot box.

It suggested a song that if radio played it, might become a hit. A Curtis Fuller song, "A Lovely Way to Spend an Evening." On the back of the ballot was written: "To a new America. God bless Mandy."

THE END.

NOTE FROM THE AUTHOR.

The Radio Revolution really did happ~~ in Honolulu, Hawaii, from June of 1991 to March of 1997. I was the Sher~~, ~nd yeah, that monkey skit and all the programming concepts mentioned in the book really happened. And we seemed to have been black balled by the monopoly rating service even though we were voted one of the top five radio stations in the medium market for the whole nation by the readers of the Rolling Stone Magazine every year they ran the poll during our tenure.

I decided to make this a fiction account, and show where Radio Free Hawaii (the Radio Revolution) could have gone if it was able to break down the rating service. And it took me twenty years to really figured out what went wrong. The root of the problem seems to stem from the Constitution of the United States that allows big business and special interest to control Congress. Thus the amendment proposal in this book.

I need to thank all the people who fell into the Radio Free Hawaii spell and kept this station alive on Facebook and on the streets of Honolulu for all these years. Facebook calls it "I loved Radio Free Hawaii." The listeners were a big help in me getting the courage to write this story. Also, Solana Reyne (Pinkie Passion), a DJ of the Radio Revolution and my creative conspirator at the radio station, was a big help with this book, though she wishes I would add more of the crazy times we had at the station. I am more concerned in bringing back the Radio Revolution and to do it, I can only see it happening if we ratify an amendment to the constitution to force all campaign funds to be funded by the government. So I spent a lot of energy (words) in the book showing how that could happen.

All the characters in this book are fictional except for Ed Kanoi, Cindy Lau and Senator Bernie Sanders. With Ed's permission, I kept his name in this book, even though he was in Kauai when Radio Free Hawaii was flourishing in Honolulu and not connected with the station. Why? In 1977, when I was out of work, Ed would take me fishing and I would talk about all the ideas I had for programming a radio station. I guess my talking scared away the fish. As I remember, Ed never caught a fish, but we talked and talked about radio programming. And twelve years later it really happened.

Cindy Lau started Jelly's in 1983, and Jelly's was stepping stone for me to create Radio Free Hawaii. I've included her in this book, though she has passed on since.

And Congressman Bernie Sanders was one of the few who fought against the Telecommunication Act of 1996 which part of the reason for the closing of Radio Free Hawaii.

But overall, the story should be qualified as historical fiction.

Only people in Hawaii, mostly youth back then, know how precious that radio station was, even I didn't understand that then. But now that we know, hey - let's do it again. Something that beautiful must rise again.

ACKNOWLEDGEMENTS:

I'd like to thank Solana Reyne, whose words are all over this story, Shirley Neely, who told me to write this after my mouthing off about politics to her, Loya Whitmer, a great supporter of my endeavors, Lauren Hayashi, a great literature genius and supporter of my writings, Jerome James, a crazy kid who built a studio in hopes Radio free Hawaii would return and edited the audio version of this book, Cary Hayashikawa, for his technical support to this story and who stayed with me through all my madness at Radio Free Hawaii and, who, without his help, Radio Free Hawaii would never have happened. Yeala Faria, a preserver, who has a non-fiction book about the radio revolution still in the salt mine, Mel ah Ching, a preserver of the radio revolution, Caraigh Clarkson, the Radio Free Hawaii DJ who gave me the details of Caraigh's Room (Mandy's room in the book), Tony Bush, who added a bit of color to the story as a listener and Evan Tector (who wrote the poem Mandy read on the Wild Women's Weekend)., Matthew Geritz a terrific book cover artist, and Audrey Keesing, who encouraged me in the early going. And most important, for all the people who assisted me with memories of Radio Free Hawaii on facebook's I loved Radio Free Hawaii, a website that has lasted twenty years with over 2000 followers. Without your tenacity to remember those years, I doubt this book would ever had come to be.

And to Marriane Rueter, author of Amber Eyes, and Where Heaven and Hell Meet, Suin, author of Being Fifteen, and Best Laid Plans, Rebecca Vaughn author of the Pendragon books, and Rachel Parsons, author of the Rhiannon books, for their help in editing the content of this book.

Sheriff Norm Winter's new books coming soon, "The Outlaw Who Saved The World—The Autobiograffiti of Grandville Rodriquez. And The Saga of the Mighty Valentine Cosmos and the Tower of Time. Read the website, stirringneurons.com for release dates.